I0825912

Novels by Karla K Goodhouse

Hellfire
Firebird

FIREBIRD

A Novel By Karla K. Goodhouse

This is a work of fiction. Names, characters, places and incidents are the product of the author's imagination or are used fictitiously. Any resemblances to actual persons, living or dead, events or locales are entirely coincidental.

Cover Art by Paper Zombies Design Group

Dedication

To Katie, Rich, Matt and Andrew.

And for Kenneth.

Special Thanks

Loren Purcell and The Paper Zombies Design Group
For the incredible cover art.

Barbara Goodhouse

Author's Note:

This book contains aviation and military terminology which may be unfamiliar to the reader. For your convenience, a glossary of these terms has been provided at the back of the book.

~ 1 ~

This is crazy, Vince Carlton thought. He'd pulled some insane stunts in his life, he admitted to himself, but never anything like this.

*But if I don't go through with this....*Carlton shuddered to think of the consequences.

The Air Force captain looked at his surroundings, taking stock of his situation for the umpteenth time. He was lying flat on his stomach behind the cockpit of a B-1 bomber, a place that was not meant to hold a man.

Carlton didn't belong on the B-1 and he knew it. He was an F-22 pilot. He had seen B-1s and been inside the aircraft once or twice while they were on the ground, but he had never flown in one before.

He had spent the majority of the flight watching the crew and trying to see what he could of the instruments. He was intently observing the plane's course, looking for any deviation from the Bone's flight path. Up until now, the crew had been flying a picture-perfect mission. Carlton hoped that they would continue to keep their course. If they held true, he wouldn't have to act. If they didn't...

The pilot turned to the copilot and nodded slowly. Then he stood, unstrapped himself from the ejection seat, and calmly turned around. Carlton saw him reach into the cargo pocket of his flight suit. The two weapons system officers seated behind the pilot and copilot were too intently focused on their jobs to notice anything unusual.

Carlton opened his mouth to scream to the men, but he was too late. The loud crack of the 9-millimeter pistol drowned out his warning. The offensive weapons systems officer slumped forward onto the console, blood covering his instrument panel. The defensive systems officer turned as he heard the shot. The pilot twisted toward him and planted a bullet squarely between the man's eyes. He fell sideways and stayed motionless.

The pilot safed the pistol and buried it back in his cargo pocket. Then he calmly strapped himself into his ejection seat. Still squished in the back of the airplane, Carlton braced himself.

The pilot grabbed the controls of the plane and nosed it forward, sending the Bone into an erratic, nearly uncontrolled dive. Then he keyed his mike.

"Mayday, Mayday, Mayday. This is Scepter six five. We have an engine flameout and are rapidly losing altitude. Scepter six five is going down. I repeat, Scepter six five is going down."

Carlton watched the altimeter spiral downward, his body tense. Through the window, the ground seemed to rush up at an incredible rate. Carlton wasn't used to being a mere passenger, and he didn't like it. He wanted to be in control of the jet. But for the moment, all he could do was hold on and wait.

The pilot held the B-1 in the dive, jerking it left and right to make the flight appear uncontrolled. Seconds away from impact, he pulled the nose up, leveling off slightly over 200 feet above the Earth's surface, and well below any radar sites. He reached forward and activated the terrain-following radar. Then he looked over to the copilot. He smiled beneath his oxygen mask.

Slowly, Carlton crawled out from his hiding place and crept toward the cockpit, keeping low. He did not want the men to see him. The pilot had a gun; Carlton was armed only with a small knife. He reached into his pocket and withdrew the blade.

Carlton stood, carefully balancing himself behind the copilot's seat. The helmet covered the man's ears, making it impossible for Carlton to knock him out quickly. He stuck the knife blade in his mouth and wrapped his hands around the copilot's neck, then pressed his thumbs deep into his throat, cutting off the blood flow to his head. The man went rigid in surprise, then quickly slumped over, unconscious.

The pilot noticed his copilot move and turned. His eyes filled with shock as he saw him leaning sideways in his seat, motionless. Then he spotted Carlton standing behind the copilot, the knife still in his mouth. For a second the two men simply stared at each other.

"Mayday, Mayday, Mayday, any aircraft in the vicinity, this is Scepter six five. We have been hijacked and request immediate aid," the pilot shouted into the radio as he reached for his gun. "I repeat, we have been hijacked and request immediate aid."

Carlton grabbed the knife and dove for the man. The pilot swung around and tried to knock Carlton away with his free hand. The knife slashed into his flight suit, drawing blood. The pilot yelled as he pulled the gun from his pocket. Carlton ducked frantically behind his seat. The pilot attacked his straps. Carlton thrust the knife around the seat, feeling it sink into flesh. He twisted the blade rapidly. The pilot jumped to his feet and turned around. Carlton could see the knife, stuck in the pilot's chest. Blood flowed from the wound.

The pilot leveled the pistol at Carlton, who

glanced around desperately, looking for any escape. He was cornered behind the pilot's seat, with nowhere to hide. There were no other weapons within reach.

Carlton lifted his head to find himself staring down the barrel of a 9-millimeter. The pilot closed one eye, carefully sighting down the pistol at him. His finger moved toward the trigger.

Carlton lunged, grabbing hold of the pilot's wrists and pushing the gun to his left. The weapon exploded. The bullet hit the unconscious copilot in the chest. Blood spattered across the cockpit.

The pilot's body quivered, and he collapsed silently to the floor. The knife had done its deed. Carlton walked over and removed his flight helmet. He pulled the knife from the pilot's body and touched his fingers to his neck. There was no pulse.

Carlton kicked the body aside and slid into the pilot's seat, strapping himself in. Pulling the flight helmet down over his head, he checked the connections for the oxygen hose and radio. Scanning the cockpit, he quickly found the gear handle and flap lever, making note of their location. The flight controls were in the same position as in any plane. The main difference would be the avionics. The flight instruments were standard, and while he didn't know the exact power settings for the throttles, the limits on the engine gauges were clearly marked. He would need to know the correct airspeed and power settings to land the B-1 safely, but all he had to do to keep the plane airborne was to stay in the green arc on the airspeed indicator and keep the engine gauges out of the red.

Locating the autopilot, he reached over and disengaged it. The computer system in the B-1 would be much older than that of an F-22 and probably very different. Carlton didn't want to try to figure out how to work it while flying the plane for the first time, especially since he was now solo in an aircraft that required two crew members. Fortunately, the autopilot was not necessary for safe flight.

He wrapped his hand around the stick. Shoving the throttle forward, he raised the nose and put the Bone into a steady climb. He wanted to light up every radar site in the nation.

"To anyone who's listening, this is Scepter six five," Carlton called into the radio. "I have the situation under control and am requesting immediate assistance."

He hoped desperately he could somehow put the Bone back on the ground.

* * *

General Thomas Lee stepped onto NORAD's main control center. The room was filled with rows of airmen seated in front of computers. Large screens displayed satellite tracks and flights across the country.

Lieutenant Colonel Will Stevens stood near the back of the room, bent over one of the computers. He was talking to the sergeant seated in front of the screen. Hearing the door shut, Stevens lifted his head, spotting Lee. Stevens quickly walked up to the general. His face looked somewhat panicked.

"Something wrong, Will?" Lee asked.

"Yes sir," Stevens said. "We've received several distress calls from a B-1 flying near the New Mexico/Texas border."

"What kind of trouble is it experiencing?"

"We're not exactly sure. The first call suggested engine trouble, but the second reported a hijacking. The plane is armed with conventional bombs. We can have fighters from Holloman there in thirty minutes. I was about to scramble them."

"Hold off on that," Lee said. "I may have something better."

He walked over to a master sergeant seated at a nearby console.

"Are you tracking today's ghost flight?" Lee asked.

"Yes, sir," the sergeant replied.

"I need to know how fast they can get to Midland, Texas."

The sergeant hit a few keys on his computer.

"Ten, fifteen minutes, tops."

"Good," Lee said. He pulled out his Blackberry and quickly dialed a number.

"Good morning, Tom," a man's voice said.

"Good morning, sir," Lee replied. "We have a potentially hijacked B-1 in eastern Texas. The ghosts are airborne. I'd like to send them to intercept."

"We've wanted to give them a real-world test for a while now," the man on the other end of the phone said. "You have authorization. Let us know the results."

"Yes, sir. Good morning."

Lee hung up and turned to Stevens.

"Have your man give Sergeant York the bomber's exact coordinates."

"Yes, sir," Stevens said.

"Sergeant York, give them the order to intercept."

* * *

The two sleek ships hovered in the blackness of space. They were ghosts moving through the darkness. Almost no one knew of their existence. They were undetectable by radar and unseen by the human eye. Yet they were real, twisting and turning in the vacuum above the Earth like wraiths. They were phantoms dodging satellites and space debris, watching the planet as it spun beneath them, a world oblivious to their presence.

They were the secret weapon of the United States—a pair of highly sophisticated aircraft, designed and flown in secret and piloted by America's finest.

"Eat lead, Moondog!" Lieutenant Colonel Martina "Panther" Redrick shouted, diving toward the second spaceplane.

Commander Rachel "Moondog" Ansetti twisted around, rapidly checking her six o'clock position. Sure enough, Martina was perched on her tail. The Air Force pilot waved. Moondog looked away in disgust.

"I'll get you next time, Panther," she said.

"Wanna bet?" Martina said.

"Yeah," Moondog replied.

"All right, let's go."

The two pilots twisted their planes away, preparing to engage in combat. America's finest loved to dogfight.

As the pilots dove for each other the radio crackled.

"Hellcat one, NORAD Control. Silver Bullet. Repeat, Silver Bullet."

"Hold off, Moondog," Martina called. She rolled out and engaged her autopilot, settling into an even orbit. Moondog followed suit, taking up position on her wing.

"NORAD, Hellcat one," she said into the radio. "Confirm Silver Bullet. What's going on down there?"

Silver Bullet was the code for a real-world emergency.

"We've received a mayday call from Scepter six five, a B-1 flying over Texas. The exact nature of the emergency is unknown. The aircraft is fully armed. Intercept the plane and escort it to Holloman AFB."

"Where is it?" Martina asked. The controller relayed the coordinates.

Martina hit a few keys on her computer. "We can be there in fifteen minutes."

"Holloman will be waiting for you. We'll contact

them about the necessary security precautions," NORAD said.

"Thank you, NORAD, we are reentering," Martina said. "Okay, Moondog, let's go get this guy."

She hit a few more keystrokes on her computer and nosed her aircraft down toward the Earth.

They dove for the ground. An ion haze appeared, wrapping the nose and wingtips of the airplane. After a few minutes it subsided. A bright blue replaced the blackness of space. They raced across the sky, losing altitude and bleeding off speed, closing in on the distressed B-1. Traveling far in excess of the speed of sound, they reached the target in a matter of minutes. The lone bomber was flying high above the clouds.

"I have him in sight!" Moondog said. "Two o'clock."

"I've got him," Panther replied. "Can you match his speed yet?"

"Not yet," Moondog said. "I'm reading Mach 5, and I'm still on glide."

"Me too," Panther said.

"How do you propose we go about escorting this guy?"

"I say we just zigzag behind him until the rest of this speed bleeds off. Keep a decent distance. We don't want a collision, and there's no way he can outfly us."

"Let's do it, then," Moondog said. Silently, the two planes slid behind the bomber.

* * *

Carlton had managed to bring the big bomber up into straight and level flight. Holding the plane steady, he was trying to figure out what to do next.

The crackling of the radio made him jump.

"Scepter six five, this is Hellcat one," a calm female voice said. "We've currently taken up position on your six, and we're going to escort you to the nearest base. If anyone tries any fast ones, we won't hesitate to shoot you down. Understand?"

"I copy, Hellcat," Carlton said. "You guys sure got here fast."

"We pride ourselves on speed," the woman replied. "What's your situation?"

"I need some help here, Hellcat," Carlton said. "The crew of the plane is dead, and I don't know how to fly her."

"You're not a pilot?"

"I'm an F-22 pilot, not a bomber pilot. I've never flown a B-1 before."

The woman laughed. "And he thinks we can help him, Moondog?"

"Poor kid," a second woman replied. "He's out of luck."

Carlton heard laughter echoing over the airwaves as the sinking feeling in his stomach grew worse.

"You're talking to a couple of fighter jocks, Scepter. We don't know any more about that bomber than you do," Moondog said.

"Well, we do have a little experience in 'heavies,'" the first woman said.

"True," Moondog replied. "But our heavy isn't anything like the one he's flying."

"I guess the poor kid's just screwed," the other woman said. Carlton's head began to swirl.

"Just kidding, Scepter. We'll get you down," she said. "How's she handling so far?"

"I've got her under control," Carlton said. "I have no idea how to land."

"We'll figure that out when we get there," the woman said. "Let's get you turned in the right direction. Hey, Moondog—"

"Already on it, Panther. A two niner zero heading should put us there."

"Scepter, can you make that turn?" Panther asked. "We'll follow you."

Slowly, Carlton swung the big plane around. He glanced out the window, but he could not see the other planes. His radar screen, he noticed, was still blank. His escort had to be a couple of F-22s.

"Is there any damage to the plane?" Panther asked.

"Not as far as I can tell."

"Okay, back up a moment here. What exactly happened?"

"The pilot was trying to steal the plane," Carlton said. "He killed both the backseaters, and then he and the copilot were going to take her somewhere else. That's when I took control of the aircraft."

"What were you doing on the plane in the first place?" Panther asked.

"I snuck on board to try and stop them from stealing it. I overheard them planning to take the plane."

Very bizarre, Martina thought. She signaled Moondog with her hand. Both pilots switched radio frequencies so that they were speaking exclusively to each other.

"If I don't cut in my engines soon, I'm gonna drop out of the sky. What say we fire up the jets and match this guy's speed? You fly on his four, I'll take his eight."

"Will do," Moondog replied.

Martina reached up and ran through her engine restart procedures. The spaceplane's dual jet/rocket engines fired back to life for the first time since the plane had left the atmosphere, giving the aircraft a slight kick. Jet noise filled the cockpit. Martina slid the plane into formation with the B-1.

"Push guard," she told Moondog before switching the radio back to the emergency frequency.

"Have you got that course all right, Scepter?" she asked the B-1.

"I'm holding fine," Carlton replied.

"Hey, Panther, how's your fuel?" Moondog called. "I'm running low."

"Yeah, me too."

"There's no way we can make it back home," Moondog said.

"Yeah, and there's no way they'll get the tanker over here this soon." The spaceplane's dual jet/rocket engines required a special type of propellant. "Let's just set her down at Holloman and get some fuel over there. I'll contact the SOF. You stay on guard."

Martina switched her radio frequency, calling up the airbase.

"Holloman SOF, Hellcat one."

"Hellcat one, this is Holloman. Go ahead."

"We're heading your way with an Emergency B-1."

"Roger, Hellcat. NORAD has already contacted us. The base is on lockdown until after your arrival."

"Good," Martina said. "The B-1 isn't damaged, but the crew is dead. The man flying is a pilot, but he has no time in a B-1. Have the crash trucks standing by. If you could find someone to talk him through the landing that would be very helpful."

"Will do, Hellcat."

"Also, we are flying F-22 Raptors with Top Secret modifications. We'll need to have the planes secured in a hangar immediately."

"NORAD has already informed us of your needs, Hellcat. We have a hangar waiting for you."

"Good," Martina repeated. "ETA twenty minutes."

Martina switched to the satellite radio the Hellcats used to communicate with NORAD while in orbit. "NORAD, Hellcat one. We've intercepted Scepter and are en route to Holloman. We're low on fuel, and we won't be able to make it home on the gas we have."

"Roger, Hellcat one," NORAD said. "Edwards has already been informed of the situation. We'll let them know not to expect you."

"Thank you, NORAD." Martina switched back to her UHF radio, changing the frequency again so that she could talk to both Moondog and the B-1 pilot.

"They know we're coming, Moondog," she said. "And home knows we're not coming back."

Sitting alone in the bomber's cockpit, Carlton peered out the window. Now he could catch glimpses of the two planes flying behind him. At first, they appeared to simply be F-22 Raptors. But Carlton had flown the Raptor most of his career, and he knew there was something different about these planes. They had a strange black covering on their underbelly and nose and on the edges of the tail and wings. There were subtle differences in the body. Carlton studied the planes. They were not F-22 Raptors. What on Earth was flying beside him?

"Out of curiosity, Hellcat, just what are you flying?" Carlton asked.

"None of your business, Scepter," Panther barked. "If anyone asks, two Raptors escorted you down."

"But you're not flying Raptors."

"Don't ask questions or I will shoot you down," Panther said. "These planes are Raptors. Got it?"

"Yes, ma'am," Carlton said. The cold, hard edge in her voice left him with no doubt that she wouldn't hesitate to fire if he persisted with his questioning.

He glanced back out the window. The mysterious planes had dropped back out of his line of sight. Most likely the pilots would not let him see the strange craft again. He sighed and turned his attention back to the Bone's controls. He found it difficult to stop wondering just what was flying on his wing for the remainder of the short flight.

~ 2 ~

The strange trio of planes began their slow descent. Holloman Air Force Base appeared in the distance. Panther and Moondog hung off the bomber's wing as someone on the ground guided the B-1's pilot through his approach. The Earth drew closer. The Bone descended and lowered its landing gear. The fighter pilots pulled off slightly, watching the larger plane descend to the runway. The bomber's wheels touched the asphalt, and it rolled to a stop.

The Hellcats raced above the tarmac as the B-1 landed and looped back around to a second, narrower runway. They screamed over the base, setting up for an overhead pattern. Martina threw Moondog a salute and rolled into the break. The second Hellcat followed her a moment later. Lowering her gear and flaps, Martina began to descend off the perch. She aligned the jet with the strip, backing out more power. The Hellcat slipped gently toward the Earth. Crossing the threshold, she flared the aircraft, holding it just above the asphalt until the rear wheels touched down. She brought the nose onto the ground, and the Hellcat rolled to a smooth stop. Following ground control's instruction, she taxied to a small hangar and quickly ran through her shutdown procedures.

Martina raised the plane's cockpit and leaped to the ground. Straightening her tall, thin body, she pulled off her helmet, shaking loose her long brown hair. Glancing back, she saw Moondog's plane come to a halt beside hers. Already a pair of airmen were hooking her plane up to a tug and pulling it to the hangar.

Moondog climbed from her jet and pulled off her own helmet. Her shoulder length golden-brown hair framed her blue eyes and stunning face.

Motioning for Moondog to follow, Martina strode up to the Security Forces sergeant standing at the edge of the hangar. The man came to attention as the two pilots approached.

"Good afternoon, ma'am," he said.

"Afternoon," Martina replied. "Are you in charge here?"

"Yes, ma'am."

"Good. I want an armed guard on this hangar twenty-four hours a day. No one is to be allowed inside but Commander Ansetti"—she pointed to Moondog— "and myself."

"Yes, ma'am," he repeated.

Martina turned around to see the tail of the second Hellcat disappear inside the small hangar. The airmen began to pull the door shut.

"C'mon," she said to Moondog. "Let's lose the pressure suits and go see how our friend the terrified bomber pilot fared."

The pair walked inside the hangar. They quickly stripped off the thin outer garments they wore, tossing them into the cockpits of their respective aircraft before walking back outside.

Martina swept her hair up as they crossed the short distance to the main landing strip. The B-1 sat silently on the runway, surrounded by crash trucks. Several airmen had already gathered around the big plane. The two pilots pushed their way to the front of the small crowd.

After a second, the bottom hatch of the Bone

swung open and a man dressed in a flight suit dropped to the ground. He landed unsteadily, barely managing to catch himself before he fell on his face. Hands on his knees, he gasped for air before slowly straightening his body. He stood about four inches shy of six feet. His young face had gone pale, and sweat slicked back his light-brown hair. He was visibly shaking.

Martina nodded to Moondog and walked up to the bomber pilot. Their movement caught his eye. He looked up at the two women and, surprisingly, smiled. His eyes sparkled when he grinned.

“That was a hell of a ride,” he said.

“I’ll bet. I’m Martina Redrick. This is Rachel Ansetti.”

“Vince Carlton,” the pilot said. “You were flying those...um...Raptors?”

“Yeah,” Martina said. “That’s us, your friendly neighborhood F-22 pilots.”

“Thanks for helping me,” Carlton said. Despite his smile and dancing eyes, the kid was still trembling. “I don’t know how I’d have managed to get this thing on the ground without you.”

“It was nothing,” Martina said.

“C’mon,” Moondog said, putting her arm around the young pilot’s shoulders. “We’ll buy you a drink and you can tell us how you managed to end up flying that mother anyway.”

She steered him gently toward the nearest building.

As the three pilots stepped out from the shadow of the bomber’s wing, a group of armed Security Forces stepped up. One man grabbed Carlton forcibly and spun him around, clamping handcuffs on his wrists.

“What’s going on here?” Martina demanded.

“This man is under arrest for attempting to steal

an armed Air Force plane," the policeman said.

"By order of whom?"

"Colonel Carmichael, the base commander."

"Where are you taking him?"

"If you have any questions, go talk to the colonel," the man replied, dragging Carlton away.

Martina glared at him for a second and then began to walk away. "C'mon, Moondog," she said. "Let's go find the colonel."

One of the onlookers offered to lead the two pilots to the wing commander's office. They found the wing headquarters building easily. Martina explained who they were to Carmichael's secretary, who told them he was in a meeting.

"We'll wait," Martina informed her. She and Moondog sat down in the chairs outside his office.

It was almost a half hour before Colonel Carmichael returned. The two pilots stood as he walked in.

"You ladies are the pilots of the planes that escorted the stolen bomber?" he asked as they sat down.

"Yes, sir," Martina replied.

"Come inside," he said, walking into his office.

He sat down behind his desk and motioned for the Hellcat pilots to sit across from him.

"I'm Lieutenant Colonel Martina Redrick. This is Commander Rachel Ansetti," Martina began.

Carmichael arched an eyebrow. "A Navy pilot?"

"I'm doing an exchange tour," Moondog said.

"It is a joint world these days," Carmichael said.

"We're test pilots operating out of Edwards," Martina explained. "We're currently experimenting with a pair of specially modified F-22 Raptors. We were on a test flight when we got the Mayday call. Needless to say, our planes are Top Secret, and it's necessary that no one other than myself and

Commander Ansetti be allowed anywhere near them."

"I'll make sure my people stay clear of your planes," Carmichael said. "How long do you expect to be here?"

"We shouldn't be longer than a day or two," Martina said. "We'll have to get in touch with Edwards. Because our planes have modified engines, they require a special type of fuel. As soon as we get a fuel truck out here and gas up we'll be able to leave."

"All right," Carmichael said. "I'll have my secretary give you directions to the lodging office so you can get a room for the night."

"Thank you."

"If there's anything else—"

The door swung open, cutting Carmichael off. A large man wearing a general's star strode in, followed by his executive officer, a tall major with black hair. The major's face was tanned, and his eyes were dark. Something sinister lurked in his presence. Carmichael looked at the pair of intruders for a moment, then turned his attention back to Martina.

"Colonel, may I present General Miles?" he said. "General, allow me to introduce Lieutenant Colonel Redrick and Commander Ansetti, the pilots who escorted your bomber here."

"Pleased to meet you, General," Martina said, standing.

"I am forever in your debt," Miles said, smiling widely as he gripped Martina's hand with both his. "The loss of that bomber would have been devastating."

"I'm sure it would have, sir. Do you have any idea what happened?"

"We believe Carlton was trying to hijack the bomber," Miles said.

"What would a fighter captain want with a B-1?" Martina asked.

"The bomber was on its way to the range and fully armed. A loaded B-1 is a very attractive prospect for a terrorist group."

"Terrorists?" Martina exclaimed.

"We believe he has links to a terror cell."

"Really?"

"We found a note in his luggage promising a large sum of money if he was to deliver the bomber to a group in South America."

"He told us he was trying to stop the pilot from stealing the plane," Martina said.

"The bomber pilot made a Mayday call, saying he was being hijacked," Miles explained. "A military aircraft hijacking is enough to call in all nearby fighter aircraft, as your arrival proved. Carlton knew that in a matter of minutes a swarm of armed planes would surround him and he wouldn't be able to fight back. His only option was to blame the theft on the other pilots and claim he was trying to stop them."

"So he was trying to fool us into believing him innocent. I guess that would explain why he was so cooperative," Martina said.

Miles nodded.

"So what happens to him now?" she asked.

"We'll hold him here for a few days, then take him to a court-martial on charges of theft of government property, hijacking, and possibly treason and murder."

"Pretty heavy charges," Martina said.

"Indeed."

"Well, unless either of you gentlemen have anything for us, we need to make some arrangements with Edwards," Martina said.

"I have no objections," Carmichael said.

"Me neither," Miles said.

"It was a pleasure to meet you gentlemen," Martina said. She began walking toward the door. Moondog stood and followed

"Thank you again," Miles said as Panther and Moondog slipped through the door.

"Does this whole thing strike you as a bit strange?" Martina asked as they stepped out of the building.

"Very strange," Moondog said.

"Oh, well, it's not our problem. Let's go talk to Edwards."

* * *

Martina dropped down in a chair inside her visiting officers' quarters. Moondog was lounging on the couch in her friend's room. Panther reached down and began to pull off her combat boots.

"I got ahold of Edwards," she said. "They said the tanker truck should be out here the day after tomorrow."

Moondog looked up at her. The Navy woman was lying on her stomach with her nose in a paperback novel. She had stripped off her flight suit and was wearing only a t-shirt and shorts.

"What do we do till then?"

"Chill here, I guess. Try to stay out of trouble."

"In other words, see how much I can take from the Air Force boys in a poker game," Moondog said. "Hope I can find some good-looking ones," she added.

"You would do that," Martina said.

"Do have a better idea?"

"Not really."

Moondog turned her attention back to her book. Martina pulled the elastic from her hair, shaking it down across her back, then slowly peeled off her flight suit above her waist, revealing a t-shirt beneath.

"Hey, Panther?" Moondog said, looking up from her novel.

"Yeah?"

"What do you think about that kid?"

"Carlton? What do you mean?"

"Do you think he's guilty?" Moondog asked. "Do you think he was really trying to deliver that bomber to a terrorist organization?"

"I don't know," Martina said. "He didn't seem like the type."

"How so?"

"He was relieved to get back on the ground," Martina said. "He didn't have a frightened or guilty look in his eyes. If he thought he was in trouble he would have been very scared. What do you think of him?"

"I don't think there's any way," Moondog said.

"Why not?"

"It just doesn't fit. I can't picture that kid doing anything like that."

"How can you be so sure?"

Moondog shrugged. "Something just doesn't feel right."

"I don't see how we can possibly judge this," Martina said, leaning back in the chair and folding her arms behind her head. "We don't know a thing about this kid. We can't say what he would or would not do."

"I suppose," Moondog said.

"And they do claim to have evidence against him. What does that say?"

"I don't know what their evidence is."

"All we can do is let the justice system work," Martina said. "If the kid is innocent, they'll set him free."

"I guess so," Moondog said, turning back to her reading. "But doesn't something about this seem off to you?" she asked, lifting her head again.

"There is something odd about this whole mess," Martina said. "But I haven't the faintest idea what."

"You don't think this is going to turn into a big fiasco like that satellite thing, do you?"

Martina laughed. “I doubt it. We’re out of here in two days. Our involvement probably ended the minute we touched down. The only thing we have to do is get home.”

“I suppose.”

“Quit worrying about it. You got some cards or something?”

“Yeah, somewhere,” Moondog said. “Why?”

“We don’t have to get up and do anything tomorrow,” Martina said. “I figured I could take some of your money in a poker hand or two.”

“You’ll be the only one losing money,” Moondog said, rummaging through a small bag at her feet for her cards.

“Right,” Panther said sarcastically. “We’ll see about that. Deal ’em up.”

~ 3 ~

Night lay over Holloman like a thick blanket. The darkness hung heavy and silent. Airman Bobby Hall stared out across the base, looking at the myriad of sparkling stars in the night sky. He slowly scanned the area around him. The black outlines of buildings sat quietly in the distance. Nothing on the entire base was moving.

Hall shifted the M-16 resting across his lap and moved his back. He sat against the corrugated metal of the smallest hangar on base. He checked his watch. The green illuminated dial read one a.m. His body was sore from sitting in the same position for hours. The slow cooling of the night air made him wish he had brought his Apex jacket.

He should have been asleep now, curled up under a soft, warm blanket, instead of sitting outside a near-empty hangar. Recent events did not seem to favor the airman. He was about to get out of work for the day when this crisis arose. The base commander wanted a twenty-four-hour guard on some Top Secret plane from Edwards Air Force Base. And Hall had the good fortune to be stuck with the graveyard shift. He had been sitting in the same spot outside the hangar for two hours, soaking in the night and the cold. He hadn't seen anything—not so much as a rodent scurrying around in the dirt. He was beginning to wonder if he wouldn't die of boredom before the night was over.

Soft footsteps crunched on the gravel beside him. He turned to see Airman Sam Johnson walking around the building, returning from his patrol. Johnson unslung his M-16 and slumped down next to Hall.

“See anything?” Hall asked.

“Nothing,” Johnson replied, blowing on his hands. “Nobody in their right mind would be out here at this time of night.”

“Makes you wonder why we are,” Hall said.

“My thoughts exactly,” his friend agreed. “What did we do to get this shit shift? I don’t think I pissed anyone off lately.”

“Do you really think the sergeants are going to sit out here in the middle of the night, when they could go home to their wives and make some airmen do the shit jobs?” Hall asked. “We simply have the misfortune of having no rank.”

“Wonderful,” Johnson muttered.

“Well, guard duty is an airman’s job.”

“What are we guarding that’s so damn important?”

“Airplanes.”

“What kind of airplanes?” Johnson asked.

“Some special modified fighters,” Hall said. “Some type of F-22.”

“Did you see them?”

“No. No one can. Only the pilots are allowed inside.”

“The pilots?”

“Yeah. Two female light birds. Fighter jocks from Edwards.”

“Female light birds?”

“Yeah, that’s what the sergeant said, anyway. I didn’t see them myself,” Hall replied. “Their names were Redrick and Ansetti or something like that.”

“How long are these things going to be here?”

Johnson asked.

"Only a few days, supposedly. They just need fuel or something, and then they're flying home."

"That's good," Johnson muttered. "I don't want any more of this extra two a.m. guard shit."

"Me neither," Hall agreed. "The front gate is bad enough."

The two men fell silent, gazing out at the dark buildings and the motionless base. Hall surveyed the area in front of him, wishing a mouse or something would dash across the sand. Maybe even a possum or a raccoon. Something worth watching, at least. There was nothing. Not even a breeze to move the dust around. Only the stars were out tonight. The still, cold, silent air surrounded everything.

A faint semblance of motion in the corner of his eye caught Hall's attention. He turned his head. The figure of a man was moving between the buildings at the end of the runway. Hall nudged Johnson with his elbow.

"Hey, you see that?" he whispered.

"See what?" Johnson asked.

"That guy over there." Hall pointed toward the figure.

Johnson squinted into the darkness, searching for the man. After a moment he spotted the figure.

"Probably just some drunk coming from the club."

"Yeah," Hall said. He turned his attention back to the figure. The man was moving slowly between the buildings, staying mostly in the shadows. He didn't seem to be weaving or stumbling. And he was gradually moving in the direction of the two airmen.

"Hey, Sam, he's getting closer."

"Yeah, so? He's probably heading over to the transient quarters. They are over there."

"He isn't moving like he's drunk."

"Maybe he just got back late or something,"

Johnson said. "He's all the way over there. I don't think you need to get all excited yet."

Hall didn't reply. Sam was probably right. The guy was probably nothing to worry about. But at least he was something to watch, and Hall was incredibly bored.

The man was moving slower now, trying to stay hidden in the shadows. He surveyed the area, then darted quickly across the open area between two buildings and back into the shadows. He edged cautiously along the side of the building, watching for any signs of life and stopping periodically. He clearly wasn't drunk. All of his actions were calculated. He was trying to keep from being seen.

Hall watched as he walked to the building next to the hangar the two airmen were guarding. He paused in the shadows, waiting a full five minutes before moving again. This time he stepped forward, creeping cautiously to the hangar. As he stepped forward, Hall realized his face was covered by a black ski mask.

"Halt. Who goes there?" the Security Forces airman said, standing and leveling his M-16 at the man.

The intruder jumped back in shock. For a brief moment he simply stared at Hall, surprised at seeing the airman appear out of nowhere. The man glanced about anxiously, then took off, running back into the dark shadows of the nearby buildings.

Hall dashed after the masked man, rushing into the night. The fleeing man had a good lead on him. He raced past the hangars on the flight line and ran to the right, along the edge of a building. Hall reached the outskirts of the shadows, sprinting past the hangars. Reaching the main road, he stopped dead in his tracks, searching for his quary. The man had disappeared. The silent night air hung still.

Hall ran quickly down the street, searching

between the buildings. Everything was silent. The intruder was gone. He walked slowly back to the hangar, checking every door along the way. His quarry was nowhere to be found.

Johnson was standing where he had been when Hall left, carefully scanning the area.

"You catch him?"

"No." The guy disappeared."

"I guess we better wake up the sergeant," Johnson sighed.

"Yeah," Hall said, unclipping his radio. "He is gonna be pissed, too," he commented before calling over the radio and reporting the situation.

* * *

"General Peters' office," Edwards Air Force Base's commander's secretary answered the phone in a casual tone.

"This is Lieutenant Colonel Redrick. May I speak with General Peters?"

"One moment please." There was a pause.

"Peters," a voice said.

"Sir, this is Lieutenant Colonel Redrick."

"Good morning, Martina," Peters said. "How is everything?"

"Not so good, sir," she said. "There was an incident with the Hellcats last night."

"What happened?" Peters sounded very concerned.

"A man tried to sneak into the hangar where they're being housed. SF chased him off."

"Did he see anything?"

"No, he only got within about fifty feet of the hangar," Martina said. "The planes are safe."

"That's a relief," Peters said. "Did they catch him?"

"No," Martina repeated. "He ran when SF confronted him. They chased him, but he got away. He had a mask over his face, so they couldn't identify him."

"So he's still out there?"

"Yes, sir."

"That's unfortunate," Peters said. "Do you think he'll try to see the planes again?"

"It's possible, sir," Martina said. "But don't worry, Commander Ansetti and I will see to it that he doesn't."

"I have no doubt you will, Martina," Peters said.

"Thank you, sir. What's the status on the fuel truck?"

"It left here this morning with a few of the technicians. They should reach you sometime tomorrow."

"Good," Martina said. "As soon as we get that fuel we'll be home."

"All right," Peters said. "Keep me informed of anything that happens."

"Will do, sir."

"Keep those planes safe, Martina."

"Yes sir."

"Have a good day," Peters said.

"You too, sir," Martina said before putting the phone down.

"What did he say?" Moondog asked from the door of the room.

"He wasn't happy," Martina said. "The fuel truck will be here tomorrow. As soon as we get gas in those things we're out of here. Did you find Carmichael?"

"Yeah, he's in his office."

"Let's go talk to him, then," Martina said, stepping out into the hall and walking the short distance to the wing commander's office. His secretary waved the two women in. Martina stepped inside and saluted.

"I'm terribly sorry about this, Colonel," he said, returning the salute.

"It's not your fault, sir," Martina said. "However, I do need your help to ensure this doesn't happen again."

"I'll do anything I can," Carmichael said.

"First, I'd like the guard on the hangar doubled," Martina said. "And I'm going to need some camo netting."

"I'll have my exec see to it that you get everything you need."

"Thank you, sir. It's greatly appreciated."

"I'll let you know if we catch the culprit," Carmichael said. "I have my Security Forces looking for him."

"I hope they find him," Martina said. "Our fuel truck should get here tomorrow, and as soon as we're gassed up, we're out of here."

"If there's anything you need before then..." Carmichael offered.

"I'll be sure to let you know, sir," Martina said.

"Good morning, ladies."

"Good morning, sir."

"Camo netting?" Moondog asked as the two women stepped outside. "What the hell are you up to?"

"You'll see," Martina said, walking down the hall. "Let's go find the exec. We've got some work to do."

"I swear, Panther, I'll never figure how your mind works," Moondog said, following her friend.

"I hope you're up for an all-nighter."

"You want us to pull guard duty?" Moondog asked, incredulous.

"Yup," Martina replied. "Go take a nap this afternoon if you want. We should have plenty of time to rest tomorrow morning before the fuel truck gets here."

"Why not just let Security Forces do their job?"

"Those planes are our responsibility," Martina said. "It's our necks if something happens to them."

Moondog shook her head. “I know you better than that, Panther. You’re curious about what’s going on. You want to catch this guy. And I’m not going to be able to talk you out of it.”

“Of course not.”

Moondog sighed. “Guess it’s going to be a long night.”

* * *

The Hellcats sat motionless in the darkness, the ghost planes mere shadows in the hangar. Several camouflage nets draped the planes, hiding their true form. The black-tiled, sleek bodies were nearly invisible beneath the army drab covering.

Two Security Forces troops armed with M-16s sat outside the front door, guarding it closely and watching the road. Another two were calmly making their rounds, walking slowly around the building. Their boots crunched softly across the stones surrounding the hangar.

Panther and Moondog sat silently in a truck outside the hangar’s double doors. It was just one of many vehicles parked neatly in a row on the flight line side. They kept a vigilant eye on the hangar, watching the Security Forces troops make their rounds.

It was almost three a.m. Martina was carefully surveying the surrounding area. Moondog stifled a yawn and tried to get comfortable in the truck. Even in the dim light, exhaustion was evident on both their faces.

“This has to be the lamest all-nighter I’ve ever pulled,” Moondog said.

“For some reason I find it very hard to believe that you ever stayed up all night studying when you were at Annapolis,” Martina said.

“Fuck, no. A proper all-nighter has lots of booze and plenty of hot men.”

"I should have known," Martina said, shaking her head.

"One of these days, I'm going to teach you how to have fun."

"I know how to have fun. Just because I prefer to be sober when I do doesn't mean anything."

"Maybe I should say relax and let your guard down," Moondog said.

"You mean drink."

"Yup," Moondog said. "Next time I go to a good party, I'm taking you with me."

"Okay," Martina said. "But I'm still not drinking. I'll just sit there and laugh at your drunk ass."

"Suit yourself. More booze for me, then."

Martina rolled her eyes. "Incorrigible swabbie."

She looked back outside, slowly sweeping the area. Out of the corner of her eye she caught a flicker of movement. She turned her head. A masked figure, dressed all in black, was creeping along the row of hangars, close against the side of a building.

"There," Martina said, pointing.

"'Bout fucking time," Moondog muttered. "I'd hate to sit here all night for nothing."

"Oh, hush," Martina replied. "You've got all day tomorrow to sleep."

She looked back outside. The man continued to creep toward the hangar that housed the Hellcats. He moved carefully, keeping himself hidden in the shadows. He made his way to the corner of the hangar to their left and stopped.

The two guards walked around the hangar, making their slow sweep. The intruder watched them walk past. As they disappeared around the other side of the building, he darted across the open area between the hangars.

He dashed over to a small door cut into the larger hangar doors. He gripped the handle and pulled. The door remained firmly shut. Quickly, he pulled a pair of lock picks from his pocket and inserted them into the keyhole.

"Freeze!" a female voice shouted.

He jumped, looking frantically for the person speaking to him. The voice had come from behind him, along the flight line. He saw the faint outline of two figures standing in front of a row of vehicles. Both were leveling guns at him.

He bolted from the door, running into the night. Panther and Moondog took off at a dead sprint, trying to close the distance. He darted ahead, nearly vanishing in the shadows cast by the nearby buildings.

Martina raised her gun and fired two warning shots into the air. The man looked back, almost tripping over his own feet. Stumbling forward, he ran faster. The two women were gaining on him.

He quickly turned to the left, darting between two hangars. Panther and Moondog followed closely. A road crossed beyond the hangars. After that sat a large group of dark buildings. He dashed forward, hoping to find a hiding place in the shadows.

Martina lowered her weapon, aimed for the man's leg, and fired again. The bullets skipped off the dirt beside his feet. He jumped in shock and tried to increase his stride, running for his life. The safety of the shadows was only a few footsteps away.

Martina bent down, scooped up a large rock, and hurled it. The makeshift projectile slammed into the man's shoulder, knocking him to the ground. He looked back. The pilots were a mere twenty feet from him. Scrambling, he climbed to his feet and sprinted off into the shadows, dodging around the corner and ducking into a nearby alley. He needed to find a place to hide quickly. The two women were right on his heels. And in a few minutes Security Forces would be everywhere.

"Where'd he go?" Moondog asked.

"That way," Martina replied, pointing between the buildings. "You check over there, and I'll get this side of the alley."

"Okay." The two pilots moved quickly down the road, glancing into the shadows beside the buildings.

The first two alleyways were empty. Martina looked into the blackness of the third. The faint outline of a figure stood against the wall. The pilot stepped forward, leveling her gun at his masked face.

"Make a move and I shoot," she said.

The man glanced desperately around, looking for an escape. He didn't have many options staring down the barrel of a Colt .45. He raised his hand, stepping forward and swinging his fist wide in a roundhouse punch. Martina dropped back, blocking the blow with her wrist. The man lunged at her, grabbing for her gun. As his hand wrapped around the barrel, she moved into him, punching him in the face. He reeled back, pulling her gun with him.

Martina rapped her knuckles into the side of his wrist, sharply knocking his hand to the side. He released his grip on the gun, and it flew down the alley. Ignoring the disappearance of her .45, Martina stepped forward, thrusting her hand into the man's stomach.

Angrily, he charged. Martina dropped back, grabbing him by the collar. She let her feet slide out from beneath her, using his forward momentum to throw him to the ground as she slipped between his legs. Rolling with him, she flung him onto his back and dropped onto his stomach, straddling him.

"Let's see who you are," she said, reaching to pull off the mask.

Panicked, the man drove his fist into her stomach. The blow caught Martina off guard, but she remained firmly seated on him. He thrust his fist into the side of her head. This time, Martina rolled off him. He jumped to his feet and ran into the darkness.

Martina stood quickly and ran after the man. She dashed from the shadows, her eyes sweeping the area around her. The base lay silent. Once again he had slipped away into the darkness. Panther turned and retraced her steps, bending down to retrieve her .45.

~ 4 ~

"The tanks are topped off, ma'am," the technician from Edwards told Martina. They stood outside the hangar. Moondog leaned up against the wall. The flight line was dark and still. The fuel truck and two crew chiefs had arrived a few hours earlier.

"Both planes are ready for flight," he added.

The Hellcats sat in front of the hangar, hidden in the shadows.

"Thank you," Martina said.

"Anytime."

Martina checked her watch. The hands read just after nine p.m.

"What say we make tracks for home, Moondog?" she asked.

"This late?"

"Why not? We can slip out under the cover of darkness, no one will be the wiser, and we won't have to put the whole base on lockdown. Besides, you slept all afternoon."

"Sounds good to me," the Navy woman said.

"Let's go grab our gear," Martina said.

"We'll be back in a few," she told the crew chiefs and the Hellcats' Security Forces guard. "Don't let anyone near here. Cover the planes up until we get back."

"Yes, ma'am," the crew chiefs said. They began to pull camouflage netting over the fighters.

The night was cool and clear. A thousand stars sparkled in the sky. Moondog and Panther crossed the base in silence, the only sound the crunching of their feet against the earth.

Halfway to their destination a slight movement caught Martina's eye. She stopped and turned, motioning for Moondog to keep silent. Two figures were stepping out of a nearby building. They turned toward Panther and Moondog. Quickly, the two pilots ducked into the shadows, pressing themselves against the dark surface of a wall.

The two men stopped several feet away from where the pilots stood. In the darkness Martina could see the first man's tall, thin outline. The second was short and squat. The shadows hid their faces.

"What do you have for me?" the first man asked.

"Carlton is cooperating, and the evidence against him isn't holding up. They moved him from the jail to billeting this morning after he agreed not to leave," the second man said. "He's in room 434."

"I'll just have to make him change his mind on that," the first man said. "Can you get me access to him?

"This is the master key to billeting," the second man said, handing him something. "I'll need it back."

"I'll return it," the first man said as he stuck the key in his pocket. He took out an envelope and handed it to the second man, who opened it and leafed through the contents.

"It's all there," the first man said. "Need I say that when Carlton vanishes, this transaction never took place?"

"You got it," the second man said, pocketing the envelope. He turned and walked away.

The first man waited until he was out of earshot before pulling a phone from his pocket and dialing a number.

"Carlton will be dead by morning," he reported. He lowered the phone and stuck it back in his pocket, then turned and walked off into the night, heading away from the pilots.

"Shit," Moondog muttered. "What are we going to do?"

"Call SF and tell them someone's about to kill Carlton," Martina said. "Then let's get the hell out of here."

"We can't do that," Moondog said.

"Why not? That's their job, let them do it. We need to get the Hellcats back to Edwards. Keeping those planes secret is our biggest concern."

"Martina, that guy probably *is* SF," Moondog said. "He knew where Carlton was, he had a master key to lodging, and he knew some details about the investigation. He could be the sergeant on duty tonight. If we call over there and tell him what's going on, he won't do anything about it."

"All right," Martina said. "I'll go warn Carlton. You call Carmichael and tell him what's going on."

Martina handed Moondog the key card to her VOQ room.

"Then go get our stuff and meet me back at the hangar." Because of their rank, the Hellcat pilots were staying in a different building from Carlton.

Moondog nodded.

* * *

A sharp knock on the VOQ door woke Carlton. His eyes flew open. The room around him was pitch black. Slowly, he looked around, his eyes adjusting to the darkness. He sat up, swinging his legs over the side of the cot. He was naked except for his boxers. The knock came again.

Carlton got up, stumbled to the VOQ door, and cracked it open. A tall woman with long hair pushed the door open and quickly stepped inside. It was difficult to discern any features in the darkness. After a moment Carlton recognized her as one of the pilots of the mystery planes. She hastily shut the door behind her.

"Keep quiet," she ordered. "Get dressed."

"What's going on?" he whispered. He grabbed his flight suit off the floor and slipped into it quickly.

"I'll explain later," the woman said. Her name, if he remembered correctly, was Martina. "Just hurry up."

Carlton noticed she was gripping a pistol tightly in her right hand. What the hell was going on? He bent down and pulled on his boots. Martina surveyed the room carefully, alert. Suddenly, she stiffened. Touching her finger against her lips, she slid silently back into the darkness beside the door. Carlton glanced around nervously.

The door burst open and a tall man stepped inside. He stopped in the doorway, surprised to see Carlton staring back at him. Slowly, he advanced. A dark mask covered his face. A sharp glint of steel caught Carlton's eyes. The man was clutching a knife in his gloved hand.

The man flipped the weapon back so that it lay against his forearm. He swung his arm forward, arcing the blade at Carlton's neck. Carlton bent his knees, ducking below the arc of the knife and thrusting his right arm into the air to stop the man's slash. The blow collided with the attacker's arm. Carlton drove his fist into the man's stomach. The man staggered backward, startled by the blow.

He flipped the knife over in his hand and lunged for Carlton. Sidestepping, Carlton deflect the knife blow with his arm again. The attacker punched him in the gut, knocking the wind from him. Carlton staggered back, hitting the wall.

The intruder grabbed Carlton's shirt, pressing his

forearm against Carlton's neck. He raised the knife blade, angling it toward the pilot's throat. Carlton squirmed, trying desperately to escape.

A fist collided with the assailant's temple. He let go of Carlton and staggered to the side, shaking his head, trying to clear his vision. A tall figure stood before him. Unsteadily, he stepped forward, waving the tip of his weapon at the dark silhouette.

Martina stepped into him, swinging her fists inward. Her right hand collided with the man's wrists as her left knuckles hit the back of his hand. The knife flew out of his grip and slid across the room into the darkness. The man's face registered a look of shock as his weapon disappeared. His eyes widened as Martina's fist slammed into his throat. He staggered back, gasping for breath.

Martina stepped forward, lifting his chin while sweeping his feet from beneath him. The intruder crashed to the floor. He rolled onto his stomach and quickly bolted from the room. Martina pulled the door open and dashed out into the brightly lit hallway. It was empty.

"Slippery fucker," she muttered to herself.

"C'mon, let's go," she said to Carlton as she stepped back inside. The kid was standing in the corner, looking at her in wide-eyed amazement.

"Remind me never to piss you off," Carlton said, grinning.

"If you cross me, I'll do a lot worse to you," she said, stepping out into the hall and moving quickly toward the door.

They walked outside into the blackness of night. The cool air hit Carlton. He inhaled, feeling the sharpness in his lungs. Above, a thousand stars shone brightly in the coal-black sky. Martina seemed to take no notice of them. She looked around, then began to walk through the shadows, scanning the compound all the while.

They skirted two buildings and soon reached the edge of the ramp. Two small planes sat on the tarmac, draped with camouflage nets. Several figures stood in the shadows of the small hangar behind them. Martina quickly spotted Moondog and Carmichael. A third man, a tall, broad-shoulder major, stood beside the wing commander.

"Good evening, sir," Martina said. "What are you doing out here?"

"Good evening, Colonel," Carmichael said. He turned to Carlton. "Captain, would you mind excusing us for a second?"

"Not at all," Carlton replied.

"Keep a close eye on him," Carmichael ordered two nearby Security Forces airmen. They led Carlton out of earshot.

"This is Major Gonzales," Carmichael said, "the head of my Security Forces. Major, Lieutenant Colonel Redrick."

"I've sent a few people over to Captain Carlton's room," Gonzales said as they shook hands. "Hopefully, they'll be able to grab our suspect when he shows up."

"Unfortunately, you're too late," Martina said. "He snuck in when I went to wake up the captain. I tried to catch him, but he managed to escape."

"Did you get a good look at him?" Gonzales asked.

"Tall and thin," Martina said. "It was too dark to see anything else. He was wearing a ski mask."

"Have your people do what they can," Carmichael said. Gonzales nodded.

"We've got a dangerous situation on our hands," Carmichael continued. "OSI and the FBI have been conducting a very thorough investigation into the attempted theft of the B-1. So far, Carlton has been cooperating. They no longer think he's responsible for the hijacking, but he is the most important of two key witnesses. If we're ever going to find out who the real culprit is, we need him alive.

"However, it appears this terrorist group has at least one agent here. And it looks like they may have bought off some of the people familiar with the investigation. Carlton isn't safe here any longer. He needs to disappear. I think you might be able to help."

"Are you suggesting we take Carlton back to Edwards with us?" Martina asked.

Carmichael nodded. "I've already spoken to General Peters, and he's agreed to it. He said you and Commander Ansetti should be able to bring him back with you."

An expression of shock crossed Martina's face.

"Peters gave the go-ahead for us to bring him back?" she asked, incredulous.

Moondog nodded.

"We had a quick conference call with him, and I think a few people higher up the chain gave some input. He said to blindfold Carlton and stick him in the back of the plane," she said.

"There is some extra space in the cockpit behind the seat," Martina said. "It's big enough to hold someone, but there are no restraints or anything."

"It will have to do," Carmichael said. "We've got to get him out of here as quickly and as quietly as possible. I don't want anyone else on this base to know where he went."

"Are you sure he can be trusted?" Martina asked.

"Carlton's role in the attempted theft is still under investigation," Carmichael admitted. "The investigating agents feel it's safe to release him. Whether or not he needs a guard for protection is apparently another issue.

"So far, they haven't been able to learn anything about the group that was trying to obtain the bomber. Therefore, we have no idea what they intended to use it for. It's possible they were planning an attack on U.S. soil. If that's the case, we need to find them and stop them as soon as possible. Innocent or guilty, Carlton is the best chance we have of locating them."

"Whoever's responsible realizes that too," Moondog added. "That's why they just tried to kill him."

"Sadly, right now, I don't know who, if anyone, I can trust in my organization," Gonzales said. "The man who gave Carlton's attacker the key had to have been one of mine. If Security Forces here is involved in relocating or protecting Carlton, there's a good chance the bad guys will find his location."

"It's best he go with you," Carmichael said. "That way, myself and Major Gonzales will be the only two people here who know where he's gone."

"All right, we'll take him back to Edwards with us," Martina said. "But if he makes any fast moves I'll kill him myself."

"I'll let you ladies be on your way," Carmichael said. "Have a safe flight."

"Thank you, sir," Martina said. "Goodnight."

Carmichael and Gonzales walked away.

"C'mon. Let's get the hell out of here," Panther said to Moondog once they were out of sight. She motioned to the two crew chiefs, who trotted over.

"Uncover the jets," she said in a low voice. "We're going back to Edwards. Then you guys can go get some sack time."

"Yes, ma'am," one of them said. They walked over to the Hellcats and began to pull off the netting.

"How do you want to play this?" Moondog asked as they watched the Hellcats emerge. "Regular flight, high altitude, or full-fledged space shot?"

"We've got to stay low," Martina said. "Carlton doesn't have a pressure suit or oxygen. We'll have to fly close to the ground, dodge radar and densely populated areas."

"I don't like it."

"Neither do I, but it's our only option. There's not much between here and Edwards except desert."

"Do we have enough fuel?" Moondog asked.

"As long as we don't go to burner we should be good," Martina said.

"Okay. I'll follow you," Moondog said. "Let's get airborne."

The crew chiefs had pulled the heavy nets off the fighters and were dragging them over to the corner of the ramp. Martina reached into the cockpit of her jet and pulled the visor cover off her helmet. She walked over to Carlton, who was standing out of sight of the Hellcats on the side of the hangar.

"You're coming with us. Don't ask questions. I'll explain as much as I can when we get to our destination. Here," she said, handing him a pair of earplugs.

Carlton rolled up the soft plugs and inserted them in his ears.

"Sorry about this," she said, "but for security reasons, I've got to blindfold you."

She handed him the visor cover. He wrapped it around his eyes.

"Bring him this way," Martina instructed the two airmen standing beside Carlton.

They took him gently by the arms and steered him over to the side of the Hellcat. They stopped a foot away from the fuselage. Martina reached over and pulled the blindfold off.

Carlton opened his eyes. He found himself looking up at the cockpit of a small jet with a black fuselage.

"Climb up there and squish yourself behind the seat," she said, motioning to the cockpit of her plane. "It's not going to be comfortable, but it's the best we can do."

Carlton pulled himself into the plane's cockpit and slid slowly behind the ejection seat. There was just enough space for him to sit between the seatback and the cockpit's rear bulkhead. The floor was flat. He sat sideways, pulling his knees to his chest.

Carlton had never seen a jet with such a large gap behind the seat. On most fighters there was no space at all. Unbeknownst to him, the space was actually designed to hold an occupant and their emergency oxygen supply. Should an emergency arise with one of the Hellcats in orbit, the plan was for the plane's occupant to transfer to the cockpit of the second craft for reentry. Unaware of the Hellcat's true mission, Carlton guessed that the gap between the seat and the bulkhead was most likely for storing baggage.

There wasn't much to see in the cockpit. Aside from the flight controls, several switches, and a keypad, the instrumentation was entirely glass. All the screens were dark, hiding their secrets.

Martina handed him the visor cover again.

"Sorry," she repeated.

Carlton sighed and pulled the cover over his eyes. He leaned back against the bulkhead and tried to get comfortable.

Martina climbed into the cockpit and strapped herself into the ejection seat. She pulled her flight helmet down over her ears and hooked into the oxygen supply. Lowering the canopy, she began to run through her preflight checklist. The displays came to life as she powered up the plane.

"Hellcat check," Martina said. The crew chiefs had returned. One now stood in front of each plane waiting for them to start engines.

"Two," Moondog replied. "Let's go home."

Martina gave her the signal to fire up the engines.

Martina verified that the plane was in jet mode, then ran through her engine start sequence. The plane's left engine roared to life. A moment later the right engine spooled up. Martina quickly scanned her gauges and instruments. She signaled to Moondog, then placed her hands on the controls and released the brakes. The planes began to roll. The crew chiefs threw them a salute as they passed by.

Martina turned onto the taxiway, creeping toward the runway. Moondog followed. The tower was closed for the night, so there was no need to make any radio calls. No one else was flying.

Making sure final was clear, Martina taxied out onto the runway. Moondog pulled up beside her. The two pilots flashed each other a few quick hand signals. Martina eased the throttles forward. Brilliant blue and red flames shot from the Hellcats' tailpipes, glowing brightly in the dark night. Panther flashed Moondog another hand signal and released her brakes.

The planes leapt forward. Pressed behind the ejection seat, Carlton felt the sharp acceleration as they picked up speed. Martina pulled back on the stick gently, lifting the aircraft off the ground. She gave Moondog the signal to raise the gear. Pulling her own gear handle up, she continued to climb. Moondog dropped back into a fingertip position. Martina leveled out a thousand feet above the ground and turned to the west.

The lights of Alamogordo quickly vanished behind the Hellcats. Martina stayed close to the ground. She flew the Hellcat slowly enough to see whatever lurked ahead of her and maneuvered the plane accordingly. They flew through the dark night silently, skirting the lights of cities.

She glanced back occasionally. Moondog remained in view, flying silently in position on her wing. The blackness of night wrapped the cockpit. The stars shone brightly in the moonless sky above. The Milky Way was clearly visible. Below, the desert floor was black and featureless. Occasionally, the lights of a car crawling along the road below appeared.

Behind Martina, Carlton tried to relax. He wished he was flying instead of stuffed in the small space in the back of the jet, but he would have been more than happy just to be able to see outside. He could feel the plane climb and turn as Martina made small course changes. She flew with an incredible smoothness. He shifted his weight again and closed his eyes, trying to get some sleep.

Martina scanned back and forth between her flight instruments and the route she had mapped out on her GPS. Her map displayed the topography in front of her, allowing her to climb and descend to avoid terrain. She kept the Hellcat about a thousand to two thousand feet above the ground.

They crossed the tall mountains on the eastern Arizona border, then flew over the fields between Phoenix and Tucson. Once west of the Valley of the Sun, Martina turned her plane to the northwest, putting her on a direct course for Edwards.

At length the radio crackled. "We almost home?" Moondog asked.

"Almost," Martina said. "You got GPS, you can figure that out yourself."

"Yeah, but it's easier to ask you," Moondog said.

"Lazy ass," Martina muttered.

The two ghost ships continued to slip through the darkness. Martina cleared a last ridge, then gently pushed the nose forward, leveling the plane out. She swung the aircraft north, preparing to make an approach. The altitude held constant. They were over flat earth.

She pulled back on the throttles, eased the

plane's nose down slightly, and keyed her mike. "Edwards, Hellcat One. Ten miles to the south, inbound for full stop, with the numbers."

"Cleared to land," the controller replied tiredly.

"Don't know who else would be flying this time of night," Moondog said.

Martina rolled her eyes and raised the nose of her plane slightly, lining up for a straight-in approach. Out in the distance she saw the faint lights of a landing strip. The runway drew closer. Martina reached over and lowered the landing gear. The Hellcat descended gracefully to the Earth. She gently pulled back on the stick, flaring the aircraft. The plane settled gently to the runway. Moondog touched down beside her. They turned off the runway and taxied back, stopping in front of a hangar, where another pair of crew chiefs waited. Martina quickly shut down the engines.

"Ride's over," she told Carlton, as she pulled off her helmet.

She raised the canopy and swung herself over the side, dropping agilely to the ground. Moondog jumped out of her jet and walked over.

"Help him out," she instructed the crew chiefs. They pulled Carlton out of the plane, then led him over to the side of the ramp. He stretched, trying to relieve the stiffness in his body and removed his earplugs.

"Peters said just to take him over to lodging and get him a room for the night," Moondog said.

"We will in a minute," Martina said. "I want some answers from him first. Let's take him over to my room."

"Let's go to mine," Moondog said. "I've got beer."

Martina made a face.

The crew chiefs went over to the Hellcats and began to pull the planes inside the hangar.

Martina walked up to Carlton. She turned him around so that he was facing away from the Hellcats, and pulled off his blindfold. Carlton blinked and grinned at Martina.

"Welcome to Edwards," she said.

"Some flight."

"Come with us," Martina said to Carlton, and started to walk away from the ramp. He and Moondog followed.

The night air was calm and cool. Everything was silent. The sky was clear and filled with a thousand sparkling lights. They seemed endless, wrapping the silent base in a thick blanket of stars.

"You sure can see a lot of stars tonight. Makes me wish I was flying in space. I always wanted to be an astronaut," Carlton said.

"Space is spectacular," Martina said.

"How do you know?"

"We're astronauts," Martina said. "We only fly Raptors in our spare time."

"Really?"

"Yeah."

"I just got accepted into NASA myself," he said. "I wonder if they'll still let me in after this whole fiasco."

"That depends on how this fiasco plays out," Martina said. "This could be very interesting depending on what you know."

"What do you mean?" Carlton asked.

"I'll explain in a minute."

They walked across the desert sand and into a brightly lit building. Carlton blinked as the light hit him. They were in a long hallway. Moondog pulled a key card from her pocket and opened another door. They walked through into the living room of a large suite. It was bigger than any he had ever stayed in, probably due to the pilot's rank.

"Have a seat," Martina said, motioning to the

couch. Carlton dropped down onto the cushions. Martina sat in the armchair across from him, propping her feet on the ottoman. Moondog disappeared into another room. After a moment she reappeared, holding a beer in each hand.

"I think I owe you one of these," she said, tossing Carlton a bottle.

"Thanks," he said popping off the top.

Moondog walked to the center of the room, pulled the ottoman out from Martina's feet, and sat on it. Panther glared at her. Moondog calmly opened her beer and took a sip as if Martina didn't exist. Panther eyed her for a moment longer and then turned her attention back to Carlton.

"It's Vince, right?" she asked.

"Yeah," he said. "You can call me Vinny, like my friends do."

"Okay, Vinny, start from the beginning and tell us how you came to be flying that Bone."

Carlton took a deep breath. "I'm stationed at Tyndall. I was TDY to Dyess. It was early Monday morning, and my wingman, Ray Beckett, and I were going out to our jets to go home. There was no one else around. As we walked across the ramp, we overheard a man talking with the pilot and copilot of that B-1. He said he'd give them a couple million apiece if they'd steal the plane for him. He gave them explicit instructions to kill the two backseaters and then to fly the plane to South America.

"He hadn't seen us. They were scheduled to take off in less than half an hour. Ray went to alert Security Forces. I stayed behind and kept an eye on the aircrew. But Ray never came back. Nor did anybody else. The jet was about to launch. My cell phone was dead, and I couldn't get in touch with anyone. I hadn't seen any Security Forces personnel on the ramp at all. There were only a few maintenance guys around, and I didn't know if they'd been paid off too. I didn't know what else to do, so I snuck on board the plane, hoping nothing would happen. I figured it would be better to get in trouble for stowing away than to let them take the jet.

"About halfway through the flight the pilot got up and killed the backseaters. Then he put the plane into a dive. He leveled off at about 200 feet and engaged the autopilot. That was when I got up and tried to take over the plane. I tried just to render them unconscious, but the pilot saw me and attacked me, so I fought back. He shot the right seater by accident. I killed him and took control of the plane. Then I sent out that Mayday signal that you guys answered. And you know the rest."

"Is this what you told the investigators at Holloman?" Martina asked.

Carlton nodded. "So why'd you guys get me out of there?"

Moondog glanced at Panther.

"They were going to kill you," Martina said.

"What do you mean?" Vinny said.

"We overheard the man who snuck into your room talking to someone," Moondog said. "He was going to kill you. So we broke you out before he could."

"So what happens to me now?" Carlton asked.

"We'll go get you a room here," Martina said. "You'll stay at Edwards until they can figure out who is behind all this."

"Thanks," Carlton said. "I think I owe you about a thousand times over."

"Well, if you want to repay us," Moondog said, "you could start by buying me a couple more beers."

Martina simply shook her head and laughed.

Carlton studied the two women. Panther was taller and slightly more slender. Long brown hair tumbled down her back. She was not remarkably beautiful, but she possessed a ruggedly attractive look. What struck Carlton, however, was the strangeness of her eyes. Something lurked behind her brown eyes that he could not describe.

Moondog, by contrast, was stunning. Her golden-brown hair fell to her shoulders. Carlton could discern a slim figure beneath her flight suit. Nothing seemed hidden in her blue eyes.

"You got any better ideas?" Moondog said.

"Where is he going to find a beer joint at three in the morning?" Martina asked.

"Well, he doesn't have to buy it for me now..." Moondog said.

Martina laughed again. "Incorrigible swabbie."

"Swabbie?" Carlton asked.

"Yeah, poor Moondog made the mistake of joining the wrong service," Martina said. "Can't you tell?"

"What do you mean, 'the wrong service'?" Moondog asked. "Naval aviators are the only real pilots. You never had to make a precision carrier landing."

"A controlled crash, you mean?" Martina said. "You can always tell a Navy pilot on landing because they slam the airplane into the Earth. I know how to finesse a touchdown. Plus I can whip your ass in a dogfight anytime."

"Wanna bet on that?"

"Yeah, I do."

"You just wait," Moondog said. "Next time we get airborne I'll wax your tail so fast you won't even know I'm there."

"Right," Martina said. "And I'll sell you some prime ocean real estate—in Arizona."

Moondog glared at her.

"You want another beer?" she asked Carlton, standing.

"I'm good, thanks," he said.

Moondog shrugged. "All the more for me, then."

"You really are a swabbie," Carlton said.

"Don't you start with me, air crapper," Moondog said, walking over to the fridge. "I'll whoop your zoomie ass in half a second. Old Panther may put up a decent fight, but she's still only second best."

"And you're very, very delusional, Moondog," Martina said. "I could wax your tail with one hand behind my back."

Moondog snorted in disgust and stuck her head back in the fridge.

"Do you still have your phone?" Martina asked Carlton.

"Yeah."

"Give it to me. You'll get it back. I don't want you getting in touch with anyone until I'm sure we can trust you."

Carlton dug his phone from his pocket and handed it to her. She put it on the table and stood.

"It's not far to the lodging office," she said. "I'll walk you over there."

* * *

Panther walked back into Moondog's suite, shutting the door behind her. The other pilot was sitting on her bed, sipping a beer, while she tried to pull off her boots with her free hand.

"If you sailors had any sense, you'd realize it's much easier to get those things off with two hands and let go of your precious booze for two seconds," Martina said. "But I guess they don't teach common sense at Annapolis."

"Ha ha ha," Moondog said sarcastically.

"I did think that was rather funny. I took the kid over to lodging."

"That's good," Moondog said. "What do you think of his story?"

"Sounds like something I would have done," Martina replied.

"Yeah, you are crazy like that," Moondog said, tipping her beer back.

"It seems to make sense."

"I told you the kid was innocent."

"I wouldn't go that far," Martina said. "We need to find Beckett. If Carlton's story is true, he should be able to back it up."

"You really don't trust many people, do you?" Moondog asked.

"Why should I?"

"Do you trust anyone at all?"

"I trust you," Martina replied.

"Anyone else?"

"No," Martina said simply. "I got his phone. So he can't call anyone. And I can go through his contacts and see if there's anything strange."

"Nice," Moondog said.

Martina walked to the door. Moondog went back to trying to pull her boots off. Reaching the door, Panther stopped and turned around.

"But if the kid's story is true," she said, "then he's definitely got a lotta guts."

~ 5 ~

Dan Haley stared into his glass of scotch. He fixed his eyes forward, ignoring the smoke and the loud noise of the local bar. He didn't care about the rest of the world beyond the small glass sitting in front of him. All his attention was fixed on the gold-colored liquid.

Haley had flown with the general back to Dyess Air Force Base earlier that afternoon, then had been given the rest of the afternoon off. He had been sitting on the same bar stool since about six, drinking slowly. His real intention wasn't to get drunk, but it would seem strange to sit in a bar and not drink anything. So he spent the majority of his time staring into his glass.

He lifted his hand, slowly rubbing his throat. The spot where that... person... had hit him still hurt. The attack had come so quickly that Haley didn't have a chance to get a look at his assailant, but some underlying suspicion told him his attacker was a *woman.* He couldn't be sure, though. In the near-darkness of the room it was hard to see more than a silhouette, and that silhouette moved so quickly that it was impossible to identify. All Haley knew for sure was that one moment he had Carlton cornered against the wall, and the next he was lying on his back. Realizing he was outnumbered, he had turned and run from the room without getting a good look at the second person.

Carlton knew enough to incriminate Haley. Already evidence was showing that Carlton's story held. The cops had proof that the pilot, not Carlton, had killed the two backseaters. And now that the kid was free, he had the attempt on his life to support his innocence. No one would go out of their way to kill someone who was going to be found guilty anyway.

Somehow, he had to find Carlton and stop him from talking. The kid was the only person who could identify him as the true culprit. But Carlton had vanished off the face of the Earth. His insider on Holloman had no idea where the pilot had been taken. To ask anyone else for information would be too risky. Carlton could now be anywhere in the country, probably hundreds of miles away from Dyess or Holloman. That meant the chances of Haley ever finding Carlton were slim to nonexistent. The situation seemed hopeless.

The two female fighter pilots drifted back into his mind again. There was something strange about the way they left. The two women had vanished into the night like ghosts. According to Carmichael, they had simply gone home. Yet their returning to Edwards oddly coincided with Carlton's disappearance.

In reality, it was incredibly unlikely that the two pilots had anything to do with Carlton. They had a job to do at Edwards and no involvement with Carlton or the investigation. He had no real proof; he could scarcely remember the scene in billeting last night, but for some reason he couldn't shake the feeling that a woman rescued Carlton.

He tried to picture the two pilots in his mind. Both seemed physically fit and capable of putting up a fight. The smaller of the pair was Navy. Chances were she had seen a bar brawl or two. But it was the taller pilot who stuck in his memory. He paused, trying to remember the details of their brief meeting. Redrick was her name. With her lean frame, she didn't seem as powerful. But there was something strange lurking in her brown eyes. He couldn't put his finger on it, but whatever it was, it made her appear even more formidable than her companion.

And she certainly knew how to fight. He felt her wrath firsthand while trying to escape from the hangar housing the mystery planes. The woman moved like lightning. He was lucky to get away. Martina Redrick was certainly a force to be reckoned with.

It didn't matter, he realized. He would probably never know who attacked him, let alone if it was a woman. His main concern was finding Carlton, another impossibility. From Haley's point of view, the situation seemed incredibly hopeless. For the first time in nearly forty minutes, he lifted his glass and swallowed some of the gold liquid.

"Care for some company, Major?" a male voice asked.

"I was wondering when you were going to show," Haley said, not turning to face the man behind him. The newcomer slid onto the bar stool beside Haley. His skin was dark and his hair was a thick, shaggy black. His ethnicity was hard to discern, perhaps Hispanic or even Middle Eastern.

"This is hardly the place to talk," he said. "Can I give you a lift back to your place?"

This is where it gets interesting, Haley thought.

"Why not?" he replied, draining the rest of his scotch and laying a ten on the bar. He stood and followed the smaller man outside. They cut into a side alley where a nondescript black sedan sat in the darkness.

"Get in," Haley's companion said, walking to the

driver's side. Haley opened the passenger door and sat down. The man started the engine. The headlights came to life, and the sedan pulled out into the city streets, swerving violently. Haley fought to fasten his seat belt.

"What the hell happened, Haley?" his contact said. "You were supposed to deliver that plane to us four days ago."

"It was a crazy fluke," Haley said. His fate rested on the course of the conversation. "Some fighter pilot found out about the plan. He snuck on board the plane and stopped our people from taking it."

"How much does he know?" the driver demanded, turning onto the highway and pushing his foot to the floor.

"I can't say exactly," Haley said, watching as the road rushed past him. "I think he overheard me briefing the pilots, which would mean he only knew of the plan to kill the crew and steal the plane. He might be able to connect it to me, but certainly not to you."

"Where is he now?"

"I don't know for sure. Originally I tried to frame him for the crime, but there were cracks in the evidence. Then I tried to kill him to keep him from talking, but he fought back and escaped. He's been moved to a safe house. I tried to find out where they took him, but no one seemed to know anything. It was like he vanished into thin air."

"You realize this is a complete and utter failure," his contact said. "You were supposed to perform the simple task of delivering a bomber to us, and you allow some stupid fighter pilot to ruin the whole thing. My boss is not going to be happy when he finds out about this. And he's liable to have your neck for it."

The car swerved off the road and stopped at a deserted turnoff. The driver killed the engine and the lights.

"If this guy manages to identify you as being involved, your connection to us could be revealed, and that would be the end for our organization." The driver turned to Haley, his face taking on a threatening appearance in the dim light. "Not only have you failed in your mission, but you may have compromised our entire operation. You know how necessary secrecy is."

"I know," Haley said, feeling cold sweat running down his back.

"However, the bomber is a key component of our plan. Is there any way you can deliver one now?"

"No. The loss of another bomber would raise suspicion. However, I may be able to get you a more powerful weapon."

"Such as?" His contact's curiosity was clearly piqued.

"When the bomber was hijacked, a fighter escort was called in. The planes that intercepted weren't regular fighters. They were highly classified aircraft. They stayed on the ground for a few days waiting for fuel, under guard the entire time."

"And you can get us these planes?"

"No, but I can tell you where to find the pilots, and you can get the information from them."

Haley's contact turned the key in the ignition and swung the car around and headed back for the city.

"Start talking," he said.

"The pilots are Lieutenant Colonel Martina Redrick and Commander Rachel Ansetti. They are currently on temporary assignment at Edwards Air Force Base in California, where the planes are being tested," Haley said. "I might add, they may be capable of defending themselves."

His contact scoffed. "I think our men can handle two women."

As the car sped back to the city, Haley outlined

all he knew about Edwards Air Force Base and the few facts he could give about Redrick and Ansetti, mostly physical description. He also told everything he knew about Carlton.

"I'll talk to my boss," the driver said as he pulled off the highway, "and get my people searching for these pilots. We'll try and track down Carlton and silence him too."

The car slid to a stop near the bar where he had originally picked Haley up. "But if we don't get to him in time, and he cites you as the real culprit in stealing the B-1, my men will make sure you can't talk. Get out."

Haley stepped quickly onto the curb. The door slammed behind him, and the black car took off again, tearing down the street into the darkness. Haley watched it disappear before turning away and walking along the road to his house. Thoughts of the fighter pilots and the bomber swirled in his head. He had managed to buy himself time and a second chance. They weren't going to kill him, at least not yet. Provided Carlton stayed in hiding, he was safe. If not, Haley would be arrested at best and killed at worst. His problems were far from solved, but for now his plan was still working.

* * *

The sun splashed warmly over the desert sand of Edwards Air Force Base. The air lay hot and dry over the tarmac as Panther and Moondog walked slowly away from their planes.

"That was a good flight," Moondog said, running her hand through her hair.

"Yeah," Martina agreed. "Too bad it was the last one for a while."

"And we go back to Houston and the space shuttle tomorrow. How long do you think before we get to come back here?"

"Six months at least. They'll have to sort through all the data we gathered and make some modifications before we get to fly again."

"Such a shame," Moondog remarked.

"Yeah."

Martina pushed open the door to her suite and stepped inside. Moondog followed.

"You hungry?"

"Yeah."

"What do you want to do for lunch?"

Moondog simply shrugged. Suddenly, her eyes grew wide.

"Panther, behind you!" she shouted.

Martina spun around. A small, dark-skinned man leapt for her, clutching a needle in his hand. Panther stepped into him, smashing her first into his nose. The man reeled backward. She grabbed his arm, banging his hand into the wall. He released his grip on the syringe, and it fell to the floor. Panther dug her heel into the syringe, breaking it. A few drops of clear liquid spilled on the carpet.

The door to the suite flew open and two more men rushed in. The first grabbed Moondog by the wrist. She twisted around to face him. He was holding a syringe in his free hand. He drove the needle toward her.

She stepped forward, blocking his jab. She dealt him a quick blow to the side of his head, then pulled his hand off hers, twisting his wrist downward. The man swung his free hand frantically at Moondog. The blow skimmed off her cheek, spinning her head around. She released her grip on him.

Moondog looked up to find another man standing over her. He reached for her, trying to grab her by the throat. Moondog punched him in the gut. The man staggered backward. Moondog kicked him forcefully in the stomach. The man stepped back again, tripping over the coffee table and crashing to the floor.

She stomped her boot into the thug's throat, pressing down with all her weight. His eyes grew wide with shock as he tried to breathe through his crushed windpipe. A rasping wheeze, accompanied by the gurgling sound of blood, emanated from his mouth.

He grabbed wildly for Moondog's legs, but she quickly sidestepped, turning her attention back to the first man.

Slowly, the man lying on the ground drew a small knife from his pocket and flung it at Moondog with the last bit of strength in his body. His hand fell to the ground as his eyes closed. He lay motionless on the floor. The knife flew erratically through the air, embedding itself in Moondog's right shoulder. Caught off guard, the pilot jumped, twisting around.

Seeing his chance, the other man threw his shoulder into her stomach. Moondog crashed to the floor, landing on the shattered coffee table. The man reached down and grabbed one of its detached wooden legs. He swung it forcefully at the pilot. Moondog rolled quickly. The blow crashed down beside her, narrowly missing her.

The man in front of Panther swung his fist at her head. She ducked, blocking the blow with her left arm. Keeping her arm raised against his, she punched him in the stomach. Quickly, she grabbed his right wrist and spun him around, throwing him into the other man. The two crashed together, nearly falling to the floor.

The larger man pushed aside his companion and lunged for Panther. He wrapped his arms around her waist, throwing her to the ground. The force knocked the wind out of Panther. The thug pinned her down. He wrapped his hands around her neck, digging his thumbs into her throat. She grabbed him by the ear, jerking it down and ripping the cartilage. The man screamed, pressing his hand to the bloody side of his head. Panther shifted her weight beneath him and threw him off her.

Panther leapt to her feet and turned to face the other man. He eyed the woman suspiciously, unsure of just how to approach her. Slowly, he raised his fist and stepped forward. He swung his fists at her. She dodged the first blow, but the second connected squarely with her left eye. She staggered back.

Moondog reached behind her and pulled the knife from her shoulder. She slashed at her attacker as he brought the table leg down on her again. This time the wood hit her collarbone. The knife flew from her hand, arcing above the man's head and sticking into the wall.

Moondog raised her leg, kicking him in the hand. He released his grip on the wooden block, dropping it on the floor. Moondog lunged for him, wrapping her fingers around his throat. The man rapidly produced another needle from his pocket and plunged the syringe into her thigh.

Moondog released her grip and thrust her left hand into the side of the man's head. He reeled backward, crouching on the ground. She paused, shaking her head to try and clear it. Her body swayed, her arms going limp. Her eyes closed. She crumpled to the floor and lay still.

A pair of arms grabbed Panther from behind in a bear hug, pinning her elbows to her sides. Seeing the large thug grab her, the goon in front of her dug in his pocket for what Panther guessed was another needle. Beyond him, she saw Moondog standing with her fists raised. Her friend crumpled to the floor as Panther watched in horror.

She quickly stuck her hand into her own pocket, removing a small knife. In one swift move, she flipped the blade open, thrust it deeply into the man's thigh, and twisted the handle sideways. He howled in pain and released his grip on Panther. She yanked the knife from his flesh and stepped forward, swinging the weapon fiercely at the small man advancing on her. He ducked, throwing himself into her chest at full force. The blow knocked her to the floor. The blade flew from her hand and slid underneath the couch.

Before Panther could regain her footing, the other man threw his body on top of hers, knocking her to the floor. He wrapped his fingers tightly against her throat. Behind him, Moondog's assailant produced another needle.

In an instant the other man was on her, sticking the needle into her arm. Martina struggled fiercely for a moment as the serum quickly worked its way through her body. Her movements became slower and more lethargic, until her body went completely limp. She never felt the men drag her from the room.

~ 6 ~

"Mr. President, General Peters is on the line," David Webster's secretary called over the intercom in her bored, nasal voice. "He says it's urgent."

"It's always urgent, Sherri," Webster sighed, wondering what was happening now. Redrick and Ansetti had probably found their way into some type of trouble again. "Did he say what it was?"

"No, sir."

"Fine, put him through," Webster responded, picking up the phone. "Good morning, General," he said, turning to gaze out at the Rose Garden as he spoke into the receiver. "What can I do for you?"

"We've got another crisis over here, sir," Peters said.

"The Hellcats again?"

"The pilots, sir."

I knew it, Webster thought. Those two were always getting into trouble.

"They're missing," Peter continued.

"Missing?" Webster asked. "What happened to them?"

"We're not entirely sure, sir. We believed they were kidnapped."

"Again? How?"

"It looks as if someone snuck into their quarters, knocked them out, and dragged them off," Peters said.

"All right," Webster said. "Start from the

beginning. When was the last time anyone saw Redrick and Ansetti?"

"They had just finished the final run on the Hellcats and were going back to billeting after being debriefed. I tried getting in touch with them about an hour later and got no answer, so I sent someone to their quarters. The living room in Redrick's suite was in shambles, and the pilots were gone. We found Ansetti's flight cap and bag inside the room."

"Is that all we know?" Webster asked.

"I've had OSI go through the VOQ," Peters said. "They found a broken syringe carrying traces of a knockout drug, as well as several unidentified fingerprints and drops of blood. Apparently, whoever was responsible for this drugged the coffee in the lodging office last night. When the person on duty fell asleep, they went in, stole a master key, and used the computer to locate Redrick and Ansetti."

"What about the planes?"

"The Hellcats have been sitting untouched in the hangar since this afternoon, sir."

"You don't suppose someone grabbed the pilots to try to get to the planes, do you?" Webster asked.

"The thought had crossed my mind," the general said. "It's very possible. We keep the Hellcats under extremely tight security, but the pilots are more accessible."

"Did Carmichael ever find the man who was snooping around the planes after that incident with the B-1?"

"No, sir," Peters said. "I called Carmichael almost immediately after we discovered the pilots missing. They still have no idea who he was."

"Perhaps he told someone about the planes, and they went after the pilots."

"It's highly possible," Peters said.

"What about Carlton?"

"He's missing as well."

"Wasn't he under guard?"

"We were keeping a close eye on him, sir," Peters said, "but he wasn't under guard. The base is too remote for him to go anywhere without transportation, and only six people knew he was at Edwards. We're guessing the kidnappers saw his name in the lodging computer and decided to pick him up too."

"Damn," Webster said. He spun back around in his chair, dropped his elbows on his desk, and stared across the Oval Office.

"Look, Scott," he said, "I'm going to send a few federal agents out there to help your guys track down our missing pilots. That way, you can have all the information at Langley backing you. I want those women found."

"Thank you, sir. I greatly appreciate that."

"Let me know as soon as you learn anything," Webster said. "We can't let those planes be compromised."

* * *

Slowly, Martina opened her eyes. Her head was pounding. Her vision was foggy, her eyes refusing to focus. All she saw before her was a dark blur. Her left eye wouldn't open. Her entire body ached. She tried to move her hands, only to find that her arms were held tightly in place. She could move her fingers, but her wrists were firmly pinned behind her. She felt the tight coils of ropes binding her.

Gradually, her vision began to focus. She was sitting upright in a hard wooden chair, still wearing her flight suit. She found herself in a large room with rough rock walls and an uneven stone floor. A few bare lightbulbs hung from the coarse ceiling. The room was completely empty. She glanced behind her. She was alone. Questions were slowly filling her mind. Where was she? Where was Moondog? And, more importantly, how could she get out of this place?

A door opened behind her. Footsteps echoed through the room as someone approached. A bearded man in torn camouflage fatigues stepped in front of Martina. A pair of black eyes stared at her from beneath his long hair. His skin was dark.

"Who the hell are you?" Panther demanded. "And where am I?"

"I ask the questions around here, Colonel," the man said in heavily accented English. He smiled, revealing cracked yellow teeth.

"Where's Commander Ansetti?" she asked, ignoring his statement. "What do you want with us?"

"I want to know about the planes you fly."

"What planes?" Martina asked. Anger burned inside her. That little son of a bitch had turned them in! If she ever got her hands on Carlton...

"The ones you were flying for the Air Force."

"You're mistaken," she said. "I don't fly."

She twisted her wrists. The bindings felt somewhat loose. She began to move her hands, trying to free herself.

"You are a pilot. It says so on your patch." He pointed to the wings on her flight suit. "You fly planes."

"What kind of planes?"

"Secret planes," he said.

"What's so special about these planes?" she asked.

"They are some sort of special fighter," he said. "Superior to everything. I want to know about them. You will tell me everything you know."

"I don't know what you're talking about," Martina said.

The man stepped forward, swinging his fist into Martina's jaw. The pilot's head flew back. The front legs of the chair lifted from the ground, then slammed back into the floor.

Martina fixed her cold eyes on him.

"Suppose I do tell you something," she said. "What's in it for me?"

The man stared at her. "What do you mean?"

"What will you do for me if I talk?" Martina asked. She pushed the ropes down, trying to pull them over her fingers.

"Nothing," the man said. "You will tell me what you know."

"Why should I tell you anything if I don't get something for it?" she said. "You don't compensate me, I won't help you."

"And what do you want?" he sneered.

"How about you start by telling me who you are and what you want with these planes."

"And if I do, you will tell me about them?"

Martina did not reply. She arched her eyebrows and looked at him.

"Very well," he said. "My name is Azad Kalliff."

"And why do you want these aircraft?" Panther asked.

"You have a superior weapons technology," he said. "With your planes I can destroy whole cities."

"And how would you do that?" she asked. Slowly, the rope was moving over her skin.

"That's what I want you to tell me," he said. Martina remained silent.

"I answered your questions," Kalliff said. "Now you answer mine."

"Don't know what you're talking about. Sorry," Martina said with a smile.

"Lying bitch!" Kalliff screamed. He punched her in the side of the face, twisting her head sideways.

"You will talk!" he shouted. "Now!"

"If you think I'm going to tell you anything, you're out of your mind," Panther said, smiling through bloodied lips. She had almost slid the rope over her thumb.

Kalliff drew out a small knife and flicked the blade open. “I will give you one last chance,” he said. “Tell me about the planes.”

“What planes?”

He stepped forward, stabbing the knife into her left arm.

“Talk,” he said.

“How ’bout you go fuck yourself?” she said, wincing.

“If you talk, I will stop,” he said, slowly twisting the blade in her skin.

“I don’t know anything,” Martina said.

Kalliff yanked the knife from her skin and slashed at her. Martina pulled her left hand free of the rope and grabbed his wrist. Shocked, Kalliff stepped back. Panther leapt to her feet, punching Kalliff in the stomach. As his head came down, she thrust her leg up, bringing her knee directly into his nose. She snatched the knife from his hand as he fell and scrambled for the door.

Two large men dressed in tattered fatigues and similar in appearance to Kalliff stepped into her path. Martina swung the knife in an arc, slicing open the throat of the man to her right. He collapsed to the floor, dead. She twisted toward the other man and swung the blade at him, only to have her slash blocked. His fist slammed into her stomach.

Martina stumbled back. Regaining her footing, she drove her foot into the man’s groin. As he bent over she plunged the knife into his side. She pulled the knife back as he collapsed. Martina jumped over his body. Rushing out the door, she found herself standing in a hallway. She took off at a dead sprint. Behind her, Kalliff was shouting angrily in some incomprehensible language.

The hall was dimly lit, illuminated by a string of small, bare electric lights. The connecting wires ran exposed against the stone ceiling. The floor and walls were roughly hewn rock. The sound of her boots echoed off the walls as she raced down the hall.

Straight ahead of her the hallway came to an abrupt stop. Martina ducked quickly into a side hall and continued her sprint, rapidly searching for any way out. The dark passages revealed no quick exits. She needed to find Moondog and get out.

The sound of pounding feet filled the hall behind her. Kalliff's minions weren't far away. Martina quickened her pace. She continued to scan to the left and right, looking for an escape route.

Shouts rang through the air. The echoing thud of boots hitting rock grew closer. There were no exits on either side. Martina looked over her left shoulder. The hall was still empty. She continued to run.

A rifle cracked loudly. The bullet whizzed over Martina's head, imbedding in the rock surface. Dust rained down over her. She stole another glance over her shoulder. Four or five men were racing after her, each holding a gun. They wore a combination of dirty fatigues and civilian clothes. Most had long hair and badly needed a shave. The lead man raised his weapon again and fired. They were aiming high, trying to scare her. They wouldn't kill her. She had information they needed.

She ran harder, turning down a hall to her left. The gunshots ceased behind her, but the pounding of boots continued, drawing closer. A flight of stairs rose ahead of her. She charged up the steps two at a time.

She found herself on a landing, with halls leading to the left, right, and straight ahead. She dodged quickly to the left, refusing to slow her sprint. Another door appeared to her left, and she dashed through it. Behind her, the sound of her pursuers' footfalls changed as they bounded up the steps.

A large man stepped into the hall in front of Martina, an AK-47 in his hands. Seeing her, he lowered the weapon, pointing it directly at her. She stopped in her tracks. The man kept the gun trained on her.

Panther glared at him, her lips curling upward in a fearsome snarl. The man studied her curiously. She screamed, a low, guttural war cry emanating from deep within her chest as she rushed for him. Taken by surprise, the man jumped, lowering the gun.

Martina threw her body into his, knocking him back. She pressed the small knife in her hand between his ribs as they collided, twisting the blade upward. The man gasped and collapsed to the ground.

Martina snatched the AK from his hands and flipped the safety off just as the men chasing her charged through the door. She raised the gun and depressed the trigger, spraying her pursuers with a hail of bullets and cutting them down. Their lifeless bodies fell to the ground. A brief wail of pain and surprise pierced the air before they fell silent.

Martina walked over to the bodies. All the men were motionless. She picked up a few magazines, sliding a fresh one into her AK. She turned and started to run again, leaping over the dead body of the first man and sprinting down the hall. The shots were sure to attract attention.

She ducked down the nearest hallway, winding her way through the passages, searching desperately for Moondog or an exit and finding neither. She was trapped in a maze of stone corridors and dim lights. Nothing seemed to bring her any closer to freedom.

Another set of stairs appeared before her, these leading down. Panther launched herself down the steps, leaping to the ground at the bottom of the stairs. She landed hard on her feet and stumbled forward. Catching herself, she continued to dash through the dimly lit hall.

She ducked into yet another side hall. No sooner had she turned the corner than a hand slammed violently into her neck. Her feet flew out from beneath her, and she crashed to the floor, landing flat on her back on the rough rock.

Dazed, she looked up. A huge man towered over her. He stood over seven feet tall and had shoulders like an ox. His face was clean-shaven, as was his skull. He wore combat boots and fatigue pants. The sleeves were torn from his tattered brown shirt, revealing huge arms and shoulders.

Martina threw her feet over her head, rolling backward into a crouching position. She pointed the AK directly at his chest and pulled the trigger. Nothing happened. The gun was jammed.

Martina stood, thrusting the butt of her rifle into his stomach with as much force as she could muster. The man did not react. She looked up at him. He smiled at her through broken, cracked teeth.

Reaching down, he pulled the AK from her hands, snapped the rifle in half, and threw the pieces across the room. Wrapping one giant hand around Martina's neck, he lifted her off the ground, squeezing her throat. Her toes dangled above the floor. She grabbed his wrist with both hands, swinging her feet at him. He simply moved his arm, laughing as her kick breezed past him.

He shook his hand, sending shock waves through her entire body, then flung her aside carelessly, as if she were a rag. Martina crashed into the far wall, sliding slowly to the ground. Dazed, she sat motionless against the rock, breathing hard.

The pounding of boots on stone filled the air. A large group of men swarmed into the room, surrounded Martina, and pointed their assault rifles directly at her.

Two men stepped forward. Grabbing Martina by the shoulders, they flung her to the floor. She landed flat on her stomach. One man pressed his boot against her back, pinning her down. The second pulled her arms back behind her and tightly wound a rope around her hands.

The first man took his foot off Martina. The others lowered their weapons and stepped back. She rolled onto her side. Kalliff advanced, stopping a few inches from Martina's face.

"That was very stupid," he said.

Martina looked up. Kalliff stood over her.

"You won't get out of here." His boot collided with the side of her face.

"But," he said, bending down and lifting her chin off the floor, "I can assure you, if you tell me about your planes, things will be much easier for you."

"Well, that's too bad," Martina said, her split, bleeding lips parting in a smile. "Because I ain't gonna tell you a fucking thing."

"You will talk," he said, standing slowly. "Sooner or later, you will talk."

He kicked her again, then barked something to the other men. Two grabbed Martina and pulled her off the floor. They began to drag her forward, her boots scraping along the ground. She kept her head up, attempting to memorize every detail of the maze the men were dragging her through.

They stopped before a barred metal door. One man pulled the door open. The second flung Martina inside. She stumbled forward, tripping over the rough rock and falling onto the hard floor. The door slammed shut behind her.

One of the men locked the door behind her. They turned and walked away, the sound of their footsteps fading down the hall.

Martina groaned, lifting her head off the rock and trying to move her arms. Something moved in the darkness of the cell. A thin figure sat against the wall, half hidden in the shadows.

"Moondog?" Martina said, staring at the figure. "Is that you?"

"Yeah," Moondog replied, standing and walking to where Martina lay. The Navy pilot's face was bruised. Dried blood coated the back of her flight suit below her right shoulder. A tear just above her shoulder blade revealed a cut two inches long. There were two small holes in the left leg of her flight suit and a third on her right arm. All were surrounded with blood.

"Hang on, I'll get you free."

Moondog sat down beside Panther and quickly untied the ropes binding her hands. Free from the coils, Martina pulled herself to a sitting position and rubbed her wrists.

"Thanks," she said. She looked at her friend, seeing the gashes in Moondog's arm and leg. "Are you hurt?"

Moondog shook her head. "They cut me a few times, but never deep. You?"

"I'm fine."

"What happened?"

"I got away," Martina said. "Took out a few of those bastards. They weren't very happy when they caught me."

"Any idea where we are?" Moondog asked.

"Somewhere with really hard floors," Martina said, massaging her neck. Her head was hurting worse than before, and her body still ached.

"That doesn't help."

"Sorry."

"You see any way out?"

"Unfortunately, no," Martina said. "I just found a lot of dark, rough hallways."

"Damn."

Martina rubbed her eyes. "The guy holding us here says his name is Azad Kalliff. Ring any bells?"

"No."

"Did he question you?"

"Briefly. I didn't tell them anything, so they hit me a few times and locked me back up."

She leaned over and whispered in Martina's ear, "I think they're after the Hellcats."

"I know," Martina replied in a hushed voice. "Don't tell these fuckers anything. They want information from us, and as long as we don't give it to them, we stay alive."

"Right," Moondog said. "You got any idea how to get out of here?"

"Not yet," Martina said. "But we'll find a way."

She inspected the cut on her arm. It had already stopped bleeding.

"Looks like trusting Carlton was a mistake after all," Martina sighed.

"Yeah," Moondog said. She leaned back, propping herself up on her elbows. "Hard to believe that kid sold us out."

"I guess he really was in on it all along," Martina said. "He might even have been working with the guy who tried to kill him. Maybe the whole attempted murder thing was just a ploy to get us to show him the planes."

"I suppose it's possible," Moondog said. "We set Carlton free and he leads his friends right to us."

"It's a good thing we blindfolded him on the flight to Edwards," Martina said. "Although he did get a look at them when we intercepted the bomber. I'm sure he could have guessed what they can do from the tiling."

"But if Carlton knows what they can do, then why is Kalliff questioning us about our planes?" Moondog asked.

"Carlton doesn't know the details," Martina said, "what kind of weapons they carry, stuff like that."

She paused, frowning.

"What's wrong?" Moondog asked.

"Kalliff didn't seem to know what the Hellcats were at all," Martina muttered. "He thought they were some sort of superweapon. He didn't even mention space."

"So?"

"If Carlton figured out what the Hellcats really were, Kalliff would know too. He would have asked me if they flew in space. He doesn't have any clue about their real mission. He thinks he can use them to destroy cities. Carlton saw how big the planes are. He knows that they can't carry more than two 1,000-pound bombs."

"That's only enough to take out a couple buildings," Moondog agreed.

"And Vinny saw where we hangared the planes," Martina continued. "He could have led them right to the Hellcats. They would have taken them and left us alone."

"So Carlton hasn't talked?" Moondog asked.

"Maybe," Martina muttered. "This makes no sense." She covered her face with her hands.

"How do we get into these things?" Moondog sighed.

"No clue," Martina muttered. "No clue at all." She lay back, stretching her body out along the hard rock floor.

"I'll tell you one thing, though," she said. "If I knew, we sure wouldn't be here now."

~ 7 ~

The sound of a key in the lock stirred Panther back to consciousness. She opened her eyes to see three pairs of boots standing outside her cell. Two men pointed guns at the captives while the third pulled open the door.

Martina pushed herself into a sitting position. The pain in her head had diminished, but her whole body was still stiff and sore. She watched the guards and waited, motionless. Moondog studied them with a bored look on her face.

Two of the men entered the small cell as the door swung open. The first man aimed his gun at Martina's head while the other fixed his weapon on Moondog. The pilots remained still. The third man walked into the cell, stepping behind Martina. He bent down, pushed his knee into her back, and shoved her to the floor. Yanking her arms behind her, he wrapped a rope tightly around her wrists.

He stood, grabbing her left arm. The first gunman lowered his weapon and took hold of her other arm. They dragged her from the cell, tossing her to the floor outside. The man on her right planted his foot firmly on her back. The third man walked slowly from the cell, keeping the muzzle of his gun pointed directly at Moondog. The man with the key latched the door behind him.

The two others grabbed Martina and pulled her to

her feet. They led her down the hall into a small room. Kalliff stood in the center of the floor. The men holding Martina flung her to the ground. Kalliff looked down at her, smirking. Martina snarled up at him. She rolled onto her side and raised herself onto her knees. Climbing to her feet, she met his gaze, head held high.

"So, Colonel, tell me about your airplanes," Kalliff said.

"I told you before, I don't know anything," Martina responded.

"You're lying," Kalliff snarled. "Now, tell me what you know."

"I know you're ugly as fuck and that your breath reeks." She smirked as his face tightened with rage.

One of the men standing behind her hit her in the back of the knees. Her legs buckled, and she dropped to the floor. Kalliff kicked her in the chest, knocking her on her back. He dropped down onto her stomach, straddling her. A wave of pain washed through her chest as his weight pressed against her injured body. Her hands, still bound, dug into the small of her back. She continued to grin, despite the pain evident in her face.

"You will talk," Kalliff said, drawing his face to within an inch of hers. "Or I will make this very painful for you."

"I don't know anything," Martina repeated.

"Do not lie to me, Colonel," he hissed. "You are a test pilot at Edwards Air Force Base. You fly a secret aircraft with amazing capabilities. Tell me what it can do."

"It seems you already know more about it than me," Martina said.

Kalliff smashed his fist into the side of her face, sending a flight of stars across Martina's vision. "What is the airplane capable of?"

"I don't know what you're talking about."

Kalliff struck her across the face again. He climbed off her and knelt on the floor. He grabbed her by the hair, pulling her head up to his face. She rolled onto her side.

"What is so special about your airplane?" he demanded.

"There is no plane," Panther snarled.

Kalliff released his grip on her hair, dropping her head back onto the floor.

"My sources in your country say otherwise," he said, pulling a knife from his pocket. He stuck the tip of the blade into Martina's arm and twisted it sideways. "They tell me you fly a top secret plane for the U.S. Air Force."

"I told you, it doesn't exist," she said, gritting her teeth against the pain.

Kalliff snarled. He pulled the knife from her arm and dug it into her leg, slashing it down the length of her thigh, creating a long, shallow cut.

"They are real," he said. "You fly out of Edwards Air Force Base."

"Either your skull is made of concrete or your brain is the size of a walnut," Panther said. "There is no such thing."

"Lying bitch!" Kalliff shouted. "The plane is at Edwards Air Force Base. I want to know where."

"I don't even know where Edwards is."

"You know where Edwards is, and you will tell me where to find these planes."

"I don't know what you're talking about," she said matter-of-factly.

Kalliff grabbed her by the collar and hauled her to her feet, thrusting her back forcefully into the wall.

"Tell me how to get to those planes," he snarled. "Tell me exactly where they are and exactly how to get to them."

"Even if I knew what you were talking about, it wouldn't do you any good. You probably couldn't find your way out of a paper bag with a map."

Kalliff drove his fist into Martina's chin.

"Where do I find the planes?" he demanded.

"Try looking up your ass," she said.

Kalliff slashed his knife into the side of her arm again.

"Tell me where to find them," he said angrily.

"Go fuck a cow, ape-man," Panther said, spitting blood into his face. "I'm not going to tell you anything."

Kalliff swung his fist into her face, sending her reeling. He grabbed her by the collar and threw her against the wall. Dazed by the force of the blow, Martina sank slowly to the floor. Kalliff barked something incomprehensible and stalked away angrily, leaving her on the floor.

Two men stepped forward, grabbed Martina by the arms, and hauled her up. She hung limply between them, her legs dragging along the floor as they pulled her from the room. Pain raced through her stomach and chest. She tried to stand, but her body was too close to the ground for her to regain her feet.

They dragged her through the hallways. Panther held her head up, trying to memorize the route. She kept her eyes open for anything that looked like an exit. She needed to find a way out of this maze if she ever wanted to get free.

The men continued to pull her along, ignoring her. Ahead of them, two more of Kalliff's rabble turned the corner, dragging a limp figure between them. Martina stared at the man. Slowly, he lifted his head.

His face was covered in bruises. Both his eyes were black. Flecks of dried blood surrounded his mouth and nose. The left side of his face was covered in blood, which was draining from a gash above his temple and matting his hair. His t-shirt and jeans were tattered, torn by the blade of a knife and covered with dark-red spots.

Martina watched in disbelief as the men dragged him toward her. Something sparked in his eyes as he recognized her. A soft light glowed in his light-brown irises. Martina twisted her head around as he was pulled past her, following him with her eyes until the body of the man to her left blocked her vision.

Martina's captors kept their even pace down the hall. Finally, they stopped in front of her cell. One unlocked the door, and the other threw her inside. The metal bars slammed closed behind her, and the men marched off. Moondog watched from the corner.

Martina slid over to her friend.

"Do you mind?" she asked, raising her bound hands. Moondog pulled the rope from her wrists.

Martina studied the cuts on her arm and leg. Once again, the gashes were all fairly shallow. A little blood was still oozing from her left arm.

"Carlton's here," Martina whispered.

"Why wouldn't he be if he's helping Kalliff?" Moondog asked.

"No," Martina said. "Two thugs just dragged him past me. He was all tied up and beat to hell. Covered in bruises and blood. He looks worse than the two of us put together."

"Really?"

"Yeah. I don't think he had a hand in this at all. You should have seen the way the kid looked at me, Moondog. His face just lit up, like I was about to set him free or something."

"If he didn't turn us in, then how did he get here?"

"I don't know. But it certainly didn't look like he came here willingly."

"So if he didn't hand us over to these fuckers, who did?" Moondog asked.

"I don't know," Martina said. "The guy who was snooping around the planes, most likely. Or maybe whoever tried to kill Carlton."

"Could be one and the same."

"That's possible," Martina agreed. "I never did get a good look at the guy who was trying to see the Hellcats."

Moondog sighed, wrapping the loose rope around her hands and then slowly unwrapping it. Martina stared silently at her feet.

"You don't suppose Vinny told them anything about the planes, do you?" Moondog asked after a moment.

"Not yet," Panther said. "Kalliff didn't have any more information than when I last talked to him."

"Do you think he will?"

"I sure hope not."

* * *

The two men dropped Carlton onto the coarse rock floor. Unable to catch himself with his hands tied behind his back, he landed on his face. He rolled onto his side and slowly sat up. Lifting his head, he found himself looking at the dark-haired man whom he had assumed to be either the group's ringleader or the chief interrogator.

The fighter pilot wasn't entirely sure where he was, or even how he had come to be there. The last thing he remembered was walking over to Moondog's suite to talk to her for a few minutes. He had knocked on the door. Someone had opened it, so he walked inside. Then everything went black. The next thing he knew, he was being locked in a subterranean jail cell.

He hadn't seen either of the astronauts, except for passing Martina in the hall a few moments earlier, but he had several meetings with the unshaven man in front of him. Carlton narrowed his eyes, his face twisting into a snarl.

"Who are you?" the man asked.

"Why the fuck should I tell you?" Carlton snorted.

The man stepped forward, kicking Carlton in the side of the face. The blow knocked Carlton onto his back.

"I asked you a question," the man said, leaning over him.

"Answer mine first," Carlton said.

The man shoved his foot into Carlton's stomach. Carlton rolled onto his side and doubled over. A wave of fire flashed through his chest. He grimaced, trying to show as little pain as possible.

"What do you know about planes?" the man demanded.

"They fly?" Carlton offered.

"Of course they fly, you idiot!" the man said. "Do you fly planes?"

"No, pilots fly planes."

"Are you a pilot?" the man asked.

"No."

"Liar!" the man shouted, driving his foot into Carlton's face. He rolled onto his back. The man placed his boot on Carlton's throat, applying just enough pressure so that his captive could still breathe, but just barely. Any more force would crush his windpipe.

"What do you know about special planes, fighter planes?" the man demanded.

"I don't know anything," Carlton choked. "Ask the Air Force."

"You are in the Air Force," the man said, leaning forward and pressing down harder on Carlton's' throat.

"No, I'm not," Carlton rasped.

The man lifted his boot from Carlton's neck.

"What were you doing in California?"

"Where?"

The man dropped to his knees, drawing a knife in a rapid motion. He flicked the blade open and shoved the tip of the weapon into the fleshy part of Carlton's thigh. A searing pain shot through his leg. He clamped his jaw shut, refusing to scream.

"California," he said. "Where we found you."

"Visiting my aunt," Vinny snarled.

"Your aunt lives on an Air Force base?" the man asked, twisting the knife in Carlton's leg.

Carlton gave him a quizzical look despite the pain in his face.

"You were on an Air Force base," his torturer said. "What were you doing there?"

"What are you talking about?" Carlton asked. The man drew the tip of the knife down his leg, creating a long shallow gash.

"Redrick and Ansetti, are they pilots?"

"Who?"

"Air Force pilots," the man replied. "What do you know about their planes?"

"I told you, I don't know anything," Carlton said. The man dug the knife into Carlton's skin again, then pulled the blade from his victim's leg and stuck it back in his pocket.

"Maybe he really doesn't know anything," one of Kalliff's men said in a language Carlton could not understand.

"He knows how to play dumb," Kalliff snorted in Arabic. "But maybe he doesn't know about the planes. Our man said the two women, Redrick and Ansetti, were the pilots. He didn't even mention this guy."

"What do we do with him, then?"

"Toss him back in his cell," Kalliff said. "Leave him there for a few days. If we don't get any information from him, then we kill him. Redrick and Ansetti are the important ones. He doesn't matter."

The two thugs grabbed Carlton and pulled him to

his feet. They dragged him from the room and down the winding corridors, stopping in front of his cell. One man pulled a set of keys from his pocket and unlocked the door. He then stepped behind Carlton, quickly untying his wrists. As soon as the rope fell free, the second man shoved him inside the small room. The door slammed shut behind him.

Carlton turned and watched as one of the men locked the door, trapping him inside. The guard stuck the key back into his pocket, leaving the ring protruding from the fabric. The two men turned.

Quickly, Carlton stuck his hands through the bars, hooking the key ring with his finger as the guard passed him. He held his hand still, keeping a tight hold on the key ring as the guard walked away. Slowly, the keys slid out of the guard's pocket. The two men disappeared down the hall, leaving the keys dangling in Carlton's hands.

Carlton rapidly pulled his arm back into the cell, carefully concealing his prize within his hands. He stepped back into the cell and lowered himself onto the floor. He sat silently, waiting with a smile on his face. He had a way out.

The minutes seemed to tick by slowly as Carlton sat listening. The halls were silent. He heard nothing—no footsteps, no voices. He checked his leg. All three gashes were oozing blood, but none seemed serious. His captor had been using the knife more as a torture device than as a means of injury. Almost all the cuts he had given Carlton over the past few days were shallow. The pilot was bruised and very sore, but not seriously hurt.

Finally he stood, ignoring the pain in his leg as he walked over to the door. He stuck his arm through the bars and twisted his wrist backward, fumbling to find the keyhole. After a moment, he managed to slide the key inside the lock and slowly turned it. The bolt creaked, then slid back with a thud. The door swung open. He was free.

Quietly, Vinny slipped out into the hall. He slid the door shut behind him, locking it again and pocketing the keys. He paused for a moment, listening. The corridors remained silent. He started moving slowly, keeping his eyes and ears open. He was unarmed and had no desire to encounter anyone with a gun.

The thugs holding him prisoner wanted information from Panther and Moondog, and therefore would keep the pilots alive until they talked. Carlton had no such protection. The goons would be quick to dispose of him if he became troublesome. If he didn't tell them something soon, he would probably be shot as well. He had only two chances for survival. The first was to comply with these men and tell them what he knew about the planes at Edwards in the hope that they would spare his life. But that would mean selling out his country and the women who saved him. It was an option he refused to take. That left one choice, escape.

He was free from his cell, but he still had to find a way out. Carlton knew he was being held underground. When he woke up, he found himself bound and blindfolded. Someone was dragging him across the ground. They had led him down several flights of stairs before removing his bindings and locking him up. Therefore, the exit had to be somewhere above him.

He crept down the hall in the direction opposite that taken by the two guards, looking for a way out. He kept his eyes open for anything that he might be able to use as a weapon. The dark halls were empty and silent.

Soon the wall gave way to another corridor. Vinny stuck his head around the corner carefully. The last thing he wanted was to be spotted. A light-skinned man with only a few days' worth of stubble on his face would easily stand out among these thugs. His tattered, bloodied t-shirt and jeans would further expose him as an escaped prisoner. Fortunately, the hall was an empty expanse of stone, stretching under dim light bulbs.

Carlton ducked into the corridor and began to walk down it as quietly as possible. He moved slowly, methodically checking every doorway and gap in the hall. As long as he remained undiscovered he could take his time and search out the quickest, most direct route. That luxury would vanish quickly if someone were to find him.

Halfway down the hall, a doorway led to a set of stairs. Quietly, Carlton ducked inside and slowly climbed up the stone steps. He reached the top and peered around the corner, only to find another long, empty hallway.

He slid into the hall and began to carefully sneak down it, once again checking every door for a flight of stairs heading up. The side corridors were few and far between. The first one he encountered was a cross hall. The second door led simply to a small, empty room.

A noise in the distance caught his ear. Carlton froze. The faint echo of footsteps carried through the hall, growing louder. After a moment, Vinny discerned voices speaking in some unintelligible language. They were heading toward him.

As quickly and quietly as possible, he retraced his steps. The voices were drawing steadily nearer. He ducked back inside the door leading to the empty room and flattened himself against the wall next to the door.

The footsteps rang down the hallway, approaching him. Carlton held his breath and pressed his back into the hard rock of the wall. He fixed his eyes forward, afraid to shift a millimeter. He heard the voices clearly now. The two men were speaking the same language everyone around here spoke.

Two shadows passed slowly through the small pool of light spilling in from the doorway, temporarily darkening the room. Slowly, the footsteps began to fade. The voices died away as the men moved farther and farther away from where Carlton hid.

Carlton exhaled, careful not to make a sound. After what seemed like hours he allowed his body to relax. He hadn't been discovered. The men were gone, and he remained undetected. He stayed standing against the wall for several minutes, but he heard nothing more. Finally, he cautiously looked through the door. The hall was empty again.

Carlton stepped outside and began to creep down the hall, looking for a way out. The next two doorways held nothing of interest. The third yielded another flight of stairs. He climbed it carefully. Reaching the top, he stepped onto a small landing. A short stretch of corridor ran between him and one more flight of stairs.

Carlton paused. He saw no one, and the air was still quiet. He walked slowly through the hallway. Hopefully, the exit was at the top of these steps. He knew he couldn't be too deep in the earth. Sooner or later one of these doors had to lead outside.

Suddenly, a man stepped out into the hall, turning directly into Carlton. He froze. The man stopped dead in his tracks and stared at Carlton. His eyes grew wide, and he opened his mouth to shout.

Carlton stepped forward, driving his fist into the man's stomach with as much force as he could muster. The man's words were muffled by the rush of air escaping from his lungs. Before the man could react, Carlton swung his other fist directly into his head. The thug reeled backward.

Carlton advanced toward him. He swung his fist again, catching the man squarely in the nose. Another quick blow to the stomach kept the man from shouting in pain. He straightened his back, swinging his own fist into Carlton's face. As Carlton stumbled back, the thug lunged, knocking the pilot over.

Carlton slammed roughly into the stone. The man leaned over him, wrapping his hands around Carlton's throat and squeezing. Carlton stuck his thumbs into his assailant's neck and pushed upward, but the man was too heavy to shove off.

Carlton struggled furiously, trying to free himself from his attacker's grip. He twisted his head, looking for any exposed vulnerable spot on the thug's body. A glint of silver caught his eyes. There was a knife hanging on the man's belt.

Carlton dropped his hand rapidly, pulling the blade free. He brought the weapon up, quickly jabbing it where he judged the man's heart to be. The man went rigid, his eyes growing wide. Then he collapsed onto Carlton.

Rolling the dead man off him, Carlton climbed to his feet. He pulled the knife from the man's side and stuck it in his pants pocket.

Grabbing the man by his feet, he quickly dragged the body into a small room carved into the rock, hiding him as deeply in the shadows as possible. He waited another moment, listening for the shouting of voices or the pounding of feet. Hearing nothing, he stepped outside and slowly climbed the flight of stairs at the end of the hall.

A heavy door stood at the top of the stairs. Light seeped through the rough cracks around it. Sunlight. He had found his way out.

He twisted the doorknob slowly. Hoping that the hinges wouldn't make a sound, he pulled the door open a crack, not daring to breathe as he did so. Carefully, he pressed his eye against the small opening. A man was standing beside the door, looking idly out at the jungle beyond him. Carlton reached slowly into his pocket, drawing the knife.

He opened the door a little wider, then reached through the opening and jerked the man's head backward, sliding the knife into the flesh beneath the man's ear. The man went limp as the blade pierced his brain. Carlton released him, letting the body fall slowly to the ground as he flung the door open.

A man standing on the other side of the entrance twisted around. Carlton raised the knife quickly and slashed, splitting the man's throat. He made a faint gurgling gasp and collapsed. Carlton stepped over the bodies and into the warm sunlight. He was free.

Shutting the door behind him, he quickly surveyed his surroundings. He had exited from a door cut in the rock face. In front of him stood a small metal hangar. Ahead of it stretched a narrow airstrip. Everything else was jungle.

Carlton quickly ran through his options. He could go for the hangar now, or he could hide in the jungle until dark and then sneak into the building and steal a plane to carry him home. Once airborne he could figure out where he was and find the nearest friendly air base. He would be back in the States in no time.

He glanced back at the door. That creep wouldn't get any information about the government's secret planes from Vince Carlton.

Carlton stopped dead in his tracks. The other pilots were still trapped inside the labyrinth beneath him! The thugs had Panther and Moondog to torture. He had seen Panther with his own eyes, bruised and bloody, her arms bound behind her back. If he left them in the custody of those goons, they would surely be killed, probably starved and beaten to death.

But if he went back inside, he might never get free again. Sooner or later, someone would discover he was gone. Someone would find the men he killed and come looking for him. And when they located him they would surely kill him. Now he could flee—hide in the jungle and survive. If he walked back into the lion's den, chances were he wouldn't make it out alive. He had a single knife with which to fight an army of men with guns. Trying to rescue the pilots would be sheer suicide. He was free. A ride back to the U.S. waited for him in the hangar fifty feet away. Then he could go back to the government and tell them where their pilots were.

If they believed him...

Vinny gazed out at the jungle before him. The sweet taste of freedom beckoned.

~ 8 ~

The guards roughly threw Moondog and Panther to the floor in front of Kalliff. Moondog stood slowly. Martina picked herself up, bringing her bruised face to eye level with his and glaring at him. The man looked back at her, unwilling to give an inch to her fierce gaze.

"Always the defiant one, Colonel," he said. "Still unwilling to talk?"

"If you think I'm going to tell you anything, you're insane," she said.

"And threatening you won't do any good, I suppose," he said. "So I won't."

He whirled around, driving his fist into Moondog's stomach. The smaller woman doubled over, gasping for breath.

"Every time you refuse to answer me, Commander Ansetti will suffer for it." Kalliff grinned maliciously, striking the side of Moondog's face.

"So, Colonel, how about you tell me what you know about airplanes?"

"Don't tell him a fucking thing, Panther!" Moondog shouted, seeing the look on her friend's face.

Martina glared at Kalliff, slowly turning her head to look at Moondog. The other woman stared back at her with blood running from her lips and fire in her eyes.

"I'm sorry," Martina mouthed silently to her

friend, turning back to face Kalliff.

"I don't know anything about planes," she said.

Kalliff nodded to a man beside him. Martina turned her head away and shut her eyes as the thug brought his foot down across the back of Moondog's legs, buckling her knees. He grabbed the rope holding her wrists behind her back and began to pull her arms up over her head. Moondog gritted her teeth.

"All you're doing is hurting your friend, Colonel," Kalliff said. "Tell me about the plane you fly."

"I won't tell you anything," she said.

The man pulled Moondog's hands farther over her head, eliciting a faint whimper from the pilot. Blood began to seep from the gash on her shoulder.

"You are a pilot, are you not?" Kalliff asked.

Martina remained tight-lipped, glaring at him with all the hatred and menace she could muster, as if she would tear his throat out if her arms were not bound behind her back.

"Those wings mean you are a pilot," he said, thumping his fingers against the name tag on her flight suit. "That means you fly planes."

Panther did not reply. Her cold eyes drilled into him.

"As soon as you tell me about your planes, I will stop hurting your friend. It is up to you, Colonel. The moment you start talking, her pain stops."

"Do whatever you want to me, fuckface!" Moondog shouted. "Don't tell him anything, Panther, not a fucking thing!"

"Shut up!" Kalliff barked. The man holding Moondog's arms pulled them further forward, shoving her face into the floor. Pain shot through her shoulders. Her arms felt like they would be ripped from their sockets at any moment. She clenched her teeth, determined not to give the men the satisfaction of hearing her scream.

"All you have to do is tell me about the planes," Kalliff said, walking back to Martina.

"I don't know anything," the fighter pilot said slowly. A fierce rage burned in her eyes and echoed in her voice.

Kalliff nodded to the man holding Moondog's arms, who grinned and applied more pressure, pushing her hands toward the floor. More blood oozed from the cut on her shoulder.

"Just talk to me, Colonel," Kalliff said, seeing Martina flinch, "and I will leave your friend alone."

"If you don't stop hurting her now I will saw off your legs with a butter knife, carve out your guts with a spoon, and leave you to die in agony," Panther hissed with contempt.

"Tell me about the planes you fly, Colonel."

"I will not tell you anything," Martina replied evenly. "Now leave my friend alone."

Kalliff shifted his gaze from Martina's icy face to Moondog, kneeling on the floor. He walked over to the Navy woman and reached down, pulling her off the floor by the collar. The man holding her released the pressure on her arms, allowing her hands to relax. Moondog drew a deep breath into her lungs as the pain in her back faded to a dull ache. She fixed her eyes on Kalliff with a cold stare.

"You know," he said to Martina, "Commander Ansetti really is a beautiful woman."

He stepped forward, slowly wrapping his arms around Moondog and bringing his face to hers to kiss her. Moondog leaned backward, repulsed by the stench rolling off him. To her disgust, Kalliff pressed his mouth against hers.

Moondog parted her teeth, drawing Kalliff's lower lip into her mouth and biting down hard into his flesh. The warm taste of blood ran into her mouth. Kalliff's eyes widened with pain and shock.

Moondog brought her knee up, catching Kalliff in the groin. He wailed in agony and fell to the ground, curling into a ball. Moondog spit the blood in her mouth into his face.

"Don't touch me, you disgusting, filthy pig," she hissed.

Kalliff barked something incomprehensible to the other men standing in the room. They glared at Moondog, advancing slowly toward her.

Martina quickly stepped over Kalliff, putting herself directly between Moondog and his goons.

"What the fuck are you doing?" Moondog whispered.

"I have no idea," Panther replied through clenched teeth.

She stepped forward, driving her foot into Kalliff's stomach. He grunted and rolled onto his back. Martina pressed her foot onto his neck.

"Take one more step and I crush his throat!" she shouted to the other men.

"The ropes!" she whispered to Moondog. The Navy pilot turned around, grabbing Martina's wrists. Her own hands still tied behind her back, she struggled to untie the knot binding her friend.

The man closest to Martina lunged forward. She raised her foot to crush Kalliff's throat. Before she could bring her foot down, the man crashed into her, knocking her to the floor and landing on top of her. The heel of her boot grazed Kalliff's nose. The man pressed his body on top of hers, pinning her firmly against the floor. She struggled, but to no avail.

Two other men rushed Moondog, grabbing her by the arms. A third walked up and hit her across the face. Martina twisted her head away as he swung at Moondog for a second time.

The man on top of Martina stood. He grabbed her by the arm and pulled her off the floor. She glanced over at Moondog. Her friend hung limply between the two men, blood running down her face.

A second man grabbed Martina. Her captors began to drag her slowly toward the door. They pulled her out into the hall. A moment later, the two men hauling Moondog appeared next to her. Panther looked over, seeing her friend's bruised face.

"I tried," Martina whispered.

"I know," Moondog replied.

"We'll get these bastards."

"Yeah, we will."

The goons dragged them forward, hauling them down the long, dimly lit stone halls. Martina didn't bother to watch. By now she had memorized the route the men took. She knew which doors led to other halls and which didn't. The thugs pulled the two women forward, mindlessly following the same path.

The man gripping Martina's left arm felt something tap his shoulder. Confused, he stopped and turned his head. A fist slammed directly into his face, cracking his nose. The man stumbled backward. His assailant lashed forward, splitting his throat open with a knife. The man collapsed to the floor, blood gushing from the wound.

Martina felt the man release his grip on her arm. She watched as he reeled backward, only to have his throat slit. She turned around to see Vince Carlton standing beside her, gripping a bloody knife in his hand. The young pilot smiled widely, revealing the white teeth beneath his split lips. His eyes danced.

Martina ripped her arm free from the second thug's grip and twisted back toward him. She drew her leg up, catching him squarely in the stomach. The man doubled over, crashing into one of the goons holding Moondog.

"Cut the ropes, quick!" Martina shouted to Vinny,

raising her bound wrists. He drew the knife across the ropes, severing her bindings. Panther pulled her arms apart, throwing the coils off. She swung her hands forward, hitting the thug in front of her in the neck. He dropped to the floor, unconscious.

The two men holding Moondog were fighting to keep their grip on the Navy pilot, who was struggling fiercely. Vinny lunged at the man farthest from him. He lifted his weapon and plunged the blade directly through the man's eye and into his brain.

Panther jumped behind the remaining man. She grabbed him, jerking his head around to break his spine. He went limp in her arms. She dropped him, and he fell to the floor. Carlton stepped forward, deftly dealing both men on the ground a fatal blow with his knife. He turned to Moondog, quickly cutting the ropes binding her.

"Damn, Vinny, am I ever glad to see you," she said, throwing the rope to the floor.

"Don't mention it," he said, flashing his smile.

"They got anything useful?" Moondog asked Panther, who was bent over one of the thugs.

"Not much," Martina said, lifting her eyes from the body she was searching. "A knife or two."

"This one has a pistol," Moondog said, pocketing the weapon. Martina took a handgun from one of the bodies.

"Did you tell them anything?" she asked, fixing her eyes on Vinny.

"No. They kept asking about your planes, but I told them I didn't know anything. Refused to admit I was even a pilot."

"Good. Let's get out of here," she said, standing.

"Follow me," Vinny said. "I found a way out."

"You what?" Martina said.

"I snagged some keys and got free," Vinny said. "There are some planes in a hangar outside. And they're not guarded."

"Wait a minute," Martina said, incredulous. "You got out of here and you came back for us?"

"I couldn't just leave you here," he replied. "You guys saved my life."

"Thanks, Vinny," Martina said, smiling. She put her hand on his back. "Now show us the way outta here."

Carlton's grin spread wider. "With pleasure," he said.

He walked quickly down the hall. The two female pilots followed him, each holding a gun at the ready. The trio crept quietly along, moving as quickly as they could through the empty hall.

Vinny stopped outside a second hallway and peered around the corner. Seeing no one, he stepped out into the hall, motioning for Panther and Moondog to follow. He began to walk down the long corridor. The two women stayed close beside him, ever alert. Carlton counted the doors. Halfway down the hall he ducked into a side passage leading to a roughly cut stairwell.

They quickly climbed the stairs and entered another hallway. Carlton kept his eyes open, but he saw no one. He felt more confident with Panther and Moondog walking behind him. Before, when he crept along the hall alone, the fear of being discovered was nearly overwhelming. Now he felt almost invincible. The presence of the two cocky fighter pilots made him think he could take on the entire army housed in this labyrinth. Still, he watched his step. Getting caught would only hurt them all.

A sharp noise rang loudly in Vinny's ears. He twisted around rapidly to see a few men step into the hallway behind him. The lead man looked at them, his eyes widening with surprise as he saw the three Americans. He opened his mouth and shouted something Vinny didn't understand. The thugs rushed for the pilots.

The crack of a gun broke the silence. The first man stopped dead in his tracks, a bullet hole in his chest. Carlton shifted his vision, glancing at the smoking gun in Martina's hands. Moondog quickly took aim, dropping the man to the left. The three remaining thugs drew their own weapons.

"Run!" Panther yelled, shooting another man.

Vinny twisted around, dashing toward the second stairwell. Moondog and Panther followed, periodically turning around to fire. Bullets whizzed past, zinging off the hard rock walls and ceiling. Vinny felt small bits of stone hitting him. He ventured a peek behind him. The crowd of men was growing.

Hurrying forward, Moondog took aim at the lead man, carefully planting a bullet in his chest. He fell to the floor. His companions ran past his body, firing their rifles. There were four or five now, screaming and shooting like mad. She took aim again.

A hot pain raced through her left leg as a stray bullet ricocheted off the wall and imbedded itself in her calf. Her leg gave way beneath her, and she fell, landing hard on the rough floor. The stone stung her bruised body. Quickly, she pulled herself to a sitting position and fired again, downing another of their pursuers.

Panther grabbed Moondog by the shoulder, pulling her to her feet. The Navy pilot tried to keep pace with her, half limping, half running. The crack of gunfire continued to echo behind them.

Ahead, Vinny ducked into a side door, leading to yet another flight of stairs. He took them two at a time and heard Moondog and Panther charge up the steps behind him. He quickly reached the top of the stairs to find himself face to face with four large men, all holding rifles.

Moondog and Panther appeared on either side of him, each brandishing a pistol against an AK-47. Panther raised her gun and fired, dropping the man directly in front of Vinny. The thug standing beside him flipped his rifle over and shoved the butt into Moondog's chest before she could shoot. The Navy woman lost her footing and tumbled backward, crashing down the steps.

She landed on the hard rock at the bottom of the stairs, sprawling on her back. Moaning, she sat up. She was surrounded by the thugs who had been chasing them. Immediately, she raised the gun in her hand and fired. One of the men fell forward, shot between the eyes.

Before she could fire again, the man closest to her stepped up to her and kicked her sharply across the face. The blow knocked her onto her back. He planted his foot against her wrist, pressing her hand into the stone floor. He bent down and pulled the pistol from her grip. A second man stepped forward, grabbing her left arm. They hauled her roughly to her feet.

At the top of the steps, Vinny pulled the knife from his pocket and rushed the man in front of him. He quickly stepped past the thug's gun and drew the weapon across his throat. Vinny twisted to the side, stabbing the point of the knife into a second man's side and jerking it across his stomach. The man fell to the ground, his rifle clattering beside him

Panther dispatched the last man with another quick shot and quickly surveyed the area. Four men lay dead at her feet. The hall before them was open. Vinny stood beside her, but Moondog was nowhere to be seen. Panther glanced around anxiously, looking for her friend.

Four of Kalliff's minions stood at the bottom of the stairs. Two men held Moondog by the arms between them. She struggled violently as they dragged her backward. Panther spun around quickly, about to rush down the stairs.

Before she could move, Vinny jumped in front of her, leaping down the steps. He landed hard on the floor below, nearly losing his footing. He continued to charge forward, lunging at the small knot of men, knife at the ready.

He slashed at the man directly in front of him, splitting the thug's stomach open. Vinny twirled the knife over in his hand and smashed the hilt into the man's head. He stepped past the goon as he fell to the ground. Quickly, Vinny flipped the knife blade over as he rushed for the man gripping Moondog's right arm. He plunged the knife into his throat. The thug fell, releasing Moondog as he crumpled to the floor.

Vinny lunged for the man holding Moondog's other arm. As he did, another of the thugs stepped into him, his fist smashing into Vinny's stomach. The pilot doubled over. The thug's knuckles struck the inside of Vinny's right wrist. The knife flew from his hand, landing on the stone several feet away. Vinny lifted his head, only to see the man's knuckles for a brief instant before they hit the bridge of his nose.

Her right hand free, Moondog twisted into the man on her left, driving her fist into his throat. As he gasped for air, she grabbed hold of his hand, yanking it off her wrist. Stepping back, she wrenched his arm toward the floor behind him, snapping the bones in his wrist.

Pulled off balance, the thug began to fall backward. Moondog kicked him in the side of the head as he fell. He landed on his back, dazed. Moondog quickly dropped her knee onto his stomach. She pulled a knife from her pocket and jabbed it deep into his throat.

Meanwhile, reeling from the blow, Vinny stepped

back and raised his fists. The thug advanced. Vinny punched him in the side of the head. His left hand collided with the man's nose, breaking it. The thug shouted in pain and angrily swung his fist into Vinny's stomach. He stumbled backward. His heel caught on the body of one of the dead men, and he fell, landing hard on the floor.

The thug stepped over Vinny, pointing a gun directly at his head. Vinny froze, holding his breath. His mind was racing, quickly running through any available options. But there was no escape.

The sound of a gunshot rang loudly in his ears. The man standing before him went limp and fell over, blood trickling from a hole between his eyes. Vinny lifted his back off the ground and quickly twisted around. Panther stood behind him holding an AK-47. Vinny squeezed his eyes shut and exhaled.

Panther lowered the rifle. She walked over to Vinny, extending her hand. He gripped her wrist, and she pulled him to his feet.

"Thanks," he said.

"You're welcome," she replied, glancing over her shoulder.

Moondog was bent over another body. She stood and limped over to the other two pilots.

"Let's get out of here before any more of these creeps show up," Panther said.

"Right," Vinny responded, turning. They dashed up the steps, quickly reaching the bodies lying at the top of the stairs.

"Grab a gun," Panther said.

Vinny bent down and picked an AK-47 off the floor. Moondog pulled the rifles from the two bodies closest to her. She slung the first over her shoulder and cradled the second in her arms. Panther picked up a few more magazines. Sticking the extras in her pocket, she turned to Vinny and nodded.

Vinny flipped the safety off the gun in his hands, laying his finger beside the trigger. Pointing the muzzle ahead of him, he began to walk forward. The third and final stairway rose before him. They were almost out.

He walked quickly down the hall. Panther and Moondog stayed close beside him. They crossed the remaining distance to the steps rapidly. Vinny raced up the steps, taking them two at a time. Reaching the top, he kicked the door open. Bright sunlight spilled into the dark tunnel. Vinny jumped outside, rifle at the ready. He carefully scanned his surroundings. The jungle was quiet.

"This way," he said, stepping out into the thick grass between the door and the jungle.

Panther and Moondog stepped through the door. The Navy pilot shut it behind her. Vinny turned and began to run to the hangar. Panther rushed after him, throwing glances back over her shoulder every few seconds. Moondog tried to keep pace, but struggled to run, half-limping after the two Air Force pilots.

Panther twisted around, grabbing Moondog by the shoulder. Vinny doubled back and grasped her other arm. They took off at a sprint, pulling Moondog between them while the Navy pilot fought to run as best she could.

They reached the small hangar.

"Will you quit hurting your damn leg?" Martina said as she released her grip on Moondog's arm. The Navy woman stumbled forward slightly and steadied herself. All three pilots were breathing hard. Martina looked at the long, narrow runway that stretched out in front of the hangar, then shifted her gaze to the hangar itself. The front doors were open wide, revealing several MiG-31 Foxhounds and a larger private jet.

"If only the damn Russians didn't sell their

planes so damn cheap," Martina muttered. Her voice trailed off as her eyes widened. Five more MiGs sat beside the hangar. Three F-15 Eagles completed the row of fighters.

"How in the hell?" Vinny muttered.

"I don't know," Martina replied, "but that's our ride outta here."

Vinny simply gaped at the airplanes.

"Unless you want to try flying a MiG," she said, beginning to walk toward the planes.

"These things are armed," Moondog said, limping up to the nearest F-15 and raising the canopy.

Martina quickly scanned the short flight line. All the planes, including the MiGs, carried a full complement of air-to-air missiles.

"Good," Martina said. "Get airborne as fast as you can and figure out where the hell we are. We'll be right behind you."

"Will do," Moondog said. She pulled her flight scarf off and wrapped it tightly around the wound in her left calf, then climbed into the Eagle and quickly strapped herself into the ejection seat.

"You can fly these, right?" Martina asked Vinny.

"Yeah," he said. "I've got some stick time in fifteens."

"Then get going," she said, pointing at the nearest F-15.

Vinny nodded and trotted over to the plane. Martina walked over to the other Eagle. She jumped quickly onto the plane, pulling herself up to the cockpit. She pushed the canopy open and swung inside, strapping herself into the ejection seat, then lowered the canopy as the first F-15's engines sparked to life with a roar. Jet noise filled the air.

A helmet, complete with oxygen mask, hung on the stick. Martina pulled it over her head, pleased to see that it was already connected to the plane. She powered up her F-15, scanning the gauges. The fuel tanks were full. So was the oxygen.

She shifted her gaze outside, seeing Moondog's Eagle leap off the runway. Beside her, Vinny was running through his engine start procedures. Martina fired up her own plane, smiling as the Pratt and Whitney engines came to life. A final check over her instruments showed everything in the green. She released the brakes, and the fighter began to move.

Martina taxied the short distance to the strip and aligned the plane along the runway. She looked back over her shoulder. Vinny had positioned his F-15 beside her. He flashed her a few hand signals.

Martina nodded at him and shoved the throttles to their stops, feeling the power of the engines as the F-15 surged forward. The Eagle picked up speed rapidly, racing past the trees. Vinny held his position on her wing. Sensing that the airplane wanted to fly, Martina eased back on the stick. The two F-15s jumped into the sky, climbing high into the wild blue. Free from the ground, Martina smiled as the thrill of flight and speed mingled with relief.

~ 9 ~

Panther quickly caught sight of Moondog's Eagle. The Navy pilot was circling a few thousand feet above the airstrip.

"You got a heading for me?" she asked, continuing to climb.

"Three five zero," Moondog replied.

Martina leveled out just ahead of Moondog and turned to the north. She pulled her throttles back slightly. Moondog slid her plane into position on Martina's left wing. Vinny was still beside her on the right side.

"Where are we?" Martina asked, putting the jet back into a climb.

"Colombia," Moondog said. "That heading should take us straight to Florida."

"Do we have enough fuel?"

"We should."

"Won't the Colombians do something when we show up on their radar?" Vinny asked.

"I doubt it," Martina said. "Kalliff has probably bribed someone so he can fly in and out of here when he pleases. Besides, we'll be in international airspace fairly soon."

The three planes continued to gain altitude, flying through a thick cloud layer and into the blue sky above. They leveled out at 40,000 feet and raced north. Ahead the clouds broke, revealing the uneven coastline and the Caribbean Sea beyond.

"Panther, we've got a problem," Moondog called.

"What?"

"I've got something on my radar. Six o'clock. Twenty miles out and closing. Looks like those MiGs."

"Shit," Martina said. "How many?"

"Five. And they haven't tried to raise us."

"I see them. Prepare to engage as soon as they do anything threatening," Martina said. "You ever seen combat, Vinny?"

"No."

"You're about to."

"I hope you two are as good as you say," he replied.

"Don't worry," Moondog shot back. "We're better."

"The question is," Martina said, "how good are you?"

A missile warning sounded loudly in Moondog's ears. "Let's find out," she said. "They're targeting us."

She dropped her left wing, banking sharply as she turned away from the other two F-15s. A shower of flares sparked to life behind her as she dispensed her countermeasures.

Panther glanced back over her shoulder. A single missile raced for them, creating a brilliant trail of white smoke in the blue sky.

"Stay on my wing, Vinny," Panther barked, dropping her nose and making a quick turn to the right. "When we roll out, aim for the plane on the far left."

Vinny remained in tight formation, straining against the g-forces that pressed down on his body. He focused on Panther's wingtip, holding his plane in position through the turn.

A brilliant red fireball filled the sky where the three U.S. fighter jets had been a moment before, as a heat-seeking missile impacted with the flares, exploding brightly in the clear air.

Completing a sharp 180-degree turn, Panther leveled out, targeting the lead MiG with her AMRAAM radar-guided missiles. A quick tone in her ears indicated she had a lock. She mashed the trigger with her finger, loosing the missiles. They screamed ahead of the plane, colliding with the lead MiG's nose. The MiG erupted in a cloud of flames. The other four MiGs broke formation immediately, preparing to engage the three American planes.

Out of the corner of his eye, Vinny caught a glimpse of Moondog's Eagle, flying about a thousand feet below him. One of the Foxhounds dove straight for the F-15. Moondog pointed her nose directly at the Russian plane, holding herself on a collision course for the fighter.

Seconds from impact, she pulled up slightly, raking the MiG with gunfire as she raced over it. She zoomed by the Foxhound, then stood the F-15 on its side, reversing course in a tight turn.

Leveling out, she turned back toward the MiG, depressing the trigger again. A hail of cannon fire peppered the MiG, chewing up its tailfins. The Foxhound began to spiral out of control, smoke billowing from its engines. The plane tumbled from the sky, vanishing in the thick clouds below.

Vinny selected his radar-guided missiles and set his sights on the plane to his left. A quick tone in his ears indicated he had a lock. He squeezed the trigger. A missile dropped from his right wing and shot forward with a hiss, racing for the Foxhound.

The MiG pulled up sharply. A shower of metallic sparks appeared behind the aircraft as the pilot released his chaff. The plane continued to climb. The missile dove for the chaff, exploding harmlessly below the Foxhound.

Reaching the top of his climb, the pilot pushed

the nose of the plane down, diving for Vinny's F-15. The missile warning sounded loudly in his ears as the MiG's weaponry locked onto his plane. Vinny jinked hard to the left.

"Get on his six, Vinny!" Panther shouted as she raced toward the two other MiGs.

Vinny pulled his throttles over the detent and pushed them to their stops, throwing the F-15 into afterburner. Fuel shot directly into the engine's exhaust and ignited, thrusting the F-15 forward. Vinny dashed below the MiG.

As the Foxhound zipped over his head, Vinny throttled back and pulled back hard on the stick and tensed his body as the g-forces hit him. The edges of his vision began to darken as the blood drained from his head. He had no g-suit to help keep the blood from pooling in his legs. He squeezed the muscles in his stomach and legs tighter, fighting to keep conscious as he pulled the plane up and over onto its back.

Reaching the top of the loop, he released the back pressure on the stick. The g-forces instantly vanished. He smashed the stick to the left. The plane quickly flipped over to complete an Immelmann. He was now flying straight and level in the opposite direction, about 2,000 feet higher.

The MiG was dead ahead of him. Vinny quickly switched over to his heat-seeking missiles. They locked instantly. He pressed the trigger. An AIM-9 Sidewinder dropped from his wing and raced for the MiG. Vinny immediately peeled off, diving to the left. This time the MiG's pilot had no time to react. The missile flew straight into his burner can, exploding in a large fireball and ripping the plane to shreds.

Panther dove for the last two enemy aircraft, guns blazing. They broke formation, one turning hard to the right, the other pulling away to the left. She rolled to the left, aligning her gun sights on the plane in front of her. She squeezed the trigger, peppering its tail with bullets.

The MiG rolled hard to the right, diving away. Panther stayed on his six, chopping her throttles to follow. The Foxhound jinked hard to the left and the right. Panther held her position directly behind him, continuing to fire.

Suddenly, the left side of the MiG's horizontal stabilizer broke off. The slipstream caught the large piece of metal, tossing it back at Panther. She pulled hard to the right. The tail section flew past her F-15, missing the cockpit by inches.

Below her, the MiG began to tumble end over end. Without the tail to stabilize it, the Foxhound spun out of the sky uncontrollably. It spiraled downward, vanishing into the clouds beneath.

Vinny watched the flaming scraps of metal ahead of him tumble to the ground. Holding the plane level, he scanned the sky. A few thousand feet below, he could see Panther's F-15 as she chased another MiG.

He looked back. The last Foxhound was directly behind him, bearing down quickly.

Vinny chopped his throttles and pushed his nose down. He pulled the stick hard to the left as he dove, trying to twist away from the plane. Unable to fire, the MiG pilot dove after him, determined not to let him escape.

Vinny pulled back on the stick, shoving his throttles forward again. The F-15 climbed upward, rolling onto its back. Vinny clenched the muscles in his legs and stomach tightly. The edges of his vision began to blur as he pulled through and leveled out again, completing the loop.

He checked behind him again. The MiG was still on his six, having followed him through the maneuver. Vinny mashed his stick to the right, jinking frantically in an attempt to escape. It was no use. The Foxhound was glued to his tail.

The missile warning sounded loudly in his ears as the Foxhound's weapons locked onto his plane. He pushed the stick down and yanked it hard to the left, but the tone continued. Vinny looked behind him again.

A blinding flash of light tore through the sky. Fire filled Vinny's eyes. His plane shook violently and pitched forward sharply. Instinctively, he turned his eyes back to the controls, quickly reducing the throttles and leveling out.

Everything went quiet. The missile warning was silent. Breathing hard, he rapidly scanned his instruments. They were all reading in the green. He looked up. The F-15 was flying straight and level.

Cautiously, he turned his head, checking his six. The Foxhound was gone. In its place was an F-15.

"You okay, kid?" Moondog asked.

"I think so," he said, exhaling slowly. "I owe you one."

"Buy me a couple of beers when we get back and I'll call it even," she replied. "Or better yet, some good scotch."

"That's the last of them," Martina said, climbing back up to rejoin the others. "Let's get the fuck out of here."

She pointed the nose of her Eagle back to the north. Moondog and Vinny resumed their positions on her wings.

"Hey, Vinny," Martina said, "not bad."

"Thanks. But I think that guy would have killed me if not for Moondog."

"Eh, she was just being a show-off."

"Hey!" the Navy pilot said.

"You got out alive, that's what matters," Martina said. "And you got one of 'em. That's not bad."

"He still owes me beer!" Moondog said.

Martina just laughed.

The three planes slipped over the coast of South America and raced out over the Caribbean. Vinny allowed himself to relax as they headed back to the safety of the U.S.

* * *

The coast of Florida appeared out ahead of Martina's nose. She quickly check her GPS.

"We're about to enter the ADIZ," she said to Moondog and Vinny. "Things might get a little interesting."

"How the hell are you going to explain this one, Panther?" Moondog asked. She sounded very tired.

"I have no fucking clue."

"What are we supposed to do if they fire on us?" Vinny asked.

"Eject," Martina said matter-of-factly. "Jettison the rest of your armament. We don't want to appear threatening."

She hit a few keys on her computer. The remaining missiles on her wing fell off lifelessly, plummeting to the ocean below. Moondog and Vinny quickly followed suit.

Setting her transponder to an emergency code, Martina changed her radio frequency and keyed her mike.

"Center, Eagle one one, emergency," she called.

"Emergency aircraft calling center, go ahead."

"Center, Eagle one one is a threeship sixty miles south of Florida level at 30,000, heading three five zero. We are low on fuel. Request entry to U.S. airspace," Martina said.

"Eagle one one emergency, ident," the controller said.

Martina hit a button on her transponder. There was a pause.

"Eagle one one emergency, radar contact," the controller said. "I'm not showing a flight plan for you."

"I have none, center."

"Type of aircraft and destination?" the controller asked.

"Three F-15Cs," Martina said. "We'd like to land at the nearest U.S. Air Force installation."

There was another long pause.

"Eagle one one emergency, maintain current altitude and heading. Cleared into the ADIZ. A fighter escort is on the way. They will take you to Tyndall AFB."

"Roger, center, thank you."

"Eagle one one?" Moondog said, as the radio went silent.

"I made it up, okay?" Martina said. "What the hell am I supposed to do? We don't have a call sign."

"And that's the best you can come up with?"

"I didn't exactly have a lot of time to come up with a good one."

They flew in silence for a few minutes. Martina watched as the Florida coast drew nearer. Suddenly, a gray flash cut across her nose. She glanced to the side. Two F-22 Raptors dropped down on either side of their formation, about a hundred feet from Panther's Eagle.

"Eagle one one emergency, Blackjack five one," Martina's headset crackled. "How do you read?"

"Loud and clear, Blackjack five one," she said.

"Are you armed?" the Raptor lead asked.

"Negative," Martina said. "We are low on fuel, and my wingman is injured."

"Okay," lead said. "I'm going to escort you to Tyndall. Follow me. Don't try anything fancy."

"Don't worry," Martina said. "We just want to get home."

The Raptor on Panther's right slid out ahead of

her. She trailed him as he descended toward the Florida coast, leading her formation through the visual approach to Tyndall. They flew lower, crossing over the thin strip of white sand beaches stretched across the shoreline.

"Eagle one one emergency, you're clear to land," Blackjack 51 said. "The runway is straight ahead."

The Raptors peeled off. Martina could see the air base out ahead of her. She was on a five-mile final.

"You first, Moondog," she said. "Vinny, stay on my wing."

She pulled the throttles back, allowing her wingman to pass her. Moondog gracefully aligned her plane with the runway.

Extending her landing gear, Moondog skimmed over the green earth. The small plane crossed over the tarmac, its wheels touching gently onto the runway. She pulled back on the throttle, rolling slowly off the runway.

Martina lowered the nose of her Eagle slightly. Vinny held position on her wing. Martina flashed him a quick hand signal, then lowered her gear. She watched the end of the runway draw nearer, the tarmac filling her view. Martina aligned her plane just to the left of the centerline. Easing back on the stick, she flared the plane, smoothly touching the ground. Vinny landed beside her. She gently lowered the plane's nose and applied the brakes. The F-15s rolled to a stop at the end of the runway.

Several crash trucks waited on a pad just off the end of the runway, lights flashing. Panther turned off the runway and taxied up to the trucks. Moondog's Eagle was already parked on the pad. A marshaller stood beside it, waving his wands at Martina. She pointed the nose of her plane at him and rolled slowly forward until he signaled her to stop.

Martina set the Eagle's brakes and quickly ran

through her shutdown procedures. The roar of the engines died. She raised the canopy. Warm, humid air filled the cockpit. Martina pulled her helmet off and set it on the throttles. She undid the restraints holding her in the seat and swung her legs over the side of the plane, dropping agilely to the ground.

Landing on the asphalt, she straightened up and looked around. Vinny's Eagle was parked to the right of her plane. The young captain was climbing down from his aircraft. He looked out of place in his tattered t-shirt and jeans. Moondog stood beside the nose of her Eagle. The left leg of her flight suit was soaked in blood. She looked pale. All three pilots were bruised, dirty, and disheveled. Martina's left eye was only open about halfway.

"Freeze!" a voice behind her shouted. "Put your hands in the air and turn around."

Martina complied, raising her arms and turning around slowly. A large group of Security Forces brandishing M-16s stood at the edge of the tarmac.

"Keep your hands in the air and walk forward slowly," a sergeant standing in the center commanded. All three pilots began to walk toward them.

"Stop," the sergeant said when they came within ten feet of the group. "Are you armed?"

"I've got a knife in my right pocket," Martina said.

Moondog shook her head. "I left the AK in the plane," she said nonchalantly. The sergeant stared at her for a minute, unsure whether or not to take her seriously.

"Frisk them," he ordered. Three airmen stepped forward, quickly patting down the pilots. One pulled the knife from Martina's pocket. The others came up empty-handed.

"They're clean," one of the men said to the sergeant.

"Can we put our hands down now?" Martina

asked. The sergeant nodded. The pilots lowered their arms.

"For fuck's sake, Moondog, sit down before you fall down," Martina said. "Sergeant, will you get my friend to the hospital? She's hurt."

"Help the lady," the sergeant said, nodding to two of his airmen. They stepped toward Moondog.

"Come with us, Colonel," one of the two said to Moondog, slinging her arm over his shoulder.

"Commander," Moondog said.

"Excuse me, ma'am?" the airman said.

"It's Commander, not Colonel," Moondog said as the two airmen led her away.

"Can I see your military ID, ma'am?" the sergeant asked.

"I don't have it," Martina said. "I have these." She reached down her flight suit and pulled a chain from around her neck and extended it to the sergeant, letting her dog tags dangle from her open palm. The sergeant snatched the tags from her hand.

"Lieutenant Colonel Redrick," the sergeant said, "you're under arrest for stealing U.S. government property."

* * *

"Do I get a phone call?" Martina asked as the sergeant led her and Vinny into the Security Forces headquarters.

The sergeant shrugged and pointed to a phone. Martina walked over, picked it up, and dialed a number from memory.

"Lieutenant Colonel Redrick for General Peters," she said when Peters' secretary answered the phone.

"One moment, please." There was a brief pause.

"Martina?" Peters said as he came on the line. "Where the hell are you?"

"In the jail at Tyndall Air Force Base, sir. Commander Ansetti is with me."

"What the hell are you doing there?"

"The Security Forces here seem to think I stole an F-15, sir."

"Did you?"

"Well, technically, yes," she said slowly, "but I stole it from a group of terrorists in Colombia, not from a U.S. installation. So I was actually returning it to the rightful owner."

"What?"

"It's kind of a long story, sir. I'll explain later. Can you get us out of here?"

"Hang on," he said. The line went dead. Martina set the phone in its cradle and sat back down beside Vinny.

The sergeant had just finished taking their fingerprints when a young captain walked hurriedly through the front door. He spoke quickly to the sergeant at the front desk before heading back to where the two pilots sat.

"Colonel Redrick?" he asked.

"Yes?" Martina said.

"I'm Captain Harris, ma'am," he said. "Colonel Weston asked me to pick you up. He'd like to see you."

"Certainly, Captain," Martina replied, standing. "But is there any way I can get a clean flight suit and a quick shower before meeting the colonel? I'm not exactly presentable. And I would kill for a sandwich," she added.

"Actually, Colonel, I think it would be best if I took you to the clinic first, just to make sure those bruises are the worst of your injuries," he said.

The look on Martina's face suggested that she didn't like the idea at all.

"You can get a shower there," he added quickly. "And I could run and get you a sandwich in the meantime."

"Colonel Weston won't mind?"

"Not at all," the captain said. "He's a little busy right now anyway."

"All right. Let's get outta here," Martina said. She and Vinny followed Harris from the room. A staff car was waiting outside. Vinny climbed in the back seat. Martina waited for him to close the door.

"If I may ask you one more favor, Captain," Martina said. "Do you have an F-22 pilot named Ray Beckett here?"

"I think so," Harris answered, "but I'll have to check."

"If you do, I need to talk to him. I shouldn't need more than fifteen minutes of his time."

"I'll see what I can do, ma'am."

"Thanks."

*   *   *

Feeling human again in a clean flight suit, Martina stopped in front of Colonel Weston's office. Her hair was still wet from her shower. The doctors at the hospital had thoroughly examined her and Vinny. Although they were bruised, neither was seriously injured. Their wounds had been cleaned, and the doctors had cleared them both back to flight status. Moondog had not been so lucky. They had pulled the bullet from her left calf and grounded her for a week.

Harris pushed open the door to Weston's office and motioned for her to enter.

"Lieutenant Colonel Redrick, sir," he announced as she walked inside.

"Have a seat, Colonel," Weston said after exchanging formalities with Martina, waving her into a chair. Panther gladly took the weight off her feet. She was still very sore and starting to feel pretty tired. Harris stood silently at the back of the room.

"I got a phone call about two hours ago from General Peters at Edwards, saying my Security Forces had you in custody. He said you disappeared from

Edwards about a week ago. Would you mind telling me just what happened, Colonel?" he asked. "How did you and your wingmen end up flying an unscheduled mission, with no flight plan and no call sign?"

"It's a rather long story, sir," Martina said. "My wingman, Commander Ansetti, and I are test pilots at Edwards. We were kidnapped by a group of terrorists who wanted information about our planes. Captain Carlton, who had also been nabbed by these guys, managed to steal a key from them and freed us. We found those three planes, along with a group of MiGs, sitting in the middle of the jungle. They had fuel and weapons, and we are pilots, so we grabbed them and made a beeline for the States."

"Why would these terrorists kidnap you?" Weston asked.

"They wanted information about the planes we've been testing. They wanted to steal them."

"What kind of planes are you testing?"

"I can't tell you, sir," Martina said. "That information is classified."

"This might interest you, Colonel," he said. "I had my people run a check on the serial numbers of the planes you flew in. Two of the F-15s were reported lost in an accident off North Carolina three years ago. The third supposedly crashed ten months ago in the Pacific Ocean."

"That is very interesting, sir," Martina said.

A sharp knock sounded at the door. Weston lifted his eyes as his secretary opened the door.

"Sir, Washington is on the phone," she said, sounding slightly surprised. "It's the White House."

"Excuse me for a moment, Colonel," Weston said, picking up the phone.

"Yes, sir," Martina heard him say into the receiver. "Yes, sir. Colonel Redrick is with me right now....Yes, sir, I will."

He put the phone down.

"Colonel, the White House wants you, Carlton, and Ansetti in Washington immediately. The President wants to meet with you."

"Yes, sir," she said. "Could I ask you for a couple of airplanes?"

"I'll call maintenance. Take whatever they can get airborne quickest," Weston said. "Harris, call the hospital and tell them to get Carlton and Ansetti to the flight line ASAP, and get the Colonel to her plane."

"Yes, sir," Harris said, motioning for Martina to follow. She stood, saluted Weston, and left the room.

~ 10 ~

Vince Carlton sat in the antechamber of the Oval Office staring at his shoes. They were brand-new Corframs, shining black and still completely unscuffed. The people over at Andrews Air Force Base had given him the shoes when he got off the plane. They had also handed him a blues uniform, which fit loosely because it was not tailored. The shirt was adorned with only a set of captain's bars and a pair of pilot's wings.

Promptly after landing at Andrews, the three pilots had been given new uniforms, along with fifteen minutes to shower and change. From there, they had been whisked directly to the White House. Panther and Moondog had immediately been ushered into the Oval Office. He had been told to wait outside.

Vinny had been looking at his Corframs for the better part of an hour. He was afraid of what was going to happen when he finally walked through the door. Would the Secret Service slap cuffs on his hands and haul him off to prison? He was still considered a suspect in the theft of the B-1 bomber. He wasn't supposed to leave Edwards. The Air Force didn't know that he had been kidnapped. They might assume that he had gone willingly. And he had hijacked the bomber, but only to take it back from the pilot, who was stealing it to sell to some terrorist or something.

At least he was back safely in the U.S., and not in some prison cell in Colombia. Being locked up in Leavenworth couldn't be as bad as being held by a group of thugs in South America who were likely to kill him on a whim. Maybe they wouldn't imprison him. He did have Panther and Moondog on his side. Perhaps he wouldn't be arrested. Instead he would just be discharged from the Air Force. And that would mean forfeiting the slot NASA had offered him. He was supposed to start astronaut training in two months. He would never fly the shuttle now.

He gazed at the surface of his shoes, trying to find a sliver of hope in his situation. Any way he twisted it, he could see no way out. He was in deep trouble for stealing the Bone and running. That single fact was going to ruin everything for him. He lifted his head and studied his reflection in a mirror across the way. A man with a bruised, cut face in a badly fitting uniform looked back at him. There were thick, dark lines under both his eyes. He hardly seemed fit to meet the President of the United States. Vinny sighed and went back to staring at his shoes, wondering what the hell was going to happen now.

He was still staring at his toes when the President's secretary walked into the room.

"The President will see you now, Captain," she said. Vinny stood and ran his hands along the edge of his pants, retucking the excess fabric of his shirt so that the front was taut against his flat stomach. Then he gathered his courage and pushed open the door to the Oval Office.

David Webster was sitting behind the thick mahogany desk. Vinny walked slowly across the presidential seal on the floor and stopped six inches from the front of the desk. He saluted.

"Sir, Captain Carlton reports as ordered," he said.

Webster returned the salute. "Sit down, Captain."

Vinny scanned the room, seeing a free chair across from the President's desk. He dropped into it, noticing that Panther and Moondog were sitting opposite him. Martina was dressed in the same uniform he wore. Silver oak leaves sat on her shoulders. Moondog had on a crisp white shirt with gold and black epaulets and black pants. The color had returned to the Navy woman's face. Both looked tired. The two pilots said nothing.

"It's Vinny, right?" Webster said, smiling.

"Yes, sir," he replied.

"Vinny, could you please tell me everything that's happened to you in the past week, starting with the B-1 incident? Take your time and don't spare any details."

"Okay," Vinny said, taking a deep breath. He carefully recounted everything that had happened to him between the time he left Dyess and his arrival in Florida.

Webster listened intently to every word Vinny said. Panther and Moondog were carefully watching him as well, but Vinny was too focused on the President to notice either pilot.

"I have a few questions, if you don't mind," Webster said when Vinny had finished his story.

"I'd be happy to answer them."

"The man who arranged the bomber's hijacking, could you describe him?" Webster asked.

"He was tall and thin. Dark hair and eyes. He was a major, a pilot too. When I saw him he was wearing a flight suit. I couldn't see his name, but I saw his rank and his wings."

"You don't know who he was?"

"No, I don't know his name."

"Did you mention Colonel Redrick and Commander Ansetti's planes to anyone?"

"I asked Colonel Redrick what they were flying

while they escorted me to the base," Vinny said. "She said the planes were Raptors, and not to say any more about them, so I didn't."

"Did you talk to anyone at Holloman?" Webster asked.

"Only OSI and SF."

"What about at Edwards?"

"No, sir. Colonel Redrick took my cell phone, and I didn't have access to a computer."

"Did you recognize any of the men in Colombia?" Webster asked.

"No, sir," Vinny repeated. "They were all foreigners. Dark skin, thick beards, spoke some language I couldn't understand."

"Did it sound like Spanish?"

"No, sir, not at all," Vinny said.

"And you never told them anything?"

"Nothing. They kept asking me about the planes, but I didn't answer."

"Tell me how you got free again," Webster said.

"When the guard locked me back up, he stuck the key in his pocket, but the edge of the key ring was hanging out, so I grabbed it and pulled the key from his pocket. Once they left, I unlocked the door. I knew I was underground because I'd gone down a couple of flights of stairs when they first brought me in, so I just looked for stairs going up and eventually found my way out. Then I remembered seeing Colonel Redrick. I went back inside, found her and Commander Ansetti, and we all got out."

"Did your captors tell you anything about who they were or where you were?"

"No, sir," Vinny replied. "I tried to find out, but they refused to tell me anything."

"Does the name Azad Kalliff mean anything to you?" Webster asked.

"Who?" Vinny looked confused.

"Azad Kalliff."

"Never heard of him, sir."

"Thank you for being so helpful, Captain," Webster said. "I hope you don't mind waiting for a few more minutes. I might have some more questions for you."

"Certainly, sir."

"If you need anything, just let Sherri know."

"Yes, sir," Vinny said, standing. He saluted again.

"Good evening, sir," he said.

"Good evening," Webster responded, returning the salute with a smile. Vinny turned and walked from the room.

"Well, Colonel, what do you think?" Webster asked Martina as the door closed.

"His story seems to hold, sir," Martina said. "What he told you about the bomber is the same thing he told me and Commander Ansetti when we questioned him. I spoke to Captain Beckett when we were at Tyndall. His account matches Carlton's. He said he tried to alert Security Forces, but for some reason they wouldn't listen. They let Scepter six five take off, and they refused to recall the plane once it was airborne. The part about Colombia seems accurate."

"You said you ran into Carlton before in Colombia, before he set you free?" Webster asked Martina.

"Yes, sir," she replied. "Two of those thugs were dragging him. He was covered in bruises and blood, and he looked beat to hell. As soon as he saw me, his whole face lit up. He looked as if I was about to rescue him or something."

"Did you talk to Carlton at all when he was at Edwards?" Webster asked.

"He went to dinner with us once or twice," Martina said. "He was really friendly."

"And really bored," Moondog added.

"What was your opinion of him? Is he the kind of person who would steal a bomber for a terrorist organization?"

"Not at all, sir," Martina said. "I don't think a man like Carlton would easily be swayed by money or power."

"What do you think, Commander?" Webster asked Moondog.

"No way in hell, sir," Moondog said. "That's an all-American kid."

"But he would sneak aboard a bomber to stop it from being stolen by a terrorist," Martina said.

"I have here a report by the agents who investigated the hijacking," Webster said, tapping a folder on his desk. "Captain Carlton told the same story to his interrogators that he told me and you. Furthermore, the evidence shows that the two backseaters and the copilot were killed with a gun that had only the bomber pilot's fingerprints on it. It does say that Carlton killed the pilot with a knife, just as he described. The evidence suggesting Carlton had links to the terrorist organization proved to be planted. The FBI did a background investigation on him and found no connections to any terror groups. And OSI thoroughly interrogated Captain Beckett, who confirmed Carlton's story. It appears that our captain is innocent. Do you agree?"

"Absolutely," Moondog said.

"Yes," Martina said. "But it does make me wonder what the hell is going on at Dyess. Why didn't they listen to Beckett?"

"I'll get answers from Dyess, and whoever screwed up will be held accountable," Webster said.

"I think I know who may be behind this, sir," Martina said. "General Miles' executive officer, Major Haley."

"Really?"

"He and the general are the only two people who were at Dyess at the time of the theft and at Holloman during the attempt on Carlton's life. He matches the description Carlton and Beckett gave of the man who orchestrated the theft, and the man Commander Ansetti and I saw at Holloman. It's possible he was the person snooping around the Hellcats too."

"I'll send a few FBI agents out to Dyess. I don't think the information you gave me will be enough to issue a warrant for his arrest, but it should be enough to bring him in for questioning. They'll be waiting for him when he shows up for work in the morning. Hopefully, that will get us the answers we need.

"Now that's settled, I need you ladies to go back to Edwards. Take the Hellcats and move them to Nellis. Kalliff knows where the planes are, and he may still try to get his hands on them. Make sure that no one can follow you."

"Take them straight out of the atmosphere, then?" Moondog asked.

"If that's what it takes."

"Sir, there's a problem," Martina said. "Commander Ansetti can't fly. She took a bullet in the leg when we were in Colombia, and the docs in Florida grounded her for a few days."

"How'd you get up here, then?" Webster asked.

"In the back of Martina's F-15E," Moondog muttered, obviously not pleased with the fact.

"And it took a lot to convince them to let her even do that."

Webster sighed. "And it would take far too long to train a new pilot. Plus we'd have to let someone else in on the secret. I guess you'll just have to make two trips, Colonel."

"Maybe not, sir," Panther said. Webster looked at

her quizzically.

"Carlton could fly it, sir."

"Carlton?"

"Yes, sir," Martina said. "He's an F-22 pilot. The Hellcat isn't much different from a Raptor. I could bring him up to speed in an hour."

"Are you sure we can trust him?"

"He could have saved his own neck in Colombia by talking, and he chose not to. We can trust him," she said.

"How can you be so sure he didn't?" Webster asked.

"If he had, they would have known where the Hellcats were hangared, and they would have stopped asking me and Moondog about them. But they never did. So Carlton must have kept his mouth shut. He's already seen the planes, so we wouldn't be telling anyone new."

"You sure he can fly it?"

"I'll guide him through the whole thing, sir," Martina said. "He shouldn't have a problem."

"And if he tries anything?"

"He won't, sir," Martina said. "But if he does, I'll bring the plane down. I'll have the crew chiefs at Edwards arm my plane, but not his. The weapons are internal. He won't even know."

"All right, Colonel, I'll tell the boys at Langley to have two F-22s ready for you and Carlton to fly to Edwards in the morning. And I'll get you a plane ticket back to Houston, Commander," Webster said. "In the meantime, I had Sherri book you the best suite she could find in town. Go take the rest of the night off."

"Yes, sir," Martina said, smiling as she stood. "Thank you, sir."

"Let me know as soon as the planes are safe at Nellis."

"Yes, sir," Martina repeated, saluting. "Good evening, sir."

"Good evening, ladies." Webster returned the salute. The two pilots turned and walked from the room.

* * *

Dan Haley stared down a dark stretch of highway. He stood by the side of a desolate two-lane road, surrounded by nothing but the night air. A thick layer of clouds blocked out the stars. A cold breeze blew past, running straight through him. The long, dry grass by the side of the road rustled, and the night fell silent again.

Haley glanced back along the road, wondering what he was doing there. He had been given no explanation for this meeting; he had just been told to show up. For the past twenty minutes he had gazed out into the darkness, contemplating the lonely stretch of asphalt. Not a single car passed. Except for the occasional gust of cold wind, the air was still and silent.

How had he become entangled in this mess in the first place? He ran through recent events in his mind, wondering exactly what he had done to find himself standing in the middle of nowhere on a dark night. He didn't want to think about what was about to happen to him.

Haley stuck his hands into his pockets and peered down the road in the other direction, listening for a car engine. He heard nothing. No headlights pierced the night. There was no rumbling of an engine in the distance, just an empty piece of asphalt going nowhere.

He wondered idly how much longer he would have to wait. He reached up and flipped up his collar, pulling his coat tight, trying to ward off the icy chill running through him. He crossed his arms in front of his chest and looked back down the road.

A faint glow of headlights appeared, accompanied by the low purr of an engine. A moment later a car raced into view. It screeched to a stop beside Haley. The driver leaned over and opened the door.

"Get in," he growled.

Haley stepped slowly into the car. No sooner had he closed the door than the driver smashed his foot onto the gas, sending the car flying down the road once more.

"Is it possible for you to do anything right?" the driver snarled.

Haley remained silent.

"We ask you to get a bomber for us. A very simple task. You pay off a couple of pilots and they bring us the plane. But that didn't work, did it?"

Again, Haley made no reply.

"Then you tell us about these two superplanes, and say to get those, and we won't even need a bomber," the driver hissed. "So we go after their pilots, and what do we get? Twenty dead men and not a shred of information. Those women managed to get free and go straight back to your government. The U.S. Air Force probably knows everything by now. You may have just compromised our entire operation."

He mashed the brakes, pulling the car off the road and killing the lights. He turned to face Haley, his right hand falling to his pocket.

"This is completely unacceptable," he hissed. "You may have just destroyed everything we have worked for."

He pulled a gun from his pocket, pressing the muzzle against Haley's forehead. The Air Force major stiffened and held still. So it was going to end this way.

"This must not fail," the man said, leaning toward Haley. "We need that bomber, and we need it now.

And you will get it for us. Tomorrow. You know what will happen if you don't."

Haley nodded, swallowing hard.

"Good," the man said. He pulled the gun away. "Get out."

Haley shoved the door open and scrambled from the car. The driver slammed the door behind him and stepped on the gas again, racing into the night. The taillights vanished into the darkness, once more leaving Haley standing alone on the side of a desolate two-lane road.

* * *

"Damn," Moondog muttered. "This place is fancy."

She limped into the middle of the hotel suite and turned around slowly, taking in the full splendor of the room.

"Yeah," Martina said. "You'd fit perfectly if you were a rich socialite."

Moondog laughed.

"I'll take the rich part," she said, sticking her head in one of the bedrooms. "You can keep the rest of that bullshit."

"C'mon, you'd make the perfect heiress," Martina said. "Especially with your bruised-up face."

"You don't look any better. You've still got a huge shiner."

Martina laughed and dropped onto one of the thick leather sofas, propping her feet up on an ottoman. Vinny sat down silently in a chair opposite her and stared at his shoes.

"Here we go," Moondog said, pulling open the liquor cabinet. She found a glass and opened a bottle of scotch. She poured half an inch into the glass and downed it.

"You want anything?" she asked Martina, refilling her own glass.

"Ice water," Martina replied.

"One of these days I'm going to teach you to drink," Moondog said, dropping a few ice cubes in a second glass and filling it with water.

Martina rolled her eyes as Moondog handed her the glass. She drained half of it.

"You want anything, Vinny?"

"Just give me the bottle."

Moondog glanced at Panther. She shook her head.

"What's wrong with you, Vinny?" Martina asked. "This is the first time I haven't seen you with a ridiculously huge smile on your face."

"I was just wondering..." he muttered. He lifted his head and looked at her.

"What's going to happen now, Martina?" he asked. "I mean now that we're back in the States, you and Moondog will go back to Houston, but what about me? Are they going to throw me in jail?"

"Tomorrow morning, Moondog is flying back home," Martina said. "You and I have a little job to do first."

"What?"

"I'll tell you in the morning," Martina said. "But don't worry, nothing bad's going to happen to you."

"You sure I can't have a drink?" he asked

"You can have one drink," Martina said. "Not the whole bottle. We're flying tomorrow."

"What's your poison?" Moondog asked.

"Scotch is fine," he said. Moondog half-filled another glass and handed it to him.

"You sure nothing's going to happen to me?" Vinny asked.

"Yeah," Martina says. "Webster thinks you're innocent. And the cops' investigation confirmed your story. Otherwise we'd all be in jail right now."

"More likely stood up against a wall and shot," Moondog interjected.

Vinny half-smiled. "So this is all going to work

out okay."

"It'll all be fine," Martina said.

"Hey, Panther! Look what I found!" Moondog triumphantly held up an unopened pack of cards.

Martina grinned.

"You play poker, Vinny?" Martina asked.

"Yeah," he said.

"Cool. Deal 'em up, Moondog."

Moondog tossed the pack of cards onto the coffee table in the center of the room. Grabbing her glass and the bottle of scotch, she limped around the couch and sat down beside Martina.

"I'm not flying tomorrow, so I can drink the whole bottle," she taunted Vinny, taking another swig.

"This is kinda funny," Martina leaned over and whispered to Vinny. "She'll start losing pretty bad when she gets drunk enough. Then I can take all her money."

"You can't take my money 'cause I ain't got any on me," Moondog said. "Not that you could anyway."

"Well, you'll just have to owe me, then," Martina said. "And you forgot the chips."

"Oops," Moondog said, reaching over the back of the couch and grabbing a box of poker chips.

"Happy?" she asked, slapping them down.

"I'd be happier if you deal out the cards," Martina replied.

Moondog grabbed the deck, broke the seal, and pulled out the stiff cards.

"Hand out the chips, will ya?" she asked, shuffling the cards. The deck flew easily through her fingers.

"Five card draw," she said, expertly flipping the cards across the coffee table. "Ante up."

Martina and Vinny each dropped a chip into the center of the table and swept up their cards.

"How many?" Moondog said.

"Two," Martina replied, dropping two cards face down on the table and picking up the two dealt to her.

"One," Vinny said.

Moondog handed him another card and swapped a few from her own set.

"Your bet," she told Martina.

She dropped two chips into the center of the table. Vinny put in three. Moondog saw his raise, and Martina dropped another chip into the center.

"What you got, Vinny?" Martina asked.

"A ten," he said, laying his cards on the table. His hand consisted of a ten, an eight, a seven, a four, and a two, in four different suits.

Panther and Moondog gaped at him and then exchanged glances. A grin crept across Moondog's face. She lay down a full house. Martina was holding a straight. She quickly scooped up the poker chips.

The deal passed to Martina. She called five-card stud and flipped the cards across the table, dealing two down and one up. Moondog was showing the high card with a queen. Vinny had a nine, and Martina had a five.

"High card bets," Martina said. Moondog dropped a chip into the center of the table. The other two stayed in. Martina flipped the cards across again. Vinny was holding a ten. Martina landed a nine, and Moondog held a two. She upped the bet again. Both the others chose to stay.

Martina dealt the last round. Vinny wound up with a jack, Moondog held another queen, and Martina landed an ace.

Moondog tossed two chips into the center. Martina upped it to three. Vinny stayed in.

"Well?" Martina asked. Moondog revealed a third queen.

"Shit," Martina muttered, flipping over her hidden hand. She had a pair of aces.

"What about you?" she asked Vinny. "You must really have something hidden."

"Just that jack," he said.

"You know, Vinny," Moondog said, collecting her chips. "I'm really starting to like you."

Vinny grinned broadly. Martina simply rolled her eyes.

~ 11 ~

Dan Haley slowed his pickup truck as he approached Dyess's main gate. He fished in the pocket of his flight suit, found his wallet, and pulled out his military ID. He caught sight of his reflection in the rearview mirror. His eyes were bloodshot. The skin beneath them sagged. He looked as if he hadn't slept in days.

That was because he hadn't slept at all last night.

The car in front of him rolled through the gate. He eased his foot off the brake, pulling up to the guard shack. The airman standing beside the road stepped up to the truck and verified his ID, seemingly oblivious to Haley's apparent exhaustion.

"Have a good day, sir," the kid said, giving him a crisp salute.

Haley forced a smile as he returned the salute. He put the truck in gear and drove through the gate, crawling along the main road of the base. Haley wondered idly whether he should check in with his boss first or go straight to the airfield.

Seeing Miles would do nothing, he decided, turning the truck off the main road and heading for the airfield. He watched the buildings pass without much thought. The sky above was clear, and the air was warm. He didn't notice any of it.

Haley pulled the pickup into an empty parking spot outside the bomber squadron, killed the engine, and got out. Once inside, he walked into the operations room and quickly found a list of scheduled flights. Running his finger down the list, he found a bomber that was scheduled to fly a training mission with live ammunition in a few hours and noted its location on the ramp. It was close to the end of the runway. Chances were maintenance would be finished servicing the plane, but not be there to launch it yet.

"What's the status on 3086?" he asked the dispatcher.

The sergeant sitting behind the dispatch desk looked at the computer in front of her.

"Maintenance released it to us this morning, sir," she said.

"Okay," he said.

Haley walked out of the room and down the hall to life support. He stopped at his locker, grabbing his flight bag. He turned quickly and walked outside onto the flight line.

The tarmac was bustling with activity. Two long rows of B-1B bombers sat on the ramp. People and trucks were scattered among the large black planes. Maintenance crews prepared jets for launch, while aircrews arrived for their morning sorties.

Haley walked to where tail number 3086 was parked, trying to appear calm. He had clearance to be in the area. No one seemed to notice him crossing the ramp.

As he approached 3086, he was glad to see there were no maintenance vehicles parked in front of the plane or any of the jets nearby. He climbed up the first few steps of the ladder and pulled the maintenance paperwork from the plane. A quick check revealed that it was adequately fueled and fully armed. There were no major maintenance issues. Haley tossed his flight bag into the jet and dropped back to the ground.

He glanced around again. There was still no one nearby. Maintenance was busy launching the planes at the other end of the row. Moving quickly, Haley pulled the protective covers off 3086's engines and exhausts, tossing them to the ground behind the jet. He disconnected the ground wire from the plane and kicked the chocks away from the wheels.

Racing back to the jet, he rapidly climbed the ladder. Once inside the plane, he pulled the ladder in and closed the hatch. Grabbing his flight bag, he hurried to the cockpit.

Haley swung easily into the left-hand seat of the plane and quickly strapped himself in. He removed his flight helmet from his bag and pulled it over his head. He connected the oxygen mask and audio cable to the bomber, then turned the radio to the ground control frequency. He had to get the jet moving before someone saw the engine covers on the ground and realized something was wrong.

Haley began to rapidly run through the startup procedures for the plane, working from memory. One by one, the B-1's four large engines roared to life. Haley quickly scanned his instruments. Everything was in the green. He took a deep breath and released the brakes.

Haley nudged the throttles. The big airplane began to roll forward, crawling past the bombers parked on either side. Following the taxi lines, Haley turned into the lane between the parking spots and bumped the throttles again. The B-1 surged forward.

Ground control began to scream at him over the radio, demanding that he stop moving. Haley ignored the controller, quickly switching his radio to the tower. The controllers were hurriedly vectoring all other traffic away from the runway.

Haley turned onto the taxiway, taking the

shortest route to the runway. He kept the power up, causing the plane to race across the tarmac. Flashing lights appeared at the edges of the ramp as several Security Forces vehicles dashed out onto the apron. He paid no attention them.

Haley looked quickly at the final approach path as he reached the end of the runway. It was clear. He rolled out onto the runway without stopping and shoved the throttles past the detent to their stops. The engines responded instantly. Flames shot from the tailpipe as the B-1 went into full afterburner.

The plane lunged forward, racing down the runway with ever increasing speed. The police trucks sped across the ramps and onto the taxiways, trying desperately to reach the large jet before it became airborne.

Keeping the plane in the center of the runway, Haley scanned back and forth between the end of the runway and his airspeed indicator. He watched his speed climb higher.

Suddenly, red and blue flashing lights appeared directly in front of him. A Security Forces truck pulled out onto the runway and slammed on its brakes, stopping dead center in the runway, a hundred feet from the speeding plane.

Haley yanked back on the stick as hard as he could, pulling the B-1 into the air. The nose wheel lifted quickly off the ground, and a second later the main gear left the asphalt. The bomber roared over the truck, clearing it by mere inches. The powerful exhaust of the engines and the air flowing off the wings hit the truck full force, rolling it down the runway behind the plane.

As the bomber climbed into the air, Haley raised the gear. Leveling off 200 feet above the ground, he turned the plane to the south. He pulled the throttles back, taking the engines out of afterburner and keeping the plane just below supersonic. At this speed, it would take just over twenty minutes to reach the border. He quickly engaged the B-1's terrain-following radar, although there was little need for him to use it. Western Texas was flat and treeless.

With the computer flying, Haley turned his attention to the autopilot. He quickly programmed a course that would take him directly out of the country without flying over any major population centers. Fortunately, there weren't many towns between Abilene and Mexico. But Haley wasn't taking any chances. It was several hundred miles to the border, and he did not want to be found. The B-1 was the loudest plane in the U.S. Air Force inventory. If he were to fly over a city, it would be noticed.

The autopilot programmed, Haley scanned his instruments again, then looked outside. At this altitude he wouldn't have much time to react to an inflight emergency. And while the terrain-following radar would keep him from hitting the ground, it might not pick up a large radio tower or a set of power lines, either of which would put an abrupt end to his escape.

Keeping an eye on the instruments and the terrain in front of the bomber, Haley turned on his radar, setting it to maximum range. He began to flip through the radio frequencies, listening for the chatter of fighter pilots. They would be coming. In a matter of minutes every fighter unit in Texas and New Mexico would be looking for him. His only chance was to keep low and dodge the cities. Once over the water he could go supersonic. Right now the risk was too great. It wouldn't do to leave a trail of shattered glass across Texas.

There was no hiding it now, Haley thought. He had blatantly stolen the bomber. He couldn't disguise this as an accident. There had been no time to find another crew he could buy off or to craft a plan to make the plane's disappearance look like a crash rather than a theft. All he could do was grab the plane and take off.

Haley cursed his luck as he watched the patchwork of fields pass beneath the nose of the plane. If only that damned fighter jock hadn't shown up and wrecked everything he wouldn't be sitting here, waiting to be shot from the sky. The first theft would have gone off smoothly, and no one would have been the wiser. It would just be another lost aircraft.

But the fighter captain had ruined everything—and then just disappeared. Haley had no idea who Carlton had told about his involvement in the first hijacking attempt. It didn't really matter anymore, Haley realized. He had just stolen a plane. There was no longer any way for him to hide the fact that he was guilty.

"The plane is armed. Shoot on sight," he heard the radio crackle. Haley stopped changing the channel.

"I repeat, to all aircraft in the area," the controller said. "Be on the lookout for a hijacked B-1 bomber."

Haley cursed aloud. They were coming for him. He wished that he was in a B-2. While he was flying well beneath any land-based radar, the B-1 would still show up on the screen of any fighter that got in range. The B-1 was designed to fly very low. The fighter pilots looking for him knew he would be close to the ground. They could angle their radar to sweep the ground below them. Common sense dictated he would be heading south toward the closest border. They would know where to look.

For the moment, all he could do was hope he wouldn't be found. He leaned back and listened to the chatter on the radio, closely watching his own radar screen. The airborne fighters were quickly organizing themselves to search for the stolen bomber. Using the coordinates they relayed to each other, Haley crafted a rough idea of where the planes were in relation to him. More planes were joining the search every minute. Every fighter in the area must have been called up. That was understandable, Haley thought. They didn't want him dropping those bombs on downtown San Antonio.

Suddenly, a blip appeared on the radar screen at a four o'clock position to the bomber.

"Center, Wrangler three one, I've got something!" one of the fighter pilots called over the radio. "There's a plane down on the deck." He quickly relayed the coordinates. They matched Haley's location exactly. The major cursed. The fighter had to be one of the Air National Guard F-16s out of San Antonio. It was too soon for the Holloman F-22s to have reached him.

"There are no known friendly aircraft in that area," the air traffic controller said. "Confirm aircraft is a B-1."

"Confirmed," the fighter pilot said.

"You are authorized to fire."

"I have a shot."

The missile alarm began to scream in Haley's ears. He immediately dispensed his flares and pushed the throttles to their stops. The big bomber broke the sound barrier, quickly reaching its top speed of just over Mach 1. There was no longer any point in trying to hide. The Air Force knew his exact location. The bomber could not outmaneuver the fighters or their missiles. Haley's only chance was to run.

A violent shock rocked the bomber. A wave of panic swept over Haley. The missile warning faded in his ears. No other alarms replaced it. He swept his eyes rapidly over his instruments. All systems were still in the green. The flares had done their job.

Haley could see some hills to the southwest. He

immediately turned the bomber in that direction. The hills weren't very big, but any little bit of terrain that might briefly hide him would help. With luck, he could find a riverbed to follow. At this speed he only had about ten minutes until he reached the border.

The two ship formation of F-16s watched the missile collide harmlessly with the flares. The B-1 quickly picked up speed. Small hills covered the land below. The large black jet weaved in and out of them, making it impossible for Wrangler 31's pilot to get another missile lock on the bomber.

Wrangler 31 shoved his engine into afterburner, trying to hold his position on the B-1's tail. The fighter pilot had been on his way to the bomb range, and his plane was heavily laden with external stores. The drag from the bombs prevented him from matching the B-1's speed.

Wrangler 31 pulled his plane into a climb, hoping to keep the Bone in sight as it sped away.

"I can't keep up with him," he told air traffic control. "He's heading about two zero zero."

"Roger, Wrangler three one," the controller replied. "Head back to base. We'll send someone else to intercept."

"Roger," Wrangler 31 replied.

In the B-1's cockpit, Haley exhaled with relief. For a moment he was safe. He adjusted his heading slightly to the west, hoping to put more distance between himself and the F-16s' training areas. He didn't want to stay on a known course. He knew there would be more Vipers inbound from San Antonio, as well as F-22s from Alamogordo. The Raptors were farther away but could fly much faster than both the F-16s and his B-1. He guessed he still had about ten minutes before the F-22s were in range.

The Bone raced across the earth. The terrain-following radar kept the plane exactly 200 feet above the deck. The B-1 hugged the ground, rapidly climbing and dipping back down as it screamed along at supersonic speeds.

The ground below was brown and barren. To the south, the sky was growing dark. Haley could see storm clouds billowing in the distance. He paid little attention to his surroundings, instead focusing on his radar screen and listening intently to the radio. He could hear the National Guard F-16s' chatter as they frantically searched for him. Air traffic control was vectoring them closer to his position. Haley pressed the throttles against their stops, trying to coax every last bit of speed out of the large plane.

Below him, the hills disappeared. Once again, a patchwork of fields appeared as the land flattened out. In the distance, Haley could see the border town of Del Rio and the Rio Grande. He was almost safe.

Suddenly, a gray flash raced across his nose a few hundred feet above the bomber, crossing from east to west.

"Center, Wrangler seven one," the radio crackled. "We just flew over him."

"Roger, Wrangler seven one," air traffic control said. "You're cleared to engage."

Above, the two ship of F-16s looped back toward the bomber in a tight turn. Catching sight of the large plane, Wrangler 71 aligned his Viper with the B-1 and armed his Sidewinders.

"Wrangler seven one, Ghost Rider two one," another voice cut in. "We're about two minutes west of you."

"Roger, Ghost Rider two one," Wrangler 71 replied. "We'll keep an eye out for you."

Haley tensed. If Ghost Rider 21 was coming from the west, he was flying an F-22. A loud growl sounded in his ears as the Viper loosed a heat-seeking missile. Haley immediately dispensed another set of flares. He pulled the bomber hard to the right.

Behind him, the missile collided with the flares, exploding harmlessly above the fields. The bright red explosion lit up the dark clouds with a menacing flash. The B-1 dashed across the Rio Grande. The F-16s raced over the border after the large bomber, determined not to let Haley escape.

"Wrangler seven one, Ghost Rider two one," the Raptor pilot said, "I've got a visual on you. I'm joining on your right."

"Roger, Ghost Rider two one," the Viper driver replied.

Haley glanced across his instruments in a panick. He was out of flares. There was no way he could outrun or outmaneuver the F-22s bearing down on him. He was a dead man.

A bolt of lightning cut across the sky. Haley looked up. The sky above him was covered in black clouds. A massive winter thunderstorm raged just to the south of him. Rain began to hit the bomber's windshield.

Haley immediately disconnected the autopilot. He pulled back on the stick, placing the bomber in a steep climb, and turned the B-1 toward the dark clouds.

Behind him, Ghost Rider 21's Sidewinders locked onto the B-1's exhaust. The missile warning sounded in Haley's ears.

The B-1 plunged into the clouds, vanishing into the dark storm. Ghost Rider 21 and his wingman immediately peeled off. Flying into the storm was sheer suicide for the fighter pilots.

The missile tone in Haley's ears fell silent as the black clouds engulfed him.

"Dammit!" Ghost Rider 21 cursed. "We lost him. He flew into a huge storm cloud."

"We've got it on radar, Ghost Rider two one," air

traffic control replied. “It’s at least fifty miles across.”

“Roger,” Ghost Rider 21 said. “We’ll never find him in there. We’re headed home before we get in trouble for violating Mexican airspace.”

Once inside the dark clouds, Haley quickly pulled his throttles back. The bomber dropped below supersonic speed. He continued to climb, letting his airspeed decrease until he was below the maneuvering speed for the airplane.

As he had hoped, the fighter jets pursuing him had not followed him into the storm. Fighter pilots rarely flew in bad weather. The jets weren’t equipped for it. With their small size, they would be tossed about violently in the storm.

Entering the massive thunderstorm was a gamble. There were numerous hazards associated with thunderstorms, from lightning and violent updrafts and downdrafts to icing and hail. His chances of flying through the storm undamaged were slim. But they were still better than his chances of escaping from an F-22 in clear skies.

The rough air currents tossed the bomber about as it climbed, pitching it violently. Hard rain beat against his windshield. Before him was only the blackness of the storm clouds. Haley fixed his eyes on his instruments, trying to hold his pitch.

Reaching 20,000 feet, he trimmed the bomber for a level attitude. He set his throttles to maintain a slow airspeed, which would prevent the aircraft from being overstressed and ripped apart by the violent air currents buffeting it.

He programmed the autopilot to attitude hold mode and switched on the weather radar. Finding the quickest path through the storm, he set the heading. Quickly, he cinched down the straps holding him in the ejection seat, tightening the restraints as much as he could.

Pitch-black clouds surrounded the B-1. Brilliant flashes of lightning pierced the darkness, illuminating the haze that engulfed the plane with momentary bursts of white light. Updrafts and downdrafts buffeted the jet, tossing it to the left and right. Haley watched his altimeter spin up and down repeatedly as the plane sank several hundred feet, only to be lifted back up seconds later. He gripped his shoulder straps and watched the instruments intently. The plane was at the mercy of the storm. Haley was simply along for the ride.

The only way to survive flying into a thunderstorm was to hold attitude, maintain a safe airspeed, and find the quickest route out of the storm. With the autopilot set, all Haley could do was hang on and hope he would find clear skies soon.

The big plane pitched and rocked on all three axis as the storm tossed it about. Disoriented, Haley kept his eyes fixed on his attitude indicator. Rain pelted the plane, covering the windshield in a thick sheet of water. The sound of the deluge filled his ears. It felt as if the bomber was about to tumble from the sky.

Finally, the fog surrounding the plane began to grow lighter. Suddenly, the big bomber burst from the clouds. Blue sky filled the cockpit ahead of the storm. Below, Haley could see the Mexican coastline and the water of the Gulf.

He nosed the plane down, dropping back to the deck and engaging the terrain-following radar. He adjusted his course, heading straight for the blue ocean, and pushed the throttles back up. The B-1 raced away from the storm and dashed across the coast.

Finally in international airspace and well below any radar sites, Haley allowed himself to relax. He programmed the B-1's autopilot to fly to the destination his contact had given him.

Loosening his shoulder straps, he leaned back and watched the waves slip by 200 feet below the bomber. He was safe for now. He didn't want to think about what would happen to him when he finally landed in Colombia.

* * *

"You ever hear of a black project, Vinny?" Martina asked, stopping in front of a small hangar at a remote location at Edwards.

"You mean something so secret the government denies it even exists?" Vinny asked. "Super-classified shit?"

Martina nodded.

"Yeah, sure I've heard of them," Vinny said. "I always thought they were just something out of old Cold War thrillers."

"They're real," Martina said. "You'd be surprised how accurate fiction can be."

Vinny didn't reply.

"What I'm about to show you is that classified," Martina continued. "If you breathe a word about it to anyone, you can be shot for treason, no questions asked. You understand?"

Vinny nodded slowly.

"Good," Martina said. She pushed open the hangar door and stepped inside. Carlton followed. She reached over, hitting a switch beside the door. Fluorescent lighting flicked on above, illuminating two airplanes sitting silently on the concrete.

"These are the Hellcats," Martina said.

"What are they?" Vinny whispered.

"State of the art fighters," Martina said, walking to the plane. "The latest in materials, weaponry, and aerospace design."

Vinny gaped. He had only gotten a few quick glimpses of the plane while flying the B-1, and he had been blindfolded when Panther and Moondog smuggled him out of Holloman. He had seen the cockpit very briefly when he climbed in, but with the avionics off, there was nothing to see other than the flight controls, switches, and blank screens. Now, for the first time, he was allowed a good look at the planes. He studied them closely, intrigued.

"Somewhat similar to an F-22 in design, with several major modifications, such as the black underbelly, and these." She reached up, tapping a series of holes on the nose of the aircraft, each roughly an inch across.

"Thrusters?" Carlton asked, following her.

"Exactly," Martina said, moving toward the tail. "These planes are designed to operate in space, exactly as they would in the atmosphere. These babies can fly straight out of the atmosphere, travel halfway around the world, reenter and engage enemy aircraft, or hit a target, then fly back home in space again. They can also dogfight within orbit."

"How?" Vinny stuttered.

"The engines," Martina said, laying her hand on the inlet. "Dual jet/rocket, very unique fuel. She takes off like a conventional fighter and climbs straight up to maximum altitude."

She moved to the back of the plane. "We usually do a zoom climb to get even higher. When we reach the top, we flip a switch, a panel slides in front of the inlet, the turbine shuts down, and fuel and oxidizer shoot into the afterburner compartment, turning the engines into rockets. We do a short burn, and we're in orbit."

She walked around the engine nozzles and leaned against the wing. "To get back, we just retrofire, fly as a glider until our speed drops to a reasonable Mach, then restart the engines as jets."

"And you can just shoot back up into space whenever you want?" Carlton asked.

"As long as we've got enough gas."

"How is that possible? The space shuttle needs a six-month overhaul between missions."

"Most of it is complicated engineering stuff, inner workings," Martina said. "The main reason is this stuff, though." She ran her hands along the black surface creeping over the edge of the wing. "Materials technology, a combination of metals and silicone. More resistant to heat and better at radiating it than space shuttle tiles, and much less brittle. This stuff can take some pretty hard hits and stay intact, anything short of a bullet through the wing. Remember *Columbia*?"

"How could I forget?" Vinny asked, following her as she ducked beneath the tail.

"Also excellent heat seals around everything, materials again." Martina walked toward the front of the plane, running her hand along the wing as she did so. "All weapons carried internally. Latest in stealth technology, of course. Radar in the nose." She pointed to the front of the plane. "Good for spotting MiGs and stray satellites."

Martina raised the canopy.

"Up you go," she said.

Carlton gazed at her questioningly, then slowly pulled himself into the Hellcat's cockpit. Martina followed, standing on the stairs leading up to the plane. She leaned her arms against the rim of the cockpit.

"Controls are very similar to that of a conventional fighter," she continued. "Stick, throttle, rudder pedals. You've got your jet/rocket switch, next to engines on and off." She pointed to each item. "Heads-up display, relatively similar to most fighters. The screen is connected to a supercomputer up front, and you'd be amazed what that thing can do. You fly like a standard fighter, both in and out of space."

Vinny nodded slowly.

"Martina," he asked, "why are you showing me this?"

"Because you're going to fly it."

Vinny's mouth dropped open, and he stared at her wide-eyed for a full minute.

"Hey, Vinny," Martina said, waving her hand in front of his face. He blinked and closed his mouth.

"I'm going to fly this thing?"

"Yeah. The President wants us to move them, just in case the guys who captured us decide to try and get the planes. Moondog's hurt, so that leaves you."

She jumped to the ground. "C'mon, I'll take you to the simulator and give you a crash course in how to fly them."

"Are you sure I can?" Vinny asked, climbing down from the Hellcat's cockpit.

"You can fly an F-22, can't you?" Martina asked, walking back to the door.

"Yeah, better than most."

"Then you can fly a Hellcat. There are just a few small differences, mostly dealing with space shots."

"You and Moondog have astronaut training," Vinny said. "I don't."

"You don't need it," Martina said. "Don't worry, I'll show you everything you need to know. It's only one flight anyway, and I'll be on your wing the whole time. I've got about 300 hours in these."

The pair stepped outside, back into the desert sun. Panther pulled the door shut behind her and locked it. Vinny watched as the planes disappeared, amazed at the sudden twist his life had taken.

~ 12 ~

It was the biggest kick in the pants Vince Carlton had ever felt.

He had faithfully flown Panther's wing, following her through takeoff and departure. Reaching the maximum power setting at the optimum altitude, the two pilots threw their planes into zoom climbs, trading every bit of speed for altitude. At the top of the climb, they switched the engines to rockets.

The small plane went from nearly motionless to maximum velocity in no time flat, shoving Vinny into his seat. He had practiced the transition in the simulator many times, but it had never prepared him for the g-forces that hit him when he flipped the little switch. An incredible roar accompanied the sudden thrust.

Almost immediately his vision started to darken. For a moment he thought he was going to black out. Then he realized his eyes were not failing—the sky was darkening. The altimeter was spinning in circles. He looked outside. In front of him, he saw Martina's plane, twin plumes of brilliant flames shooting from the tailpipes. He checked behind him. The Earth was rapidly falling away, revealing blue ocean and green continents. Bright orange fire shot from the tail of his own aircraft, propelling him into the ever darkening sky. Carlton could only gape.

"That's one hell of a jolt, huh?" Martina's voice

crackled over the radio.

"Yeah," he said. "Thanks for warning me."

"Where would be the fun in that?" she asked with a laugh.

"You know, you have a bit of a mean streak."

"Only towards people I don't like. Cut engines in three...two...one...mark."

Vinny reached up and switched off the engines with a gloved finger. The roar behind him died. Everything fell instantly quiet. He was hovering in darkness, with the shimmering stars above him, the glowing Earth beneath, and Martina's silver plane ahead. They were in orbit.

For a moment all he could do was stare in complete awe. He was suspended in the silent vacuum, hovering in the darkness of space. The stars shone around him, a thousand points of light glowing in the blackness. The Earth curved away beneath him. He saw swirling clouds, mountains and plains, lakes and rivers, greens and browns and blues. Satellites and space debris flashed and sparkled around him as the sun glinted off metal.

He felt himself being lifted off the seat, his body pressing up against the straps. He wanted to undo the restraints and float freely, but the cabin was far too small. He searched for the pockets in his pressure suit, found a pen, and pulled it out. He placed the object in front of his nose and released it. The pen hung freely, suspended in the air. Satisfied, Vinny snatched it and stuffed it back in his pocket.

Ahead and to the left was Martina's plane, shimmering in the sunlight. The silver craft seemed to glide along on nonexistent air currents. Her engines were cool and silent. She appeared to hang in midair, held up by nothing at all.

Martina pulled the nose of her craft up, dodging an oncoming satellite. Vinny saw small jets of flame shoot from the tips of the wings and the tail, moving the craft through the vacuum. He gently eased the stick back on his own plane. The Hellcat responded seamlessly, climbing effortlessly. Vinny pushed the stick forward, and the spacecraft leveled off, right in position on Panther's wing.

Vinny was sorely tempted to throw the Hellcat into a roll. He wanted to weave in and out of the satellites, pull a couple of loops, see just what the plane could do. If that little climb was any indication at all, this was one hell of an airplane.

But Martina kept her course steady and even, maneuvering only when necessary. Vinny could only sit and wonder at what the Hellcat would be like to fly in a dogfight.

The sun was disappearing behind him. Looking down, he could see darkness creeping over the Earth's surface. To Vinny's utter amazement, the stars grew even brighter and more numerous as the light faded away.

Lights sprang up on the Earth below, cities as bright masses of light and towns as small dots. He studied at the heads-up display. The computer indicated that they had flown across the Atlantic Ocean and were now somewhere over eastern Europe.

"So, what do you think?" Martina's voice crackled over the radio.

"This has got to be the most amazing experience of my life," he said slowly.

"It's something, isn't it? It's so beautiful up here. The stars are incredible."

"Yeah. Too bad I can never tell anyone about this."

"Gotta love the government and all its classified information," Martina said. "But you'll be able to talk about flying in space after you start working for NASA."

"You think they'll still let me in?" he asked.

"You got in, didn't you?"

"Yeah, but after all this..."

"You'll still fly for NASA," Martina said. "Webster let you in on the Hellcat project. You don't have to worry about your future."

"Wow," Vinny breathed.

He glanced down and gasped in amazement. Beneath him the sun was rising. Clouds swirled over the Pacific Ocean, tinged orange and pink by the rising sun. The blue Earth curved beneath him. The stars sparkled above. He actually was flying in space.

"Time to reenter," Martina said. "Remember how to retrofire?"

"Yeah," he said reluctantly, wishing he could go through a few more orbits.

He nudged the Hellcat to the side, putting a little space between his plane and Martina's. He mimicked her as she moved her plane into the proper orientation and adjusted the throttle settings.

"Burn in three...two...one...mark."

Vinny reached over and flipped the engines on. The roar of the rockets filled his ears again, and the plane began to move, sliding back toward the Earth.

"Cut engines in three...two...one...mark," Martina called.

Carlton shut the engines off, but the plane continued to slide, moving downward. Silence filled his ears again. He checked his alignment on Panther's wing, holding his plane in exactly the same attitude as hers. A quick glimpse at the computer revealed that he was in the perfect position.

They began to slip through the outer reaches of the atmosphere. A red ion haze appeared, creeping over the nose of the plane. He saw the plasma flowing over the wingtips. Ahead, Martina's plane was surrounded by a red shock of plasma.

He looked at the heads-up display, looking for his

airspeed. The computer told him he was traveling over Mach 20. Keeping his attitude steady, he watched the ion haze creep up and then recede. They were still sweeping over the ocean, but the blue water was closer than before. He was now gliding along at hypersonic speed. His airspeed began to bleed down.

Martina adjusted her attitude again, and Vinny moved back into a loose fingertip position on her wing.

"These things can dogfight, right?" he asked.

"Yeah," she said.

"Even in space?"

"It's what they were designed to do."

"Have you ever tried it out?

"Yeah," she said. "Me and Moondog do it all the time."

"How do they handle?"

"Beautifully. Best damn dogfighter you've ever flown."

"You don't suppose..."

"Sorry. I'd love to do it, but this one's got to be straight by the books."

"Yeah, I figured," Vinny said.

The west coast of the United States appeared over the horizon. They were still bleeding off both airspeed and altitude. Keeping steady on Martina's wing, Vinny watched as the beaches of California slipped below. They were over land once more, still higher than anything other than a Blackbird could fly. The sprawling cities of western California gave way to a mountain range. On the other side, desert stretched as far as the eye could see.

Suddenly, Martina dropped the nose of her plane, pointing it almost directly at the ground. Vinny copied the maneuver, watching as the dirt rushed up toward his plane. It was unnerving, at the least.

"Why are we diving like this?" he called to Martina.

"We're diving through Class A," Martina explained. "ATC doesn't know about us, so we want to get in and out as quickly as possible. And we don't want anyone on a passenger jet catching a glimpse of us."

Reaching 15,000 feet, Martina pulled her nose back up, leveling off. Vinny stayed in place beside her. To his amazement, he was still flying supersonic without any engines at all. But that speed was bleeding off rapidly.

"Time to restart," Martina said.

The Hellcats were capable of landing in a glide, Martina had explained to Vinny, but they usually restarted their engines before landing. If they encountered an emergency that required more thrust, such as a go-around situation, they wanted that power available.

Vinny ran through the air restart procedures. His left engine quickly came to life, followed by his right. He checked his instruments. Everything was running smoothly.

In the distance he could see a runway cutting across the desert sand. Panther aligned her plane with the runway and led Vinny through the approach.

They touched down, one behind the other, on a remote strip north of Nellis Air Force Base. The outpost was very small. A tall fence covered in concertina wire surrounded everything. There was nothing but desert visible in every direction. A few buildings sat at the edge of a small ramp. The only other aircraft present was a Huey.

Several people stood on the ramp. Martina and Vinny taxied to them and shut their planes down. As he climbed out, Vinny recognized the men on the ramp as the maintainers from Edwards who worked on the Hellcats.

With the help of the technicians, Martina and Vinny pulled the Hellcats into one of the hangars along the ramp. Then they climbed aboard the Huey, which quickly started engines and took off, flying south.

Thirty minutes later the Huey set down on the transient ramp at Nellis. Martina and Vinny jumped off the helicopter and walked through the passenger terminal.

"That's some ride, huh?" Panther said as they headed down the road beside the flight line, passing the various fighter squadrons.

"Yeah," Vinny agreed. "That is one hell of a ride. I bet a space shuttle seems tame after that."

"It's kinda like flying a cargo plane after piloting a twenty-two," Martina said as they moved toward the main part of the base.

"So that's what you meant when you said you had some experience in heavies," Vinny said.

Martina smiled.

"It's still a pretty good ride," she said. "Plus the cabin is bigger, so you can get the full feel for floating in zero gravity. And you can do spacewalks, which are incredibly spectacular."

"Martina Redrick," a voice said from behind them, "you've got a lot of nerve coming here."

Martina and Vinny twisted around. A major in a flight suit was leaning against a nearby building, arms crossed. He was tall, with a tan, rugged, handsome face, hazel eyes, and brown hair cut short. A smaller man with blue eyes and shaggy dirty-blond hair stood beside him. Gold oak leaves also adorned his shoulders. Both men wore pilot's wings.

"I'll land my plane anywhere I damn well please," Martina said, sauntering up to the man.

"Not if I have anything to say about it," he replied, stepping away from the building.

"You wanna make something of it?" she said, stopping in front of him.

"Yeah, I do," he said, raising his hands. Martina immediately shifted her weight back, lifting her own fists. Vinny glanced quickly between the two pilots, wondering just what to do. The blue-eyed major simply watched with a look of amusement on his face.

The big major swung his fist in a wide hook. Martina quickly stepped inside his reach. The man grabbed her, engulfing her in a giant bear hug. Martina wrapped her arms tightly around his neck.

"Goddamn, Panther!" the major said, grinning broadly. "It's good to see you again."

"It's been way too long, Apache," she said as he released his grip on her. She turned to the smaller major and embraced him warmly.

"How you doing, Desperado?" she asked.

"Not bad," he said with a smile, "not bad at all."

She stepped back.

"You're all bruised up," he said, pointing at her face. Most of her bruises had faded to brown, except for a thick, dark mark under her left eye. "You get in a fight or something?"

"Yeah," Martina said. "Long story."

"It's always something with you," Apache said.

Martina turned back to Carlton. "Vinny, this is George Pershing," she said, pointing to the taller man. "And Chris Vella. These guys flew my wing from my first flight in an operational squadron to the day I left for test pilot school. Guys, this is Vince Carlton."

"You been beating the poor guy up, Panther?" Apache said. "He looks worse than you."

The cuts and bruises on Vinny's face had begun to heal but were still clearly visible.

"No," Martina said. "I'll tell you guys what I can over dinner."

"I'll be damned, Apache," Desperado said, pointing to Martina's shoulders. "She outranks us."

"Holy shit, Panther!" Apache said, ogling her rank.

"How on Earth did you get silver oak leaves? Last time I saw you, you were still a captain!"

"I was only a major for about six months," Martina said. "That's another long, crazy story."

"That's a big surprise," Desperado said, shaking his head in amusement.

"I'll say," Apache agreed. "What brings you out to Nellis?"

"We're just bringing a couple planes from Edwards," she said. "I'm going back to Houston in the morning."

"You got a place to stay tonight?" Apache asked.

"I was just on my way to lodging."

"Bullshit. This is Vegas," Apache said. "You're staying with us tonight. Me and Desperado got a great apartment in town."

"Well, if you insist..."

"We do."

"All right," Martina said. "I've got to make a phone call first, though."

"You can use the phone in my office," Apache said.

"Can you get me a secure line?"

"Yeah, c'mon." He led the way back into the building. The others followed him inside.

"How's NASA?" Desperado asked.

"Not bad," Martina said as they walked down the hall. "I spend most of the time flying T-38s. Take the shuttle into space a couple times a year."

"I saw you on the news last year," Apache said. "When you and that Navy pilot brought her down after the commander got knocked out."

"Yeah," Martina said. "They made a big deal out of nothing, as usual."

"What were you doing at Edwards?" Desperado asked.

"Me and Moondog were on loan to them for a few

months. We've been test flying planes."

"Moondog?" Apache asked.

"The Navy pilot who was on that shuttle mission with me," Martina said. "She's a hell of a pilot, but don't tell her I said that. You'd like her, Apache," she added with a smile.

"My spot on your wing got taken by a swabbie?" he said indignantly.

Martina rolled her eyes. "Don't be silly. No one will ever take your spot on my wing."

Apache pushed open the door to an office. There were a few desks inside, but all were empty.

"Phone's right here," he said, handing the receiver to Martina.

She produced a small piece of paper from one pocket. "Sorry, I can't let you overhear this."

"Classified stuff, huh?"

"Yeah."

"Now, why doesn't it surprise me that you'd get caught up in some secret government work?" he asked.

"I'm stupid like that?" Martina suggested.

Apache laughed.

"We'll wait for you outside," he said, stepping from the office and closing the door.

Martina slid into the chair behind the desk and punched a series of numbers. After a moment the phone on the other end began to ring.

A woman answered on the third ring. "Oval Office."

"This is Lieutenant Colonel Redrick," Martina said. "I was told to call."

"One moment please, Colonel," the woman said. There was a long pause.

"Afternoon, Colonel," the President said as he came on the line.

"Good afternoon, sir," Martina said. "We are on

the ground, and the planes are secure."

"No trouble?" Webster asked.

"None whatsoever, sir."

"That's a relief."

"Did they get Haley, sir?" she asked.

"No," Webster said. "He must have gotten a tip or something. He stole a B-1 and fled the country."

"Any idea where he went?"

"Somewhere in South America."

"Hmmm." The pilot paused. "Would it be reasonable to assume he took the plane to Kalliff?"

"That's a possibility."

"We have the coordinates of his base, sir," Martina said. "If you gave the word, I could have a fourship of F-22s bomb that place first thing in the morning."

"You can get pilots that quickly?"

"I've got three standing outside right now who will volunteer in an instant," Martina said. "All you have to do is give me a go-ahead."

"All right," Webster said. "I'll get the authorization to the base commander."

"We'll nail 'em, sir."

"I know you will, Colonel."

"Do you want me to go back to Houston after this bombing mission, sir?" she asked. "Commander Ansetti and I are finished with this set of tests at Edwards."

"I see no reason not to," he said. "If I need anything else from you, I'll let you know."

"One more quick thing, sir. What do I do with Carlton?"

There was a pause on the other end of the line.

"Take him back to Houston with you," the President said. "Just until we find Haley, and then send him back to his old base."

"Will do, sir," she said. "Have a good evening, sir."

"Good evening, Colonel," he replied. "Good hunting."

The line went dead. Panther replaced the phone and stood.

Apache, Desperado, and Vinny were waiting when she stepped out of the office.

"How'd you boys like to go bomb some terrorists?" she asked.

~ 13 ~

They came in low and fast, racing over the treetops—four silver ships, flying through the blue tropical sky, dashing by with a roar. The slick crafts slipped through the early morning air, awakening the jungle with thunder.

Two laser-guided bombs dropped from the belly of the lead plane. A second later the three others released their own bombs.

Below, the jungle exploded in flames. Fire filled the sky. The smoke billowed high above the treetops.

The pilots never saw their handiwork. They held their course south for a moment before looping back to the north, flying parallel to their original course ten miles to the west.

"You know, of all the bombing runs I've done," Martina said from the lead Nellis F-22, "that was one of the most satisfying."

"Did you hear that, Desperado?" Apache called from her wing. "Panther just admitted to enjoying a bombing run."

"Guess I better alert the papers," Desperado said.

"Funny guys," Martina replied. "For the record, I said compared to other bombing runs, not compared to dogfighting, which is far more enjoyable than bombing anything."

"I'm still calling the press," Desperado said.

"Need I remind you two that this plane is armed,

and I can still kick both your asses out of the sky?" Martina asked.

"That sounds like a challenge," Apache said.

"When we're back in international airspace," Martina said. "But first I want to see if Vinny can hold his own against me. I already know you two are pushovers."

"Don't listen to her, Vinny," Desperado told his wingman. "She can't get either of us."

"I hope you put up a decent fight, Vinny," Martina said. "Because those two sure don't."

"Well, I can't be as bad as you say they are," Vinny replied.

"Listen to him," Apache said. "First combat mission and he thinks he's hot shit."

"Second," Martina said. "We had a run-in with some MiGs about three days ago."

"What the hell have you been up to lately, Panther?" Apache asked.

"I can't tell you, so don't ask."

"Figures."

"You wouldn't believe me anyway," Martina said.

"When it comes to you, I'd believe almost anything," Apache said.

"I second that one," Desperado called.

"Say, Vinny, how long have you known her?" Apache asked.

"'Bout two weeks," Vinny replied.

"Are you scared yet?" Desperado asked.

"Should I be?"

"Absolutely," Apache said.

"Shut up, you two," Martina said. "Let's get home."

Below, the jungle gave way to the light-blue water of the Caribbean Sea. The four silver planes crossed the coast and slipped out over the ocean, racing for home across the waves.

*   *   *

Andrew Kennedy lifted his head as the fourship of F-22s flew past with a deafening roar. The silver planes vanished into the distance as quickly as they appeared. Kennedy turned his head back to the clearing in front of him, wondering briefly about the pilots of the planes.

Ahead of him, the jungle exploded in flames as the F-22s' bombs landed on their targets. The laser-guided weaponry was amazingly accurate, for which Kennedy was very thankful. Any closer and he would be caught in the flames. He could almost feel the heat from the fire mingling with that of the jungle.

Sweat had already begun to form on his camouflaged face. Swirls of green masked his tan skin. A floppy boonie hat covered his black hair. Only his dark eyes were visible. He lay amid the long jungle grass, his tall, muscular body completely hidden as he watched the fires the Air Force had lit burn.

"I see the Air Force is on time," a voice said from behind him.

Kennedy turned his head. A shorter and slightly stockier man crouched in the foliage behind him. His face was also painted green, and he was dressed in camouflage. Kennedy easily recognized his voice.

"On time and on target, as always," Kennedy said. His voice was deep and even. "They were twenty-twos."

"Really?" Mike Hawk responded.

"Yeah. Beautiful planes," the taller man said.

"Must have flown all the way in from the States," Hawk mused. "All they got around here is sixteens."

"Everyone has sixteens," Kennedy said. "I wouldn't be surprised if the frickin' Russian Air Force flew sixteens."

Hawk laughed. "Shall we go do what we came to do?"

"Looks clear to me."

"I'll get the boys, then," Hawk said, disappearing

back into the bush.

Kennedy turned his head back to the jungle. The acrid smell of burning trees filled his nose. Aside from a few curling wisps of smoke, the area in front of him seemed lifeless. Even the air hung motionless. The lack of a breeze only seemed to add to the oppressive heat and humidity of the jungle.

"Take point," Hawk announced on his return. Two more armed, green-faced men in camouflage flanked him.

Picking up his M-16, Kennedy stood, stretching to his full height for a moment. He flicked the safety off and began to walk forward, staying within the shadows of the jungle. His boots barely made a sound as he threaded his way between the trees. The others silently fanned out behind him. All four men walked slowly, alert to the slightest movement or sound. Many creatures lurked in the Colombian rain forest, but the small group of America's finest was by far the most fearsome.

A long, now cratered runway led to the burned-out hulk of a barn. Kennedy skirted the open area surrounding the strip, walking to the side of the barn. He moved slowly, watching for signs of life. He saw none.

Reaching the side of the barn, he stopped and glanced back at Hawk. The other man nodded. Kennedy lifted the muzzle of his M-16 and stepped into the open. The air around him stayed silent. He waited a moment longer, then motioned for the others. One by one they slipped from the jungle behind him.

"What exactly are we looking for?" Kennedy whispered to Hawk.

"A B-1," Hawk replied.

"A U.S. bomber?" Kennedy asked. Hawk nodded.

"You're shittin' me."

"Nope. They didn't tell me what it would be doing

here."

Kennedy didn't reply. He started walking toward the barn.

"They also want whatever intel we can give them," Hawk said.

"There are tire tracks in the grass," Kennedy said, stopping.

Hawk looked down.

"Trucks?" he suggested.

"Can't be," Kennedy said. "The tires are too big, and they aren't aligned. There's one tire in the front and two in the back."

"Airplanes," Hawk said. "Probably fighters. They're too close together to be from a B-1."

"What kind of fighters?"

"I can't tell that from the tire tracks," Hawk said. "Check the building."

The corners of Kennedy's lips curled upward for a brief second as he walked toward the still smoking shell of the barn. Hawk and the others followed him.

The building was completely empty. The timbers that had not been incinerated by the Air Force's bombs cluttered the ground. Kennedy stepped inside and kicked through the rubble with his toe, encountering only scorched earth.

"Whatever was in here's gone too," he said. "They probably took their planes and got out of here."

Hawk followed him inside, pushing some of the burning wood away.

"See any bomber tracks?" Kennedy asked.

"The ground's too chewed up," Hawk said. "There's a hole over there. I want to check it out."

The two men picked their way through the debris and walked in the opposite direction of the woods. They stopped beside a gaping depression in the ground.

"That is one big hole," Kennedy said.

"Musta dropped a bunker-buster on it," Hawk said.

"Looks like they dropped about three."

"Will you get down there and check it out, already?"

"All right," Kennedy said, making his way into the crater.

"Stay up here," Hawk said to the other two men. "Let me know if anything moves." He followed Kennedy down into the hole.

The taller man was standing in the center of the depression, examining the rough-hewn rocks.

"There was definitely something down here," he said. "These rocks have been cut."

He stepped forward, brushing his hand along the dirt at the side of the crater. He stuck his fingers between the rocks and pulled several away. The large stones cascaded down. Kennedy stepped back quickly to avoid being hit by the falling rocks.

He glanced at Hawk, then back to where the stones had stood. In place of the rocks was a tunnel leading into the ground.

"After you," Hawk said.

"Shoulda brought my NVGs," Kennedy muttered, pulling a flashlight from his pocket. He expertly balanced his M-16 between his arm and his hip and flicked the small light on with his left hand. Slowly, he stepped into the tunnel. Hawk followed.

The flashlight cast a tiny beam along the floor. The ground and sides of the tunnel were made of the same rough-hewn rock Kennedy had found outside. Wiring ran along the ceiling. Lightbulbs appeared at sporadic intervals. He pointed upward, indicating the lighting to the man behind him.

The two soldiers walked along the dark corridor, moving slowly so as not to make noise. Their eyes darted back and forth, searching for the slightest motion in the blackness. They saw nothing.

Kennedy's flashlight fell on an opening in the rock. As the two men approached, the large hole revealed itself to be a roughly cut door. Nothing blocked the opening. Kennedy turned to Hawk, silently indicating that he was going inside. Hawk nodded.

Kennedy stuck the muzzle of his rifle into the room and waited, listening. Hearing nothing, he stepped inside, leading with the muzzle of his M-16. The flashlight revealed a poorly made wooden cot and chair. The walls were bare. Aside from the two pieces of furniture, the room was completely empty.

Kennedy stepped outside and nodded to Hawk. The two men continued into the tunnel. The small flashlight beam uncovered more doors as they moved. All the rooms were empty save for a few random items of furniture scattered about.

"No bodies," Kennedy whispered, stepping from one room.

"No signs of life at all," Hawk added. "But someone definitely lived here at one point."

"They sure don't now," Kennedy muttered.

"C'mon," Hawk said, turning around. "There's nothing to see here. Let's get the fuck out of this jungle."

~ 14 ~

"This is my place," Martina said, unlocking the front door of her house and pushing it open.

A loud meow greeted Vinny as he followed her inside. A large gray cat sauntered up to Martina and wrapped himself around her legs.

"And this is Orion," she said, setting her bag on the floor and scooping the cat up.

"Hello, Orion," Vinny said, reaching over to scratch the cat's ears. Orion pushed the top of his head into Vinny's hand.

"I'm gonna go feed him," Martina said. "Make yourself at home." She disappeared through a door off to the left.

Vinny swept his eyes over his surroundings. He was standing in a large room with a high ceiling. A patterned carpet sat in the middle of the hardwood floor. A roomy couch and two chairs were arranged around a small coffee table on the center of the rug. Pictures of airplanes hung on three of the walls. Two large windows looked out at the gravel driveway and the trees beyond it.

The wall opposite the door was covered with a large built-in bookcase. Carlton walked slowly to the shelves. A medium-size television and a stereo sat in the far right corner of the shelves. The remainder of the bookcase was filled with framed photographs and models of airplanes and spacecraft. Books appeared at odd intervals, held in place by a variety of aviation-related bookends. The volumes ranged from collections of airplane photos to military history. Fiction intermingled with engineering and a smattering of astronomy books.

Vinny turned his attention to the pictures. There were several shots of Martina standing beside the space shuttle or seated in the cockpit. Moondog appeared in a few photos. He found some of a very young Martina standing with a group of kids, all in Air Force Academy uniforms. The vast majority of the pictures came from Panther's career in the Air Force. He recognized Apache and Desperado in several photos.

"See anything you like?" Martina's voice interrupted his exploration.

"Some of these pictures are pretty interesting," Vinny said. "Like this group of cadets here." He pointed to one picture. "How old were you?"

"Pretty young," Martina said. "That was a long time ago." She walked over to the bookshelves.

"I remember that day." He pointed to a picture of Martina standing in parade dress, with a yellow sash around her waist and butter bars on her shoulders. She was grinning broadly, and her eyes were dancing.

"How could you forget?" she asked.

"What about this one?" He picked up a photograph showing Martina standing beneath the nose of an F-22 Raptor. Her name was inscribed below the canopy. Beneath it were five emblems, each indicating an enemy kill. Panther was gesturing toward the emblems with her hand.

"That was when I became an ace."

"How many kills did you end up with?"

"A lot."

Vinny set the picture down. "Do all these have stories?" he asked.

"Some do," she said. "Others are just people I know. Old friends."

Vinny nodded.

"C'mon, I'll show you where you can drop your stuff. The little that you have."

She led him away from the pictures and through another door, into a smaller room with a bed and a dresser.

"It's not much," she said, "but it's a place to crash. There's a bathroom through there." She pointed to another door near the one leading to the living room. "Remind me to find you some soap."

Vinny dropped his stuff and followed Martina back to the living room. Orion had reappeared. He was sitting on the center of the carpet, licking his paws.

"I spent the last month and a half at Edwards," Martina said. "There's not much food in the house, but you're welcome to whatever you can find. I've got to run to NASA tomorrow, so I'll pick up some groceries on my way back. It's way too late to go out now."

After landing back at Nellis, Martina and Vinny had caught a flight into Houston, touching down at the airport just after nine. From there, it was an hour's drive to Martina's house, tucked back in a rural area outside the city.

Martina dropped onto the couch, sprawling across it with her head propped on a small pillow at one end and her feet hanging off the other. Orion jumped onto her chest. She began to run her fingers along his soft fur. The cat lay down and curled up on top of her.

"So what does he do when you're gone?" Vinny asked, sitting in one of the armchairs.

"Whatever it is cats do," Martina said. "I have some neighbors down the road who stop by and feed him every day or so."

"How long am I here for?" he asked, changing the subject.

"Not sure," Martina replied. "Webster wants me to keep you safe until Haley is caught."

"So what am I supposed to do until I can go back to Tyndall?"

"I don't know," Martina said. "Figure out how Orion spends his days?"

"Maybe I can even join him," Vinny said with a smile.

Martina laughed. "I suppose if you promise to be good I can take you to NASA with me."

"Really?" Vinny's eyes lit up. He grinned broadly.

"Yeah. I probably won't be doing anything exciting for the next two days, but you're welcome to tag along. It's better than watching the cat." Orion purred loudly.

"You got anything to drink?" Vinny asked.

"Check the fridge. There might be a few beers or some juice. Barring that, there's always tap water."

"I thought you didn't like beer."

"I can't stand the stuff personally, but I usually keep a few in the fridge just in case someone who does stops by."

"So they're Moondog's?"

"Yup," Martina said. "The kitchen is through that door." She pointed over her shoulder.

"Thanks," Vinny said, walking in the direction she indicated.

Martina turned her attention back to Orion, running her hand over the back of his head and down his back. The cat was fast asleep. Panther stifled a yawn.

"If I'm not careful I might end up like you," she said to the cat.

The long flight to South America and back had

taken the edge off the pilot. She had spent far too much time catching up with Apache and Desperado the night before. While she had been wide awake for the early mission, the lost hours of sleep had caught up to her. Add to that a commercial flight back to Houston...

She heard Vinny rummaging through the kitchen, probably searching for a glass or something. The soft, rhythmic rise and fall of Orion's body beneath her hand relaxed her. His deep, rumbling purr rolled into her fingers. She felt her eyelids growing heavy and falling shut.

Suddenly, the cat perked his head up and bolted from Martina's lap. Startled by his sudden motion, Panther jolted back to consciousness. She opened her eyes to find herself staring down the barrel of a gun. A tall man with dark hair was standing behind the couch, pointing a pistol at her head. Haley.

Martina's hand instinctively dropped to her side, searching for her Colt .45. Her pockets were empty. She hit her leg again, realizing she had packed the gun in her luggage before getting on the plane. It was sitting in her bag beside the door, on the other side of the room. She would have to go through Haley to get the weapon.

She leapt to her feet and threw her hand against the side of Haley's arm, knocking the weapon away from her. He kept his grip on the pistol. Before he could bring it back to bear on Martina, she jumped over the back of the couch, tackling him. They crashed to the floor. Haley landed flat on his back, with Martina sprawled on top of him.

Quickly, Martina collected herself, drawing her body into a sitting position and pressing her thumbs into his throat. Haley gasped and swung the pistol around, hitting her in the shoulder blade with the butt of the weapon. She grunted but kept her grip.

Haley swung the gun at her again, this time catching her in the elbow. Martina's hand flew free. Haley planted his palm against her shoulder and shoved her off him. He tried to roll on top of her, but Martina thrust her leg into his stomach with enough force to push him back.

She jumped agilely to her feet as he rolled onto his back. Before he could stand she was on top of him, dropping her knee onto his wrist and pinning the gun against the floor. She slapped the side of her hand against his temple with enough force to daze him and quickly pulled the gun from his hand.

"What the hell...?" Vinny said, emerging from the kitchen.

Martina twisted her head around. Seeing an opportunity, Haley rolled onto his side, driving his fist into her stomach. She rocked backward. Haley climbed quickly to his feet, kicking her in the chest. The pilot fell onto her back, the gun sliding from her hand. She rolled with the blow, letting the momentum carry her onto her feet.

"Grab that!" she yelled to Vinny. He scrambled for the gun.

Haley stepped forward, punching her in the face. He swung his other fist at her. Martina stepped to the inside of the punch, grabbing his wrist lightly. She stepped forward quickly, planting her heel behind his foot and digging her other hand into the opposite side of his throat. She flung him down. He hit the hardwood floor with a thud and lay still.

Martina jumped back, standing just outside his reach. Blood ran from her mouth and nose. She glared at Haley contemptuously, then ran the back of her hand across her mouth.

Haley moaned and attempted to sit up.

"Don't move," Vinny hissed. The young captain was standing to Martina's right, pointing the gun at

Haley's head. The look on Vinny's face made it clear that he wouldn't hesitate to pull the trigger. Haley's eyes darted back and forth. He could not move quickly enough to reach either pilot before a bullet reached him. He froze.

"Why the hell are you here?" Panther said. The blood on her face only accented the anger in her eyes.

"I need your help," Haley said. A hint of surprise crept into Martina's face. Vinny's expression read somewhere between confusion and shock.

"Please hear me out, Colonel," he said. "You're the only one who can get me out of this."

Martina glared at him. "Talk fast."

Haley stared at the floor for a moment, half opening his mouth as if to speak, then closing it. He looked up at the two fighter pilots. They stared back at him silently.

"I have a family, Colonel," he said finally. "A wife and two little girls. They're five and three."

"I really don't give a shit about your personal life," she said. "Get to the point."

"I want you to know why I did what I did," he said. Martina's stony gaze remained unchanged.

"A few months ago, General Miles approached me and told me there was a man he wanted me to meet," Haley began. "I didn't think much of it. I mean, that's the kind of stuff executive officers do sometimes. So I went to see this guy. He told me he belonged to some organization based in South America. He said he wanted me to deliver a B-1 to them and that he'd give me the how and why of it all later.

"I told him I didn't want any part of it. He told me if I refused or told anyone they would kill my wife and my girls in front of my eyes. Then he said they'd be watching me. What the hell was I supposed to do, Colonel? I couldn't let them hurt my family."

Martina remained impassive. "So what happened

next?"

"I went to Miles and told him everything. He told me he wanted me to act as a liaison between himself and this group and that I was to give them whatever they wanted. He wanted me to keep him informed. Then he echoed the same threat and said if anything ever happened I was to completely deny his involvement."

"So he wanted to use you as a fall guy, keep himself clear of the matter if the shit hit the fan," Vinny said.

"Exactly," Haley said. "They had me organize the theft. I paid off two pilots and told them to deliver the plane to a specified location in Colombia and to make it look like an accident. But you showed up and kept them from getting away."

"Which is why you tried to kill him," Martina said.

"Miles ordered me to," he said. "At first we tried to frame you, but the evidence we manufactured didn't hold. He told me to kill you to keep you from talking. He also told me to find out whatever I could about your planes, Colonel. He said since we didn't deliver the bomber, we had to give them something in return."

"And it was us," Martina said. "You told them we flew out of Edwards, and they came and found us."

"But that fell through too," Haley said. "So they sent me back to steal a bomber, which I did."

"Did you deliver it to them?" she asked.

"I did. If I didn't, there's no telling what they'd do to my girls."

"So what do you want from me?" Martina asked.

"I need you to get my family away from them," he said. "I know you have connections. You've got to be able to talk to someone who can help me." Haley's voice took on a panicked tone. "I'll tell you everything I know. I know where they are. I know what their plans are. Just get my girls to safety."

"Don't you think the terrorist cell will suspect something when you disappear?" she asked.

"I told Kalliff I needed to get back to the States so I could continue my role as a liaison," he said, "but I didn't talk to Miles before I left. Hopefully, he won't miss me for another day or two. If you act quickly enough you should be able to save them."

"And what do you know?" Martina said. "What is Kalliff planning?"

"He's going to take that bomber and the rest of his arsenal, fly into New York City, and drop every bomb he can."

"Shit," Martina muttered, closing her eyes. "When?"

"As soon as possible. Two, three days," Haley said. "He's moving the planes up to Canada. As soon as everything's in position he'll strike."

"Canada, this time of year?" Martina said in disbelief. It was the middle of January.

"It's not much colder than Ellsworth," he said. "And I don't know what facilities they have."

"What about Miles?"

"He doesn't know yet. At least, I don't think he knows. When he does, he might try to join Kalliff."

"All right," Martina said, chewing on her lip. "Vinny, watch him. I'm going to make a few phone calls."

She walked past Vinny and disappeared through the kitchen door. A moment later he heard her talking to someone. He leaned up against the back of the couch, keeping his gun fixed on Haley. The other man made no attempt to move. He remained seated on the floor, staring at the hardwood.

Vinny glanced behind him. Orion had materialized again and was curled up in the center of the couch. He raised his head to look at Vinny and meowed loudly.

"Hello to you too," he said, reaching back to scratch the cat's ears with one hand. He kept his other tightly on the gun and his attention focused on Haley. The dark-haired man stayed still.

"Your family will be fine," Martina said, walking back into the room. Vinny noted that she had washed the blood from her face.

Haley looked up.

"I just talked to some of my connections. They're sending a team in to bring them to safety. I told them to keep it discreet," she said. "We have to catch the red-eye to Washington. Hope you didn't get too comfy, Vinny. Grab your stuff."

"Yeah, well, I didn't really want a decent night's sleep anyway," he said with a smile. Placing the gun in Martina's open hand, he walked back into the spare bedroom.

"What about me?" Haley asked.

"You're coming with us, and you're under arrest," she said. "Get up. And don't try anything fast."

Haley climbed slowly to his feet.

"Moondog is meeting us at the airport," she said to Vinny as he emerged from the spare room, bag in hand.

"Really?" he said, taking the gun back.

"Yeah, she'd kill me if she got left behind," Martina said, walking to the door, and picking up the small bag she had left beside it. Vinny and Haley followed her outside.

"Bye, Orion, be good," she called to her cat before shutting the door and locking it.

"Here we go again," Panther muttered to herself, walking to her Jeep.

~ 15 ~

The earliest rays of sunlight were creeping through the windows of the White House conference room as Martina stepped inside. She quickly looked around her. The chair at the head of the table was empty. On either side of it sat the Secretary of Defense and the Secretary of State. The Director of Homeland Security and the Chairman of the Joint Chiefs of Staff occupied the next two chairs. The secretaries of the Army, Navy, and Air Force sat opposite several empty chairs.

"Holy brass hats," Martina whispered under her breath. She peered behind her. Vinny had a slightly shocked expression on his face. Moondog didn't so much as bat an eyelash at the generals. The Navy pilot looked as if she were about to join the boys for a beer in the local pub. Dan Haley, led into the room in shackles, looked frightened.

The three fighter pilots walked to the chairs opposite the Joint Chiefs. Moondog was still limping slightly. The bruises on Moondog's and Vinny's faces had almost completely faded away, except for the dark circles under Vinny's eyes. The thick line under Martina's left eye was still visible, although it was now a reddish-brown color. There was a smaller bruise surrounding the left corner of her mouth.

The Secret Service agent escorting Haley positioned him behind an empty seat and stepped back, standing silent against the wall.

The door opened and the President entered, walking to the head of the table.

"Good morning, everyone," David Webster said. "Sorry to drag you out here again Colonel, Commander. Please have a seat.

Everyone at the table sat down.

"Well, Colonel," Webster said. "Tell us what you know."

Martina stood slowly, sweeping her eyes over the group of men before her.

"Sir, this man approached me last night," she said, pointing to Haley. "He is Major Dan Haley, the executive officer to General Miles, who is the commander of Dyess Air Force Base. Haley stated that for the last several months he has been working, against his will, as a liaison between the general and a terrorist organization operating out of Colombia under the direction of a man named Azad Kalliff. Haley organized the theft of a B-1 bomber from Dyess, which Captain Carlton thwarted. Once the plot failed, he arranged to have Carlton arrested for hijacking, and then tried to kill him.

"Three days ago, he personally stole a second bomber and delivered it to the terrorist cell. He then managed to regain entry to the United States, and he turned himself in to me, saying he would tell us everything he knew. He claims that Kalliff is planning to attack New York City in one or two days using the bomber and several other fighter aircraft."

For a moment the room fell silent. Everyone stared at Martina, wide-eyed and slack-jawed. Only Webster, Moondog, and Vinny didn't appear shocked, having heard the story before. Haley simply looked at the table. Martina calmly sat back down.

"Obviously, gentlemen, we can't let this happen," Webster said.

The men seated around the table began to fire off questions in rapid succession, demanding as much detail as possible. Most of the questions were directed at Haley, and he answered to the best of his ability. A few were flung toward Martina. The Secretary of State wanted to know if the information could be trusted and what her involvement was in the issue. Martina said that, as far as she knew, everything Haley had said was true, but she had no concrete proof, and expertly skirted the issue of the Hellcats.

Webster leaned back in his seat, taking in all the information being tossed about the table. He let his staff grill Haley for a good fifteen minutes, until the questions approached redundancy. Finally, he raised his hand, interrupting the conversation.

"Gentlemen, I think we have enough information to work with," he said. "If there are no further pressing questions, I'd like to move on."

"Sir, I have a question," Martina said, standing.

"Yes, Colonel?"

"After the second B-1 was stolen I led a flight of F-22s to bomb where we suspected Kalliff's headquarters was located," she told the Joint Chiefs. "I was told a team was being sent in to inspect the damage. However, I left Nellis before receiving any word of their findings. I was wondering, sir, if you knew the results."

"The site was abandoned, Colonel," Webster said. "The troops we sent in found evidence that people had lived there at one point and that aircraft had been at the site, but that they left several days before the bombing run. There was nothing to indicate where they had gone."

"Thank you, sir," Martina said, sitting.

"Sir," Haley said timidly as he stood, "what about my family?"

"Your family is safe," Webster said, smiling. "They

are on their way to Washington under the escort of several Secret Service agents."

"Thank you," Haley said softly, dropping back into his chair.

"Anything else?" Webster asked. The room was silent.

"All right," the President continued. "I want General Miles arrested immediately. With any luck, he can lead us to Kalliff, and we can stop this attack before it even gets airborne. However, we need to be prepared if we can't stop the planes on the ground. Colonel, I want you to set up a defense around New York. These gentlemen will give you everything you need." He motioned to the Joint Chiefs.

Now it was Martina's turn to gape in shock.

"I don't want those planes to enter our airspace," Webster said.

"Yes, sir," Martina replied.

"Bill," he said to the Director of Homeland Security, "raise the national threat level. I also want the military on a higher alert. But don't tell them why. All your work will be done in secret, Colonel. I do not need the millions of people in that city panicking."

There was a chorus of "yes, sirs" from around the table, along with several nods.

"Colonel, do you need any information from Mr. Haley?" Webster asked.

"I questioned him thoroughly on the way here, sir," Martina replied. "He's told me everything he knows."

"All right," Webster said. "I'm going to turn him over to my people. If you need any more information from him, let me know."

"I will, sir."

"I'll let you get to work then, Colonel," the President said, standing. The scraping of chairs filled the room as everyone rose. The President walked the length of the table and disappeared through the doors. Several members of his staff followed him. As soon as the group had exited, the Secret Service agent led Haley from the room. The door closed, leaving Martina, Moondog, and Vinny alone with the Joint Chiefs.

For a moment the room was silent.

"We can stay here, or we can move to the Pentagon, Colonel," the Air Force Chief of Staff said after a moment, "whichever suits you better."

"It doesn't matter," Martina said, speaking quickly. "I need a map, a big one, showing from D.C. to Canada and from Rhode Island to Ohio."

"I think that can be arranged," the Air Force Chief said. He stood and walked to the door, speaking briefly to someone outside before returning to his seat. A moment later a projector on the ceiling hummed to life, casting a map of the northeastern United States on the far wall.

"Will that work, Colonel?" he asked.

"That's perfect," Martina said, standing. She walked over to the wall and studied the map. After several minutes she began pacing back and forth, keeping her eyes fixed to the display.

"All right," she said finally, stopping and collecting herself. "We know Kalliff is somewhere up here, in northern Canada." She pointed to the top of the map. "He's probably pretty far north so nobody finds him. According to Major Haley, he has one B-1 bomber, about twenty Russian MiGs, and five or so older American planes. Fifteens, sixteens, and the like. None of these aircraft has any stealth capability. The B-1 has terrain-following radar, so it can stay low and fly under the radar, but the others can't.

"The most direct route would be to fly straight in through here, down the Hudson River Valley." She swept her hand from the Great Lakes to New York

City. "The bomber alone might be able to make it through, but the other planes would be spotted for sure. I don't know how much this guy knows about the aircraft's capabilities, so he might be foolish enough to try it.

"But if I were running this show, I'd fly down the Atlantic coast and come in through here." She swept her hand over the area beneath Long Island. "Right over the water. The Sound is too close to land, so I'd fly right along the Atlantic, stay low to avoid the radar until it's too late. The bomber could fly lead, keep right on the deck using its radar, and the others could follow. The surface of the ocean is flat enough to allow that, right, Moondog?"

"Did it all the time flying off carriers," the Navy pilot said.

"That's the angle from which the city's most vulnerable," Martina said. "Now, as far as defenses..." she paused, glancing back at the map. "I'll need a squadron of F-22s, General," she said.

"I'll get you the top one from Langley, Colonel," the Air Force four-star said.

"All right," Martina continued. "I want the squadron split in half. The first flight needs to be somewhere in here." She laid her hand on the center of Connecticut. "The others should go to McGuire. We'll have two planes flying combat air patrol over the city at all times. The others will be on alert. I want an AWACS out here around the clock." She motioned to the water to the east of Rhode Island.

"I have a carrier in Norfolk with two AWACS sitting on it," the Navy Chief of Staff said. "The carrier isn't ready to sail yet, but I can easily put the planes on station."

"Thank you, Admiral," Martina said. "We'll also need to coordinate with the Canadian air traffic control centers and our own in the States. I want an alert out as soon as anything strange shows up on the radar. We should also tell the border patrol to notify us if any low-flying aircraft enter the U.S."

Martina paused and turned to face the generals.

"Does that cover everything?" she asked.

"I think we can make that work," the Air Force general said.

"Just let us know if you need anything else," the admiral replied.

"I do have one question, Colonel," the Air Force Chief of Staff said. "Where do you plan to be during all this?"

"I can't speak for Commander Ansetti or Captain Carlton, sir," Martina said. "But with your permission I'd like to join the fighter squadron."

"I reviewed your record before coming here this morning," the general said, "and I think a pilot of your caliber belongs in the sky."

"Yes, sir," Martina said.

"Now, as for the Commander and the Captain..." He turned to face the other two pilots.

"Panther, there is no way you are flying without me," Moondog stated.

"Count me in," Vinny chorused.

"All right," the Air Force general said. "Let's make this happen."

* * *

The sharp ringing of the phone cut through the silence of the room. Vince Carlton lifted his head and glanced at it, then looked back at his companions. The three fighter pilots were sitting in the visiting officers' quarters at Langley AFB, having spent the day making preparations to deploy a handful of F-22 Raptors.

The phone rang again.

"Get that, will you?" Moondog said to Panther, shuffling the deck of cards.

"Why me?" Martina asked indignantly.

"Because you're the one they want to talk to," she replied. "You're the one running this show."

"Fine," Martina said, standing. "Deal me out of this hand."

She walked from the room.

"All right, big money for me!" Moondog said, eagerly flipping the cards to Vinny, intent on taking everything she could from him in the short time Martina was out of the poker game.

She was well on her way to depleting his supply of poker chips when Martina returned. The Air Force pilot dropped back into her seat, silently watching the card game.

"Well?" Moondog asked, lifting her head.

"They sent a team to bring Miles in," she said.

"And?" Vinny asked.

"He's vanished. His wife said he left this morning on a fishing trip, and she hasn't been able to get in touch with him since. Apparently someone tipped him off."

"Haley?" Vinny said.

"They don't think so. Haley claims he came straight to my place after he left Colombia. He didn't want Miles to know he was back in the country. Someone else must have warned him."

"So now what?" Moondog asked.

"He probably joined Kalliff in Canada. Haley said Miles has a cabin up there that his wife doesn't know about. It's on a lake, hence fishing. Most likely that's where they're running the operation from. We're sending a spec ops team up there tonight to try and apprehend them."

"That's a lot of guessing," Moondog said.

"Right now it's all we've got to go on. Northern Canada is a pretty big place."

"We still deploying the fighters?" Moondog asked.

"Everything else is on schedule."

"Okay," Moondog said, beginning to shuffle the cards again.

"Deal me back in," Martina said. The three fighter pilots turned their attention back to the card game.

* * *

"I think that about wraps it up," the man sitting across from Haley said.

The Air Force major sat in front of a plain folding table at the center of a small, windowless room. Haley's hands, still in cuffs, rested in his lap. Opposite him sat a man in a gray suit. Two men in black suits leaned against the wall behind him.

After leaving the White House, Haley had been driven to the FBI's headquarters and escorted into the small room where he now sat. The man in the gray suit had entered after a few minutes and proceeded to question him for hours. All the while the two men had stood silently behind him.

"You will be taken to Quantico," the man in the gray suit continued, "where you will be held until your court-martial."

Haley said nothing. The man in the gray suit rose and walked from the room. The two men standing behind Haley stepped forward, grabbing him by the arms and pulling him to his feet. He hung his head as they led him through the door and out into a hallway.

They stopped in front of an elevator. The men remained silent as they waited for the car to arrive. Once the doors opened they pushed Haley inside. One of the men pressed a button. The elevator began to descend.

After a moment, the car stopped and the doors opened, revealing an underground parking garage, half-filled with nondescript black sedans and SUVs. The two men led Haley to a nearby car. One opened the rear driver's side door. Ducking his head, Haley sat down in the backseat. The door closed behind him.

The two agents got in the front seat. Haley wasn't sure if they were FBI, Secret Service, or plainclothes military police. It didn't really matter, he decided as the car's engine came to life.

The sedan pulled out of the parking lot. Haley looked around. A soft evening light bathed the city. Haley stared out the window as they drove slowly down the road through the National Mall. There wasn't much traffic. The sun was sinking, turning the cloudless sky a pale, hazy red. The Washington Monument rose high above, piercing the air.

The car came to a stop at a light. Haley continued to gaze outside. He didn't know how long it would be until he saw daylight again. He had been told that he would be offered a deal in exchange for his testimony against Miles, but that didn't mean he wouldn't see jail time. And he had no idea how much time it would be before his court-martial convened.

A loud shot interrupted his thoughts. Haley quickly looked forward. The driver was slumped over the wheel. Half his head was missing. The man in the passenger seat was covered in blood and brains. He quickly drew his gun as a second shot rang through the air. The bullet caught him squarely in the chest, knocking him back against the door. He gazed forward motionlessly, a large red spot spreading across his shirt.

Two dark-skinned men jumped out of a white van parked across the street and dashed for the car.

Haley looked around hysterically, unsure what to do next. His hands were still bound. There was no way for him to grab a weapon. He wouldn't be able to put up much of a fight with his hands cuffed. His only chance was to run.

Haley awkwardly unclipped his seatbelt and slid over to the passenger side door. Twisting sideways, he managed to grab hold of the door handle and open it a crack.

The first man reached the car and pulled the driver's side door open. Haley stared at him, eyes wide with fear. The man ducked inside the car. Moving rapidly, he plunged a needle into Haley's thigh, injecting the contents into his leg.

Haley flung the passenger door open and bolted from the car. He took off running across the grass, the needle still stuck in his leg. He made it about five steps before he tripped, crashing to the ground. The sky around him began to swirl, fading to gray. His eyes closed, and he lay motionless.

The two men ran over to Haley and grabbed him. Lifting him off the ground, they quickly carried him to the van and tossed him in the back. Once the rear doors were closed, the men walked around to the front of the van and climbed in. The vehicle drove down the road and turned onto the interstate, blending in with the other cars on the freeway.

~ 16 ~

Hundreds of miles north of civilization, away from the lights of the cities, the night air hung still and cold. The stars shone brilliant in the black sky, a million points of ice set against the infinite blackness of the universe.

The giant trees loomed into the night sky, their huge branches reaching up to touch the stars. The tall firs seemed large enough to dwarf mountains. Beneath the thick branches, the night slipped into a darkness so black it was impossible to see anything.

The only sound was the muffled call of an owl, carried on the faintest breeze. The bird's song echoed through the air even after the singer had fallen silent.

The owl's eerie cry had no effect on the group of men surrounding Jason Wagner. They seemed oblivious to the night's chill and the darkness, moving so silently that Wagner was convinced that if he closed his eyes for the briefest of seconds they would vanish in the forest, simply melting into the air.

This was Wagner's first mission with the Special Forces. He had completed his training the week before. He had expected his first assignment to be somewhere overseas. Instead he found himself creeping through a cold Canadian forest in the dead of night.

They had been walking in complete silence for the better part of an hour, weaving wordlessly through the trees. Wagner watched the faint outline of the man in front of him, following his large shadow. In the blackness he could not see the point man, ten feet ahead of him. He knew two more men followed him, but in the silence of the night their presence was impossible to detect.

They wound through the trees, feet padding on a soft bed of pine needles. The tall firs blotted out the sky, hiding the stars with their thick branches. A road led to the cabin that was their final objective, but the Special Forces team had elected not to take it. Instead they walked through the forest for miles, hoping to catch the cabin's occupants by surprise in the middle of the night.

The point man led the way through the night, following the GPS in his hand. The others simply walked behind him. Wagner hoped the point man knew where he was going, because Wagner wasn't sure he could find his own way out of the trees. Despite all his training, the woods were so dark and thick that he felt completely disoriented.

The forest seemed to go on forever. Finally, the trees parted, revealing the star-covered sky and a large, open clearing. The silhouette of a cabin sat along the edge of a lake. The frozen surface of the water mirrored the sparkling stars and the tall tips of the pine trees. A road parted the trees and ran up to the cabin. An old truck sat near the cabin, and a little boat lay upturned on the shore beside a small pier encased in ice.

The Special Operations men fanned out along the tree line, stopping just inside the trees. The lead man pulled a pair of night-vision goggles from his pack and slowly surveyed the building. The group crouched in the woods for what seemed like hours as the point man systematically scanned the clearing.

Finally he lowered his goggles and nodded to the

other men. Silently they slipped their weapons off their backs. A barely audible succession of clicks followed as the men slid magazines into their guns and armed the weapons. Wagner followed their lead, unslinging his own M-16 and inserting a magazine in place. He chambered a round.

The lead man stood slowly and the others followed, creeping along the clearing, staying just within the tree line. Nothing moved in the shadows of the clearing. The air hung still. From somewhere in the distance, the solitary owl's wild cry pierced the night. Wagner shivered involuntarily.

The small group crept around to the back of the cabin. The lead man halted the advance again as they reached the point where the woods came closest to the small building. Once more, the men crouched down among the trees and waited while the lead man pulled his night-vision goggles over his eyes and carefully scanned the clearing for a second time. The others strapped on their own night-vision goggles while they waited. Wagner raised the bulky device to his face and tightened the strap around his head. The world around him shifted instantaneously from black shadows to a strange scale of green.

The lead man stood and walked slowly into the clearing. The others followed, moving cautiously across the dead grass. Reaching the little building, the men quickly flattened themselves against the timbers of the wall.

Three steps led up to the back door. The point man walked slowly up the stairs and placed his hand on the doorknob, carefully twisting it. He slid the door open an inch before thrusting it open with the muzzle of his gun. He carefully stepped into the building, leading the way with his rifle. One by one the other men filed inside behind him.

Wagner made his way up the steps and walked

cautiously into the cabin. He found himself standing in the living room. His night-vision goggles revealed a green coffee table sitting on a circular braided rug. A large fireplace, composed of green stone, was set into the wall to his right. Across from the hearth was a comfortable-looking couch with a chair beside it. A row of bookshelves lined the left wall.

The Special Forces men ignored the décor, concerned only with the fact that the room was unoccupied. Seeing no signs of life, the lead man moved on, followed by the others.

The door from the living room led into a kitchen. Wagner stepped inside slowly, carefully surveying the surroundings. A green wood table sat in the center of the floor, surrounded by four green chairs. A large refrigerator and stove stood beside a long counter. A window over the sink looked out over the lake. Cabinets lined the walls.

The two broad-shouldered men who had entered the room ahead of Wagner seemed out of place standing between the table and the wall, their guns shifting left and right as they searched for any sign of habitation. But the room was devoid of life. The point man walked over to the cabinets and pulled several open, finding only dinner plates and glasses. The drawers simply revealed silverware.

The men moved on, walking through another door. Wagner shifted his M-16 in his hands and followed, stepping into a bedroom. A large rug lay across the wood floor. A lamp sat on a table beside an unoccupied double bed. A thick comforter was wrapped over the pillows, untouched.

The lead man walked across the room, sticking his gun into the closet and finding nothing. A door on the opposite side of the room revealed only an unoccupied bathroom. The point man surveyed it carefully and then walked back out of the room.

A set of stairs led up to the second floor. The point man motioned for Wagner to follow and began to climb the stairs, rifle at the ready. The other three men remained behind, taking up positions to watch both doors leading into the cabin. The point man walked slowly up the steps, moving quietly so as not to make the old steps creak. Wagner followed in silence.

He reached the top of the steps and walked into another bedroom almost identical to the one downstairs. Although this room was larger, it was also empty. The big bed appeared undisturbed. The picture window in the far wall looked out across the lake, framed by green curtains.

The point man began to systematically search the room, looking in the closet and through the bureau drawers, and finding no signs of life. Wagner kept his rifle raised, scanning the room, but everything was still and quiet.

He waited while the point man pushed open a door leading to another bathroom, disappeared inside for a moment, and conducted his search. After a moment he reappeared, having found nothing.

"Base," he said, touching his headset as he spoke for the first time in hours. "Cabin is unoccupied. Negative on cabin."

He dropped his hand back to his weapon and slowly crossed in front of the large bed. He started down the stairs. Wagner followed.

The lead man reached the bottom of the stairs quickly and began to walk toward the front door. The three men waiting on the first floor moved from their guard positions and fell in behind him. Wagner stepped back onto the hardwood, easily finding his place with the others.

The small group walked down the steps of the cabin. They quickly made their way across the clearing, vanishing into the dark forest beyond, leaving no trace of their presence. The night air hung silently around the deserted cabin. A soft breeze ruffled the pines, blowing a few flakes of snow across the frozen surface of the lake. Above, the brilliant stars filled the black sky. The only sound was the distant hoot of an owl, echoing through the sky.

* * *

Langley Air Force Base was a hub of early morning activity as the fighter wing prepared to launch into its daily operations. F-22 Raptors lined the ramp. Out on the tarmac, maintenance crews prepared their planes for flight. Trucks sat out on the apron as they busily fueled and armed the planes. A few pilots had already arrived and were conducting walk-arounds on their aircraft. Maintenance had begun the day's repair work on a few of the planes sitting outside and several more housed within the large hangars.

Inside the fighter squadron, the pilots were getting ready for their flights. A large group of pilots filled the life support shop and were pulling on their gear. A few were still inspecting their equipment, but most were ready to fly. The group chatted idly as they organized their equipment and prepared for the short flight up north. All the pilots agreed this was one of the strangest assignments they had ever been handed. Deployments were fairly routine, but they had always been sent overseas. The idea of deploying only 500 miles for a few days seemed absurd, but everyone agreed it was far better than a trip to the sandbox.

Panther had just finished strapping on her g-suit and was giving her helmet a last check before stepping to her jet. A major wearing a flight suit entered the room and walked over to her.

"Colonel, there's a phone call for you," he said. "It's important."

"All right," Martina replied, setting down her helmet. She followed the major from life support to the squadron's main desk at dispatch.

A few of the Raptor pilots, receiving their aircraft numbers, watched as she walked to the telephone and picked it up. They craned their necks to hear the conversation, but all they caught were a few "yes, sirs." After a moment Martina replaced the phone and walked back to life support.

All eyes turned to her as she reentered the room.

"I just got a report from the team in Canada," Martina began. "The cabin was a dead end. No one's been there for months. They're expanding their search, but it's unlikely they'll find Miles or the missing Bone anytime soon."

She stopped and swept her gaze slowly across the room. All fifteen Raptor pilots had their eyes fixed on her.

"It's all up to us now," she said.

Martina walked over to Moondog and Vinny. Moondog had been cleared back onto flight status earlier that morning. The two pilots were inspecting their life support equipment. They lifted their heads from their parachutes as Martina approached.

"Haley's vanished too," she told them.

"What happened?" Moondog asked

"The car he was in was ambushed en route to Quantico," Martina explained. "The two Secret Service agents guarding him were shot and killed. Witnesses say two men dragged Haley into a van and took off."

"I guess Miles went looking for him. Maybe they're trying to shut him up before he tells us too much," Moondog said.

"Or he went back willingly," Vinny stated.

"Either way," Martina said, "if Kalliff doesn't already know what Haley told us, he will soon. They know we'll be waiting for them."

* * *

Dan Haley opened his eyes. The morning sun falling on his face was near blinding. He squeezed his eyelids shut and slowly opened them again. After a moment his eyes adjusted to the brightness. He found himself staring at the ceiling of a log cabin.

Lifting his head, he quickly surveyed his surroundings. He was lying on a thin ground mat thrown on a rough wood floor. The sunlight was streaming in from a dirty window on the opposite wall. A small table and a few chairs made for meager furnishings. An open door led from the room.

He pushed himself to a sitting position. His head was pounding, but he was unharmed.

He raised his arms over his head and leaned back, holding a stretch for a moment. Relaxing, he dropped his hands back into his lap and looked at his feet. He reached up and massaged the back of his neck, followed by his temples, wishing his head would stop aching.

"Good morning, Major," a voice said.

Haley lifted his head. Miles was standing in the doorway. He stepped into the room and dropped into a chair opposite Haley.

"Good morning, sir," Haley said, hesitantly.

"I take it you had a nice talk with Colonel Redrick and her friends," he said.

"Yes, sir."

"And what did you tell them?"

"Exactly what you told me to, sir," Haley said.

"Good," Miles said, grinning. "I think it's time we put this plan of ours into action."

"Let's do it, sir," Haley said, climbing to his feet.

~ 17 ~

Bradley International Airport's terminal afforded passengers a view of the Connecticut Air National Guard wing on the opposite side of the runway. A small group of helicopters sat on a pad beside the National Guard building. Directly across from the commercial terminal, a row of C-21 Learjets sat in a line facing the jetliners.

The C-21s were a typical sight to frequent travelers through Bradley, but the line of aircraft parked beside the Learjets were rarely seen there. Eight F-22 Raptors filled the strip that ran in front of the National Guard building, nearly pushing the C-21s into the grass on the edge of the tarmac.

The small group of fighter pilots had not only taken over the Air National Guard's runway and parking spaces, but also occupied their building. For the most part the National Guardsmen didn't mind. Most weren't around very often, and those that were had welcomed the chance for a close-up look at a Raptor.

"I had no idea sitting on alert was this boring," Vinny said. He sat at a long table in the squadron's break room. Moondog sat across from him with her nose in a paperback.

"What did you expect?" Moondog asked, looking up from her book. "We sit around here until something happens."

"I don't know," Vinny said. "Something other than being locked up in this building."

"It's called sitting alert for a reason, you know," Moondog said. "You just sit around. Didn't you ever sit alert at Tyndall?"

"Yeah. But we had an hour callout, so we just had to be somewhere on base."

"Well, our callout time is a lot shorter," she replied

"This is mind-numbing," he complained.

"You want to play cards?" Moondog asked.

"No. You already took all my money."

"Well, you should have brought a book or something," Moondog said, turning her attention to the paperback in her hands.

"There's nothing to do around here anyway, even if you could leave," one of the National Guard pilots said. "Trust me, I live here."

"That's comforting," Vinny told the local pilot. "Where'd Martina go?" he asked Moondog.

"I don't know," she replied, not lifting her eyes from her novel. "She's around here somewhere."

"Is that the only book you got?"

"Yup."

"That doesn't help me."

"Nope."

"Ugh," Vinny said, dropping his head on the table.

Moondog reached down and rummaged in her flight bag, which sat by her feet. She slapped a deck of cards in front of him.

"Here," she said.

"What am I supposed to do with these?" Vinny said.

"Play some solitaire. Stop bugging me."

"Good book?"

"Yes. If people would only leave me alone I might actually be able to read it." She buried her nose in the paperback again.

Vinny sighed, pulled the cards from the pack, and began to deal a game of solitaire across the table. He flipped the cards over idly, wondering just what else he could possibly find to do in the small building. He let his eyes play across the face-up cards, then began to put some cards on top of others and flipped over the ones that lay beneath.

"Let's go!" Martina announced, stepping into the room. "We got bogeys incoming!"

The three F-22 pilots and the few National Guard pilots present raised their heads and looked at her for a moment. Then the scraping of chairs filled the room as the Raptor pilots grabbed their gear and bolted out the door.

In five seconds the room was empty except for an overturned paperback novel, a half-finished solitaire game, and a magazine or two scattered about. Several cards fluttered to the floor. The National Guard pilots gazed in amazement at the open door. A moment later the loud roar of jet engines filled the air as the Raptor pilots started their planes.

Sitting at the end of the main taxiway, a large 737 was about to turn onto the runway for its takeoff roll when the pilot's radio crackled.

"American four eight six," Bradley tower said, "takeoff clearance canceled. Stay where you are and do not go onto the runway. I repeat, do not go onto the runway."

"Why not?" the pilot demanded, somewhat irritated. "I was cleared a minute ago."

"Nutmeg one one, cleared for takeoff runway one five," tower said, ignoring the 737 pilot.

A thunderous roar filled the air. A silver flash flew down the runway, racing in front of the 737's nose as it shot forward on twin columns of fire. Both the pilot and the copilot of the passenger liner gawked in amazement as a second jet zoomed past their window, followed by a third and then a fourth.

Everyone at Bradley International Airport stopped and stared as four F-22 Raptors screamed down the runway and leapt into the sky.

Airborne, Martina put her Raptor into a broad turn to the east. Keeping one eye on her radar for incoming passenger jets, she followed air traffic control's instructions as they vectored her to the threat. The other three planes quickly fell into place on her wing.

"Here's the situation," Panther said. "AWACS just picked up a formation of eight to ten aircraft flying over the Atlantic Ocean. The flight is unscheduled. They just confirmed all planes have a radar signature of fighter aircraft. Standard intercept procedures. Any questions?"

"What about the B-1?" the Langley pilot asked.

"There's no sign of it, according to the AWACS," Panther said. "But keep your eyes open. We can't let that bomber slip by. Anything else?"

The airwaves stayed silent.

"All right," Panther said. "We're five minutes to target. Everyone get ready."

"Third time out, Vinny. You good to go?" Moondog asked.

"Hell, yeah!" the young captain replied.

"Hey, Vinny, you got a call sign?" Panther asked.

"No," he said slowly.

"How the hell do you get to be a captain without a call sign?" Moondog wondered.

"I guess we'll just have to remedy the situation," Panther said nonchalantly. "What do you think?"

"Hijack?" Moondog suggested.

"Oh, that'll go really well over the radio."

"It should have something to do with the fact that he's always smiling for no good reason. The guy's in the lockup in fucking Colombia, and he's still grinning about something or other."

There was a pause on the radio as Panther mulled over the idea for a moment.

"Phoenix," she said. "What do you think?"

"I like it," Moondog said.

"All right, Vinny," Panther said. "From now on you're Phoenix."

"Cool!" Phoenix replied, his trademark grin spreading even wider beneath his oxygen mask.

The four Raptors raced over the winter landscape, reaching the coast in seconds. Following the vectors of the AWACS, they dashed across the water, heading for the large group of aircraft approaching the shore.

A flash of silver against the waves caught Panther's eye. Below, a formation of planes was flying across the ocean, heading southwest. She turned her plane toward the lead aircraft. The Raptors quickly closed the distance.

"MiG-29s," Moondog said.

"And they're armed," Panther replied. "You three take up position on their six."

The other three Raptors peeled off from Panther's aircraft, circling around behind the flight of MiGs. She chopped her throttles and pushed her nose down, descending. She put her plane into a gentle turn, maneuvering to put herself just behind the lead MiG-29 Fulcrum.

"Unidentified aircraft, you are approaching U.S. airspace," she said, keying her mike as she flew toward the formation. "Turn to a zero nine zero heading and state your destination."

There was no response. The planes continued along their course. For a moment, Panther held her position a few hundred feet above the Fulcrums. She could see that all the aircraft were armed with missiles and bombs.

"Unidentified aircraft, please acknowledge," Martina repeated.

Again there was no reply.

Panther nudged her throttles forward, dropping down in front of the first aircraft. She kept her plane slightly above the formation of MiGs. She wanted to make herself clearly visible to the pilot of the lead aircraft without presenting an easy target.

Panther waggled her wings and quickly looked behind her. There was no reaction from the Fulcrum's pilot. She rocked her wings again and made a shallow turn to the right. The Fulcrums held their course. Panther turned her plane back, once again putting it in front of the MiGs.

A missile warning sounded loudly in her ears as the MiG's missiles locked onto her plane. She pulled sharply back on the stick and thrust her throttles past the detent into afterburners. The Raptor immediately stood on its tail and shot skyward. The g-forces pressed against Panther's chest as the plane climbed. The missile tone immediately died.

"Shoot the fuckers!" she called to the others through clenched teeth.

Safely out of range of the MiG's missiles, Panther pulled her throttles out of afterburner. She kept the back pressure on her stick, completing a loop to come down behind the other F-22s. The other three aircraft quickly armed their heat-seeking missiles and fired. Three AIM-9 Sidewinders shot forward, racing for the flight of MiGs.

The enemy planes immediately broke formation, scattering in all directions. Red fire and white smoke filled the sky as several of the Fulcrums released their flares. Two of the Sidewinders impacted harmlessly with the flares, exploding.

The last missile flew directly up the tailpipe of a MiG-29 and detonated. The plane burst apart, the flaming remains of its wings and fuselage tumbling to the ocean below.

Fire shot from the tailpipes of the first four Fulcrums as they went into afterburner. They leveled out on a direct heading for New York City. The other three planes looped back on the four Raptors, diving for the pursuing aircraft.

Panther shoved her throttles forward, sending her own jet into afterburner. She pointed her nose at one of the fleeing MiGs.

"Moondog, keep them off my back," she said. "Phoenix, follow me."

Phoenix pushed his throttles past the detent, taking up position on Martina's right wing. Loaded with stores, the Fulcrums had no chance of outrunning the F-22s. Even if the MiGs had been in a clean configuration, they were still slower than the sleek Raptors. The American fighters easily kept pace with the Russian-made jets.

The other three Fulcrums doubled back. One angled straight for Phoenix. The second headed directly for Panther. The third MiG looped up over the top of the Raptors. Panther ignored the approaching planes, arming her heat-seeking Sidewinders and aiming the missiles at the plane on the far left.

Out of the corner of his eye Phoenix saw one of the Fulcrums bearing down on his Raptor from eleven o'clock. He tapped his stick, rolling slightly to the right.

"Hold your position," Panther said calmly in his ear. "Moondog will do her job."

Her missiles locked onto the MiG's tailpipes, and she fired. The MiG pilot shoved his nose down, diving away from the others in a desperate attempt to escape the Sidewinder. The missile clipped the top of his right tailfin and exploded, shredding his vertical stabilizer and the trailing edge of his wing. Its flight controls destroyed, the plane began to spiral downward uncontrollably.

Moondog put her plane in a climbing turn to the right, pointing her nose on a course straight for the MiG to the left of Panther's Raptor. The Fulcrum was quickly bearing down on her friend, trying to get in position to fire. Moondog armed her guns, racing for the MiG as it closed in on Panther.

Phoenix rolled back into formation, aiming his Sidewinders at the MiG directly ahead of him. He continued to fly straight. The MiG at his eleven o'clock was drawing closer. He stayed tightly on the tail of the Fulcrum ahead of him, keeping a close eye on the second fighter bearing down on his plane. He would be in range of its guns in seconds.

Suddenly, a missile raced past Phoenix's cockpit, leaving a trail of white smoke in its wake. An instant later the Fulcrum headed for him exploded in a ball of fire. Phoenix glanced back over his shoulder. The Langley pilot's F-22 was perched just above and to the right of his aircraft.

The missile lock sounded in Phoenix's ears. He quickly squeezed the trigger, loosing one of his own missiles. The Sidewinder raced at the MiG-29 at the center of the formation. Unable to turn to the left or right, the Fulcrum had nowhere to go. The AIM-9 Sidewinder hit it directly between the burner cans and exploded, destroying the plane's empennage. Its back half gone, the MiG tumbled toward the ocean.

The MiG aiming for Panther's Raptor dove for the F-22. Moondog kept the nose of her plane fixed on its cockpit. As soon as the MiG came within range, she opened fire with her cannon. Bullets pelted the Fulcrum, breaking through the canopy and killing the pilot. He fell forward on his stick, pushing the plane's nose down. It dove for the ocean below at supersonic speed, breaking to bits as it hit the water.

The remaining two MiGs heading for New York broke formation. They continued to run for the coast, with the two F-22's in hot pursuit. Phoenix took off after the jet on the right, and Panther kept her plane aimed at the Fulcrum on the left. The Fulcrum's pilot began to jink to the left and right, preventing her missiles from locking on his heat signature.

The missile warning blared in Panther's ears. She quickly peered back over her shoulder, checking her six. The final Fulcrum was perched on her tail, having looped over top of the Raptor. She looked back at her heads-up display. Her Sidewinders almost had a lock. Arming her flares, she held her course.

A second alarm sounded. Panther looked behind her once again. This time she saw the bright orange flame of a missile headed straight for her F-22. She immediately released her countermeasures. Flares spewed out from her F-22, burning brightly behind the plane. Trusting her defenses to work, Panther held her course, waiting for her own missiles to lock onto one of the MiGs in front of her.

The hot-burning flares gave off a much larger heat-signature than the Raptor's tailpipe. The heat-seeking missile quickly locked onto the flares, exploding harmlessly behind Panther's F-22. The Fulcrum pursuing her raced past the flares, bent on bringing down her plane.

Panther ignored the MiG chasing her, focusing her attention on the Fulcrum ahead of her, which was still jinking wildly. Finally, her heat-seeking missiles locked onto the MiG. She smashed down her trigger, sending a Sidewinder flying for the Fulcrum.

Almost instantly a shower of smoke and fire appeared behind the MiG-29 as its pilot released his own flares. A second later he put his plane in a tight turn to the left, breaking away sharply from the Sidewinder flying toward him. The missile kept flying straight, headed for the flares.

Panther pulled her throttles back, keeping her nose pointed at the Fulcrum. The MiG-29 could not outmaneuver the Raptor. The Fulcrum turned sharply, rolling almost to ninety degrees of bank. The steep turn exposed most of the aircraft's back. Panther immediately opened fire with her guns, raking the Fulcrum from nose to tail with bullets.

The Langley pilot broke off from Phoenix's wing, turning back to the Fulcrum that was chasing Panther and arming his radar-guided AMRAAM missiles. From his vantage point a few hundred feet above the MiG, the Russian fighter gave off a larger radar signal. The AMRAAMs quickly locked on, and he fired.

Seeing the incoming missile, the MiG pilot broke off Panther's six and put his plane into a steep dive. But it was no use. The AMRAAM followed the Fulcrum down, hitting his right wing and exploding. The burning remains of the plane tumbled to the water below.

The MiG in front of Panther leveled out, flying away from the others. She dropped onto its tail, continuing to pepper the damaged plane with gunfire. The bullets flew up the Fulcrum's exhaust, chewing its turbines to bits. The engines seized in rapid succession. Unpowered, the plane nosed down and began to glide steeply toward the water.

Panther pulled her plane around in a tight turn, searching for any remaining fighters. The first plane she caught sight of was the Langley pilot's F-22, just to her right. He quickly dropped into position on her wing. Further to the west, Moondog and Phoenix were chasing the remaining Fulcrum. The MiG was now racing for its life, trying to escape the pursuing fighters.

Panther pushed her throttles past the detent and

to the stops, racing for the other aircraft. The Langley pilot followed close behind.

She watched as Moondog and Phoenix closed in on the last MiG. The plane was jinking quickly to the left and right, but with two Raptors on his tail he had no chance of escape. It was only a few more seconds before his plane fell from the sky, cut to pieces by Phoenix's and Moondog's bullets.

"That's the last of them," Moondog reported.

Martina chopped her throttles, reducing her speed below Mach one.

"All right," she said. "Form back up."

She changed her radio frequency.

"Whaler one seven, Nutmeg one one," she said, calling the AWACs as Moondog and Phoenix dropped back into position on her wing.

"Go ahead, Nutmeg," Whaler replied.

"We intercepted and destroyed eight MiG-29s armed with missiles and bombs," Martina reported. "I suggest you dispatch search and rescue to look for any survivors."

"Will do, Nutmeg," Whaler said.

"Any sign of the B-1?" Martina asked.

"Negative," the AWACs reported. "I haven't picked up any more unscheduled flights, and the CAP over New York hasn't seen anything."

"All right," Martina said. "We're heading back to Bradley. Call us if you need us."

"Roger," Whaler 17 said.

The fourship of F-22s turned back toward shore, flying home.

~ 18 ~

Moondog entered the break room carrying a Styrofoam cup of steaming coffee and a copy of the *Hartford Courant.* She tossed the paper on the table and slid into a chair. Setting her coffee down, she unfolded the paper and began to scan the headlines.

After a moment she looked around. Phoenix was rummaging through the fridge, searching for something to eat. Martina was sitting with her arms on the table, gazing at the far wall. None of the Langley pilots or the National Guard boys were anywhere to be seen.

Moondog opened the front section of the paper and began to look through it. The only noise in the room was the sound of Vinny moving stuff around in the refrigerator.

"All right, Panther," Moondog said after a moment, setting her paper down. "What's bugging you?"

"I can't figure it out," Martina said.

"The B-1?" Moondog asked.

Martina nodded. "It's Kalliff's most powerful weapon. I can't understand why he didn't use it."

"The attack was a feint," Moondog said. "He's going to send it in later."

"He would have done it already," Martina said. "The most effective strategy would be to attack at the same time as those fighters but from a different angle. Hit the city while we're tangling with the MiGs. We've been flying CAPs over New York for two days and we haven't seen anything other than a Cessna."

"Maybe he figured out we know his plan and he's waiting a month or two until we give up. If he has Haley, we have to assume he knows we were warned of the attack."

"If he waits, we'll find the plane. He has to know we're looking for it."

"What if he's going to use it to attack another city?"

"Again, he would have done it while the MiGs were offshore, distracting us. Besides, New York is symbolic of America."

"Maybe the plane broke," Vinny said, shutting the fridge and sticking his head into a nearby cabinet.

"What the hell are you looking for?" Moondog said.

"Anything edible. I'm starving."

"And you can't find anything?"

"All they've got in the fridge is a couple of bottles of ketchup and some moldy buns," Vinny replied, pulling open another cabinet. "They really need to restock the snack bar."

Moondog turned her head back to her paper.

"Maintenance problems are the only thing that makes any sense," Martina said.

"But Miles probably has people who could repair it," Moondog said. "He is up there with Kalliff. They should be able to fix anything short of a major problem."

"Miles..." Martina muttered, looking at the top of Moondog's newspaper.

"Of course!" she said, smacking her palm flat against her forehead. Moondog lifted her eyes and stared at her. Vinny turned around and gave her a strange look.

"We've been approaching this all wrong!" Martina said. "What if Kalliff isn't in charge, and Miles is?"

"How does that make a difference?" Vinny asked.

"Kalliff is a terrorist. His aim would be to scare people, kill civilians. He'd attack a population center, a major city," Martina said. "But Miles is a general. Therefore, he'd select a military target, something that would impact our nation's ability to wage war."

"What could he possibly do with a single bomber?" Moondog asked. "An attack on any one base would be insignificant. If he wanted to have an effect on our war-fighting ability he'd need a hundred bombers."

"He could take out the entire government," Martina said, reaching across the table and laying her finger on Moondog's newspaper, indicating an article beneath the TV listings. The headline read "State of the Union Address to Air on NBC."

"Holy shit!" Moondog said. Her face went pale.

"One bomber," Martina said, "and he could kill the President, every member of Congress, the Joint Chiefs, and God knows who else. If that won't plunge the country into complete chaos, I don't know what will."

"Nuking a major city?" Moondog suggested.

"This place is going to get pretty chaotic if I don't find something to eat damn soon," Vinny said.

"Oh, go take a walk to that convenience store across the street," Moondog said. "I'm sure they have something."

"Maybe I will."

"You better make it quick," Martina said, standing. "I have a feeling we're going to be heading back to Washington very soon."

"What are you going to do, try to convince Webster to cancel the State of the Union address?" Moondog said.

"Hopefully," Martina replied, walking out the door.

"You're crazy," Moondog called as the door closed behind her friend. She turned her attention back to the *Courant*. After a moment she lifted her eyes over her the paper and looked at Phoenix.

"If you're going to get some food, I'd suggest you get moving," she said, "unless you want to eat that moldy bread."

* * *

The speakerphone on David Webster's desk buzzed. He reached across the desk and pressed a button.

"Yes, Sherri?"

"Sir, Colonel Redrick is here," his secretary said.

"Send her in, please."

A moment later the door to the Oval Office opened and Martina strode in. She was dressed in blues, adorned only with a pair of pilot's wings and her name pinned over her right breast. Silver oak leaves sat on her shoulders. Her long brown hair was tied up behind her head and was still visibly wet. There was a small mark under her left eye, but the rest of her face had healed.

She crossed the presidential seal. Stopping in front of Webster's desk, she raised her hand to the corner of her right eye in a crisp salute. He returned the gesture casually. The room's two other occupants, the Secretary of Defense and the Secretary of State, simply watched the slim, long-legged woman.

"Thank you for seeing me, sir," she said.

"I've learned that when you have something to say, it's worth listening, Colonel," he replied.

Martina smiled.

"The Air Force Chief of Staff told me you successfully predicted the attack on New York."

"Military training mingled with a little dumb luck, sir," she said.

"And that you repelled the attack before the planes were even within sight of shore," Webster continued.

"We stopped one attack, sir," Martina said. "But we haven't stopped Miles and Kalliff. The attack on New York was a ruse."

"What makes you think that?"

"They only sent a group of MiGs armed with bombs," Martina said. "There was no sign of the B-1. That bomber is the most powerful weapon they have. If attacking New York had been their main objective, they would have used it. They're saving it for something else."

"They're going to attack New York again?" Webster asked.

"I don't think New York is the target at all," Martina said. "I'm sure the MiGs would have bombed the city had they gotten through, but the main purpose of that attack was to distract us from the real target."

"Why do you say that?" Webster asked. "Haley told us Kalliff intended to attack New York."

"I don't think Kalliff is in charge of the operation. I think Miles is. He's a military man, and plans on attacking a military target."

"Which is?"

"Washington," Panther said. "During the State of the Union address. He can destroy the entire government with one bomber."

"What makes you think Miles is leading Kalliff's group?" the Secretary of State challenged.

"The fact that he didn't send the bomber to attack New York," she said. "He had one chance, and if that was his intended target, he would have used the B-1. He didn't."

"But Haley only mentioned New York," the Secretary of Defense said.

"Sir, Haley was just a pawn, used to give us false information," Martina replied. "Either Miles ordered him to warn us of an attack against New York, or he purposefully told Haley the wrong target, knowing Haley would turn himself in the first chance he got. The end result is the same. We're guarding the wrong city."

"Do you have any concrete proof?" the Secretary of State asked.

"No," Martina said. "It's just a hunch."

"Are you looking for this bomber?" the Secretary of State asked.

"We have a team searching for it," the Secretary of Defense said. "But northern Canada is a very big place. They haven't found anything yet."

"You think Miles will attack Washington?" Webster asked, shifting the conversation back to the original topic.

"I'd put money on it, sir," Martina said.

"All right," Webster said. "What you suggest we do about it?"

"Cancel the State of the Union address."

"You want to cancel the most important national address on an unfounded whim of yours, Colonel?" the Secretary of State asked, incredulous.

"Sir," she said, "as long as that bomber is in the hands of a group of terrorists, it poses a very credible threat to this nation. Washington, D.C., is a nice target, especially when all the government and military leaders are in one room."

"You honestly think that bomber can get through?" the Secretary of State asked.

"Bin Laden successfully attacked New York with two passenger jets, flying below Mach One and visible to radar," Martina said. "A B-1 bomber can fly above the speed of sound 200 feet off the ground. Flown by an experienced pilot, that plane can strike anywhere in the world, and no one would know until the bombs exploded."

"Washington is very well protected," the Secretary

said. "There are fighters on alert twenty-four hours a day, and we have hired additional security personnel for the address."

"By the time you scramble the alert jets, it will already be too late," Martina replied. "That is if you're even able to detect the B-1 in the first place. It will fly right up the Chesapeake Bay under the radar and you won't even know it's there. If you want to stop them from attacking this city, you have to cancel the address."

"Even if we do, won't Miles simply select another target?" the Secretary of Defense asked.

"He may," Martina said. "But no other location would have such an impact. The losses would be significantly less. And it may give us the time we need to find the plane."

"Sir, this is ridiculous," the Secretary of State said to Webster. "Do you honestly believe this woman?"

"Colonel Redrick is very intelligent," Webster replied. "I trust her judgment, and I think her fears are well founded.

"That said, Colonel, I cannot simply cancel the State of the Union address," Webster said to Martina. "It's completely unprecedented. The speech is too important."

"Yes, sir," Martina said slowly. "In that case, let me fly a combat air patrol over Washington during the address. That way, if Miles does attack, I'll have planes in the air, and hopefully I can stop that bomber."

"Where will you get the planes?" the Secretary of Defense asked. "Between your operation over New York and routine deployments, Langley has almost no fighters left."

"I have the three F-22s sitting on the ground at Andrews. All I need is one more Raptor and a tanker."

"And who would fly them?" Webster asked.

"Myself, Commander Ansetti, and Captain Carlton," she said. "I can find a volunteer from the squadron guarding New York to fly the fourth."

"Only four planes?" the Secretary of Defense asked.

"That's all I really need. It would be nice if I had the local alert force for backup, but I can fly the mission without them."

"All right, Colonel," Webster said. "Do whatever you think is necessary."

"Yes, sir."

"And Colonel, don't let one bomb hit the ground."

"The only thing that will hit the ground will be that B-1, sir," she said.

"Good," Webster said with a smile. "I'll let you get to work."

"Good evening, sir," Martina said, saluting again.

"Good evening," he replied, waving his hand in a salute.

Martina turned and walked from the room, letting the door close behind her.

"Well?" Moondog asked as Panther walked into the Oval Office's antechamber. She and Phoenix had made themselves as comfortable as possible on the hard benches.

"They're fools," Martina said, walking toward the door.

"Wouldn't listen to you, huh?" Moondog said, jumping to her feet and following Martina. Vinny fell in beside her.

"No," Martina said.

"I told you they wouldn't," Moondog said. Martina glared at her.

"So what happens now?" Vinny asked.

"We fly a CAP over Washington tomorrow night," Martina said. "And we stop Miles."

"So we're going back to Andrews?" he asked.

She nodded. "I have some arrangements to make. We need a fourth pilot, a tanker, and hopefully I can land an AWACS."

"Man," he muttered. "Since I met you guys, it's been nothing but action. I've never seen so much combat in my life."

"If I remember correctly, Phoenix," Martina said with a smile, "it was you who dragged us into this mess."

~ 19 ~

The large B-1 bomber seemed out of place sitting beneath the tall Canadian pine trees. Even in daylight the firs seemed ominous, stretching upward to scrape the sky. The small clearing where the bomber sat was washed in shadow, hiding its black shape against the ground.

The forest itself smelled of dirt, pine needles, and sap. A crisp, cool breeze blew across the earth, shifting the tree branches and making a few dappled patches of sunlight dance. The only sound was the swish of pine boughs mingled with the occasional bird call.

The dark shadow of the bomber seemed more like an apparition in the woods, a black wraith hiding beneath the trees. The plane was an object of modern society lost in the wilds, a creation of the imagination, a mirage.

Yet it was there, sitting motionless beneath the trees. Pine boughs brushed the tips of its wings, and green needles covered its back. Its wheels sank ever so slightly into the thick, brown earth. The metal of its skin felt hard and cold to the touch.

Dan Haley reached up and touched the bomber's nose as if to confirm that the giant black plane shrouded beneath the trees was real. He ran his hand along the smooth surface, feeling the cold, black skin. The plane didn't belong here. It belonged on a runway, in the civilized world, with crew chiefs running around to service it and keep it working. It belonged behind a fence, with Security Forces to protect it from men like the ones who brought it here. It belonged in a world that smelled of asphalt and gas, oil and grease, where the breeze carried the roar of jet engines, a world of pavement and hangars, not trees and dirt.

But somehow this plane had found its way here, into a place where it did not belong, to perform a mission it should never have been assigned. There were no crew chiefs or Security Forces, only Dan Haley and a ragtag band of foreigners.

Haley sighed and walked slowly around the B-1, carefully inspecting the plane. There was no maintenance crew to do a proper preflight on the bomber. That left Haley to make sure the aircraft was safe to fly. He wanted to be extra observant during his walk-around. His life depended on it.

"How does she look?" a voice interrupted his inspection. Haley turned to see Miles standing behind him.

"Fine, sir," he replied. "She'll fly."

"All the way to Washington?" Miles asked.

"As long as she's got the fuel,"Haley said.

"They gassed her up this morning."

"Then there shouldn't be any problem getting there."

"Getting there?" Miles asked. "You think there will be a problem when you get there?"

"Maybe," Haley said. "They know we have the bomber. They might have guessed what we're going to use it for."

"I doubt it," Miles said. "You never mentioned Washington, did you?"

"No, sir," Haley replied. "I only told them what you wanted me to."

"Then we have nothing to worry about."

"That doesn't mean they don't suspect something, sir. I doubt Redrick fully believed me, and I know Carlton didn't."

"So they have suspicions, not concrete proof," Miles said. "Just fly the mission, and you'll get through."

"Yes, sir."

"Everything is ready for tomorrow night?"

"Yes, sir," Haley repeated.

"Good," Miles said. "Is there anything else concerning you, major?"

"No, sir."

"All right, I'm leaving, then. If you need anything from now on, talk to Kalliff's people." Miles turned, heading toward the forest.

"Will do," Haley said as Miles walked away.

"Oh, and Dan," Miles turned around. "I wouldn't worry about Colonel Redrick or her friends. They won't give you any more trouble."

Haley watched as Miles disappeared into the pine trees. He fixed his eyes on the trees until the forest fell silent again, then turned his attention back to the bomber.

* * *

"How come I never get to drive?" Phoenix asked as Martina pulled their rental car onto Constitution Avenue.

"Because I outrank you," she replied jokingly.

"Is that why I have to sit in the back?"

"Yep," Moondog said.

"Man, I need to stop hanging out with light birds. I always get shafted," Vinny grinned.

"Don't worry, I'm sure there will be some lieutenants you can screw over when you get back to your base," Moondog said.

"Yeah, if I ever get back to my base," Vinny said.

Moondog laughed.

"That's what you get for hanging around Panther."

"Oh, so it's all my fault now, is it?" Martina asked.

"Of course," Moondog said.

"Some terrorist group decides to steal a bomber, and it's my fault. Explain to me how I caused this again."

"You attract trouble," Moondog said. "Did I ever tell you about the first mission I flew with her, Phoenix?"

"Don't think so."

"You know, Moondog," Martina said, "this stuff never happened to me before I met you."

"So?"

"So maybe you're the trouble magnet."

"Oh no, not me," Moondog said. "I don't attract trouble, I just cause it."

"Crazy drunken sailor," Martina muttered.

"Hey!" Moondog said, indignantly. "I say we go back to blaming Vinny. He was the one who got us into this."

"All right," Martina said. "Phoenix, this is all your fault."

"Why is it my fault?!"

"Because we outrank you," Moondog said.

Martina laughed, keeping her eyes focused on the road ahead of her. The sun was sinking behind the buildings, casting long shadows across the Mall. Many of the cars on the road had switched on their headlights. Traffic overall was fairly light. Most people had probably already gone home for the day, Martina reasoned as she turned right down Fourteenth Street.

"Any chance we can go find someplace to eat?" Vinny asked.

"Can't you wait until we get back to Andrews?" Martina asked, checking the rearview mirror.

"I'm pretty damn hungry. All I've had to eat all

day is some orange juice and donuts from the convenience store outside Bradley."

"And whose fault is that?" Moondog asked.

"Panther's. She dragged us down here before I could find any lunch."

"And do you know any place nearby to eat?" Martina asked, turning onto Independence Avenue.

"No," he said.

"Then you'll have to wait until we get back to Andrews. Us light birds have work to do."

"You know, there really is no such thing as a light bird in the Navy," Moondog said. "I'm a commander."

"You're an O-5, aren't you?" Martina asked.

"Yeah."

"Same difference"

"No," Moondog said. "You don't call commanders light birds, you call them commanders."

"It's the same damn pay grade."

"That doesn't mean you call me a light bird."

"I really don't give a shit what they call you, swabbie," Martina said, "but your rank is equivalent to mine."

"So I guess the real question is who has more time in grade," Vinny said.

"Neither one of us does," Moondog said.

"What do you mean?" Vinny asked.

"Moondog and I were both promoted to O-5 on the same day," Martina said.

"How is that?" he asked.

"It's a long story," she said, turning left onto Seventh Street.

"Hey, Panther, you do know Andrews is south of here, right?" Moondog asked.

"Yeah, I know," Martina said, pressing the gas pedal.

"Then why are we going north?"

"Because I think we're being followed," the Air

Force pilot replied.

"Followed?" Vinny asked.

"That silver sedan has been tailing us since we left the White House."

Phoenix and Moondog peered out the back window. There was a silver car a hundred feet behind them.

"What makes you think he's following us?" Moondog asked.

"Why would he turn south and then go north?" Martina replied.

"How can you be sure he's not just a lost tourist?" Vinny asked.

"There's one way to check," Martina said, flashing a smile.

Catching the look in her eyes, Moondog quickly grabbed hold of the door as she grinned. Martina twisted the wheel sharply to the right. The car swerved over a lane, skidding through a yellow light onto Pennsylvania Avenue. Martina mashed her foot to the floor. The engine revved wildly, and the car shot forward. Several seconds later the silver sedan careened onto the road after her.

"He's following us," Martina said, nonchalantly.

"Great," Vinny said, picking himself off the backseat. "Now what?"

"We lose 'em," Martina said, jerking the wheel to the left. The small car rose up on two wheels, twisting onto Sixth Street.

A pair of headlights met Martina immediately. She swerved to the right as the oncoming car blared its horn. Martina dodged back into the left lane and stepped on the gas. A glance in the mirror revealed that the sedan was still behind them. Hitting the brakes and twisting the wheel to the right again, she pulled the car through a red light, merging with the traffic of Indiana Avenue.

The silver sedan pulled onto the road behind them, nearly colliding with the oncoming traffic. A driver in the left lane slammed on his brakes, only to have the car behind him crash into him.

Martina turned her car to the left and was met with headlights and the blaring of horns. She spun the wheel rapidly to the left, then back to the right, finding the small gaps between the oncoming traffic.

“This is a one-way street!” Vinny screamed. “And we’re going the wrong way!”

“Yep,” Martina said, twisting back to the right to dodge another car. “He’d be crazy to follow us.”

“He’s definitely crazy,” Moondog remarked, glancing in the rearview mirror.

Martina stomped on the gas pedal, making the oncoming cars rush forward with increasing speed.

“He’s not the only crazy one, either,” Moondog said.

“Oh, shut up. You drive like this when you’re not being chased,” Martina said as she wove through traffic.

“I never claimed to be sane,” Moondog said, flashing a maniacal grin. “If I did, I certainly wouldn’t be anywhere near you.”

“I really need to stop hanging around with crazy light birds,” Vinny said.

“Like you can talk,” Moondog said. “You hijacked a fucking bomber.”

“Yeah, but I didn’t play chicken with it.”

Moondog looked back. The silver sedan was still trailing them, somehow managing to navigate its way through the traffic.

“Can’t this damned thing go any faster?” she asked.

“I’m flooring it,” Martina said. “This is a rental piece of crap, not your Corvette.”

“It’s obviously not my Corvette,” Moondog said as

they made a quick right turn. "Because if it was I'd be the one driving, and we'd have already lost these guys."

Martina swung around another car, taking a sharp right.

"But I'd rather have the Dodge Viper. It's faster," Moondog said, as Martina turned the wheel to the left again, racing onto I-395.

"Taking the freeway, huh?" Moondog said.

"At least I'm going the right way."

"Where the hell are the cops?" Vinny asked. "With the way you're driving I'd expect there to be about ten of them behind us."

"Don't know," Martina said. "I was kinda hoping we'd pick up a couple. Figures. The one time we need 'em, they ain't around to nab us."

The car accelerated again, racing through ninety. Martina swung into the far left lane, dodging between the slower cars moving at the speed limit.

"Is he still back there?" she asked.

"About three cars behind," Moondog said. "And he's gaining."

"Fuck," Martina said. The freeway dipped down, entering a dark tunnel running beneath the Mall. Martina kept her foot to the floor as the lanes narrowed.

"Two cars," Moondog said. Martina threw the small car around a slow-moving truck.

"Still gaining," Moondog called.

Martina twisted the wheel to the right again, sliding in front of the truck and rapidly racing ahead of it.

Something crashed into the back of the car, throwing the three pilots forward. A sickening crunch of metal accompanied the jerk. A glance in the mirror revealed the silver sedan directly behind them, headlights crumpled from the impact.

"Hope nobody had anything important in the trunk," Moondog said.

Another impact shook the car. The silver sedan swung to the left, racing alongside the rental car. Martina looked to the right. Two men rode in the front seat of the car.

The driver turned the wheel to the right, smashing the side of the car into Martina's rental. The force pushed the car toward the wall. The right rearview mirror smashed against the concrete and snapped off.

Martina turned the wheel back to the left, forcing the silver car back to the left lane. The driver of the sedan pulled away, then moved right again. Martina twisted the wheel hard to the left. The two cars hit each other along the center line, running together for a moment. Flying sparks accompanied the scraping of metal as the cars pressed against each other before breaking apart.

"Open the glove compartment!" Martina shouted.

"What's in the glove compartment?" Moondog asked.

"My .45. Get it out and try to shoot that fucker's tires."

Moondog jerked the glove compartment open and pulled out the pistol. She chambered a round and flipped the safety off just as the silver sedan crashed into them, sending yet another tremor through the car. She leveled the pistol at the front tire of the other car, trying to take aim.

"I can't get a clear shot!" she shouted. "Your head's in the way."

Martina lifted her foot off the gas pedal and stepped on the brakes. The silver sedan shot out ahead of them. She pressed the gas back to the floor as Moondog quickly leaned out the window and fired off several rounds. One hit the sedan's trunk. The other two smashed through the taillights.

The sedan's brake lights flashed on as the driver swerved back into the right lane.

"Fuck!" Martina shouted, jerking the wheel to the left. The black car scraped the side of the silver sedan as it raced past. The screech of metal on metal echoed through the tunnel.

In an instant the silver car was behind them again, accelerating. The sound of gunfire suddenly filled the air. Panther twisted her head around. The passenger in the other car was leaning out the front window, firing at them.

"Moondog!" she shouted.

"I can't get a good shot!"

"Give the gun to Vinny," Martina said.

"Break the fucking window and aim for the driver," Moondog told him.

"The rental agency won't be too happy if I break the window," he said.

"They won't be any more angry than they're already going to be. Look at the shape this fucking thing's in."

"Right," Vinny grinned. He flipped the Colt over and slammed the butt into the rear window. The glass shattered, covering the backseat. He quickly took aim and fired off several rounds that hit the hood and the center of the windshield. Vinny adjusted his sights and pulled the trigger. The Colt clicked empty.

"You got another clip?"

"Not on me."

"I guess we're screwed, then," Vinny said, smiling.

"Give me my gun back," Martina said.

He passed the .45 forward. She grabbed it and dropped it in her lap, then focused her attention on weaving through a band of traffic. For a moment the gunfire ceased as the silver sedan disappeared among the cars.

The tunnel rose sharply, climbing back into the falling twilight. Ahead, the road split. At the last second Martina pulled the car into the left lane and merged onto 695 heading east. She mashed her foot to the floor, hoping to put as much distance between herself and the silver sedan as possible.

"They still back there?" she called.

Vinny tossed his head back as the sound of gunfire filled the air. He ducked down beneath the seats.

"Yep," he said. Slowly, he lifted his head, peeking through the broken glass.

"They're gaining, too," he said, ducking again.

"Fuck," Martina said.

She twisted the wheel to the right, cutting through two lanes of traffic. The driver in the far right lane slammed on his brakes as she skidded in front of him, turning onto the exit ramp with only feet to spare.

The driver of the silver car hit his brakes, slid to a stop just past the exit, then spun the sedan around, heading backward to the exit ramp.

"Still back there?" she asked, racing through the turn and pressing her foot on the gas, speeding over the Eleventh Street bridge.

Hanging on for dear life, Vinny looked back and saw the silver car cut its way through the approaching traffic and pick up speed on the ramp.

"Four cars back."

"Double fuck," Martina said.

"Where the hell are we going?" Moondog asked as they pulled out onto 295, sliding through three lanes of traffic. Horns and squealing brakes filled the air as Martina straightened the wheel and hit the gas again.

"Back to Andrews as fast as fucking possible," she said. "If we can get to the gate, SF can nab those fuckers."

"How far is that?" Vinny asked.

"A little under ten miles," Martina said, jerking the wheel to the right to avoid a slower-moving car. She cut back in front of the car as soon as she had passed it. The driver stepped on his brakes.

"He's gaining again," Vinny called.

"Shit," Martina said, dodging left again. The taillights were rapidly thinning as they raced into the suburbs.

"We are not going to get back to Andrews before this guy catches us," Vinny said.

"I know, I know," Martina replied.

"Can't we go any faster?" Moondog asked.

"This is it," Martina said.

"Maybe if Vinny could shoot," Moondog said.

"Or if Martina had more bullets," Phoenix said.

"At least I had the sense to bring a gun," Martina retorted. "How far back are they?"

"Fifty feet and gaining."

"You must have some tricks left up your sleeve, Panther," Moondog said.

"Just one," Martina replied, glancing at the road sign. "Vinny, hang on tight," she called as the exit blurred past.

Vinny hurriedly braced himself against the handhold on the door. Martina twisted the wheel to the right and slammed on the brakes. The car turned crosswise into the center lane just as the silver sedan smashed into the trunk, rotating the black car around to face oncoming traffic.

Martina mashed the gas pedal again. The tires spun, then caught the asphalt, launching the car against the traffic. Several pairs of headlights met Martina. Rubber squealed against the road as the oncoming drivers desperately tried to stop or swerve.

Martina hit the brakes and turned the wheel hard to the left, spinning the car onto the exit ramp and nearly missing being clipped by a truck. She floored the gas again. Surprisingly, the little car responded, accelerating through a cloverleaf and charging onto the Suitland Parkway.

"Holy shit!" Vinny said, relaxing his grip on the handhold.

"Are they still back there?" Martina asked.

"Don't see them."

"Good."

"You can probably slow down," Vinny said.

"No way," Martina replied. "If those guys are still back there, I don't want them catching up."

"So now we get nabbed by the cops?" he asked.

"I can get us out of jail," she said. "Those guys probably won't be nearly as reasonable."

"If that car isn't totaled, I'd be amazed," Moondog said. "You probably cracked the fucking engine block."

"You're going to be pretty amazed, then," Vinny said with a wry smile.

"Oh, you have got to be shitting me," Moondog said, glancing back over her shoulder. The lights along the freeway illuminated a silver sedan creeping up slowly through the traffic. Its hood was crumpled, and it had only one headlight.

"How is that thing still running?" she asked.

"I don't know," Vinny said. "Looks like you did some damage, though. He isn't going nearly as fast."

"Keep an eye on him, Vinny," Martina called, pressing the gas pedal further into the floor. "Maybe we can outrun him."

"How far is it to Andrews?" Moondog asked.

"Maybe five miles. We should be able to make it."

"Panther! Brakes! Now!" Vinny shouted.

"Wha—?" Martina turned her head to the left to see a large pickup truck racing directly at them, bearing down rapidly.

The truck rammed into the car, pushing it to the

side of the road. The car crashed through the guard-rail and flipped, rolling down the embankment. It slid to a stop at the bottom of a hill, resting on its roof. The revving of the engine died, leaving only the sounds of the freeway in the darkness of the night.

~ 20 ~

Martina blinked. She closed her eyes, drew a deep breath into her lungs, exhaled slowly, and opened her eyes again. The rapid succession of sky-ground-sky-ground-sky had stopped. Only now the ground was where the sky should be. She fixed her eyes on the piece of earth in front of her, staring at it for a moment. The grass stayed still.

The car had come to a halt lying upside down at the bottom of the embankment. Panther hung from her seat, held in place by the safety belt. Her head dangled inches from the roof of the car. Quickly, she took stock of the situation. She was upside down and breathing rapidly, but nothing seemed to hurt.

"Are you guys okay?" she asked, glancing to her right.

"Everything still works," Moondog said. The Navy pilot was looking at her feet. "I bet my back's going to be sore in the morning."

"I'm not hurt," Vinny called, wriggling around in the backseat. "But I think I'm stuck."

"Undo your seatbelt," Martina said. She reached up and freed herself, carefully extracting her legs from beneath the steering wheel and lowering herself to the roof of the car.

"I can't!" he said, tugging at the straps holding him in place.

"Moondog, help him," Martina said, seeing that

the Navy pilot had already untangled herself.

"Hold still," Moondog said, reaching into the backseat and unclipping Vinny's seatbelt. Unprepared, he crashed down, landing on his head.

"Ow! Hey!" he shouted.

"I got you free, didn't I?" Moondog asked.

"C'mon, let's get the hell out of here," Martina said.

"Don't have to tell me twice," Moondog said, pulling herself out through the window. Vinny was already wriggling out of the rear window. Martina punched out the shattered glass nearest her and rolled out onto the soft grass. She ran her hand over the earth, feeling the cool blades against her fingers.

Something moved in front of her. Martina looked up. The faint outline of a pair of boots stood before her in the darkness. Slowly, she stood, drawing herself up to her full height. A large man was standing in front of her, pointing a gun to her head.

Panther threw a glance behind her. Moondog and Phoenix were climbing slowly to their feet. Five dark figures surrounded them, all holding guns. The silver sedan, a pickup truck, and a third car sat on the embankment.

Slowly, Panther spread her hands out at her sides. The man in front of her reached forward, grabbing her wrist with his free hand. Panther sidestepped rapidly, using the force of his lunge to propel him forward and pulling him toward the ground at the same time. His head smashed into the car, and he reeled back, dropping to the ground.

Seeing Panther move, Moondog and Phoenix sprang into action. Stepping to the inside, Moondog grabbed the hand of the figure nearest her, crushing his fingers against the butt of the gun. She jerked his hand up just as the gun fired, sending a bullet wildly into the sky. Moondog pressed his hand toward the ground behind him, wrenching his arm from the socket. The man yowled and dropped the gun. Moondog dove for it. Her fingers narrowly brushed the cold steel.

Before she could lock her hands around the gun, something smashed into her stomach, knocking her away from the weapon. She landed hard on her left shoulder and rolled onto her back. As she tried to regain her feet, someone grabbed her by the collar and pressed her up against the side of the car. Her arms were yanked behind her and bound tightly.

Two of the men leapt for Phoenix. He sidestepped the first attacker, causing him to stumble and roll into the grass, then quickly turned to the second man, punching him in the center of his chest. The attacker staggered back. Phoenix stepped forward, smashing his fist directly into the man's nose.

The man wailed and swung his hand wildly at Phoenix. The blow grazed the side of Phoenix's head, knocking him sideways. Something collided with the back of his legs, causing his knees to buckle. In an instant someone was on top of him, pulling his hands together and twisting a short length of rope around his wrists.

Panther quickly reached for the unconscious man's gun. Her hand found the small weapon just as someone tackled her from behind, knocking her flat into the cool grass. Panther struggled but found herself unable to move.

The man planted his knee in the center of her back, forcing all of his body weight down on her. He grabbed her arms and tugged them backward. Panther kept her grip on the gun. She tried to aim the weapon at the man behind her as she squeezed the trigger. The shot went wild.

Her captor immediately pulled the gun from her grasp and flung it away. He quickly bound her wrists together, gave the ropes a final tug, then stepped off her, roughly pulling her to her feet.

Martina looked behind her. Both Moondog and Phoenix were being held between the remaining men, hands bound. One of their captors was bleeding from a crushed nose, blood oozing over his chin and onto his shirt. A second's attacker's right arm hung limply at his side.

"Move!" the man holding Martina said, shoving her forward. She began to walk up the embankment. The other thugs hauled Moondog and Phoenix up the hill after her.

Martina watched as the freeway drew closer. Her captor steered her to the undamaged sedan, and a second man pulled the rear door open. Martina's captor wrapped a strip of cloth across her eyes, tied it tightly behind her head, and shoved her forward. Her legs caught the soft cushion of the backseat, and she fell across it. After a moment Moondog and Phoenix were thrown into the car on top of her. The door slammed shut.

She heard the front doors open and shut again as two men climbed into the vehicle. The engine roared to life, and the car pulled back onto the freeway. The man in the passenger seat turned around and pointed a gun at the three pilots.

"Try anything and I shoot you all," he said.

Martina remained still. Pinned beneath Moondog and Phoenix, with their combined weight crushing her, it was nearly impossible to move. Her face was pressed against the door, twisting her neck at an awkward angle. Her legs had been pushed between the front passenger seat and the rear door. The strange position was causing both her feet to fall asleep.

She had no idea how long they drove. The blindfold prevented her from seeing anything. She could feel the motion of the car, accelerating and then braking, turning the occasional corner. Their captors stayed silent, and Moondog and Phoenix kept still.

After what seemed like hours, the car slid to a stop and the driver killed the engine. Martina heard the front doors open in succession and shut again. Then the rear door opened. The men pulled Moondog and Phoenix off her, relieving the pressure on her legs and shoulders.

Someone grabbed Martina by the arm and yanked her out of the car. Her feet hit soft ground, and she stood, wondering idly where she was.

"Walk," one of the men said, shoving her away from the car. Martina stepped forward slowly. She was walking across grass or dirt, not asphalt. The earth gradually sloped away beneath her feet. The air around her was cool and silent. The sound of traffic and the noises of the city were gone. All she could hear were the soft footfalls of the men around her and what sounded like water lapping gently against the shore of a lake. She could feel the moisture in the air. They were probably somewhere along the Potomac or Chesapeake Bay, she decided.

The man holding Martina's arms pushed her sideways. Her feet hit something solid. The sound of footfalls on wood filled her ears. Her captor pulled her to a stop and shoved her to the side. Her back banged into something hard. The man grabbed her wrists and pulled them away from her body, working with the bindings. After a moment he released his grip. Panther stepped forward cautiously, only to be yanked back by the ropes.

Martina stood still, listening as the men walked around. The sound of their footsteps against the wood floor made it easy for her to guess their location. After a few minutes, she heard them walk away. The door slammed shut just as the smell of gasoline reached her nose. For a moment everything was silent.

"Are they gone?" Moondog asked.

"I think so," Martina said, stepping back until her body touched the object she had bumped into earlier. She turned into it, pressing her face against it. It felt like a thin metal rod. Finding an edge, she hooked the blindfold over it and moved her head down. The piece of cloth slid off, returning her sight.

Martina scanned her surrounding and gasped. She was in a long, thin building. There were double doors at each end. Four rowing shells lined the wall directly across from her, stacked from the ceiling to the floor. Four larger shells were behind her. Oars hung on the walls next to the smaller boats.

Moondog and Phoenix stood to her left, each blindfolded and tied to the supports holding the boats in place. Martina's own hands were tied to the boat rack with about a foot of rope. Her blindfold hung on the rigger of a boat behind her.

A spark of light caught her eye. She glanced to her left, seeing the door through which they had entered burst into flames. In a flash, the fire raced along the shells opposite her to the far door, consuming it.

"Do you smell smoke?" Vinny asked.

"Yeah," Moondog said.

"I've got some bad news, guys," Martina said. "This place is on fire."

"Oh, fuck," Moondog said.

Martina twisted her hips, grabbing hold of the right side of her pants. She pulled the fabric back until she could reach into her pocket. For a moment she wriggled her fingers into its depths, finding her Swiss Army knife. She pulled the small weapon free.

Working quickly, Panther turned the knife over in her hands and pulled it open. She flipped the handle over, pressing the blade against the rope holding her wrists together, then frantically began to cut into her bindings. The tip of the knife nipped at her skin, drawing blood, but the blade quickly broke through the fibers.

Finally, the fibers gave way. Martina pulled her arms free as the rope fell off her wrists. She walked over to Moondog, grabbing her friend by the arm.

"Hold still," she said, quickly cutting through Moondog's bindings.

Her hands free, Moondog ripped the blindfold from her eyes.

"How the hell did you get loose?" she asked, astounded.

"Never leave home without it," Martina said, showing her the knife.

She quickly cut through the ropes holding Phoenix.

"I take back everything I ever said about light birds," Vinny said, pulling off his blindfold.

"How the hell are we going to get out of here?" Moondog asked. Both doors leading out of the boathouse were engulfed in flames from floor to ceiling, as was much of the right wall.

Martina stomped her right foot, feeling the give in the wood.

"I think this is built on the water," she said. "If we can get through the floorboards, we should be able to swim free."

"And how the hell are we going to do that?" Moondog asked. "I know your pocketknife is versatile, but I doubt it can undo those nails before that fire gets us."

All three of them desperately looked around the room. The boats on the right were blazing, but the left wall was still relatively untouched. The burning logs that had been oars a few minutes earlier were resting in a rack against one wall. On the opposite wall hung a variety of toolboxes, a few crates, and some extra riggers.

"There might be something we can use over there," Martina said, pointing at the crates.

Phoenix dashed over to the toolboxes and began to rummage hurriedly through the drawers.

"Here," he said, pulling out a saw.

"Over here," Martina said, walking as close to the flames on the far end of the boathouse as she could.

Phoenix handed her the saw. She immediately began to cut through the floor. He grabbed a hammer and rushed over to Martina. He shoved the back of the hammer into the cut she had made, prying the boards up.

They quickly ripped several boards from the floor, creating a two-by-three-foot hole. Phoenix and Moondog tossed the boards to the side. The three pilots peered down into the hole. All they could see was dark water beneath.

The fire was crawling up over the ceiling and along the far wall. More than half the floor was ablaze, filling the air with thick black smoke. The blaze was rapidly encroaching on the remaining patch of wood where the pilots stood.

"Strip off anything you don't need," Martina ordered, ripping her shirt off. "The dock's probably on fire too, and we've got to get past it. Grab anything you value and get rid of the rest."

Phoenix pulled his wallet from his pocket and kicked off his shoes. Sticking the leather billfold between his teeth, he flung his shirt away and quickly dropped his pants. Straightening his back, he caught sight of Panther and Moondog standing in only their underwear. The roaring flames revealed the lean muscles twisting through their slim, toned bodies. Fading bruises were still barely visible on their stomachs and chests. Both had several healing cuts on their arms and legs. The wounds showed up as stark red lines. Phoenix noticed that they had quite a few older scars as well. Moondog's back was crisscrossed with faint lines.

"Damn," Vinny said, with a grin. "I don't think I've ever gotten one woman naked that quickly, let alone two."

Moondog and Panther turned and looked at him.

"Shut up, Phoenix," they said in unison.

"You've probably never even seen a naked woman," Moondog added.

"Yes, I have!" Phoenix retorted indignantly.

"Shut up and take a swim," Martina said as she tucked her Victorinox and her wallet into her bra and cinched up the straps.

Vinny needed no further prodding. He jumped into the hole feet first, vanishing into the dark water. A second later his head popped up.

"It's deep."

"Good," Martina said. "Get out of here."

Vinny took a deep breath and vanished again.

A loud crack reverberated through the air. Panther and Moondog turned to see a flaming beam fall from the ceiling. The timber smashed into the boats, crushing them.

The two pilots glanced at each other. The flames were less than three feet from them. All four walls were fully ablaze, and most of the roof had caught fire.

"After you," Martina said.

"If you insist," Moondog said, grabbing her wallet. She drew three quick breaths into her chest, exhaling rapidly. She filled her lungs and dove through the small hole.

The cold water hit her, sending a quick shiver through her body. She opened her eyes, seeing the faint outline of the bottom below. She pulled her arms down along her sides while kicking rapidly, propelling herself forward. She watched the shadow of the dock sliding over her head.

Her lungs began to cry for air. She exhaled forcefully, temporarily relieving the burning sensation in her chest. She continued to swim forward, determined to put as much distance as possible between herself and the boathouse before surfacing.

Her chest was screaming from lack of oxygen, and her head was beginning to swirl. The frigid black water threatened to engulf her. She forced her hands through one more pull, then angled her body to the surface.

The darkness above her seemed infinite, pulling her down into a black abyss. Her lungs felt as if they were on fire. It seemed as if she was hardly moving, crawling upward at an agonizing pace.

Then she broke through the surface, gasping for air. The cool night filled her lungs. For a moment she treaded water, breathing hard.

Phoenix was floating a few feet away from her. They were a hundred feet from the bank of a large river. The blazing fire lit up the sky, illuminating the riverbank as if it were daylight. The orange and red flames reflected brilliantly against the dark water and faded out the stars in the clear night sky. The entire building was engulfed in flames. The fire had spread onto the dock over the river. Burning bits of wood tumbled into the water.

Everything else was quiet and still. The cold water of the river flowed slowly, lapping gently against the shore. The banks of the river were lined with trees. There were no other buildings and no signs of life.

“Where’s Panther?” Phoenix asked.

Moondog glanced around hysterically. Martina was nowhere to be seen.

“I don’t know,” she said. “I thought she was right behind me.”

A loud rumbling sound filled the air. Both pilots looked back at the boathouse, watching in horror as the timbers supporting the ceiling gave way. The roof caved in with a reverberating crash, crumbling into the center of the burning building. The sparks flew into the sky as the walls crumpled, leaving the boathouse a smoldering pile of logs.

"Panther..." Moondog said.

"Oh, no," Phoenix whispered.

For a moment neither spoke. They simply gazed in disbelief at the flaming pile of debris that had once been the boathouse.

"No," Moondog said. "This can't happen."

Her gaze was fixed on the fire. Try as she might, she could not free her eyes from the burning rubble that was her friend's tomb. The air hung deathly silent except for the crackling of the fire and the hiss of burning wood falling into the water. The water moved slowly along the shore, and the smell of smoke drifted on the wind.

"Damn, did that thing collapse?" a voice said. Moondog and Phoenix turned around. Martina was floating behind them.

"Panther!" Moondog shouted with a grin.

"You're alive!" Vinny exclaimed.

Before Martina could move, they jumped on top of her, embracing her tightly.

"Of course I'm alive," Martina said, struggling to keep her head above water. "Get off me, you crazy, naked freaks, before we all drown!"

"We thought you were in there," Moondog said, as they released their grip on Martina.

"Nah," Martina said. "I'm faster than that."

"You scared the hell out of us," Vinny accused.

"Sorry," Martina said. "Let's get the fuck out of here. I'm freezing."

"With you on that one," Moondog said, starting to

swim to shore. The others followed her, paddling to the riverbank slightly upstream of the burning boathouse. The water was still, with hardly any current.

Moondog's feet touched solid ground, and she stood. Martina and Vinny climbed onto the riverbank behind her. All three were shaking violently from the frigid water. They sprawled across the cool, soft grass, watching the smoke rising to the stars. The heat from the fire rolled slowly over their drenched bodies, warming them. For a moment no one spoke.

"Now what do we do?" Vinny finally asked, keeping his eyes focused on the stars.

"We've got to get back to Andrews," Martina said, staring forward.

"We have to figure out where the hell we are before we can do that," Moondog muttered, gazing at the sky.

"At least the guys who tried to kill us are gone," Vinny said, glancing at the flaming remains of the boathouse.

"They probably didn't want to be around if the fire department showed up," Moondog said, not turning to look.

"I don't suppose anyone thought to grab their phone," Martina said.

Vinny shook his head.

"I doubt it would have survived the swim," Moondog said.

"I've got some change if we can find a payphone," Vinny said.

"I guess we'll just have to wait," Martina remarked, watching a plane move across the sky.

"Whoever owned that place isn't going to be happy when they find it," Moondog said. "There must have been thousands of dollars worth of shells in there. Those things are expensive."

"Yep," Martina agreed.

"Any idea where we might be?" Moondog asked.

"Along some river about three hours from Washington."

"That helps."

The group fell silent again. Downstream, the fire from the boathouse glowed bright orange in the night sky. The three pilots continued to gaze at the stars above.

Far off in the distance, a siren began to wail. It quickly grew louder, the blaring noise cutting sharply through the calm night air. After a moment, flashing lights appeared as several fire trucks raced toward the river.

"How are you going to explain this one?" Moondog asked.

"Why am I always the one who has to explain things?" Martina asked indignantly.

"'Cause you are, " Moondog replied.

"We're lying on the bank of a river by a burning building in our underwear, with no believable excuse whatsoever for being here," Martina said. "For some reason, Moondog, I think you're better suited to come up with an explanation for this one than me."

"They're going to lock us up again, aren't they?" Phoenix asked.

"Probably," Moondog said.

"As long as they bring food, I don't care what they do!" he said. "I'm starving."

~ 21 ~

Moondog and Phoenix sat in a corner booth of a nearly empty all-night diner. The restaurant was quiet. There were only a few other patrons scattered throughout the large dining room. The windows revealed a quiet street outside. Most of the nearby businesses were closed. A few cars sat in the diner's parking lot. Headlights appeared at odd intervals as the occasional vehicle crawled down the deserted roads.

The two pilots were far too focused on the food in front of them to pay much attention to their surroundings. Vinny was devouring a large plate of steak and eggs. Moondog was halfway through a chicken breast smothered with cheese. Both were dressed in ill-fitting clothes that looked like they came from a secondhand store. An untouched cheeseburger sat on a plate across the table from Moondog.

After arriving at the burning remains of the boathouse, the fire department had taken the three pilots to a nearby hospital. Once the doctors looked them over and found them unhurt, they were brought to the local police station. The cops questioned them for about an hour before releasing them. Then Moondog and Phoenix made a beeline for the nearest open restaurant.

The door opened and Martina entered. She was

also dressed in loose, worn clothes. She walked over to the table and sat down across from Moondog. The Navy pilot stopped eating for a second and shifted her eyes to her friend. Vinny didn't even lift his head.

"I got you a burger," Moondog said, nodding toward the plate in front of Martina.

"Thanks," Martina said, picking it up and taking a bite.

"They're sending a chopper to pick us up," she said between mouthfuls. "The cops offered to give us a ride over to the airport. We should be back at Andrews around two."

"That's good," Moondog said. "Any sign of the guys who tried to kill us?"

"None so far."

"How did Kalliff's goons even know we were back in Washington?" Moondog asked.

"Obviously Miles has more spies than just Haley," Martina said.

"Yeah, but who?"

"Could be anyone," Martina said. "White House aide, Secret Service agent, a vendor parked on the street. It's a public building. It wouldn't be too hard to find out who comes and goes. A camera hidden across the road would do the trick."

"That's true," Moondog agreed.

"The FBI's investigating," Panther said. "Hopefully, they'll be able to track down whoever's involved. In the meantime, let's finish eating and get back to Andrews. I don't know about you two, but I'm exhausted."

* * *

The setting sun elongated the shadows of four F-22 Raptors sitting silently on the tarmac alongside the large transports at Andrews Air Force Base. The big fighters reflected the last few rays of light. The sun glinted off their silver wings, flashing across the glass of their cockpits as the blue sky faded slowly to black.

The transports easily dwarfed the Raptors, making the Air Force's large fighter seem small to their pilots as they stepped onto the tarmac. Dressed in clean flight suits and rested, Panther, Moondog, and Phoenix walked across the ramp. The fourth flier, Captain Paul Doran from the Langley squadron, fit in easily with the small group.

Martina approached her aircraft. She circled the plane, inspecting the landing gear and the airframe. Satisfied the F-22 was ready for flight, she climbed into the cockpit. Strapping herself into the ejection seat, she lowered the canopy and ran through the prestart checklist, methodically bringing her Raptor to life.

Lifting her head, Martina shifted her gaze to the three planes to her left.

"Guardian check," she said.

"Two," Moondog replied.

"Three," Vinny called.

"Four," Doran said.

Martina gave the signal to start engines, then quickly powered up her plane. Beside her, the other three pilots did the same. The F-119 turbofan engines roared to life, filling her ears with jet noise. Carefully, she scanned her gauges. Everything read in the green.

Martina keyed her mike. "Andrews ground, Guardian one one. Request taxi to the active with November."

"Guardian one one, taxi to one left."

"Taxi to one left, Guardian one one," Martina said.

She gave the crew chief the signal to pull chocks. He did so and then stepped back, marshaling her out of her parking spot. The other three planes fell in line beside her as she taxied to the end of the runway. Reaching the hold short line, Martina braked and changed her radio frequency to tower.

Receiving her takeoff clearance, she taxied onto the runway, positioning her aircraft just to the left of centerline. Moondog aligned her plane beside Martina's. Panther flashed Moondog the signal to power up, pushing her throttles to their stops and holding the brakes. All instruments read in the green. Martina fixed her eyes on Moondog's cockpit, watching for the signal that she was ready. Seeing the thumbs-up, she signed for her friend to release brakes. Simultaneously, they let go of the brakes and shoved their throttles into afterburner. The Raptors' engines roared. Blue flames shot from their burner cans, stretching brilliantly behind the planes as the fighters raced down the runway.

Martina kept her eyes focused on the end of the runway, keeping her plane aligned just to the left of centerline. Reaching rotation speed, she pulled back on the stick, and the sleek fighter leapt into the air. Martina held the nose up, climbing easily into the twilight sky.

She looked over to see Moondog in place on her wing. They raised their landing gear at the same time. Martina glanced back. Below and behind them, the other F-22s were completing their takeoff roll. She throttled back slightly, allowing the two planes behind her to catch up. A moment later, Phoenix and Doran fell into position, completing the fourship formation. Still gaining altitude, Martina turned her Raptor to the west, flying along the path the tower relayed her. The others held their places in formation.

In a matter of seconds they were over the city. Martina settled her Raptor into an easy circle, keeping the flight directly above Washington, D.C. Below, she could see the Mall and the marble monuments that dotted the city, brightly illuminated in the night.

Reaching her desired cruise altitude, Martina set her throttles to maximize her time in the air. She switched her radar to the greatest range. Flying a racetrack course over the city, she began scanning outside and alternately checking her radar, alert for anything out of the ordinary. The sky was empty except for the four Raptors. Martina hoped it would stay that way.

* * *

This was a suicide mission.

Dan Haley looked up at the ominous dark shadow of the B-1 bomber, studying it. The aircraft was going to carry him to his death. In a matter of hours the magnificent plane would be a burning ball of fire with Haley trapped inside. Even if he accomplished his mission, he would not make it out alive. Fighters waited for him in the sky above Washington, and when they found him it would be the end.

It didn't seem right that this bomber would be destroyed attacking the country she was built to defend. This cause was hardly worth the B-1's destruction or the life of its pilot. But the small renegade group that stole the plane was hell-bent on using it to further their purpose, the fall of the nation that designed and constructed the plane.

Haley ran his hand along her cold black underbelly as he walked slowly to the ladder leading to the cockpit, wondering again how he ended up here. Everything was out of place. The B-1 was preparing to attack her homeland.

Haley sighed and climbed into the Bone's cockpit. He strapped himself into the left-hand seat. His backseater, one of the weapons system officers from Dyess, followed and began to perform his own prestart checklist.

Haley wondered what his companion's motivation

for flying this mission was as he brought the engines to life. A quick scan of the computer and the instrument panel revealed that the plane was functioning perfectly. The B-1 would fly tonight.

"Everything good?" Haley asked his backseater.

"Working fine," the man replied. "Let's go."

Haley released the brakes and allowed the bomber to roll onto the makeshift strip. The deafening roar of the B-1's four engines flaring into full afterburner shook pine needles from the trees as it shattered the silence of the Canadian wilderness. Tongues of fire shot from the exhaust, lighting up the dark sky like rocket plumes. The big plane sped down the strip and climbed into the night sky. Leveling off just above the tree line, the bomber turned south, disappearing into the darkness.

* * *

Panther rolled away from the tanker and pointed her Raptor back toward Washington. Leveling out over the city, she resumed her circling pattern. The others fell in behind her, refueled and ready for combat.

Night had fully settled in over the city, revealing a sparkling sea of lights below and the small pinpoints of stars above. A long line of limousines and cars stretched to the Capitol, carrying members of Congress and other important government figures to the old marble building to hear Webster's speech.

Martina checked her watch. The address was scheduled to begin in thirty minutes. The speech would take about an hour. Once it concluded and the building's occupants had left, the F-22s would finally land.

Off to the east, Martina made out the small moving point of light that was the KC-135 Stratotanker. Aside from the occasional satellite passing overhead, the sky was devoid of the lights of air traffic. The only aircraft authorized to fly within fifty miles of Washington airspace were the fourship of Raptors and the tanker. The fighters ran without their lights, making them invisible in the blackness. Out over the ocean, an AWACS was scanning the coast for approaching aircraft.

So far, everything was quiet. All commercial and military traffic avoided the area above D.C., leaving Martina with little to do other than circle above. She alternated her gaze between the sky and the radar, but the black expanse above Washington was empty. The only visible blip was the large tanker, circling slowly over the Atlantic.

The moon had risen, casting a pale light across everything it touched. A few bright stars appeared in the blackness above, but most had been washed out by the lights of the city and the nearly full moon.

"Guardian one one, Watchdog three six," the radio crackled. Watchdog 36 was the AWACS flying off the coast.

"Go ahead, Watchdog," Martina said.

"I've got a flight of five to six planes approaching from the northeast," Watchdog reported. "Radar signature indicates fighter aircraft. They're headed straight for Washington. Negative IFF."

"Roger, Watchdog. We're on our way. Any sign of the B-1?"

"Negative."

Martina put her plane into a turn to the northeast, following the vectors given to her by the AWACS. She nudged her throttles up, wanting to reach the approaching aircraft before they got close to the city. The other three pilots held their positions in the formation.

A small cluster of blips appeared on her radar screen. She pointed her nose straight toward the echoes, scanning the sky for the planes as she raced closer.

A flash of moonlight off metal caught her eye. Out ahead of her she saw the faint outlines of six aircraft, rapidly growing as the two groups neared each other. All their lights were off. Martina raised her nose slightly. She peered down as the Raptors raced over the planes with a roar.

Below she could see six MiG-31 Foxhounds. All were armed to the teeth with missiles. Carrying solely air defense weapons, the group of planes could serve only one purpose: to destroy the fighters guarding Washington so that the bomber could safely make its attack.

She chopped her throttles and rolled onto her back. Tugging back on the stick, she pulled the plane down in a split S. Bringing the nose of her Raptor up, she leveled off, flying in the opposite direction a few hundred feet lower. The others stayed in place on her wing, following her through the maneuver.

Martina armed her Sidewinders. The missiles quickly locked on the lead MiG-31's tailpipe.

"Unidentified flight, you are nearing restricted airspace," she hailed the nearing formation. "Divert to a heading of zero six zero degrees or you will be shot down."

The radio stayed silent. The planes held their heading.

"I repeat: Flight approaching Washington, divert to a zero six zero degree heading or you will be shot down," Panther said. "Acknowledge."

The aircraft in front of her suddenly broke formation, all turning back on the flight of Raptors. They raced for the F-22s, guns blazing.

Panther shoved her throttles into afterburner, dashing past the older fighters. The other Raptors stayed with her. Once beyond the others, she pulled her nose up and turned back toward the other aircraft.

"Watchdog three six, bogeys are hostile," she reported. "We're taking them out. Suggest you scramble the alert jets. Put them over the city. We'll take care of these guys."

"Roger," Watchdog replied.

"Shoot 'em down," she told her wingmen. "Keep them over the water."

Panther armed her AMRAAMs and pointed her nose at a MiG directly in front of her. The missiles locked on, and she squeezed the trigger. Beside her, the others released their own weapons.

The missile warning sounded loudly in Panther's ears as the enemy planes loosed a volley of their own. Brilliant red trails of fire filled the sky as the missiles crossed in the night. The group of F-22s immediately released their chaff and broke formation. Their attackers did the same. Jets scattered across the sky.

Most of the missiles collided with the chaff, exploding harmlessly. Bright fireballs appeared in the sky, then vanished. One projectile struck a Foxhound's wing, sending the Russian-made fighter spiraling toward the dark ocean below.

The missile warning in Panther's ears died. She scanned the sky. The three other Raptors were still airborne. On her right, Moondog was diving for a MiG, guns blazing. The Foxhound's pilot jinked rapidly, trying to shake her, but the F-22 was a far more maneuverable plane. She stayed easily in place, peppering his tail with gunfire.

Doran immediately spotted a second MiG and rolled toward it, maneuvering aggressively to get in position on its tail. The Russian fighter twisted and turned, trying to keep his missiles from locking on. The pilot pulled up sharply into a loop. Doran pulled back on the stick, staying close behind the MiG.

Reaching the top of the loop, the MiG's pilot

chopped his throttles and rolled away, tumbling toward the ocean. Doran copied the maneuver, still fighting to get a clear shot.

Two of the remaining MiGs dove for Phoenix's F-22. He pulled hard to the left, banking sharply away. The MiGs followed, trying to get behind him. Tracers lit up the sky as the lead Foxhound fired. Phoenix jinked sharply to the right, pulling his Raptor into a tight, climbing turn. The bullets narrowly missed the fuselage of his fighter.

Panther rolled to the left and pointed the nose of her F-22 at the second Foxhound. She nudged her throttles forward, quickly closing the distance between her plane and the MiG. She carefully aligned her Raptor and squeezed the trigger, sending a quick burst of cannon fire at the Foxhound. The bullets flew straight up the MiG's tailpipe, colliding with the engine. The turbine blades broke apart as the bullets ripped into them. Pieces of metal scattered everywhere, tearing through the fuselage.

Panther loosed a second burst of fire. This time the bullets collided with the tail, damaging the control cables. The Foxhound pitched nose-down and began to spiral toward the black ocean below.

Phoenix rolled onto his side and pulled back hard on the stick. G-forces immediately pressed against his body. He tensed his leg muscles and held his breath, feeling his g-suit inflate. Despite the incredible force pressing down on his helmet, he lifted his head, searching for the remaining MiG.

The Foxhound clung tightly to the Raptor's tail, attempting to follow him through the maneuver. But the Raptor had a much tighter turn radius. Try as it might, the MiG could not hold position.

Phoenix finally released the back pressure and rolled wings level. He checked over his shoulder. The Foxhound was now slightly ahead and to the right of him. He immediately jinked, pointing the nose of his F-22 at the MiG's tailpipe.

Panther looked to the right, to see another Foxhound racing at her. She jerked her nose toward the plane, rolling out so that she was heading directly at the MiG. Rapidly, she armed her radar-guided AMRAAMs. The missile locked immediately, and Panther mashed the trigger.

The MiG's pilot reacted quickly, pulling his nose straight up and throwing his plane into afterburner. The missile hit him squarely in the underbelly and exploded. A brilliant fireball ripped through the night as the MiG was torn to pieces.

Panther rolled sharply to the right, temporarily blinded by the explosion. She felt the shock wave hit her plane. A loud bang resounded through the cockpit as a fragment of the MiG's fuselage collided with the underside of the Raptor. The plane shook again as another bit of shrapnel bounced off the wing.

Panther rolled wings level. She quickly scanned her instruments. Everything was still in the green. Any damage the Raptor had sustained was superficial. Satisfied her aircraft was functioning properly, she turned her eyes back to the sky.

Moondog was still tenaciously following one MiG, peppering it with cannon fire whenever it crossed her path. Try as he might, the Foxhound's pilot could not shake her. Fuel was streaming from holes in his wing and fuselage, and his left engine was no longer running. Finally, a burst of gunfire caught his right aileron, ripping it off. The MiG's wing dipped down, and it tumbled away.

The Foxhound in front of Phoenix quickly chopped his throttles and dove for the ocean. The Raptor pilot followed, trying to line up a shot. The MiG leveled out for a brief second and turned hard to the right. Phoenix copied the maneuver, staying close behind. The Foxhound's pilot threw his plane into afterburner and pointed his nose at the sky, climbing sharply.

Phoenix quickly armed his Sidewinders. A tone sounded in his ears a second later, and he pulled the trigger, loosing a missile. He pulled away sharply as the heat-seeking missile raced for the Foxhound. It collided with the MiG, exploding violently.

Another explosion ripped through the sky a second later as Doran fired on the remaining MiG. The MiG pulled hard to the right at the last second, and the missile ripped through its wing and tail. The plane immediately tumbled from the sky, rolling uncontrollably downward.

Panther checked her radar. The only aircraft visible were the three other Raptors. She pulled her throttles back and gave the signal for them to rejoin. One by one they fell into formation on her wing.

"Anybody hit?" she asked.

"Negative," Doran replied.

"I'm fine," Phoenix said, sounding slightly out of breath.

"Of course not," Moondog answered calmly.

"All right. Let's head back," Martina said.

She put her Raptor in a shallow bank, turning back toward Washington.

"Guardian one one, Watchdog three six," the AWACS announced. "You've got another five or six aircraft approaching fast."

Panther glanced back at her radar screen. A small group of echoes appeared on the edge of the scope. She rolled out and looked up. In the pale moonlight she saw the silhouettes of a formation of fighter aircraft racing for the city, fire blazing from their tailpipes against the black sky.

"Get ready," she said to the others. "It looks as if this fight isn't over."

~ 22 ~

Dan Haley watched the lights of the East Coast cities slip past, one by one. The bomber flew down the eastern seaboard over the Atlantic Ocean, just far enough from the coast to remain undetected. Maine and Boston had slid by in the darkness, followed by New York, New Jersey, and then Baltimore. No one took notice of the plane's presence as he flew southward well below the radar, 500 feet off the waves.

Haley sat at the controls, letting the autopilot hold the B-1 on course. He had said very little to the backseater the entire trip, riding in silence. Instead he watched the city lights pass by off his right wing while he gazed into the black night, looking at the dark ocean beneath him and the stars above. He monitored the radio frequencies, checking to see if his southward passage had been noticed. All he picked up was the chatter of air traffic controllers moving airliners around and the occasional private pilot flying on the Victor airways.

The GPS indicated that he was directly east of Washington, D.C. Haley saw the bright city lights glowing to the west. He checked the time. He had ten minutes until the State of the Union address started. Everyone attending should be in their seats by now.

He reached over and reprogrammed the computer to bring him on a heading directly over the Capitol.

Nosing the big plane down, he descended to 200 feet off the ground and engaged the terrain-following radar, shoving the throttles forward into full afterburner. If he was low and fast enough, nobody would see him until it was too late.

"We're going in. Get ready," Haley informed his backseater. The man simply nodded in acknowledgment.

The B-1 raced toward Washington, D.C.

* * *

Martina watched as the incoming jets drew closer. The dark silhouettes quickly resolved themselves as they neared. She recognized two F-15 Eagles and four F-16 Falcons heading for them.

"Watchdog three six, Guardian one one, those incoming planes are U.S. fighters," Panther said, watching them closely. "Are they talking to you at all?"

"Negative, Guardian," the AWACS replied. "I'm only in contact with Knife Edge one one, a flight of F-22s over D.C."

"Those F-15s are old C models," Doran said. "I don't think there are any based around here anymore."

"Something tells me these guys aren't friendly," Panther said.

She switched frequencies and keyed her mike.

"Unidentified flight, you are approaching U.S airspace," she said, sounding slightly annoyed. "Divert to a zero six zero heading or you will be shot down."

There was no answer. The flight of fighters turned toward the Raptors. Tracers lit up the sky as the lead F-15 fired his cannons. The F-22 pilots immediately broke formation. The bullets flew harmlessly between the big fighters.

"Watchdog, bogeys are hostile," Panther called. "We're taking them out. Keep Knife Edge over the city."

"Roger, Guardian," the AWACS replied.

She rolled sharply to the right. Phoenix stayed in position on her wing. Moondog and Doran quickly turned to the left, heading toward the formation of approaching fighters.

Panther set her sights on the lead F-15 and armed her radar-guided missiles. The AMRAAMs quickly locked on, and she squeezed the trigger. The Eagle's pilot immediately released his chaff and shoved his plane into afterburner, racing away from the missile. The AMRAAM collided with the countermeasures and exploded, filling the sky with a brilliant flash of fire.

Panther pointed the nose of her Raptor slightly ahead of the F-15's path. There was no way the older fighter could outrun her, and she knew it. She switched to her cannons and fired a long burst. The bullets slammed into the F-15, raking the fuselage from nose to tail. They ripped through the cockpit, killing the pilot instantly. He slumped over the stick. The F-15 nosed over, diving rapidly for the ocean below.

Phoenix pulled his plane into a steep climb and rolled over on his back. He pulled through, dropping down behind an F-16, and armed his AIM-9 missiles. The heat-seeking Sidewinder locked onto the Viper's exhaust. Before Phoenix even had a chance to fire, the F-16's pilot jerked the aircraft hard to the left. Phoenix held his position on the little fighter's tail, trying to get a clear shot.

The F-16 dove, racing toward the dark water below. Phoenix followed him. In frustration he flipped his guns on and fired. The F-16 leveled off just a few hundred feet over the water, jinking to the left and right. Phoenix chopped his throttles and pulled back as he saw the ocean rushing up. Staying right behind the little fighter, he continued to fire short bursts.

The F-16 wove back and forth across the water, trying to shake him. Somehow the little plane was avoiding his gunfire. Phoenix was not about to let it get away. Keeping a close eye on his altimeter, he chased the Viper as it twisted and turned.

Moondog pointed her nose at the second F-15 and armed her AMRAAMs. Before they even locked on, she heard a sharp warning in her ears. Two F-16s were racing at her tail. She immediately pulled back on the stick and shoved her throttles forward. The F-22 raced skyward, climbing rapidly. The F-16s were very maneuverable, but they could not match the Raptor's rate of climb. They tried to follow, but their speed bled off quickly, and they fell behind.

Reaching the top of the climb, Moondog pulled back sharply on the stick and looped over. A few thousand feet below her she could see the two Vipers. She pointed her nose at the little fighters and dove for them, letting loose a burst from her cannon. The two F-16s split, racing away from her bullets.

She followed the F-16 on the right, leveling out on its tail and arming her AIM-9 Sidewinders. The second Viper executed a quick, high-g turn, rolling out on Moondog's tail. Its pilot fired a short burst from his cannon. Moondog felt her plane shudder as a line of bullet holes appeared in her right vertical stabilizer. She quickly rolled away, trying to shake the little plane. She shoved her throttles into afterburner, rapidly putting distance between her and the Viper.

Chopping the throttles, she executed a tight turn and raced back to the battle. Quickly, she scanned the sky. The two F-16s were once again flying straight for her. Panther was racing after the remaining F-15. Phoenix was nowhere to be seen. Doran was maneuvering, trying to line up a shot on an F-16's tail. The agile plane jinked to the left and right, trying to shake him. He stubbornly chased the small jet, refusing to let it get away.

The Viper pulled up sharply in a tight loop. Doran clung to the little plane's tail, holding position closely as both aircraft went over the top. The F-16 leveled out for a brief second, then quickly executed a high-g turn. The Raptor followed it.

The F-16 Phoenix was following pulled up abruptly, climbing rapidly. Ahead he saw another F-16 roll sharply on its side and turn quickly. The Viper in front of him didn't see the other F-16 until it was too late. The plane shot upward, colliding with the second F-16 behind its cockpit.

A brilliant fireball filled the sky as both planes exploded. The shock wave hit Phoenix's F-22, pushing the plane back. Already at a high angle of attack, the wings of his plane stalled, and the F-22 tumbled backward, falling uncontrollably downward.

Panic gripped Phoenix for a split second. All he could see outside was blackness. He couldn't tell if he was descending or climbing. Quickly, he turned his eyes back to his heads-up display. His attitude indicator showed that he was nose-down. His altitude was decreasing while his airspeed climbed. He immediately retarded his throttles. Slowly, he rolled wings level. The Raptor continued to dive but was no longer tumbling. He gently brought his nose up, advancing his throttles as he did so. The aircraft leveled out. He quickly scanned his instruments. Everything was functioning properly. He raised his nose, climbing back toward the battle.

Doran saw the Vipers collide and tried to roll away. The shock from the explosion hit his plane, and the flames seemed to be only inches away. A large chunk of metal flew into his right engine intake, destroying the compressor blades.

A warning began to scream in his ears. He immediately shifted his eyes to his engine gauges.

The RPMs on his right engine were rapidly dying. He quickly pulled his right throttle into the cutoff position and shut off the fuel to the engine. He checked his engine instruments again. The right showed a successful shutdown. The left was still functioning properly. One engine provided more than enough thrust to keep the sleek fighter airborne. Doran turned his eyes back to the sky, looking for another enemy fighter.

Panther rolled out behind the second F-15 and fired a Sidewinder. The F-15 released its flares and turned sharply to the left. The missile hit the flares and exploded harmlessly. Panther quickly fired again, releasing an AMRAAM. The F-15 had its back to her. The radar-guided missile quickly locked on to the big fighter. This time the F-15's pilot didn't have time to react. The missile hit the plane directly between the tailfins and exploded.

The two remaining F-16s were racing for Moondog's F-22. She set her sights on the plane on the right and was flying straight for it, firing her cannon. Doran pointed his nose at the Viper on the left and armed his Sidewinders. The heat-seeking missiles quickly locked on. He fired.

The F-16 immediately released its flares. The missile headed for the countermeasures. Doran kept his position on the Viper's tail as it turned sharply to the left. The other F-16 twisted to the right, with Moondog chasing it.

The first Viper rolled out, only to find Panther's F-22 bearing down on it rapidly. The pilot rolled the opposite way, exposing his back to Doran. The F-22 pilot fired a quick burst from his cannon. The bullets ripped through the F-16's wing, and it began to tumble.

Doran glanced back at the final F-16. Moondog had lined up directly on its tail. A quick burst from her guns hit the plane squarely in its burner can, destroying the turbine. Powerless, the F-16 nosed down, gliding sharply toward the water below.

Once again the F-22s were alone in the sky. Panther signaled the others to form back up. They quickly fell into position on her wing for a second time.

"Watchdog three six, Guardian one one," Martina reported, "bandits are destroyed."

"Roger, Guardian," Watchdog replied.

"Any sign of the B-1?"

"Negative."

A sinking feeling hit Martina in the pit of her stomach.

"Roger," she said. "We're heading back to the city. Let us know the instant anything else shows up on the radar."

"Wilco," Watchdog replied.

Martina pulled her throttles over the detent and shoved them into afterburner, racing back toward Washington as fast as she could. She hoped she wasn't too late.

* * *

The lights of Washington rushed toward Haley, filling the window of the big bomber. The city shone, casting its lights into the black sky. The glow washed out the stars, causing all but the brightest to fade from view. Haley stared forward, watching as the expanse of lights grew larger and larger before him. The computer told him he would be over his target in two minutes. So this was it.

Haley reached into the pocket of his flight suit and pulled out his pistol. Flipping off the safety, he twisted around and placed the sight directly over his backseater's head.

"Hands up," he ordered, "or I shoot."

"What the hell?" the backseater said, twisting

around.

"We're aborting this mission, now," Haley said.

"No, we're not," the man said, quickly pulling a gun from his pocket. Before he could raise his weapon, Haley squeezed the trigger. The explosion reverberated off the walls of the small cabin. The backseater's chest exploded in red, and he slumped forward, dead.

Haley disengaged the autopilot and grabbed the Bone's controls. He pulled the big bomber skyward, throttling back as he did. Washington, D.C., fell away beneath him as he climbed to 20,000 feet, where every radar beam in the area would paint him, including those of the Raptors above.

No sooner had he leveled out than he saw them, eight black wraiths diving directly for him, intent on killing him.

"Don't shoot. Don't shoot," he screamed into the radio. "I surrender. I surrender. Don't shoot."

"Turn to a zero nine zero heading and give me one reason why I shouldn't blow your ass out of the sky," a cold female voice hissed in reply. The Raptors raced closer.

"If you kill me, everyone in the Capitol will die," Haley responded.

"How do I know you won't kill them if I let you live?" she challenged.

"If I was going to drop my bombs, I would have already done it, when I was 200 feet off the ground and you didn't see me. If I make one move now, you'll shoot me down," Haley said.

The Raptors screamed past his cockpit, four racing by each wing with a roar. The plumes shooting from their tails illuminated the night. Haley watched apprehensively as they disappeared behind him.

"Damn right I will," the Raptor pilot replied. "We're flying on your wing. Any fast ones, and you're a fireball. Turn to a zero nine zero heading."

"All right," Haley said, putting the bomber into a sweeping turn. "You have to listen to me. The President still isn't safe. If you don't act now, everyone in that building will be dead."

"What are you talking about?" the fighter pilot asked.

"This bomber is a diversion," Haley said. "It's only carrying half the bomb load it left Dyess with. Miles and Kalliff used the other half to build a bomb of their own. They've planted it beneath the Capitol. It will explode forty-five minutes into the address."

"And how did they get that through security?" the Raptor pilot asked sarcastically.

"There are miles of tunnels under Washington," Haley explained. "They planted the bomb down there, under the building. They've got inside help. Please, you've got to alert someone."

"Why should I believe you?" the fighter pilot challenged.

"You can't afford not to. If I'm wrong, nothing happens. If I'm right, and you don't act, the entire government will be destroyed."

"And who are you with all this information?"

"Dan Haley, General Miles' executive officer. I was in on the planning."

"You sonofabitch," the Raptor pilot muttered. "Where is Miles?" she demanded.

"He's waiting right outside the Capitol, ready to take over as soon as that bomb explodes," Haley said.

"All right, you got your wish," the pilot said. "We'll tell them what's going on. Hold steady for a minute."

Martina peered at the city below her. To fly back to Andrews and alert them would take too much time. She needed to get the word to the people on the ground, and she needed to do it now. Time was in short supply.

"Knife Edge one one, can you spare one plane?" she asked the second flight of F-22s.

"Affirmative," Knife Edge 11 replied. "Three, follow Guardian one one's direction."

"Guardian four, Lead," she said to Doran.

"Go ahead, Lead," he replied.

"You and Knife Edge one three escort the bomber back to Andrews. Have the pilot put under arrest the instant he lands. He tries anything, blow him out of the sky. You copy?"

"Copy, Lead, will do," Doran replied.

"Watchdog three six, did you hear that?" Martina asked the AWACS.

"Affirmative, Guardian one one," Watchdog replied.

"Alert the authorities."

"Wilco."

"Knife Edge one one, continue the CAP. Moondog, Phoenix, follow me," Martina ordered.

She dropped her wing, rolling away from the bomber and back toward the city. She chopped her throttles, putting the Raptor into a steady descent. Behind her Moondog and Phoenix peeled away from the B-1 and followed.

Martina flew low over the city, scanning the roads carefully. To her delight, a roadblock was set up on the street running alongside the Mall, leaving a wide stretch of asphalt completely open. Martina carefully judged the distance with her eyes.

"Let's get going," she said, turning tightly and flying parallel to the road, away from the Capitol.

"She is not going to..." Phoenix said.

"Oh, yes, the crazy woman is," Moondog replied. "And so are we."

She quickly copied the maneuver.

"This could get interesting," Vinny said, rolling after Moondog so that the three planes flew one behind the other.

Panther lowered her landing gear. She swung the plane through a descending 180 degree turn, aligning herself with the big six-lane road as she bled off altitude and speed. Streetlights illuminated the long, straight stretch of asphalt. Martina centered her plane over the dividing yellow line.

The police officers standing at the roadblock turned as the sound of a jet engine grew louder in the sky. The large gray underbelly of an F-22 Raptor immediately filled their vision. The plane was only about twenty feet above them and descending rapidly. The jet glided toward them, its nose pointed in the air and its wheels down, showing only the slick undersides of its massive wings.

The police dove away, flattening themselves against the ground as the large plane roared above their heads, its wheels missing the roadblock by mere inches. The Raptor was over them in a flash as the noise of the engines filled their ears. A powerful gust of wind hit them, toppling a few of the sawhorses in the street. They felt the heat from the tailpipes roll over them as the big fighter swept past.

The F-22's rear wheels smoothly touched the asphalt, and the pilot expertly brought the nose down, placing the gear easily on the ground. The engines throttled back to idle, and the flaps and speed brakes extended fully, bringing the aircraft nearly to a stop.

As the roar died, the police officers lifted their heads and stared in disbelief and shock at the large plane sitting on the road, too stunned to move. As the aircraft crawled up the road, the sound of jet noise filled the air once more. The cops twisted back around to see another plane angling for them. They hit the ground again as the second Raptor flashed overhead, followed by a third.

"Guardian one one, Watchdog three six,"

Martina's radio crackled as she rolled out.

"Go ahead," she said.

"We've alerted fire rescue and the local police," Watchdog reported. "But no one can get through to the Capitol. The phone lines are down and all cell phone and radio signals are being blocked."

"I'm on my way there, Watchdog," Martina said. "I'll let them know."

Martina quickly taxied the plane up the road. She turned down another street, stopping in front of the Capitol. Quickly, she shut down the engines. Unstrapping from her ejection seat, she swung her legs over the side of the plane and dropped to the ground.

Moondog and Phoenix taxied up and stopped beside her. They killed their engines and raised their canopies, climbing from the aircraft. They jogged over to Martina, who was waiting for them on the sidewalk.

"This is one hell of a party you decided to crash, Panther," Moondog said, strolling up.

"Should be a good time," Martina said.

"Hope they got some good booze," Phoenix said. "Some good-looking women would be nice too."

"It was the quickest way I could think of to tell them," Martina said, ignoring him. She turned and ran down a paved footpath to the Capitol and up the marble steps. Moondog and Phoenix followed close on her heels. Several police officers stood on the landing outside the main entrance to the building, watching the three pilots suspiciously. Martina walked up to the nearest man.

"You've got to evacuate the building immediately," she said. "A terrorist group has planted a bomb in the tunnels underground, and they're going to blow it up any minute now."

The policeman stared at her as if he hadn't heard anything.

"Are you deaf?" Martina said, incredulous. "There is a bomb in the building! You need to evacuate now!"

"No one is going anywhere," the man replied, coldly.

"What the hell?" Martina said, not believing what was happening.

"If we evacuate the building, Colonel," a voice behind the guard said, "then the bomb underneath it won't kill anyone."

Panther lifted her head to see Miles step out from the shadows.

"And that would spoil everything," he said, walking up to the three fighter pilots. "So we will keep everyone where they are, and in a matter of, oh," he checked his watch, "thirty minutes, President Webster and every other member of the government will be dead, leaving me in control. Unfortunately, you won't be around to see the fireworks."

Miles turned and walked back toward the building.

"Kill them," he ordered.

~ 23 ~

Five men slowly closed in around the three unarmed pilots like a pack of wolves encircling their quarry. Panther felt Moondog and Phoenix draw closer to her until the three stood almost shoulder to shoulder, facing the approaching men. She glanced to each side, looking for any potential weapons. But the landing was open and empty. Her Victorinox was buried in the pocket of her flight suit. She quickly dismissed the idea of going for the knife. The guards would shoot her before she had a chance to pull it from her pocket.

Panther watched the men approach. Reflexively, she shifted her weight, sinking down onto her heels. Moondog and Phoenix held their ground beside her.

"Where's your .45?" Moondog whispered.

"I left it at VOQ," Panther whispered back. "It was out of bullets."

"Oh, shit," Moondog muttered.

The men stopped a few feet from the pilots. The guard standing directly in front of Panther dropped his hand to his hip, pulling his gun from the holster. He raised the pistol. His movements were slow and deliberate as he flipped the safety off and prepared to fire.

The other men reached for their own weapons as the first man leveled his gun at Panther, depressing the trigger.

She lunged for the guard across from her as Moondog and Phoenix leapt to the side. Panther jumped forward, brushing the man's arm aside with her hand as she stepped quickly inside his reach. The gun exploded, sending the bullet screaming past her ear. She felt the breeze of the projectile against her skin.

As Moondog dove for the man immediately to the left, Phoenix rushed to the right, hell-bent on stopping the approaching guard from drawing his gun. The bullet from the first man's pistol sailed harmlessly between them.

The man in front of Panther stepped back, surprised by her speed. She moved with him, hitting him in the side of his neck with enough force to daze him. Grabbing his wrist with her left hand, she slid her fingers quickly down to his hand, grabbing the gun.

The thug drove his fist into Panther's stomach, causing her to step back. The pistol came away in her hand. As she moved away, he thrust his foot into her chest. She stumbled, lost her footing, and hit the ground. The gun flew from her hand, clattering down the marble steps. She rolled with the blow, feet flying over her head as she tumbled.

Her boots hit the ground again, and she drew herself up into a crouch. Her back heel hung over the top step. Behind her a long flight of marble stairs stretched to the ground. The gun lay halfway down the stairs. Panther ignored it, jumping to her feet and rushing at the man ahead of her, fire blazing in her eyes.

Seeing her charge, he stepped to the side and swung his fist at her nose. She easily dodged the blow, and the punch flew harmlessly past her. She stepped behind him and twisted around. She raised her leg, driving the heel of her boot into his back just above his kidney. He collapsed with a wail of pain, falling to the ground and curling into a ball. Panther turned away from him. A route to the Capitol lay open before her.

Moondog lunged at the man to her immediate left as he tried to unsafe his gun. She stepped inside of his reach, smashing her fist into his jaw and twisting his head to the side. His hand dropped, pistol pointing to the marble surface of the landing.

A second guard standing to the left of Moondog raised his weapon, aiming for her. She quickly stepped to the right, placing the first guard between her and the second man. The guard shifted his aim but was unable to get a clear shot at her. Frustrated, he squeezed off a round. The bullet whizzed by Moondog's head, missing by inches.

The first guard raised his hand again, swinging his gun toward Moondog. She quickly grabbed his wrist, stopping him from bringing the weapon to bear on her. Instead the muzzle of the gun pointed harmlessly out at the Mall.

The man looked down at Moondog. She flashed a quick smile and thrust her fist into his stomach. He doubled over, gasping. Moondog grabbed the back of his head and pushed his face down at the same time she raised her leg, forcefully slamming her knee into his nose.

He yelped with pain. She released her grip, shoving him back, pulling the gun from his hand at the same time. He dropped to the ground, splayed out along the marble. Blood gushed from his broken nose. Wailing in agony, he covered his nose with his free hand, trying to stem the flow of blood.

Moondog glanced at the second gunman. Seeing her in the open, he adjusted his aim, pointing his gun at her chest. His finger curled around the trigger. Moondog quickly raised her gun and fired, hitting him in the thigh. His leg gave way as he fired, and he dropped to his knees.

The bullet ricocheted off the stone two inches in front of Moondog, spraying her with shards of flying marble. Most pieces collided harmlessly with her flight suit, but several hit the exposed skin on her wrists, leaving scratches on her hands and bare arms. A small piece of shrapnel cut the skin beside her left eye, leaving a deep gash.

Blood began to trickle down the side of Moondog's face. She ignored it, adjusting her aim and firing again. The projectile hit the guard's left shoulder, spinning him around. He landed on his side and lay motionless.

As Moondog jumped to the left, Phoenix ran at the guard standing to his right, who was in the process of drawing his own weapon. Seeing the pilot rush him, the man let go of the pistol, realizing Phoenix would be on top of him before he could fire. Leaving his weapon in the holster, he settled back into a fighting stance. Phoenix squared off opposite him

The man threw a roundhouse punch, catching Phoenix in the side of the head. Phoenix sidestepped, slightly dazed. He shook his head, trying to clear it. The guard quickly threw a second punch, aiming for Phoenix's jaw.

Phoenix ducked to the side, dodging the blow. He smashed his fist into the man's nose, snapping his head backward. Phoenix moved forward, grabbing the man by the shoulder and throwing him to the ground.

The sentry landed flat on his back on the hard marble surface. The force of the impact knocked the wind from him, and he lay stunned on the ground, gasping for air as he stared at the sky. Phoenix immediately stepped forward and dropped down onto the guard, pinning him to the ground with his knees.

He reached for the guard's gun while the man struggled.

Phoenix rapped his knuckles against the man's temple, dazing him, then quickly pulled open the leather flap covering the man's weapon, yanking the gun from its holster. As he raised the weapon to flip off the safety, something stung his left arm. He glanced at his sleeve and saw a small hole in his flight suit. Blood trickled from a shallow cut. He lifted his head to see another man five feet away aiming a pistol at him.

Jumping to his feet, Phoenix raised his own weapon, pointing it at the other guard. Behind him the first guard rolled over and grabbed Phoenix's ankle. He jerked Phoenix's foot up as he depressed the trigger. Phoenix lost his balance and toppled backward, landing hard on the marble.

The first man quickly leapt on top of him, pinning him to the ground. He grabbed Phoenix's wrist, struggling to regain his gun. Phoenix tightened his grip on the weapon as the man attempted to pry his fingers loose.

Miles stood in the shadows of the Capitol, watching the fight. He did not know how the three pilots managed to survive his earlier assassination attempt, but he was determined to see their demise this time. He would ensure they did not make it through his men.

He watched Redrick fighting with his agent with a pleased expression on his face. Although embroiled in the fight, she kept her eyes on Miles, glaring angrily at him when her gaze met his. Fire burning in her eyes, she dispatched his minion with a quick kick to the back, knocking him to the ground, and rushed forward.

A loud gunshot stopped her in her tracks. She turned to her right. A guard leveled his pistol at her.

Behind him, Phoenix was grappling with another one of the fake policemen. Panther immediately stepped back, standing beside the first guard, who was still moaning on the ground.

Miles watched her with a bemused look on his face. Her inability to reach him humored him. He grinned wider, knowing she would be dead in a matter of minutes.

Panther shot Miles a fierce glare, then turned her attention back to the shooter. He sighted his weapon carefully and fired again. Panther ducked instinctively, dropping to a crouch. The bullet sailed above her.

Hearing the gunfire, Phoenix lifted his head, careful not to loosen his grip on the weapon in his hand. He was surprised that the second guard was still trying to shoot him. With the other man kneeling on top of him, Phoenix did not present a good target.

He twisted his neck to get a better view of the shooter. The man was standing several feet away, with his back to Phoenix. He was aiming at a target about five feet off the ground and slightly to the left of where Phoenix lay. Phoenix quickly glanced to the left, to see Panther duck from the oncoming fire. He was trying to kill Panther!

Furiously, Phoenix punched the guard in the temple. The man wavered from the force of the blow, but stayed firmly planted on Phoenix. He drove his knuckles into the guard's throat with as much power as he could muster. The man gagged. Phoenix wrapped his hand around the side of his neck, pressing his thumb deep into his throat. Pushing his hand up, he extended his arm, lifting the man off him.

The guard struggled for a moment, grabbing for the gun with both his hands as Phoenix's thumb pressed deeper into his throat. Unable to grasp the weapon, he rolled off Phoenix and collapsed to the ground, rubbing his neck.

Ignoring the man lying to his side, Phoenix swung his gun toward the guard standing in front of him, firing off several rounds. The bullets caught the guard squarely in the back, and he fell forward. He hit the ground and lay still.

In an instant Phoenix was standing over the corpse, pulling the gun from his loose grip. Standing, he turned to Panther. The man in front of her rolled onto his hands and knees, trying to stand. She quickly struck him across the midsection with her boot. He doubled over from the blow. She kicked him hard in the side of the head, and he crashed back to the ground.

"Panther!" Phoenix shouted. Martina lifted her head, fixing her eyes on him.

"Catch!" he shouted, flinging the weapon toward her.

Panther reached up and snatched the gun out of the air. The small weapon twirled easily in her hand, sliding into her grip. Her fingers curled around the butt of the gun.

The man lying on the ground at her feet rolled onto his side, doubled over. Slowly, he unwound his hand from his stomach. Planting his hands on the ground, he gazed up at Panther. His eyes met the muzzle of a pistol pointed directly at his forehead.

"If I were you, I wouldn't move," she hissed.

The man went limp, fear in his eyes. The look on her face left no doubt in his mind that she would pull the trigger if he disobeyed. Quickly, Panther stepped over him and grabbed a pair of handcuffs off his belt. She stepped on his back, flattening him on the stone. Yanking his arms back sharply, she slapped the cuffs on his wrists.

Panther scanned her surrounding. The man between her and Phoenix was climbing to his feet. Anger blazed in his eyes, which were locked on Vinny.

Martina quickly trained her weapon on him and fired. The bullet hit his knee. His leg collapsed, and he crashed to the ground. He knelt on the hard stone, unable to regain his feet. Intense pain immediately replaced the fury in his eyes.

Moondog was bent over the final man, whom she had already handcuffed. She reached down, pulled two extra magazines of ammunition from his belt, and stuck them in her flight suit pocket. Straightening her back, she turned to her companions.

"Hey, Moondog," Panther said, touching her finger to the side of her face.

Moondog brushed her left hand along her cheek. Her palm came away covered with blood.

"Shit," Moondog muttered. "That's a bloody little scratch." She wiped her hand on her flight suit, leaving a red print across the drab green fabric.

"C'mon," Panther said, turning her attention back toward the entrance to the Capitol.

Standing between the marble pillars, Miles watched in horror. Martina turned and raised her weapon, aiming it directly at his head. Miles did not wait around to hear the weapon fire. He spun on his heel and ran, dashing back into the relative safety of the building.

"Shit," Panther said, surprised at the speed with which the large man moved.

"Let's go," she said to her friends, lowering her weapon and taking off after Miles. The sound of combat boots on stone filled her ears as Moondog and Phoenix followed on her heels.

The three pilots rushed into the foyer, skidding to a stop in the center of the room. The trio surevyed their surroundings, eyes playing over the large, open area. The ceiling rose high above their heads into the high dome. Bright lights illuminated the clean white walls and the polished marble floor. Miles was nowhere to be seen.

"Where the hell did he go?" Moondog whispered.

"Shhh," Panther replied. The other two fell silent. The echo of footsteps drifted to their ears, the sound rapidly diminishing as the runner sprinted away.

"That way," she said, pointing.

Moondog and Phoenix turned their heads toward the sound, about to run after Miles.

"Wait," Martina said. "Vinny, get to the House chamber. That's where the President and everyone else are. Get them the hell out of this place."

"Right," Phoenix nodded, immediately running in the opposite direction.

"Moondog," Panther said as he disappeared down the hall, "let's get the bastard."

They rushed after Miles.

~ 24 ~

The long, polished corridors of the Capitol were silent and empty, devoid of the normal activity of tourists moving reverently through the halls and of congressional aides going about their business. Even the expected scattering of security guards was absent, raising Panther's suspicions as the two pilots raced down the hallway, weapons drawn, boots pounding against the stone floor.

As they sprinted from the foyer into the hall, Panther caught sight of Miles rushing away from them. Hearing their rapid footfalls, he glanced over his shoulder at the two pilots. He ran faster, trying to put as much distance between himself and them as possible.

The two pilots were slowly gaining. Despite Miles' initial speed, he was quickly tiring. He struggled to keep up his pace, knowing full well he was running for his life. Equally determined to stop him, the pilots followed, gradually closing the distance on him.

Martina fired off a round as she ran, and the loud shot echoed through the long, empty halls. The bullet missed Miles by inches, hitting the wall beside him. Hearing the gun go off, he ducked into a nearby hallway.

Panther cursed under her breath as he disappeared. The two pilots slid to a stop in front of the doorway, boots fighting for traction on the slick tile surface. They turned to race down the hallway after him.

The walls of this hall were narrower. Ahead of them, Miles dashed down the corridor. Seeing him, both Moondog and Panther raised their weapons.

Miles stopped in front of a small door near the end of the hall. Quickly, he grabbed the doorknob, fighting with it for a second. Panther squeezed the trigger of her pistol again. The gun exploded just as the door swung open and Miles stumbled through it. He disappeared, unharmed.

Panther and Moondog ran through the door after him. A long, black metal staircase stretched out before them, leading down into the ground below the Capitol.

Panther heard the ringing of boots on metal as Miles ran down the stairs beneath them. The two pilots followed, leaping down the stairs. They barely managed to keep their footing as they jumped from landing to landing. Through the openings between the steps, Panther saw Miles below them, rushing ever downward.

Reaching the bottom of the stairs, Miles took off at a run again, dashing away from the stairwell. Two flights above him, Martina saw him rush off. She quickened her pace, leaping down the steps and barely managing to land on her feet. One false step, and the resulting tumble was sure to twist her ankle or worse. Despite that fact, she jumped from flight to flight with as much speed as she could muster. Not to be left behind, Moondog stayed close on her heels, seemingly unconcerned with the danger of falling.

Panther's boots hit the hard concrete floor at the bottom of the stairs, and she ran in the direction Miles had disappeared. Before her stretched a dimly lit tunnel, with walls, ceiling, and floor all made of the same gray concrete that her boots now dug into.

Wiring and pipes ran along the walls and ceiling. The tunnels under Washington, D.C., supposedly ran for miles.

Miles was nowhere to be seen. Panther rushed into the tunnel, glancing from side to side as she ran. Ahead of her, the tunnel ended, opening up into a wider area. As she ran out of the tunnel, something hit her in the side of her face, knocking her to the ground.

Panther tumbled back across the concrete, rolling into a crouch. Her head was spinning from the blow. Shaking her head, she looked up. A group of men dressed as security guards surrounded her. They seemed unarmed. A large collection of assault rifles leaned up against the wall, but the men left the weapons in place. Moondog skidded to a stop beside her and trained her gun forward.

Panther slowly drew herself up to her full height, eyeing the crowd surrounding her without lowering her weapon. They drew closer, tightening the circle around the pilots. Two men stepped in front of the tunnel leading back to the stairs, closing off the way back to the Capitol. Panther and Moondog moved closer together until they stood back to back, guns pointed toward the crowd. For a moment no one spoke. The group of men stood motionless, staring at the pilots in the damp, cold silence.

Miles was talking in a low voice to a man in a guard uniform. The man nodded and motioned for most of the others to follow. They passed Panther and Moondog, each picking up a rifle before vanishing into the tunnel behind them. At least twenty men remained, surrounding the two pilots.

"Drop the gun, Colonel," Miles' voice echoed from outside the circle.

Panther shifted her weight, as she glared threateningly at the crowd surrounding her.

"Drop the gun or I'll kill you," Miles repeated, stepping from the shadows to stand between the two men holding the guns.

"Why should I?" Panther demanded. "You're going to kill me whether or not I do."

"True," the general said. "I am going to kill you, and the Commander, and everyone else in this building who isn't loyal to me."

"If you kill everyone who isn't loyal to you, you'll wipe out the majority of this country's population," Panther replied coolly.

"The others will fall in line once I crush the leadership," Miles replied. "You forget that I will control the military."

"And you forget that most people who join the military do so to protect this nation from power-hungry scumbags such as yourself."

"Insult me all you want, Colonel," Miles replied. "The facts still stand. In a matter of moments you will be dead, and I will control the most powerful nation on Earth."

"Do you seriously think you can hold this country and the rest of the world at bay with a ragtag group of poorly trained terrorists?" Panther askcd. "Every freedom-loving nation on the planet will band together with the American people to overthrow you, even if you somehow manage to succeed."

"And who is going to stop me from succeeding, Colonel?" Miles challenged. "You and the Commander?"

"You bet your ass we will!" Moondog said.

"I admire your determination, Commander, but it's foolish," Miles said. "Can't you see I've already won?"

"That's what you think," Panther said. "Even if you do kill us and everyone here, you will eventually be overthrown."

"I could argue this with you all day, Colonel," Miles said. "It doesn't really matter, because in a few minutes you'll be dead. Now, if you don't mind, I have to take over a country." He stepped out of the circle and walked back toward the stairs.

"Kill them," he said, speaking to another man standing in the shadows. "Make it as brutal as you want." Miles disappeared from sight. After a moment Panther heard the echo of shoes on metal as he climbed the stairs back to the Capitol. Some of the men followed him. A dozen remained behind, surrounding the two pilots.

Panther shifted her weight, preparing to fend off an attack as a second man stepped from the shadows. As he came into the light, she recognized him as the man who held them captive in Colombia. He had traded his tattered fatigues for more American attire and had trimmed his beard, but he still had the same cracked yellow teeth in his sadistic smile. He approached the two women slowly, looking at them with malicious glee.

"So what do you get out of all this?" Panther asked before he could speak.

"Excuse me?" Kalliff stopped in his tracks.

"I said, what do you get from this?" Panther asked. "You do all the work, Miles walks in and takes over the country, and you get nothing from it. Looks to me like you got a bad deal."

Kalliff laughed. "Don't try to trick me," he hissed. "The downfall of the United States is something I have wanted for years. Once your country crumbles, all the Arab nations of the world will be free from its oppression."

"Free to oppress their own people and slaughter innocents," Panther said.

"You're lying," Kalliff hissed.

"Do you think your situation will improve at all if

Miles takes power? It won't. You'll get nothing from this."

"I know what you're up to, you crafty bitch," Kalliff snorted, "and it won't work. You can't talk your way out of this."

"I know," Panther smirked. "There's no reasoning with thick-skulled imbeciles like yourself."

"You have caused me far too much trouble," Kalliff said. "I'm going to enjoy watching you die."

"You're going to be disappointed," Panther said.

"Kill them," Kalliff ordered his men.

"What do you think, Moondog," Panther asked calmly as the men moved toward them. "Should we kill him?"

"Absolutely," Moondog said, smiling. "I think we should kill them all."

"Down in flames," Panther said, fire dancing in her eyes.

"Damn straight," Moondog replied, her maniacal grin accented by the blood on her face.

The man in front of Panther lunged for her. She immediately pointed her pistol at him and pulled the trigger. The shot caught him in the center of the stomach, and he staggered back, gripping his gut. He pulled his hand away, looking at the blood covering his fingers before falling backward and landing against the concrete with a loud thud.

The group of thugs surrounding Panther and Moondog moved in, closing the gap created by the fallen man. Panther shifted her weapon, firing off a second shot and then a third. The two men directly in front of her dropped to the ground, each with a bullet in the chest. Behind her gunfire echoed as Moondog easily dispatched two others.

Panther shifted her aim to the left, squeezing off a fourth round. At the same instant someone tackled her from the right, knocking her to the ground. The shot went wild, flying harmlessly into the far wall.

Panther's left shoulder banged into the concrete. She rolled onto her back as the man crashed on top of her, pinning her right arm to her chest. Her weapon lay at her left side, muzzle pointed at her arm, still in her grip.

The man on top of Panther pushed himself into a sitting position, swinging his legs over her chest and straddling her. He pressed his weight down onto her, crushing her arm against her chest. Panther struggled to move her hand, twisting her wrist around and trying to aim the gun.

Seeing her move the weapon, the man thrusted his hand on top of hers, keeping it pressed firmly against her chest. The gun remained aimed at her left arm. Panther carefully relaxed her index finger, removing it from the trigger so that she wouldn't shoot herself as she struggled with her assailant.

Panther ran her eyes quickly over her adversary, spying a knife hanging from his belt. She reached up with her free hand, whipped the blade from the sheath, thrust the tip into his thigh, and twisted the blade ninety degrees, eliciting a sharp wail of pain. Then she jerked the blade toward her, pulling the knife the length of his thigh. The man screamed again, momentarily releasing his grip on her other hand.

Panther immediately shifted her weight. She pulled the knife from his thigh and grabbed his shirt, yanking him down as she shifted her hips up, throwing him off her. The man crashed to the side, holding his bloody leg. Panther leapt back to her feet.

Meanwhile, Moondog watched the men drawing in around her as she slowly stood, waiting for the next attack to come. She kept her gun trained forward, aiming into the gang encircling her. *If I have to go down, I'm taking as many of you with me as I can.* The manifestation of her thoughts blazed within her eyes, highlighted by the blood running down her face. Her lips curled up in a menacing smile.

Her challenge did not go unanswered. A man standing directly in front of her rushed for her. Moondog waited until he was within an inch of her before rapidly sidestepping and firing. The bullet caught him in the chest, killing him instantly.

As the dead man fell forward, two others lunged for Moondog. One grabbed her left wrist. Before she could twist to get free, the second took hold of her right wrist. She struggled to get loose as the second man reached forward and yanked the gun from her hand.

A third man stepped forward, striking her sharply in the side of the neck. Her eyes fell shut. She slumped to the ground and lay still.

One of the thugs grabbed Panther from behind, looping his arm around her neck. Panther flipped the knife over again and rammed the point into the flesh behind her. The man grunted sharply as the metal slipped into his leg, but held his grip on the pilot.

A second man dove forward, catching her right arm against his body and pulling the gun from her hand before leaping back. He flipped the weapon over in his hand, bringing the butt of the gun down hard against the side of her throat.

Her eyes shut and her body went limp.

The man holding Martina released her and she fell to the ground, lying motionless on the concrete.

~ 25 ~

Phoenix ran through the silent corridors of the Capitol. His heavy footfalls echoed through the empty halls as he dashed across polished tile floors. He ignored the large marble statues and the paintings on the walls, heading for the chamber of the House of Representatives as quickly as he could.

Suddenly, the thunder of applause drowned out the loud ringing of Vinny's combat boots on the stone. He turned toward the sound, reaching the door to the House chamber just as the ovation died down. He stopped outside and gazed at the pistol in his hand. Realizing he would be shot without question if he entered the room holding a weapon, he stuck the gun in his pocket and zipped it closed, then pushed the door open and stepped inside.

In sharp contrast to the deserted hallways of the Capitol, the brightly lit House of Representatives was packed. For a second Phoenix stared in awe at the size of the room. He had seen the State of the Union address televised before, but that didn't compare with actually being there.

Each tier of the large room was filled with desks. The desks were occupied by the 300-plus Congressmen and Congresswomen. Joining them were the United States Senators, the Joint Chiefs, various cabinet members, and many others. The room was absolutely packed with people.

President Webster stood at the center of the chamber, behind a large podium. Behind him were the stars and stripes of the American flag, as well as several other flags bearing symbols of the United States government. The row of chairs behind Webster was occupied by the Vice President and other important members of the government.

Vinny ran his eyes along the walls of the House. Dozens of cameras, complete with crews, were filming the speech, either pointed at the President or sweeping the crowd. Vinny noticed a few men in simple black suits spaced throughout the room.

The applause faded away and the scraping of chairs filled the room as everyone sat down. At the front of the room, Webster adjusted his notes and continued his oration, speaking in a loud, clear voice that rang through the chamber. As soon as the President started to talk, everyone immediately fell silent, listening intently.

Phoenix didn't pay attention to Webster's words. He turned to the tall African American man standing beside him. The man's hair was combed back neatly, and he wore an impeccably tailored black suit and a black tie. He stood motionless by the door, face set in stone. He was not listening to the speech either. Instead he was eyeing Vinny suspiciously. No one else had even noticed the pilot slip into the room.

"Are you Secret Service?" Vinny whispered to him. Miles may have been able to replace the hired security detail with his people, but there was no way he would be able to infiltrate his minions into the Secret Service, especially the President's personal security detail.

"What?" the man responded, surprised by his question.

"Are you Secret Service?" Vinny repeated, quietly.

The man looked at him for a moment, then

nodded.

"Agent Hayes," he said.

"Good," Vinny said, speaking softly so that only the agent could hear him. "Listen to me. There's a bomb planted under the building. It's going to explode in a matter of minutes. You have to get President Webster and everyone else out of here now."

"Follow me," the agent whispered, opening the door and slipping out of the chamber. Vinny slid through the door after him, shutting it silently. He turned and followed Hayes, who was walking quickly through the halls around the large chamber.

The agent ducked through a side door, dashed down a short flight of stairs, and then raced through another hall. Vinny stayed close behind him. Hayes stopped in front of a door. He pushed it open and peered through, motioning for Vinny to look inside. The agent whispered something terse into the cuff on his right wrist.

Vinny stuck his head through the door. He was standing on the floor of the House. In front of him, President Webster stood at the podium, with his side to Vinny, continuing with his speech. Everyone except the Secret Service agents were focused too intently on the President to notice Vinny and Hayes peering through the door.

Phoenix watched as four men seated in the front row stood simultaneously and approached the podium. All were dressed just like the man beside him and were just as neatly groomed. They moved quickly, walking up the steps on either side of the President. Webster stopped his speech, a look of surprise on his face. The men quickly surrounded him and led him from the podium toward the door where Vinny and the agent waited.

Suddenly, a loud staccato pulse of gunfire filled the room. Instinctively, Vinny threw himself to the floor. Hayes dropped into a crouch beside him, his face registering shock. Vinny cautiously lifted his head, surveying the room in horror.

At least a dozen gunmen had burst through the doorways throughout the House chamber. Each clutched a semiautomatic weapon. They opened fire, spraying bullets into the thick crowd.

The room instantly erupted into complete chaos. Screams of horror and pain filled the air. People leapt to their feet and began to run toward every available exit, but the sheer number of people in the room made it nearly impossible for anyone to reach the door.

All the while the gunmen loosed their fire, spraying bullets into the crowd indiscriminately, trying to cut down as many people as possible. The shots ricocheted into the crowd, bouncing off the hardwood desks and the walls of the House. But the vast majority of the projectiles hit the people rushing for the exits, cutting down civilians, Senators, Representatives, and military men, as well as the cameramen, who were frantically trying to get footage of the attack while trying to avoid the flying bullets.

The room was covered in blood. Many people lay dead or motionless on the floor or slumped over the desks. Others were writhing in pain, screaming as life ran from them. Still more ran for the doors, holding bloody wounds. Some had flattened themselves against the carpet or were huddled beneath the desks, hoping to escape the rain of bullets. A few stood motionless, too petrified to move.

Vinny watched one woman who froze in the center of the House floor, screaming in stark terror. Others rushed past her or dropped to the floor, trying to save themselves, but the woman simply stood in middle of the room and wailed until the spray of bullets cut her down and she fell to the floor lifeless and silent.

Only the Secret Service agents managed to keep their cool. The four men escorting Webster away from the podium pulled him to the floor as the initial shots rang through the air. Two of the men lay to either side of him, and the other two were on top of him, shielding the President from the flying bullets.

The remaining Secret Service agents in the room immediately drew their weapons and trained them on the shooters, picking them off one by one. The sheer size of the frantic crowd made it hard for the agents to get many good shots. However, they took every clear chance they had. The number of gunmen slowly began to diminish.

The two Secret Service agents pressing Webster to the floor moved off him, taking up position beside him. One of the agents whispered something to the President, pointing to the door where Phoenix and Hayes crouched. Webster nodded and began to crawl toward the door. The four Secret Service agents moved with him, shielding his body with theirs.

Hayes had drawn his own weapon as soon as the shooting started. Vinny pulled himself into a crouch and carefully removed the pistol from his pocket, aiming it at the room.

"I thought you said they had planted a bomb," the agent whispered to Vinny.

"That's what I was told. They knew we were trying to warn you. They must have decided to do something before we got the chance."

"How did they get through the guards out front?"

"The guards outside were replaced."

"How on Earth..."

"I don't know," Vinny said, shaking his head.

The bullets continued to fly through the room, a few hitting the door frame where Vinny and Hayes crouched. They ignored the sharp crack of metal and wood, watching Webster as he crawled forward.

The other Secret Service agents had managed to kill two men standing in front of one of the larger doors, opening a path to the outside. Seeing a clear route away from the bullets, the people in the room began to rush for the door, flooding out of the chamber. The gunmen rapidly shifted their fire, aiming for the fleeing crowd. They tried to block the door with bullets. Despite the gunfire, people continued to run for the door, trying to escape the carnage.

The President was now within a foot of the door. Hayes glanced at Vinny and nodded. The two men reached down, each grabbing one of Webster's arms, and pulled him rapidly from the room. The other four Secret Service agents leapt to their feet and rushed out of the House chamber. Vinny and Hayes slammed the door shut behind them.

Safe from the flying bullets, President Webster took a deep breath and brushed off his suit. He stared back toward the door, making no attempt to disguise the horror and shock on his face as he tried to control his breathing. The Secret Service agents immediately reformed their human wall around him.

Webster slowly turned to face Vinny.

"I'd ask you what the hell is going on, Captain," he said, "but I think I can figure out why you were trying to pull me out of there. Thank you."

"You're welcome, sir," Vinny stuttered.

"Sir," Agent Hayes said to Webster, "we really need to get out of here. There's a bomb under the building."

Webster nodded.

"Please come with us, Captain," he said to Vinny.

"Yes, sir," Vinny replied.

The five Secret Service agents immediately tightened their circle around the President and began to walk rapidly down the hall, leading him away from the House chamber and the gunmen. They moved fast, scanning the area around them much as fighter pilots on a combat mission would, weapons drawn. Phoenix guessed they were headed for a back exit where Webster could slip away quickly and safely.

At a loss for what else to do, Vinny fell in silently behind the Secret Service agents, matching their pace as they hurried through the vast, empty corridor. He kept his own gun drawn, watching the hall behind him for gunmen. But the corridor remained empty except for the small party spiriting the President to safety.

The tall, black Secret Service agent led the way, navigating through the halls. The agents moved quietly, needing little direction to perform their duty. When they communicated at all, it was simply to point out the direction to take. No words were spoken as they moved. Webster and Vinny were left to watch the scene play out before them as they hurried along with the agents.

Hayes pushed open a door, revealing a set of stairs. Two other Secret Service agents proceeded up the steps, with Webster on their heels. The next two agents stayed close behind him. Vinny and Hayes brought up the rear.

As the door shut behind Vinny, the screams and gunfire died away, leaving only the sound of their footsteps. They made their way quickly up the steps.

The Secret Service agent at the head of the small group pushed open the door leading away from the stairwell and stepped out onto the main floor. Webster followed, only to have the four men circle around him once more. The agent leading the group pointed down the hall, and they started to move again.

Screaming and gunfire filled Vinny's ears again as he stepped out into the hall. The distant wail of sirens floated above the commotion. The local police were finally on their way.

Better later than never, the pilot thought as he turned and followed the Secret Service agents down the empty halls away from the chaos. He vigilantly checked behind him every few steps but saw no one.

The agent in front of Webster stepped out into a cross hallway. As he did so, several loud gunshots rang out. The agent did not have time to react. The bullets caught him in the side. He was dead before he hit the ground.

The two men on either side of Webster grabbed him, pulling him away from the gunfire. The hidden shooter continued to depress the trigger, sending a stream of bullets into the far wall and blocking their path.

"That way," said Hayes, pointing back in the direction they had come. The two agents holding Webster spun the President around, hauling him away from the shooter. He followed without protest.

They had taken only a few steps when a stream of bullets burst from another door, cutting off their only escape route. The small group stopped dead in their tracks, surrounded. The four remaining Secret Service agents and Vinny quickly surrounded the President, shielding him with their bodies. Guns pointed outward, they stood and waited.

The gunfire stopped abruptly. The sharp, slow ringing of boots against tile replaced it as five men with pistols stepped from the door in front of Phoenix. A sixth carried an M-16. They moved across the hallway and stopped, leveling their guns at the small party trapped in the center of the room. Another group of men stepped from the second hall. Walking in front of the dead agent, they lined up across the hall and pointed their weapons at the President.

For a moment no one moved. The agents glared

coldly at the gunmen, refusing to lower their weapons. The intruders simply glared back. The hall remained silent except for the sirens wailing in the distance.

The sudden bark of a pistol cut through the silence. The gunman standing in front of Vinny with the M-16 toppled backward, cut down by a Secret Service agent's bullet. He landed flat on his back against the hard tile surface. For a moment everyone looked at his body.

Then gunmen on both sides of the hall opened up with their weapons. At the same time two Secret Service agents pulled Webster to the floor, covering him with their bodies. The remaining three agents and Vinny dropped to a crouch and began to fire at the gunmen.

The spray of fire immediately cut down a second agent. The other agents managed to momentarily avoid the hail of bullets as they began methodically shooting at the attackers. One of the two agents shielding Webster rose to a crouch and began to fire at the men behind Vinny.

Bullets zipping around him, Vinny carefully selected a target and squeezed off a round. The bullet caught the man ahead of him in the chest, killing him. Vinny shifted his fire to the right and pulled the trigger again, dropping another man to the floor.

The Secret Service agents' well-placed shots killed a fourth man, and then a fifth. Hayes ended another's life. The bullets cut down a third Secret Service agent who stood opposite Vinny.

As if on cue, the remaining gunmen ceased fire. Several ejected their magazines and reloaded their weapons. Surprised by the sudden silence, Vinny and Hayes glanced around, unsure how to react. The second agent moved away from the President to face the men standing behind Vinny. Webster rose into a crouching position.

"President Webster, what a pleasant surprise," a voice said from the door.

"I thought I was going to have to let a bomb do my dirty work," Miles said, stepping into the hall. The large man held an M-16 across his body. He stepped to the center of the corridor in front of his henchmen and smiled. "Instead I get to kill you myself."

"Not if I have anything to say about it," Phoenix challenged. The young pilot drew himself up to his full height, placing himself between Webster and the gunmen. Anger blazed in his eyes as he pointed his small pistol at Miles' chest.

"Vince Carlton, isn't it?" Miles asked, aiming his own weapon at the pilot. "The little punk who hijacked my bomber and nearly ruined everything. Do you have any idea how much trouble you've caused me, Captain?"

"Obviously not enough," Vinny snarled, leaning toward Miles.

"And I suppose you think you're going to stop me all by yourself, don't you?" Miles challenged. "Your friends Colonel Redrick and Commander Ansetti thought they could stop me too. And now they're both dead."

Vinny's face visibly paled. His expression turned to one of shock. He stepped closer to Miles, channeling the fierce anger building within him at the large man.

"Then it's going to be even more enjoyable when I kill you," Vinny hissed.

Miles laughed. "Gutsy and determined, but foolish. In fact, downright stupid. Just like your dead friends." He smiled at the rage burning in Vinny's eyes. "If you had any sense at all, Captain, you would never have stuck your nose where it didn't belong."

"And let you take over this nation? I'd hijack that plane again in an instant."

"You didn't stop me," Miles laughed. "In a matter of minutes everyone in this building is going to be dead, and I'll have won. All you did was get yourself and your friends killed."

"This isn't over yet," Vinny snarled, tightening his finger around the trigger.

Phoenix was quick, but Miles was quicker. The sound of gunfire erupted in the hallway once again. A bullet slammed into Phoenix's right thigh, and a second hit his shoulder. The young pilot gasped, his eyes growing wide with pain. He dropped to his knees, eyes blazing with fire as he stared wildly at Miles.

"Foolish," Miles said with a laugh. "And dead. Just like your friends."

"Then I'll watch you burn in hell," Vinny hissed, trying to raise his pistol. His arm refused to move.

Vinny's eyes shut, and he fell forward, face down. Blood spread out along the polished tile floor. The pilot did not regain his feet.

~ 26 ~

Martina slowly opened her eyes. Her head was throbbing with a terrible dull ache, and her throat felt as if it had almost been crushed. She blinked, trying to focus her vision in the dim light. All she saw was the gray walls of the tunnel and her own feet, splayed out along the concrete floor. She was sitting upright, propped against something.

Panther attempted to move her arms, only to feel a thick coil of rope dig into her biceps. Startled, she glanced down. A length of rope was curled twice around her chest, pinning her arms to her sides. Her hands were pulled across her chest. The coils were wrapped around her wrists, binding her hands together.

Slowly, she turned her head, looking over her shoulder. Moondog sat with her back against Martina's. The Navy pilot's head was slumped forward and her eyes were shut, but she was breathing slowly and evenly. The rope wrapped around Martina's chest was also pulled around Moondog's body, binding them.

Martina looked around. Kalliff and his minions had disappeared, leaving the two pilots tied together on the floor of the tunnel. She turned her head to the left and saw a large device sitting on the concrete beside them. Wires ran around it, connecting the lights of a glowing digital timer to the center of the massive object. The red diodes displayed the digits 8:31. Martina watched in horror as the numbers slowly ticked down.

"Moondog!" she hissed into the Navy pilot's ear, trying to keep her voice as low as possible. Moondog moved her head slightly but did not open her eyes.

"Moondog!" Martina repeated, slightly louder.

Moondog lifted her head and muttered something incomprehensible, then dropped her chin back onto her chest and remained still.

"Wake up, dammit!"

"Huh?" Moondog lifted her head and opened her eyes. "What's going on?"

She looked around, her dazed mind trying to make sense of her surroundings.

"We're strapped to a fucking bomb!" Martina replied.

"What the hell..." Moondog said, her eyes landing on the large device beside the two women.

"Oh, fuck," she said simply, staring at the glowing red numbers. "Please tell me you've got that pocketknife."

"I've got the knife," Martina said. "It's in my pocket, and I can't reach it."

"Shit. How the hell are we going to get out of this?"

"I'm working on it, I'm working on it," Martina said, studying their surroundings. The tunnel was completely empty save for the two pilots, the bomb, and the wiring and pipes running along the walls. A few dim light bulbs barely managed to illuminate the darkness.

Martina twisted her hands, trying to see if she could wriggle free of the ropes, but they were coiled so tightly that she couldn't move. After a moment she gave up struggling, turning her attention back to the tunnel.

"You better come up with something damn quick,"

Moondog replied. "I really don't like the idea of being blown to tiny pieces and buried down here."

A glint of metal on the far wall caught Martina's eye. One of the pipes had broken from the wall, leaving the sharp fastening exposed. The jagged metal edge protruded several inches from the concrete, about four feet off the ground.

"Over there!" she said.

"Where?" Moondog asked. She scanned the far wall with a puzzled look on her face.

"Can you walk?" Martina asked.

"Yeah, my head hurts like hell, but my legs feel fine," Moondog said. "What do you see?"

"There's a jagged piece of metal sticking out of the wall over there. We can use it cut the ropes."

"Let's do it," Moondog said, pulling her legs up underneath her.

"All right. Stand up on three," Martina said. "One...two...three." The two women pushed themselves slowly off the ground so that they stood back to back. The rope remained tightly coiled around their bodies.

Moving as quickly as they could, the pilots made their way to the far wall. They moved awkwardly, tripping over each other's feet, and nearly toppling over several times. Finally, they managed to stumble to the broken bracket.

Panther turned to face the wall. She placed her wrists directly over the broken metal protruding from the concrete. The jagged edge caught the rope. Martina moved her hands back and forth, sawing through the rope with the edge of the broken pipe fastening. The metal nipped at her skin, drawing blood along her hands and wrists, but it slowly managed to cut through the rope fibers. One by one they broke apart. Martina could feel the rope around her wrists loosening. After what seemed like ages, the final strand snapped, freeing her hands.

Pulling her hands apart, Martina ripped the coils from her wrists. She pulled the rope up over her head and stepped free. The Navy pilot quickly freed her own wrists and tossed the rope to the ground.

"Let's get the fuck out of here," Martina said.

"Where the hell are the stairs?"

Martina swept her eyes around the tunnel, looking for the nearest exit. "That looks like them," she said, pointing to a door on the far wall.

The Air Force pilot quickly set off toward the door. Moondog shrugged and followed her friend. A few feet from the door, Martina suddenly stopped, freezing in her tracks. Moondog turned, giving her a quizzical stare. The sound of voices drifted to her ears, coming from their escape route.

Martina took the knife from her flight suit and flipped open the blade. She nodded to Moondog and walked forward again slowly. Moondog followed.

Two men stood just inside the door, chatting idly in a slightly nervous tone as they blocked the path to a metal staircase. Panther saw their outlines as she drew closer. Quickly, she raised her knife and stepped toward the man on her left. She hoped to catch the men off guard and dispatch them quickly with the small blade.

As she lunged for her target, the man to her right turned, catching sight of her. He shouted to his companion, who immediately jumped back and spun around to face his attacker. Panther quickly slashed at him with the blade.

She nicked his shoulder with the knife as he leapt back again. A trickle of blood ran down his chest, the cut too shallow to do more than sting. The man stepped forward and reached for her wrist, grabbing her hand before she could turn the weapon back to him. At the same time, he swung his left fist at the side of her head. Unable to move in time, Panther took the blow on her right cheek.

Panther staggered back awkwardly, twisting to the side as she did. With his opponent temporarily off balance, her attacker quickly tried to pry the knife from her fingers.

Shaking off the blow, Panther drove her foot into his shin and raked the edge of her boot down his leg. The man yelped. He ripped the knife from her hand as he leapt back in surprise and pain.

As Panther grappled with the first sentry, the second man turned to Moondog. The Navy pilot stopped several feet from him, cocked her head to the side, planted her hands on her hips, and waited for him to advance, a faint smile tracing across her lips.

The guard studied her for a moment, unsure of just how to react to her strange challenge. Slowly, he stepped forward, sizing her up. Balling his right hand into a fist, he threw a punch straight for her nose. The Navy pilot quickly sidestepped, blocking the blow with her left arm as she punched him in the jaw.

He stumbled to the side, gripping his chin with his hand. Moondog advanced, swinging her foot up and kicking him squarely in the stomach. The man lost his balance and toppled over, landing flat on his back on the hard concrete.

Before he could regain his feet, Moondog was standing over him with a sadistic grin. His eyes grew wide as the pilot drew her foot up and smashed her boot down on his throat. The blow was forceful enough to crush his windpipe, but Moondog held her foot on his neck as he fought to draw air into his lungs. He wriggled desperately for a few moments, grasping her boot with both hands and trying to lift it from his throat. Moondog leaned her weight further into his neck as his strength ebbed away. Finally, his eyes closed and his body went still.

The first man lunged for Panther, slashing at her with the knife. The blade sank into the flesh on Panther's upper left arm, leaving a deep cut. She let out a sharp cry of pain as the knife dug into her muscle. She thrust her fist into the man's stomach, stopping his forward motion. He gasped and stepped back, leaving the knife sticking in her arm.

Panther quickly reached up and grabbed the blade's protruding hilt, pulling the Victorinox from her flesh. She swung the weapon at the man in front of her. He jumped back, avoiding the knife. Panther flipped the blade over in an instant, slashing toward him again. Again the man leaped backward, barely avoiding the knife. As he did, the back of his heel caught on the edge of the first step, and he crashed onto the flight of stairs behind him.

Panther turned the blade over in her hand and dropped her knee onto the man's chest, planting him against the metal stairs. She plunged the knife behind his ear, killing him quickly. Martina stood, wiped the blood off her knife, folded the blade, and stuck it back in her pocket.

Moondog watched the man on the floor in front of her for a moment. Convinced he was dead, the Navy pilot removed her boot from his throat. She turned around, finding herself face to face with Kalliff's huge henchman. The broad-shouldered man easily dwarfed the pilot, his shadow covering her body. Before she could react, he reached down and grabbed her by the throat, flinging her into the wall.

Panther stepped back into the tunnel to see her friend fly past her and crash into the concrete, sliding inertly to the ground. Moondog lay still, moaning slightly. Panther turned her head. Kalliff stood against the far wall, smiling his malicious grin as the huge man advanced toward her.

As he approached, Panther swung her foot up.

The toe of her boot caught him squarely between the legs, seemingly with no effect. He stepped forward and grabbed Panther by the collar, hauling her into the air with one arm.

Martina gasped, her eyes growing wide with surprise as she stared into the face of the massive man holding her above the ground.

"I remember you," she choked.

The giant man wrapped his other hand around her left leg and lifted her over his head so that she was perpendicular to the ground, eight feet in the air. He straightened his arm, forcefully throwing Panther's entire body into the ceiling, creating little cracks in the concrete. He lowered her about a foot before smashing her back up against the hard stone. He immediately released her and stepped back.

Panther crashed to the floor in a rain of dust and debris. For a moment she lay splayed face down, trying to gain control over the pain running through every inch of her body. As the fog began to dissipate from her brain, she managed to push her left arm off the floor, rolling herself slowly onto her side.

Looking up through half-focused eyes, she saw the huge man step toward her. He kicked her in the face, knocking her onto her back. Leaning down over her, he smiled with a wide, broken-toothed grin and reached for her throat with his massive hand. A muffled warning in the back of Panther's head screamed for her to move, but her body refused to comply. Instead she stared dazed and wide-eyed as the man grabbed for her.

Suddenly, something crashed into the back of the man's head. He slowly straightened his back and turned. As he did, Moondog's fist collided with his temple. He stepped back and shook his head, glaring angrily at the Navy pilot. He backhanded her across the face as if he were flicking away a pesky insect.

The blow lifted Moondog off her feet, and she crashed to the floor several feet away.

Moondog fell and skidded across the ground, coming to a stop in the center of the tunnel. As she pushed herself off the concrete, her fingers curled around the rope that had bound her wrists minutes ago. Picking it up, she stood and began to walk back to the huge thug.

The man turned his attention back to Panther, only to find her standing face to face with him. Moondog's brief attack had bought her the few seconds she needed to regain control of her senses and get back on her feet. Pain and fire danced in her eyes as she glared at her assailant.

Panther stepped forward, smashing the heel of her palm into the bridge of his nose. The bone cracked as her hand hit it, and blood began to pour from his nostrils. He never even flinched. He grabbed Panther by the collar and flung her into the far wall.

Panther fell to the ground, landing hard on her side. The large man moved toward the dazed pilot, thrusting his foot into her stomach. She doubled over with a gasp, wrapping her arms across her body.

The man reached for her throat. His fingers brushed Panther's skin as Moondog threw the rope around his neck. She yanked back hard, jerking him away from Panther. He stepped back. Panther was now just beyond his reach. The Navy pilot crossed the rope behind his neck and pulled the ends in opposite directions with all her might.

The thug's eyes grew wide as the rope bit into his throat. His hands flew to his neck, and he desperately tried to dig his fingers underneath the thick coil, but the rope was too tight. He spun around wildly, trying to throw Moondog, but she refused to loosen her grip. She only tugged harder on the rope. The man gagged and gasped for air, tearing at the rope with all his strength. Moondog twisted the rope tighter, holding fast until his body went limp and he dropped to the floor like a sack full of bricks.

Releasing the rope, Moondog stepped over the large man's body to where Panther lay curled on the floor, looking up at her. She extended her hand to Martina. The Air Force pilot reached up and grabbed her wrist. Moondog pulled her to her feet.

"Thanks," Martina said, her voice raspy.

"You all right?" Moondog asked.

"Yeah," Martina said, looking at the large man's inert form. "Just got the wind knocked out of me a few too many times. Let's get outta here." She turned back to the door.

"Not so fast," a voice behind her said.

Moondog and Panther turned to see Kalliff standing a few feet from them, gun in hand.

"You're not going anywhere," he said.

"I suppose you're going to kill us both now, aren't you?" Martina asked tiredly.

"That's right," Kalliff said.

"I don't think so," Martina replied. She stepped into him quickly, knocking her left hand into his right as she pressed her fingers into his throat and forced him to the ground. He landed on his back, his gun pointing harmlessly at the wall.

Moondog planted her foot on Kalliff's chest, leaning into him. The terrorist exhaled sharply as the blow forced the air from his chest. Martina bent down, pulled the gun from his hand, and stood.

"Don't move," she said, leveling the weapon at his head. Moondog slowly lifted her foot. She took a step back, standing beside Martina and crossing her arms. Kalliff remained frozen on the floor.

"What do we do with him?" Moondog asked.

"He's not good enough for a bullet," Martina said, a sadistic grin spreading across her face. "Get that rope. I've got an idea."

Kalliff looked up at the pilot in apprehension, unable to hide the growing fear in his eyes as Moondog jogged back across the room. She quickly snatched up the rope and returned to where Martina stood.

"Roll over. Slowly," Martina said to Kalliff. He did as ordered.

"Tie him up. Tight," she said told Moondog.

The Navy woman dropped to her knees beside Kalliff. She pulled his arms behind his back and tightly wound the rope around his wrists. She looped the excess around his ankles, knotting it firmly.

Martina stuck the gun in her pocket and reached down, grabbing Kalliff by the feet. She dragged the terrorist across the concrete by his feet, letting his head bump against the hard floor. The rough surface scraped the skin on his face. She dropped his body next to the bomb. The timer now read just over four minutes.

"What are you doing?" Kalliff demanded.

"Making you a proper terrorist," Martina said, walking away.

"You're just going to leave me here?" he nearly screamed.

"Yep," Martina said, glancing over her shoulder. "Terrorists have a long history of suicide bombings."

Kalliff let out a long wail. Panther ignored him. She stepped over the large man and touched her fingers to his neck. There was no pulse.

"Let's get the fuck out of this place," she said to Moondog.

The two pilots raced for the stairs, leaving Kalliff screaming in the tunnel.

~ 27 ~

David Webster lifted his eyes from the young pilot lying face down on the polished tile floor to the large man leveling an M-16 at his chest.

"It's a shame to think that so many innocent people have died for nothing," he said to Miles, a slow, roiling anger reflected in his eyes and his voice. "You know, even if you kill everyone here, the United States government will still be in place. You won't have accomplished anything."

"Really?" Miles replied, cocking an eyebrow.

"The lines of succession are well established," Webster replied. "There is always one member of the cabinet who does not attend the State of the Union address, so this nation will have a leader just in case something like that happens. Anyone who went to middle school knows that."

"I know. Your Secretary of State," Miles laughed, "who has been working for me all along. How do you think I got in here in the first place? Somehow I replaced all your hired guards with men who were loyal to me. Everyone protecting this building, with the exception of your Secret Service agents, is under my command. And it doesn't take much to kill two men."

"And you think the American people and the American military will stand for something like this?" Webster said. "They will come together and overthrow you as soon as you claim power. All you've done is murder innocent people. Good people, like Captain Carlton."

"Carlton was a pest," Miles replied. "I'm glad I got to kill him."

"Carlton was a patriot," Webster said. "He put his country before himself. Unlike you."

"Spare me the bullshit," Miles said. "The kid's dead because he was stupid and stuck his nose where it didn't belong. And now I'm going to kill you too. Because in, oh—" Miles checked his watch—"two minutes the bomb beneath us is going to go off, and this whole building is going to come down. And I really don't want to be here when that happens."

He flipped off the safety on his weapon and let loose a volley of fire. The three men standing behind him also depressed their triggers, sending bullets flying toward Webster and the two Secret Service agents. The three thugs standing behind Webster stepped aside, careful to avoid the gunfire, and pointed their own weapons at Webster and the Secret Service agents.

Hayes leapt on top of the President, dragging him to the floor, and the gunfire narrowly missed Webster. The second agent was not so lucky. Caught in the crossfire, he was torn to pieces by the bullets, and he collapsed to the floor, his lifeblood spilling from several different wounds.

Covering Webster's body with his own, Hayes raised his gun and took careful aim at the nearest man. He squeezed the trigger, hitting his target squarely in the chest. The other men immediately shifted their fire toward him. Aiming his weapon again, the Secret Service agent waited for the bullets to cut through him.

Suddenly, one of the men in front of him fell to the ground, bleeding from a hole just above his ear. A second man dropped immediately after him as a bullet sliced through his chest. Three rapid shots dispatched the men standing behind him. In an instant Miles was alone, standing in the center of the room. He looked around in panic, a shocked expression on his face. The Secret Service agent stared in amazement as the gunfire ceased.

Two women leapt from the side hallway, placing themselves between Miles and Webster. Both wore the same dull-green flight suits as the young captain, except that silver oak leaves adorned their shoulders. The first woman stood a few inches shy of six feet, with a trim figure. Her long brown hair was pulled back, and her brown eyes seemed to be on fire. The left sleeve of her flight suit was soaked with blood from her shoulder to her elbow. She carried a pistol, which she leveled at Miles.

The second woman was shorter, but just as slim. Blood trickled from a cut at the corner of her left eye, covering the side of her striking face and matting her shoulder-length golden-brown hair. She reached down and snatched up the M-16 from the floor. She rested the rifle on her hip, also aiming at Miles. Specks of dust clung to their flight suits.

"You? How?" Miles stuttered, staring at the pair in disbelief.

"We're not that easy to kill," Moondog replied, flipping her hair over her shoulder with a twist of her head.

"Vinny..." Panther gasped, catching sight of Phoenix's limp, bleeding body. She turned her head back toward Miles, her eyes filled with a new, fearsome rage. The blazing ire sent a shiver of terror through the Secret Service agent.

"Where's Kalliff?" Miles demanded.

"About to be blown to the deepest pits of hell," Panther hissed. "Just like you."

She leveled her pistol directly at Miles' head.

Miles glanced anxiously from Panther to Moondog. The two women glared at him, faces set in stone. Neither moved. They each pointed the muzzle of their weapon at him, fire and rage burning in their eyes.

"Now, Colonel, be reasonable," Miles said, stepping back.

"That's right, beg me to spare your life," Panther hissed. "All your goons are dead. And you've got no one to protect you."

Miles opened his mouth to speak, then closed it again, seeing the expression in Martina's eyes. He was looking into the face of a cold-blooded killer, he realized, and there was nothing he could do to save himself.

Panther slowly curled her finger around the trigger and pulled it back.

A sudden pulse ripped through the entire building, knocking everyone to the floor as the bomb in the tunnel beneath the Capitol exploded, sending shock waves through the entire structure. A loud rumbling filled the air. The floor shook violently.

Statues toppled and pictures crashed from the walls. The hundreds of people fleeing the building fell to the ground, pitched off their feet by the violent tremors rocking the building. Cracks appeared in the walls, ceiling, and floors. The crashes from walls collapsing reverberated throughout the Capitol, echoing down the long hallways.

Directly above the small group around the President, cracks materialized in the marble walls, running up through the ceiling. The entire section collapsed with a thunderous clap. Debris rained down, covering the people on the floor with chunks of plaster and dust inches thick.

The rumbling gradually subsided. The floor and the walls stopped shaking, and the cracks ceased to grow. A last few crashes echoed through the long halls, and then everything fell silent. For a moment, nothing moved. Then the remaining, panicked people within the Capitol scrambled to their feet and ran for the doors.

Panther lifted her head, pushing the debris off her. She drew her sleeve across her eyes and opened them. By some miracle, the bomb blast had not brought down the entire building. Large cracks ran along the walls, branching out along the stone. A huge chunk of the ceiling directly overhead was missing, and the material that had once composed that ceiling lay scattered over the floor, burying Panther, Moondog, Webster, Miles, and the surviving Secret Service agent in several inches of debris. But the building itself was intact.

To Panther's right, Moondog pushed herself out of the rubble and into a kneeling position. The Navy pilot was covered in dust, mingled with the blood on her face. Her hair was tangled and disheveled. She shook her head and spit the dust from her mouth, then glanced at Martina. The crazy grin on Moondog's face told Panther she was no worse for the wear.

Behind her, the Secret Service agent and Webster were pushing the wreckage off themselves. Both were covered in the same fine gray powder. Blood ran from a small cut on Webster's forehead. Hayes appeared unharmed despite the dust in his black hair and the rips running through his suit.

"Don't move, Colonel," a voice said.

Panther lifted her head. Miles was standing over Webster, gun in hand. He pointed the muzzle of his M-16 directly at the President's head and looked at Panther, a look of triumph on his face. His lips spread into a grin as everyone around him froze, afraid to move for fear of the President's life.

Panther looked around desperately. Moondog had

dropped her weapon, and the Secret Service agent was also unarmed. Her own gun had vanished from her hand. Out of the corner of her eye she caught sight of the butt of the pistol, buried in the debris a few inches away. Keeping her eyes fixed on Miles, she slowly reached for the gun.

"I said don't move, Colonel," Miles repeated. Panther froze. Her hand was almost touching the pistol. She could have it in her grip in a second if she lunged for the weapon, and could save herself, Moondog, and the Secret Service agent. But no matter how fast Panther moved, she could not have the gun in hand before Miles squeezed the trigger, killing Webster.

"You move and the President dies," Miles said, confirming her fears.

"And if I don't?" Panther said, stretching slowly for the gun.

"I kill you all anyway," Miles said. "I've won."

"You'll only be dictator of America for a few hours at most," Panther said. The tips of her fingers brushed the metal of the gun. She stretched her arm further.

"You're an idealist," Miles said. "The military will fall in line. And with the power I wield, so will every other nation."

"You can kill us all," Webster said, staring up the barrel of the M-16 to meet Miles' gaze, "but it won't accomplish anything. You're the fool."

"Then at least I'll have the satisfaction of killing you all," Miles replied, grinning sadistically. "Goodbye, Mr. President. I'm in charge now." He slowly pulled the trigger back.

The loud crack of two gunshots echoed through the room, breaking the deathly silence. Both bullets caught Miles squarely in the chest. He staggered backward, dropping the M-16 and staring in disbelief at the two holes in his body.

"I told you I'd send you to hell," Vince Carlton said through gritted teeth. The young pilot lay half buried in the rubble, barely lifting his head off the floor. The small pistol in his hand was pointed directly at Miles. Every muscle in his body strained to hold the weapon in place. Fire and pain raged in his eyes.

Miles gaped at him in shock for a moment before collapsing to the floor in a bloody, lifeless heap. Phoenix watched him fall with a look of satisfaction on his face before his own strength gave out. His eyes closed, and he slumped back to the floor. The sinews in his body relaxed again, and he lay still.

"Vinny!" Martina shouted, jumping to her feet and crouching down beside the young captain. She ran her fingers along his throat, feeling for a pulse.

"Is he?" Moondog asked, standing.

"He's alive," Martina said.

"We've got to get out of here," the Secret Service agent said as he pulled Webster to his feet. "This whole place could come down at any minute."

"What's the quickest way out?" Martina asked, lifting her head to look at him. Her hand still rested on Vinny's shoulder.

"If you go straight it will take you to the center of the building. Go right and you'll be on the Mall," the agent said. "But we're going that way." He pointed down the hall. "The motorcade is waiting for the President there."

"All right," Martina said. "Moondog, go with the President."

Moondog nodded. Reaching down, she scooped up Miles' M-16, cradling the weapon in her arms.

"Ready when you are," she said to the Secret Service agent.

"Follow me," he said to Webster and Moondog.

"You bring up the rear," he told Moondog. She nodded again.

Holding his gun at the ready, the Secret Service agent took off down the corridor, making his way over the debris as quickly as possible. Webster followed, staying close behind him. Moondog was on the President's heels, glancing over her shoulder periodically. The hall was deserted. They did not see another living soul as they leapt over the rubble toward safety.

The Secret Service agent ducked into another side hallway, racing quickly to the end. Webster and Moondog kept pace. The agent pulled open the door at the end and motioned for the others to go through the exit.

The cool, fresh night air hit Moondog as she stepped outside. The sky was black, and the lights of Washington shone brightly. The wail of what seemed like thousands of sirens filled the air, drifting from the other side of the Capitol.

Three long, black stretch limousines sat in a row along the curb, motors running. A pair of motorcyclists led the cars, and two more sat at the rear. The Secret Service agent rushed to the center car and pulled open the rear door. Webster quickly slid inside.

The agent motioned for Moondog to join him. The Navy pilot dropped her M-16 on the curb and jumped into the car. The agent shut the door, and the lead motorcycles instantly took off, followed by the first limousine. The agent jumped into the third car as the second limo raced away.

President Webster kept his eyes on the Capitol until it disappeared. Then he turned his eyes forward, watching the city speed by. He tried to gather his thoughts as the motorcade whisked him to safety.

"I guess you're along for the ride, Commander,"

he said, finally turning to Moondog.

"That's okay, sir."

Webster studied the Navy pilot for a moment. She had made herself comfortable in the backseat of the presidential limousine. Her flight suit was covered with dust and dried blood. Her hair was disheveled and tangled. A trickle of red ran from the cut by her left eye. Yet none of that seemed to concern Moondog. She looked perfectly relaxed on the leather seat.

"Are you hurt?" Webster asked.

"Not really. Most of this blood isn't mine. I'm only bleeding here," she said, touching her cheek. "I think," she added, studying the red on her fingers.

"What about Colonel Redrick?" he asked.

"Panther could live through anything," Moondog said with a grin. "You could shoot her in the heart and she wouldn't die." She reached up and wiped more blood from her cheek.

Webster reached forward and pulled a cocktail napkin from the limousine's minibar.

"Here," he said, handing it to her.

"Thanks," Moondog said, pressing it to the cut.

"Is there anything else I could do for you, Commander?" Webster asked.

"Well," Moondog said slowly, a smile creeping across her face, "you could offer me a drink."

"What's your poison?" Webster asked, smiling for the first time.

"Scotch is fine."

"Scotch it is, then." He broke open a bottle and poured two glasses half full of the gold-colored liquid. He handed one to Moondog and downed the other. Moondog smiled and easily did the same.

The motorcade sped away from the chaos surrounding the Capitol through the streets of Washington, D.C., taking the President to safety.

* * *

"Hang on, Vinny," Panther said. "I'm going to get you out of here."

She quickly brushed the debris off the unconscious pilot. Rolling him onto his back, she scooped him up in her arms. Phoenix lay limp against her body. His head dropped onto her shoulder. She could feel the steady rise and fall of his chest against hers.

Carefully, Martina stood. Turning in the direction the Secret Service agent had indicated, she began to pick her way through the rubble, moving as fast as she could. While she could have quickly navigated the rubbish alone, Vinny's weight made it difficult for her to hurry without tripping over the sharp debris. The last thing she wanted was to fall and further injure him on the hard, broken marble littering the floor. So she moved as quickly and as carefully as she could, barely able to keep her own balance.

The entire floor was covered in rubble, with pieces of the ceiling and the walls lying several inches thick over the tile. Paintings and broken statues intermingled with the litter. Cracks ran through the walls and overhead.

Martina could hear the building breaking apart as she moved through it. The structure creaked and moaned. Crashes reverberated through the empty halls, growing more frequent with every second. The long cracks running through the walls and ceiling began to slowly grow again.

A loud crash directly behind Martina startled her. She looked back to see a huge section of wall crumble. She quickened her pace as the sounds of the dying building filled her ears and the dust filled her eyes and nose.

After what seemed like an eternity, she broke out of the long hall into the massive foyer where they had first entered. A glance up revealed that the large dome was intact for the most part. However, the entire surface was covered in huge cracks, snaking up through the dome like a thousand spider webs. The black night was visible through several large holes where pieces of the dome had fallen to the floor.

Martina turned toward the Mall and nearly ran. The floor of the foyer was clearer than that of the hallways, allowing her to move faster. The increasing crashes, echoing through the building, spurred her on.

Finally, Martina burst free of the building. She raced out from between the marble pillars and hurried for the long steps leading to the Mall. As she stepped outside she felt the cool night air on her skin. The sky stretched black and clear overhead, complemented by the million shining lights of the city.

The Mall was lit up with the flashing red and blue lights of countless fire trucks, police cars, and ambulances. Sirens of all tones filled the air, wailing ceaselessly into the night. It looked as if every emergency vehicle in the city was present. Beyond, the night sky was lit with the myriad city lights from the buildings and monuments in the distance.

Hundreds of people were crowded on the Mall. The vast majority were those who had escaped from the Capitol. Some stood and gazed at the building, while others rested on the grass. Still others wandered aimlessly through the crowd. Firefighters, EMTs, and rescue workers were doing their best to help the injured. A few spectators and many news crews had arrived on the scene. The police had formed a barricade around the victims of the attack and were trying to keep the onlookers away from the building and the victims.

Martina ignored the flashing lights, blaring sirens, and human voices that drifted up to her ears. She made her way down the steps to the Mall, careful not to trip. All that mattered to her was saving the man resting in her arms.

No sooner had Panther set foot on the second step than a loud rumbling filled the air. With a horrendous crash, drowning out every other noise in the city, the Capitol caved in on itself. The walls gave way and crumpled. The roof fell in, filling the air with the sounds of falling rock. The large dome shattered, falling to the ground.

Dust flew into the air, completely engulfing the ruins of the large structure. The haze rolled down, covering Martina and Vinny and temporarily blinding them in a fog. For a moment all Martina could see was gray dust. The lights of the city vanished, and the crashes behind her muted the sounds of the sirens. Even the steps beneath her feet vanished. She stopped moving, waiting for the fog to dissipate.

Slowly, the dust settled, revealing the wreckage of the Capitol as it covered the debris. The once-beautiful white marble structure was now little more than a glorified rock pile. Jagged white stones lay in a huge heap. In places, pieces of the walls still stood. The magnificent dome had vanished completely, leaving only rubble.

As the dust rolled down the steps, a dark figured appeared in the fog, moving slowly toward the Mall. Martina emerged from the dissipating cloud. Vinny rested limply in her arms. Both were covered in dust.

Martina glanced over her shoulder as she made her way down the last few steps and walked onto the Mall. Shaking her head, she knelt down, laying Vinny on the grass. Slowly, she ran her eyes along his body, inspecting his injuries thoroughly for the first time.

Vinny's eyes were closed, and his face was relaxed. His chest rose and fell evenly. His right leg was covered in blood, as was his right shoulder, which was still oozing blood.

"Hey, we need an ambulance over here!" someone shouted. Martina's ears heard the call, but her mind ignored it. She pressed her hands against Vinny's shoulder, trying to stem the flow of blood.

"Vinny," she whispered. "Vinny, can you hear me?"

He remained motionless. Martina touched his neck. His pulse was still strong.

"C'mon, Vinny, talk to me." His chest continued its gradual rise and fall, but he did not move.

"Phoenix," she said softly.

Vinny's eyes fluttered open.

"Martina?" he asked, turning his head to look at her.

"Yeah," she said, smiling. "Don't move. You're going to be all right."

"Where am I?"

"The Mall. Outside the remains of the Capitol."

"Must have been some crash," he said, looking past her at the wreckage.

"It was really loud," Martina said, half-grinning.

"Did Webster get out?"

"Yeah."

Vinny looked around. "Where's Moondog?"

"She took a temporary assignment with the Secret Service," Martina said. "She's fine."

"Miles?"

"Dead. Kalliff too."

"Good," Vinny said, relaxing.

Panther lifted her head to see a pair of EMTs running toward her, holding a stretcher between them.

"Looks like they're going to haul you off to the hospital now," she said to Vinny. "Hang in there, okay? I'll see you in a little while."

Phoenix nodded. Martina watched as the paramedics dropped the stretcher on the ground beside him, then carefully moved the pilot on top of it. They lifted him into the air and ran to the nearest ambulance. Martina watched them go. For a moment she sat motionless on the ground, looking at the bustle around her.

Martina felt two sets of hands grab her by the arms and haul her to her feet. The world began to spin in circles. The flashing colored lights whirled together as the grass spun to the sky and back. Her legs quivered, threatening to collapse. She shut her eyes and fought to steady herself, drawing in a deep breath. Her vision gradually returned to normal.

"Come with us, please, ma'am," she heard a voice say gently. Slowly, she turned her head. A pair of EMTs were holding her up by the arms.

"I'm fine," Martina said. "I don't need to go to the hospital."

"We just want to stitch your arm up, that's all," the EMT on her left said.

Martina gazed down. The entire left sleeve of her flight suit was soaked with blood. Her hand was covered in red. Blood dripped from her fingertips onto the grass below. She watched the little drops tumble from her fingers.

"That's all you're going to do?" she asked.

"And give you a little blood. That's it."

"All right," Martina said. She let them lead her across the grass to a waiting ambulance.

~ 28 ~

"Are you sure this is a good idea, sir?" Webster's chief Secret Service agent asked. "It might not be safe for you to go out in public."

"Yes, I'm sure," Webster said to Hayes. "It's safe enough. Everyone responsible for the attack is either dead or under arrest."

"There might be some we don't yet know about still around," the agent said.

"If that's the case, I still have you to protect me," Webster replied. "This is something I have to do."

The agent simply nodded, pushed open the door, and held it for Webster. The President stepped into the hospital where most of the victims of the attack had been taken. He walked through the sterile, brightly lit halls toward the main lobby. Hayes stayed a few steps behind him.

The receptionist had vanished from the desk, leaving it empty. A round clock over the desk showed the time to be just before two in the morning. The lobby itself was deserted save for one woman. Martina Redrick was slumped in a chair by the far wall, staring listlessly out at the black night through the automatic glass doors.

The pilot sat motionless, like a rag doll cast aside by a child. Her entire body sagged in the chair. Her hair was untied and fell limply past her drooping shoulders, half covering her face. Her arms rested in her lap. Her long legs stretched out across the white tile floor. Exhaustion was etched on her face. Several bright-blue bruises had appeared on her face and neck.

A clean white t-shirt and a pair of jeans that were too big for her had replaced her bloody flight suit. She still wore her combat boots. A white bandage was wrapped around the wound on her left arm. Blood from the gash had soaked partway through the dressing, creating a bright-red spot on the white strip. Several small cuts on her wrists had been cleaned but not bandaged.

Seeing Webster approach, she placed her hands on the armrests of the chair and shifted her weight to stand.

“Stay down, Colonel,” the President said, waving her back to her seat.

Panther gladly relaxed her body, slumping back into her seat.

“What are you doing here, sir?” she asked, unable to hide the exhaustion seeping through her voice as she looked up at Webster through half-closed, half-dead eyes.

“I felt I should see how the victims of the attack are doing,” Webster said, sitting down beside her. “After all, I’m partially responsible for this.”

Martina turned her head toward him, giving him a questioning look.

“I should have listened to you, Colonel. You told me to cancel the address, and I didn’t. Now at least fifty people are dead and twice that many are injured, all because I was too foolish to heed your warning.”

“You did what you thought was right, sir,” Martina said. “As far as we knew, all they had was the plane. There was no way to know about the bomb or the gunmen.”

“I still can’t shake the feeling that this was my

fault," Webster said, shaking his head. "There must have been something I could have done to stop it."

"You can't change the past, sir," Martina said softly. "All you can do is learn from it and make sure something like this never happens again."

"I guess you're right," Webster said, pausing for a moment. "It's a good thing you were there. Otherwise a lot more people would be dead."

"Just doing my job, sir," Martina replied simply.

"Your job was to stop the bomber. You did much more than that."

"My job is to ensure this country stays free," she said softly. "And that's all I was doing."

"Well, if you look at it that way…" Webster said. "But I still think your actions were far above the call of duty."

"Do me a favor, sir. Don't tell the press I was involved," Martina said. The exhaustion in her voice was clear. "I still haven't been able to live down that shuttle mission last year. I don't need to see my name in the papers again."

"I don't know if I can, after that landing you made. You certainly know how to make an entrance, Colonel. The Air Force has no idea what to do with those Raptors parked off Maryland Avenue."

"That was pretty fun," Martina said with a chuckle. "All they have to do is start the engines. I'm sure they can find a road long enough to use as a runway."

"I guess so," Webster said. "But honestly, Colonel, thank you for saving my life, and everyone else."

"Just doing my job," Martina repeated.

"You're going to say that no matter what I do, aren't you?"

"Yes, sir."

"Did Captain Carlton survive?" Webster asked, changing the subject.

"Yeah," Martina said. "The doctors patched him up. They think he's going to be fine."

"That's good."

"Where did Commander Ansetti go?" Martina asked.

"I think she caught a ride back to Andrews."

Martina simply nodded, too tired to say more.

"So why are you sitting here, Colonel?" Webster asked.

"I'm just waiting for my own ride."

"For this long?"

"I wanted to make sure Captain Carlton was all right before I left."

"How did you fare?" Webster asked.

"They put a few stitches in my arm and pumped a couple of pints of blood into me," she said, with a shrug.

"Does it hurt much?"

"Honestly, sir, they shot me so full of painkillers that I can't feel a damn thing. The only thing I feel right now is dead tired."

"What will you do once you get back to Andrews?"

"I'm going to sleep for two days straight," Martina replied. "Then I'm going to catch the first plane to Houston. I was supposed to be back at NASA over a week ago."

The sound of the automatic doors sliding open cut through the air before Webster could respond. Panther turned her head to see a young second lieutenant standing in the center of the doorway, a look of surprise on his face. He had not expected to encounter Webster and had absolutely no idea how to react upon seeing his commander in chief.

"Looks like your ride's here, Colonel," Webster said.

"Yes, sir," she said. "If you don't mind."

"Go get some sleep."

“Yes, sir.” Moving her body for the first time since seeing Webster, she summoned all the strength in her arms and pushed herself out of the chair.

“Good luck sorting out this mess, sir,” she said to Webster.

“Thank you, Colonel,” he replied, standing.

Martina turned to the young lieutenant.

“You here to take me to Andrews?” she asked him.

“You’re Colonel Redrick?” he managed to stammer. She nodded.

“Yes, ma’am,” he said.

“Good,” Martina said. She turned and walked slowly to the door, barely lifting her feet with every tired step. Her shoulders continued to droop, and her arms hung limply at her sides. At a loss for what to do, the young lieutenant turned and followed the exhausted woman as she moved through the doors and vanished into the night.

* * *

TWO MONTHS LATER:

“And this is your office,” the man giving Vince Carlton his introductory tour of NASA’s facilities said, opening the door. “You got any questions?”

“Not at the moment,” Vinny said.

“Good,” the man replied. “Training starts tomorrow at eight. Be on time.” He turned and walked away.

Vinny looked at the door. His name had been stenciled across it. He pushed the door open. The room was empty except for a desk and a chair. He shrugged and walked inside. Dropping into the chair, he propped his feet up on the desk and scanned the room.

So this is it, he thought as he surveyed the room. After all these years, Vince Carlton had made it to NASA.

A voice interrupted his reverie. “Will you look at

that, Moondog?" He lifted his head to see two women dressed in blue NASA flight suits standing in the door.

"Another wet behind the ears rookie," Panther continued.

"And I guess it's up to us to show him the ropes," Moondog said.

"Yep," Panther said. "What do you suggest we do about it?"

"I say we take him down to the airfield and whip him into shape," Moondog replied.

"Sounds good to me," Panther said.

"I'd be glad to beat your ass in a dogfight," Vinny said, standing and walking around his desk.

Moondog laughed.

"Not that you could," she said, wrapping her arm around his shoulder. "Welcome to NASA, Phoenix." She steered him down the hall. "Let's go fly."

Panther appeared on his other side. Talking among themselves, the three pilots walked down the hall, heading for the airfield.

Coming Soon From Karla K. Goodhouse

LONE WOLF

While on a mission to launch a weather satelitte, the space shuttle re-enters without warning, landing in a remote area of Russia. A rogue faction of the Russian army seizes the shuttle for their own mysterious purposes.

It's clear the Russians have inside help, and all evidence points to the mission commander, veteran astronaut Martina Redrick. Accused of treason, Martina soon finds herself on the run and fighting against her closest friends.

Targeted by Russia, and marked for death by her own nation, Martina must clear her name, while saving the country she loves from certain destruction.

Also Available From Karla K. Goodhouse

HELLFIRE

Air Force fighter pilot and rookie astronaut Martina Redrick is flying the space shuttle when disaster strikes. A satellite about to be repaired explodes above the cargo bay, damaging the shuttle and knocking the mission commander unconscious. But the explosion was no accident. When an unmarked spacecraft attacks the defenseless, crippled shuttle, Martina must save the ship and crew. And she soon discovers, returning to earth will not put them out of danger.

The shuttle isn't the only target. Someone is systematically destroying US communication and surveillance satellites. Determined to protect America's assets, the President sends Martina and Navy pilot Rachel Ansetti back into space, flying top secret space-fighters on a search and destroy mission.

However, the attacks are only the beginning of a far more sinister plan, which threatens the heart of the free world. Now it's up to Martina and Rachel to stop them before it's too late.

About the Author

Karla K. Goodhouse grew up in beautiful rural New England. A natural born storyteller, she was fascinated by all things air and space. She graduated from the US Air Force Academy in 2005 with a degree in Aeronautical Engineering. While at the Academy, she also throughly enjoyed studying martial arts. Today, Karla is a maintenance officer in the US Air Force Reserve and is a rated commercial pilot.

Firebird is the second of three Martina Redrick novels written to date. Karla is currently working on a fourth.

Visit her website: www.karlakgoodhouse.com.

Glossary of Military and Aviation Terms

ADIZ – Air Defense Interdiction Zone. The boundary between international and U.S. airspace.

Afterburner aka **Burner** – The section of a jet engine behind the turbine where fuel can be injected and ignited to produce extra thrust.

AIM-9 Sidewinder – A heat seeking missile. Designed to lock onto the infrared signature from an enemy aircraft's engine exhaust.

AIM-120 AMRAAM – Advanced Medium Range Air to Air Missile. A radar guided missile. Designed to lock onto the radar signature of an enemy aircraft.

ATC – Air Traffic Control.

AWACS – Airborne Warning and Control System. An airborne radar platform used for aerial battle management.

B-1B Lancer aka **"Bone"** – A long range, multi role bomber with a large payload capacity.

B-2 Spirit – The U.S Air Force's stealth bomber.

Bandit – A confirmed enemy aircraft.

Bogey – An unidentified aircraft.

Bone – See B-1B.

Burner Can – An aircraft's tailpipe.

CAP – Combat Air Patrol. A mission flown over a designated area to guard it from aerial attack.

Center – An Air Traffic Control agency which oversees a large section of enroute airspace.

Chaff – Countermeasures used against radar guide missiles.

Class A – Controlled airspace above the continental United States from 18,000 to 60,000 feet MSL. This is where most commercial traffic flies.

F-119 – The jet engine used in the F-22 Raptor.

F-15 Eagle aka **"15"** – A tactical fighter jet.

F-16 Fighting Falcon aka "**Viper"** aka **"16"** – A compact, multi role fighter jet.

F-22 Raptor aka **"22"** – A multi role stealth fighter jet capable of supercruise, or supersonic flight without the use of afterburners.

Flares – Countermeasures used against heat seeking missiles.

Fingertip – A position in formation flying in which the number two aircraft flies to the side and slightly behind of the lead aircraft. The distance separating the two planes can be as little as three feet in this position.

Full Bird – A Colonel.

G-Force – Gravity force. Force of acceleration experience by pilots during aerobatic maneuvers.

G-suit – A garment worn by fighter pilots to prevent loss of consciousness due to g-forces. When the g-force on a pilot increases, the g-suit inflates, putting pressure on the pilot's legs and preventing blood from rushing to his or her feet.

Guard Frequency – The emergency frequency used by military aircraft.

Ident – An instruction given to pilots by Air Traffic Control to identify their aircraft on radar by highlighting the signal from their transponder.

IFF – Identification Friend or Foe. Similar to a transponder, used to identify military aircraft.

Immelman – A course-reversal maneuver executed by pulling back on the stick, so the aircraft climbs. The back pressure is maintained until the aircraft is on its back at the top of a loop. Then the pilot rolls the aircraft upright, completing the maneuver.

In the Green – Within safe operating limits.

In the Red – Out of safe limits.

Jink – To maneuver erratically in an attempt to shake an enemy aircraft.

KC-135 – An aerial refueling aircraft also used for cargo transport.

Light Bird – A Lieutenant Colonel.

Mach – The measurement of an aircraft's speed as a ratio relative to the speed of sound.

Maneuvering Speed – The maximum airspeed at which an aircraft will not be overstressed if it encounters a sudden jolt.

MiG 29 Fulcrum – A Russian made multi-role fighter jet.

MiG 31 Foxhound – A Russian made interceptor.

NORAD – North American Aerospace Defense Command. The agency which oversees U.S. and Canadian airspace.

O-5 – Officer pay grade equivalent to the rank of Lieutenant Colonel in the Air Force, Army or Marines and Commander in the Navy.

OSI – Office of Special Investigations. An Air Force agency similar to the FBI.

Over the Top Maneuver – Any aerial maneuver in which an aircraft executes a pull up to inverted flight.

Push – Term used to notify a wingman of a radio frequency change.

Security Forces aka **SF**– Air Force police.

SOF – Supervisor of Flying. The individual overseeing the day's flying activities at an Air Force Base.

Split S – A course-reversal maneuver executed by first rolling inverted and then pulling back on the stick, as if completing the second half of a loop.

SR-71 Blackbird – A spy plane used by the U.S. Air Force capable of flying Mach 3 at 80,000 feet MSL. Now retired.

TDY – Temporary Duty. A short assignment at a location other than one's home station.

Transponder – A device used to identify an aircraft to air traffic control.

UHF – Ultra High Frequency. The radio bandwidth on which most military aircraft transmit.

Victor Airway – A set route between radio navigation aids used by pilots.

Viper – See F-16.

VOQ – Visiting Officer's Quarters. Lodging on a military base for officers who are there for a short stay, usually on TDY.

White Arc – The airspeed range on at which an aircraft's flaps can be lowered, as marked on the airspeed indicator.

Wilco – Short for will comply. Used by pilots to inform controllers that they will follow the instructions given.

Zoom Climb – A maneuver in which an aircraft pitches nose up, trading all excess speed for altitude very rapidly.

www.ingramcontent.com/pod-product-compliance
Lightning Source LLC
LaVergne TN
LVHW020528100826
845148LV00010B/1387